THE VENETIANS

THE VENETIANS

MARY ELIZABETH BRADDON

WILDSIDE PRESS

Originally published in 1893.
Published by Wildside Press LLC.
wildsidpress.com

CHAPTER I.

IN THE CITY BY THE SEA

Little golden cloudlets, like winged living creatures, were hanging high up in the rosy glow above Santa Maria della Salute, and all along the Grand Canal the crowded gondolas were floating in a golden haze, and all the westward-facing palace windows flashed and shone with an illumination which the lamps and lanterns that were to be lighted after sundown could never equal, burnt they never so merrily. It was Shrove Tuesday in Venice, Carnival time. The sun had been shining on the city and on the lagunes all day long. It was one of those Shrove Tuesdays which recall the familiar proverb—

"Sunshine at Carnival,
Fireside at Easter."

But who cares about the chance of cold and gloom six weeks hence when to-day is fair and balmy? A hum of joyous, foolish voices echoed from those palace façades, and floated out seaward, and rang along the narrow Calle, and drifted on the winding water-ways, and resounded under the innumerable bridges; for everywhere in the City by the Sea men, women, and children were making merry, and had given themselves up to a wild and childish rapture of unreasoning mirth, ready to explode into loud laughter at the sorriest jokes. An old man tapped upon the shoulder by a swinging paper lantern—a boy whose hat had been knocked off—a woman calling to her husband or her lover across the gay flotilla—anything was food for mirth on this holiday evening, while the great gold orb sank in the silvery lagoon, and all the sky yonder towards Chioggia was dyed with the crimson afterglow, and the Chioggian fishing-boats were moving westward in all the splendour of their painted sails.

At Danieli's the hall and staircase, reading-room, smoking-room, and saloons were crowded; English and American for the most part, but with a sprinkling of French and German. Shrewd Yankees were bargaining on the sea-washed steps below the hall-door with gondoliers almost as shrewd. Quanto per la notte—tutte la notte, sul canale? To-night the gondoliers would have it all their own way, for every one wanted a gondola to row up and down the Grand Canal, with gaudy Chinese lanterns, and singing men, twanging guitar or tinkling mandoline to that tune which is almost the national melody of Venice fin de siècle—"Funicoli, funicola."

The dining-rooms at Danieli's are capacious enough for all ordinary occasions, but to-night there was not space for half the number who wanted to dine. The waiters were flying about wildly, trying to appease the hungry crowd with promises of tables subito, subito. But travellers in Italy know what subito means in an Italian restaurant, and were not comforted by these assurances. Amiable Signor Campi moved about among his men, and his very presence gave comfort somehow, and finally everybody had food and wine, and a din of jovial voices rose up from the table d'hôte to the grand old rooms above, on that upper story which is called the noble floor, a place of strange histories, perhaps, in those stern days when these hotels were palaces.

* * * *

The ubiquitous Signor Campi was near the door when a gondola stopped at the bottom of the steps, and two ladies came tripping up into the hall, followed by a young man who was evidently English, handsome, tall, broad-shouldered, and clad in a suit of rough grey cloth, whose every line testified to the excellence of an English tailor.

The ladies were as evidently not English, and they had a Carnival air which was totally different from the gaiety of the American young ladies in their neat tailor gowns, or the English ladies in their table d'hôte silks. One wore ruby plush, with a train which trailed on the wet steps as she came up to the door. The other wore black velvet, with a wide yellow sash loosely knotted round a supple waist. The ruby lady was masked, the black velvet lady dangled her lace-fringed mask on the end of a finger, and looked boldly round the crowded hall with her big black eyes—eyes which reflected the lamplight in their golden splendour.

Signor Campi was at the Englishman's side before the ladies could pass the threshold.

"You were thinking of dining with those two ladies, sir?" he inquired, in excellent English.

"Certainly. You can give us a private room, if you like."

"There is not a room in the house unoccupied;" and then, in a lower voice, Signor Campi murmured, "Quite impossible. Those ladies cannot dine here."

The Englishman laughed lightly.

"You are not fond of your own countrywomen, it seems, Monsieur Campi;" and then to the hall-porter, "Keep that gondola, will you?" and then in Italian, to the larger lady in ruby plush, who might have been mother or aunt to the lovely girl in black velvet, "They have no room for us anywhere. We should have to wait ages, ages for our dinner. Shall we try a restaurant?"

"Yes, yes," cried the girl eagerly. "Ever so much more fun. Let us go to the Black Hat. No gha megio casa per el disnar."

"Where is the Black Hat?"

"On the Piazza. We often dine there, la Zia and I. We shan't want the gondola, it is only five minutes' walk."

"Shall I engage him for the evening?"

"No, no. You are going to take us to the opera."

"As you will."

He offered the girl his arm, and left la Zia to follow him across the hall to the door opening on to the Quay of the Slaves—that quay whose stones are beaten nowadays chiefly by the footsteps of light-hearted travellers drunken with the enchantment of Venice. They crossed the bridge, the girl hanging on the young man's arm, chatting gaily, and holding up her long black skirt with the other hand, revealing glimpses of feet and ankles which were far from fairy-like, feet that had been widened by the flip-flopping shoe which the damsel had worn when she was a lace-maker on the island of Burano.

If he wanted a good dinner—a real Venetian dinner—nowhere would he get it better than at the sign of the Black Hat, and good wine into the bargain, the girl told her cavalier.

They turned by the Vine Corner, and then threaded their way along the crowded Piazzetta, whence the sacred pigeons had been banished by the tumult of the throng. They crossed the Piazza in front of St. Mark's Moorish domes, and entered a low doorway under the colonnade, only a few paces from the Torre del Orologio, with its ultramarine and gold clock and its bronze giants to beat the time. At the end of a long, narrow, stuffy passage, they found themselves in a low-ceiled room where there were numerous small tables, and where the heat from the flare of the gas, and the steam of cooked viands, was too suggestive of the torrid zone for comfort.

The waiters were evidently devoted to the dark-eyed Si'ora in black and yellow, for room was speedily found where there was apparently no room. Some diners were hustled away from a snug little table in a corner by a window, where by opening one side of the casement one might get a breath of cool air—flavoured by sewage, but still a boon.

"May I order the dinner?" pleaded the dark eyes, smiling at the young man in rough grey woollen, while la Zia looked about her, turning her head to survey the groups of diners at the tables in the rear.

The waiter set a huge flask of Chiante on the table unbidden, and stood, napkin in hand, waiting for Fiordelisa's orders. Fiordelisa—otherwise Lisa—was the name of the dark-eyed damsel, who to the Englishman's eye looked as if she had just stepped out of a story in the Decameron.

She ordered the dinner, discussing the menu confidentially with the waiter; she ordered, and the dishes came, and they all ate, Vansittart being too hungry to be daintily curious as to the food set before him after a long day on the lagoons and an afternoon on the Lido, and all the fun and riot of the Grand Canal at sunset. He never knew of what his dinner at the Black Hat was composed, except that he ate some oysters and drank a pint of white wine, and helped to finish a couple of bottles of champagne—which he ordered in lieu of the big flask of Chiante—that they began with a frittura of minnows, and that the most substantial dish which the brisk waiter brought them was a savoury mess of macaroni, with shreds of meat or choppings of liver mixed up in an unctuous gravy. Lisa was in high spirits, and ate ravenously, and drank a good many glasses of the sparkling wine, and told him, half in broken English and half in her Venetian dialect, of the old days when she had worked in the lace factory, where her earnings were about seven soldi per diem, and where she lived chiefly on polenta.

This was the sole knowledge Mr. Vansittart had of her history, since he had only made her acquaintance three or four hours ago at the concert hall on the Lido, where he had offered this young person and her aunt a cup of coffee, and whence he had brought them back to Venice in his gondola. He knew nothing of their histories and characters, cared to know nothing, had no idea of seeing them ever again after this Carnival day. He had taken them to his hotel without stopping to consider the wisdom of such a course, thinking to feast them in one of those grand upper rooms overlooking the broad sweep of water between the Quay of the Slaves and St. George the Greater, meaning to feast them upon Signor Campi's best; but Signor Campi had willed otherwise, and here they were feasting just as merrily upon a savoury mess of macaroni and chopped liver at the sign of the Black Hat.

After the savoury dishes Fiordelisa began upon pastry, with an appetite as of a giant refreshed. She rested her elbow on the table, and the loose sleeve of her velveteen gown rolled back and showed the round white arm. All the little crinkly curls danced upon her pure white forehead and over her dancing eyes as she ate chocolate éclairs and creamy choux to her heart's content, while Vansittart thought what a pretty creature she was, and what a pity Mr. Burgess or Mr. Logsdaile was not there with palette and brushes, to fix that gay and brilliant image upon canvas for ever.

Vansittart was not in love with this chance acquaintance of an idle afternoon. He was only delighted with her. She amused, she fascinated him, just as he was amused and fascinated by this enchanting city of Venice, which had always the same charm and the same glamour for him, come here at what season he might. She impressed him with a sense of her beauty, just as one of those wonderful pictures in the Venetian Academy would have done.

His heart was unmoved by this sensuous, eager, earthly loveliness. Her vulgarity, all her words and gestures essentially of the people, interested him, yet kept him worlds away from her.

He was rich, idle, alone in Venice, and he thought it was his right to amuse himself to the uttermost at this Carnival season. That offer of a cup of coffee, arising out of mutual laughter at some absurdities among the crowd, had been the beginning of the friendliest relations.

He strolled on the loose, level sands with Lisa and her aunt, those sands over which Byron used to ride, the poet of whose existence Lisa had never heard, yet who had wasted lightest hours with just such girls as Lisa. And then how could he go back to Venice alone in his gondola and leave this black-eyed girl and her chaperon to struggle for standing room among the crowd on the twopenny steamer, in their fine clothes and jewels, those jewels in which lower-class Venetians love to invest their savings? No; it was the most natural thing in life to offer them seats in his gondola, and then to see the fun of the Grand Canal in their company; and what young man with his note-case plethoric with limp Italian notes, and a reserve of English bank-notes in a close-buttoned inside pocket, could refrain from offering dinner, and then, hearing that Lisa was pining to go to the opera, a box at that entertainment? No sooner had she expressed her desire, while they were on the Grand Canal, than he sent off a Venetian guide, whom he knew of old, to engage a stage box for the evening.

Fiordelisa told him about her life at Burano, while she devoured her pastry, the aunt listening placidly, replete with dinner and wine, caring for nothing except that those old days were a thing of the past, and that neither she nor her handsome niece need toil or starve any more—not for the present, at any rate; perhaps never. La Zia was not a woman to peer curiously into the future while the present gave her a comfortable lodging and meat and drink.

The girl talked her Venetian, and Vansittart, who had spent most of his holidays in Italy, and had a quick ear for dialects, was able to understand her. Now and then she spoke English, better than he would have expected from her youthful ignorance.

"How is it that you can talk English, Signorina mia, and how is it that you left Burano?" he asked in Italian.

"For one and the same reason. A young English gentleman fell in love with me, and brought my aunt and me to Venice, and is having me educated, in order to marry me and take me to England with him."

Vansittart did not believe in the latter half of the story, but he was too polite to express his doubt.

"Oh, you are being educated up to our idea of the British matron, are you, bella mia?" he said, smiling at her, as she wiped her coral lips with the coarse serviette, and flung herself back in her chair, satiated with cream and pastry. "And pray in what does the education consist?"

"I am learning to play on the mandoline. A little old man with a cracked voice comes to our lodgings twice a week to teach me—and we sing duets, 'La ci darem' and 'Sul aria.'"

"The mandoline. Ah, that is your English friend's notion of education," said Vansittart, laughing. "Well, I dare say that it is as good as Greek or Latin, or the pure science that gave Giordano Bruno such a bad time in this very city."

He leant back with his head in an angle of the wall, idle, amused, interested, taking life as it seemed to him life ought to be taken—very lightly.

He had been in Venice only a few days, days of sunshine and sauntering in gondolas to this or the other island, to dream away an idle afternoon. It was his third visit, and he seemed to know every stone of the city almost as well as Ruskin—every palace front and Saracenic window, every mouldering flight of steps, every keystone of every bridge which he passed under almost every day with lazy motion, drifting as the cabbage leaves and egg-shells drifted on the dark green water. He never stayed very long anywhere, being free to wander as he pleased at his present stage of existence, and having a dim foreshadowing of the time when he would not be free, when he would be bound and fettered by domestic ties, and travelling would be altogether a different business from this casual rambling. He pictured himself at the head of his breakfast table discussing the summer holiday with his wife, while perhaps his mother-in-law sat by and put various spokes into the family wheel, opposing every preference of his on principle.

He would have to marry some day, he knew. It was an obligation laid upon him together with the family seat and comfortable income to which he had succeeded before his two-and-twentieth birthday. The thing would have to be done—but he meant to delay the evil hour as long as he could, and to be monstrously exacting as to the fairy princess for whose dear sake he should put on those domestic fetters.

He had enjoyed this particular visit to Venice with a keener relish than either of his previous visits. Though the year was still young, the weather had been exceptionally lovely. Sun, moon, and stars had shed all that they have of glory and of glamour over the romantic city, painting the smooth lagoons with a rare splendour of colouring which changed city and sea into something supernal, unimaginable, dreamlike.

His windows at Danieli's looked over an enchanted sea, where the great modern Peninsular and Oriental steamer moored between the Riva and St. George the Greater seemed an anachronism in iron. All else was fairy-like, historic, mediæval.

The steamer was to sail for Alexandria in the afternoon, they had told him, whenever he made any inquiry about her; but the days and afternoons had gone, and she was still lying there, blocking out a little bit of the opposite island and the famous church.

"And so you sing as well as play, Fiordelisa?" he asked, presently, after a silence in which they all three smoked their cigarettes.

"Sing! I should think she did sing," answered the aunt. "She warbles like a nightingale. Signor Zefferino, her master, says she ought to come out at the opera."

Vansittart smiled. Idle flattery on the maestro's part, no doubt; the flattery of the small parasite who knows where the macaroni is savouriest, and where the salad reeks with oil.

And yet, if this girl sang at all, she should sing sweetly. Those dark, sunny eyes of hers gave promise of the artistic temperament. The tones that came from that round, full throat, ivory white against the tawdry black and yellow of her gown, should be rich and ripe.

He asked no questions about her English lover. Had he been ever so little in love with her himself he would have been full of curiosity—but for this flower of a day, this beautiful stranger, with whom he ate and drank and made merry to-night, and whom he might never see again, he had no serious concern. He cared not who were her friends or followers; whether the life she lived were good or evil. She had a fresh youthfulness, a look of almost childlike innocence, in spite of her tousled hair and tawdry raiment, and although Signor Campi's keen eye had condemned her. The aunt, too, fat, common, too fine for respectability, seemed a harmless old thing. No word of evil had come from her lips. She had not the air of laying snares for the stranger's feet. She thought of nothing but the enjoyment of the moment.

"Pray, where may your Englishman be to-day?" asked Vansittart, as it flashed upon his idle mind that there might be peril in such a city as Venice in being seen with another man's sweetheart. "Why didn't he escort you to the Lido?"

"He went to Monte Carlo a fortnight ago," she answered. "I am afraid he is a gambler."

"Is he rich?"

"No, not as you English count riches. He is rich for a Venetian. He gave la Zia and me our gowns—she chose red, I black—last Christmas. There are few Venetians who would give such handsome presents. He is very generous."

"Yes, he is very generous," echoed the aunt.

"It is time we went to the opera," cried Fiordelisa. "I want to be there at the beginning."

The opera was "Don Giovanni;" the artists were third-rate; but they sang well enough to lull la Zia into a comfortable slumber and to lift Lisa to the seventh heaven. She sat with clasped hands, listening in a rapture of content. She only unclasped her hands to applaud vehemently when the house applauded. The theatre was crowded, the audience were noisy, but Fiordelisa craned her long neck out of the box to listen, and drank in every note with those quick ears of hers, and was perhaps almost the only person in the Rossini Theatre that night who listened intently: but before the second act was over the crowd and the heat had increased to such a degree that women were fainting in the boxes, and even Fiordelisa was resigned to leaving before "Don Giovanni" was half done. She wanted to walk in the Piazza before the shops were shut, or the crowd began to thin, or the bands ceased playing.

There was to be a masked ball at the same theatre on the following night.

"Shall I take you to the ball, Lisa?" asked Vansittart, as they came out of the heat and the glare into the cool softness of a Venetian night.

"No, I don't care about dancing. I only care for the opera. The

12

girls at Burano were mad about dancing, but I liked to hear the organ at High Mass better than all their dances."

Vansittart thought of bidding his new friends good night at the door of the theatre. Had Venice not been Venice, and had there been any vehicles in waiting, he would have put his fair companions into a coach, paid their fare, and bade them good night for ever, without so much as inquiring where they lived. But Venice has a romantic unlikeness to every other city. There was no coach. To say good night and leave them to walk home unescorted was out of the question.

"In which direction is your house, Signora?" he asked the elder lady.

"Oh, we are not going home," cried Fiordelisa. "We are going to the Piazza. This is the time when there will be most fun. You'll take us, won't you?" she asked, slipping her hand through his arm, and boldly taking possession of him. "Come, come, aunt, we are going to the Piazza."

Her feet threaded the narrow ways so swiftly that Vansittart scarcely knew by which particular windings of the labyrinth they came to the Bocca di Piazza, and emerged from the shadow of the pillars upon the broad open square, all aflame with lamps and lanterns, and one roar of multitudinous voices, squeaking punchinellos, barking dogs, blaring trumpets, tinkling guitars. They pushed their way through the crowd, the two women masked, each hanging on to his arm, and making progress difficult.

The Piazza was a spectacle to remember, full of life and movement, a military band braying out brazen music, music of Offenbach, loud, martial, insistent, above the multifarious squeakings and shoutings, the laughter and the clamour of the crowd. In the long colonnades the throng pushed thickly; but Vansittart had been one of the strong men of the 'Varsity, a thrower of hammers, a jumper of long jumps, a man with a name that was famous at Lillie Bridge as well as at Oxford. He parted the throng as if it had been water, and would have made his way quickly to the brightest, largest, and gayest of the caffès, if it had not been for Lisa, who hung back to look at the lighted shop windows, windows that she could have seen any night of her life, but which had a particular attraction at Carnival time.

The touters were touting at the shop doors, with that smiling persistence which makes the *Procuratie Vecchie* odious, and recalls Cranbourne Alley in the dark ages. Lisa made a dead stop before a shop where gaudy wooden figures of Moorish slaves, garish with crude colour and much gilding, were grilling in the glare of the gas. It was a kind of bazaar, half Venetian, half Oriental, and one window was full of bead necklaces and barbaric jewels. At these Lisa looked with such childish longing eyes that Vansittart would have been hard as a stone if he had not suggested making a selection from that sparkling display of rainbow glass and enamel.

The spider at the door was entreating the flies to go into his web, a young Venetian with smiling black eyes and a Jewish nose—a lineal descendant of Jessica, perhaps—a very agreeable young spider, entreating the Signora and Signorina to go in and look about them. There would be no necessity for them to buy. "To look costs nothing."

They all three went in. Fiordelisa fastened upon a tray of jewels, and lost herself in a bewilderment as to which of all those earrings, brooches, and necklaces she most desired. Vansittart was interested in the Moorish things—the bronze cups, the gold and scarlet slippers, the embroidered curtains, and, most of all, the daggers, of which there were many curious shapes, in purple-gleaming Damascus steel.

While Fiordelisa and her aunt were choosing brooches and necklaces—necklaces which by a double twist became bracelets—Vansittart was cheapening daggers, and, as a young man of ample means, ended by buying the dearest and perhaps the best, a really serviceable knife, in a red velvet sheath.

He paid for as many things as Lisa cared to choose; for a bead necklace and an enamel brooch; for a square of gold-striped gauze to twist about her head and shoulders; for a dainty little pair of Moorish shoes which might admit Lisa's toes, but which would certainly leave the major part of her substantial foot out in the cold; for a gilded casket to hold her jewels—for a fan—for a gilt thimble—and for a little set of Algerian coffee-cups for her aunt.

All these things were to be sent next morning to the Signora's lodgings near the Ponte di Rialto. Vansittart paid the bill, which disposed of a good many of his limp Italian notes, put his dagger in his breast pocket, and left the shop, cutting short the compliments and thanks of the Venetian youth.

The Caffè Florian—of which tradition tells that it closeth not day or night, winter or summer—was filled with people and ablaze with light. Lisa pushed her way to a table, making good use of those fine shoulders and elbows of hers, and a little group of men who had finished their coffee got up and made way for the brilliant black eyes, and the red lips, which the little velvet mask did not hide. Those finely moulded lips looked all the lovelier for the fringe of lace that shadowed them, and the white teeth flashed as she smiled her thanks.

She talked loud, and laughed gaily while she sipped her chocolate. Vansittart himself was somewhat exhilarated by champagne, music, and two or three little glasses of cognac taken between the acts at the Rossini Theatre, and he was unashamed of his companion's laughter and general exuberance, even although she was attracting the attention of every one within earshot. Beauty and vivacity are not attributes to make a man ashamed of his companion, although she may be only a Burano lace-maker disguised in a tawdry velvet gown.

"Show me the dagger you chose after all your bargaining," she said, leaning over towards him, with her elbows on the table.

He obeyed. She drew the dagger from its sheath and looked at it critically. The red velvet sheath, embroidered with gold, took her fancy much more than the damascened blade.

"It is too heavy to wear in one's hair," she said, throwing down the sheath, and taking up the weapon.

"Take care. The blade is as sharp as a razor. It is not by any means an ornament for a lady's toilette table. I bought it against an excursion to the Zambesi, which I have been thinking about for the last two years."

"The Zambesi," she repeated wonderingly; "is that in Italy?"

"No, Signorina. It is on the Dark Continent."

She had never heard of the Dark Continent, but she only shrugged her shoulders, incuriously, and leant further across the table to examine a black pearl pin, shaped something like a death's head, which Vansittart wore in his tie, and thus brought her smiling lips very near his face.

While she leant thus, with the tip of her finger touching the pearl, and her eyes lifted interrogatively, a heavy hand was laid upon Vansittart's shoulder, and he was half twisted out of his chair—tilted after the manner of chairs on which young men sit—by sheer brute force on the part of the owner of the hand.

"Come out of that!" said a voice that was thickened by drink.

Vansittart was on his feet in an instant, facing a man as tall as himself, and a good deal more bulky—a son of Anak, sandy-haired, pallid, save for red spots on his cheek-bones, spots that burnt like flame.

He was scowling savagely, breathless with rage. Lisa had risen as quickly as Vansittart, and Lisa's aunt had moved towards the newcomer in evident trouble of mind.

"Signor Giovanni," she faltered, "who would have thought to see you in Venice to-night?"

"Not you, evidently, you wicked old hag—nor you, hussy!" cried the man, furious with jealousy and drink. "I've caught you at your games, have I, you good-for-nothing slut! You couldn't stay indoors like a decent woman, but you must needs walk the streets late at night with this Cockney cad here."

"Take care what you say to her—or to me," said Vansittart, in that muffled bass which means a dangerous kind of anger.

He put his arm round Fiordelisa, drawing her towards him as if she belonged to him and it were his place to guard her from every assailant. The crowd made a ring about them, looking on, amused and interested, with no thought of interference which might spoil sport. The comedy some of them had seen at the Goldoni Theatre that night was not half so amusing as this bit out of the comedy of real life—the cosmopolitan comedy of human passion.

"You infernal blackguard!" cried the stranger, trying to tear the girl from Vansittart's protecting clasp; "I'll teach you to carry on with my——"

A foul word finished the sentence: a blow from Vansittart, straight in the stranger's teeth, punctuated it. Then came other foul words, and other blows; and the men were grappling each other like pugilists fighting for the belt. The unknown was of heavier build, and showed traces of former training, but Vansittart was in much better condition, and was nearer sobriety, though by no means sober. He had the best of it for some minutes, till the other man by sheer brute force flung him against the table, crashing down among the shattered glasses and coffee-cups, and dealt him a savage blow below the belt, kicking him as he struck.

The table reeled over and Vansittart fell. Under his open hand as it struck the floor he felt, the unsheathed dagger which Fiordelisa had flung down, in careless indifference, after deciding that it was too big for an ornament.

Infuriated by that foul blow, maddened by the brutality of the attack, excited to fever heat by the surrounding circumstances, even by the very atmosphere, which reeked with tobacco and brandy, Vansittart sprang to his feet, clutched his foe by the collar, and plunged the dagger into his breast. In the moment of doing it the thing seemed natural, spontaneous, the inevitable outcome of the assault that had been made upon him. In the next moment, as those angry eyes grew dim, and the man fell like a log, Vansittart felt himself a coward and a murderer.

A sudden silence came upon the crowd, tumultuous a moment ago. A silence fell upon the scene, like a dull, grey veil, gauzy, impalpable, that had dropped from the ceiling.

"Dead," muttered a voice at Vansittart's elbow, as the man lay in the midst of them, motionless. "That knife went straight to the heart."

A shriek rent the air, wild and shrill, and the vibrating glasses echoed it with a banshee scream. Lisa flung herself upon the body, and tried to staunch the bubbling blood with her poor wisp of a handkerchief. A man pushed his way through the crowd with an authoritative air—a doctor, doubtless; but before he reached the little clear space where the victim lay with Lisa crouching over him, and Lisa's aunt wringing her hands and appealing to the Madonna and all the Saints, a rough hand pulled Vansittart's arm, and a man whispered in Italian, "Run, run, while you have the chance!"

"Run?" Yes, he was a murderer, and his life belonged to the law, unless he used his heels to save his neck. Quick as lightning he took the hint, clove his way through the crowd, and made a dash for the door nearest the Piazzetta. The crowd were busy watching the doctor as he knelt beside that prostrate form—interested, too, in Fiordelisa, with her mask flung off, her loosened hair falling about her ivory neck, her dark eyes streaming, her red lips convulsed and quivering. Vansittart was at the door, past it, before a man cried—

"Stop him; stop the assassin."

There was a sudden tumult, and twenty men were giving chase, a pack of human bloodhounds, perhaps as much for the sake of sport as from actual horror at the deed. They rushed along the Piazzetta, knocking down more than one astonished lounger on their way. They made for the Pillars of St. Mark and St. Theodore—for that spot where of old the Republic put her felons to death, and where now the gondolas wait in sunshine and in starshine for the holiday visitors in the dream-city.

He would make for the water naturally, and jump on board the first gondola he could find, thought his pursuers; but when they reached the quay there was not a gondola to be seen. The gondoliers had all got their fares to-night, and all the gondolas were on the Grand Canal, with flaunting paper lanterns flying at their beaked prows, and coloured fires burning, and mandolines and guitars tinkling and twanging, and "Funicoli, funicola," echoing from boat to boat.

"We shall have him!" cried the foremost of that yelping pack, and even as he spoke they all heard the sound of a great splash, by the steps yonder, and knew their quarry had taken to the water.

The Venetians, warm with macaroni and wine, and in no humour for an improvised bath under those starlit ripples, pulled up, and began to chatter; then whistled and shouted for gondolas, hopelessly, as to the empty air; and anon, by common consent, ran to the bridge hard by the furthermost corner of the Doge's Palace, and from that vantage point looked over the water.

It was covered with holiday craft. Far as the eye could see the gaily decked boats were crossing and recrossing the broad reach between the Riva and the island church, and in the midst of them, like a sea-girt fortress, rose the dark hulk of the P. and O. steamer, her lights showing bright and high above those fantastical Chinese lanterns, her boilers throbbing, her cables groaning, all prepared for instant departure.

There was a deep-toned blast of the steamer's whistle, the clamour of the donkey engines suddenly ceased, and the beating of the screw lashed up the water: and, lo, all the gondolas were tossed and swung about like a handful of rose-leaves on a running brook.

"She's off!" cried one of Vansittart's pursuers, almost forgetting the chase in the pleasures of watching that big ship getting under way.

"Do you think he could have got on board her?" asked another; "he" meaning their quarry.

"Not he, unless he were a better swimmer than ever I knew."

* * * *

He was a better swimmer than anybody among that Venetian's acquaintance—or, at any rate, he was good enough to swim out to the P. and O. steamer and to get himself on board her before the engines began to beat the water with their first deliberate pulsations. The last boat had left the side of the vessel; the sailors were drawing up the accommodation ladder, as he called to them with a voice of command which they did not question. In three or four minutes he was on deck, and had made his way, dripping as he was, to the captain of the vessel.

He explained himself briefly. He had got into a row—a Carnival frolic only—and wanted to get clear of Venice, and knowing the steamer was to sail for Alexandria that night, had swum out to her at the last moment. He had plenty of money about him, and as for change of clothes, he must do the best he could.

"I hope it wasn't anything very bad," said the captain doubtfully, looking at this dripping stranger from top to toe.

"Oh no; a man hit me in a caffè just now, and I hit him."

The steamer was imperceptibly moving seaward at every steady throb of those ponderous engines, threading her way along the tortuous channel so slowly and cautiously at first that Vansittart wondered if she were ever going to get away. Venice the lamplit, the starlit, the beautiful, glided into the distance, with all her domes and pinnacles, her gondolas and Chinese lanterns, torches and skyrockets, music and laughter. Vansittart's heart ached as he watched the fairy city fading like a vision of the night. He had loved her so well—spent such happy, light, unthinking days upon those waters, in those labyrinthine streets, laughing and chaffering with the little merchants of the Rialto, following Venetian beauty through the mazy ways and over the innumerable bridges—happy, uncaring. And now he was an escaped murderer, and would never dare to show his face in Venice again. "Good God!" he said to himself, in a stupor of horrified shame, "that I, a gentleman, should have used a knife—like a Colorado miner, or a drunken sweep in Seven Dials!"

CHAPTER II.

AFTER-THOUGHTS

There was nothing but fair weather for the P. and O. steamer *Berenice* between Venice and Alexandria—fair weather and a calm sea; and John Vansittart had ample leisure in which to think over what he had done, and to live again through all the sensations of his last night in Venice.

He had to live through it all again, and again, in those long days at sea, out of sight of land, with nothing between him and his own dark thoughts but that monotony of cloudless sky and rolling waters. What did it matter whether the boat made eighteen or twenty knots an hour, whether progress were fast or slow? Each day meant an eternity of thought to him who sat apart in his canvas chair, staring blankly eastward, or brooding with bent head, and melancholy eyes fixed on the deck, seeing nothing, hearing nothing, irritated and miserable when some officious fellow-passenger insisted upon plumping down by his side in another deck chair, and talking to him about the weather, or his destination, with futile questionings as to whether this was his first voyage to the East, and all the idle inquisitiveness of the traveller who has nothing to do, and very little to think about.

Captain and steward had been very good to him. The former had asked him no questions after that first inquiry, content to know that he was a gentleman, and had a well-filled purse; the latter had put him to bed in the most comfortable of berths, and had given him a hot drink, and dried his clothes ready for the next morning. And in that one suit of clothes, with changes of linen borrowed from the captain, he made the voyage to Alexandria in the bright spring weather, under the vivid blue that canopies the Mediterranean. Perhaps the fact of living in that one suit of clothes all through those hot days intensified his sense of being a pariah among the other passengers; he who had come among them with a hand red with murder.

Hour after hour he would sit in his corner of the deck, always the most secluded spot he could find, and brood over the thing that he had done.

He had an open book upon his knee for appearance's sake, and pretended to be absorbed in it whenever a curious saunterer passed his way. He smoked all day long for comfort's sake, the only comfort possible for his troubled brain, and all day long he thought of his last evening in Venice and the thing that he had done there.

To think that he, a gentleman by birth and education, should have slain a man in a tavern row; that he, who in his earliest boyhood had been taught to use his fists, and to defend himself after the manner of Englishmen, should have yielded to a tigerish impulse, and stabbed an unarmed foe to the heart! He, the well-bred Englishman, had behaved no better than a drunken Lascar.

He scorned—he hated—himself for that blind fury which had made him grip the weapon that accident had placed in his way.

He was not particularly sorry for the man he had killed; a violent, drunken brute, who for the sake of the rest of humanity was better dead than alive. A profligate who had betrayed that lovely ignoramus under a promise of marriage, a promise which he had never meant to keep. He hated himself for the manner of the brute's death rather than for the death itself. If he had killed the man in fair fight he would have felt no regret at having made an end of him; but to have stabbed an unarmed man! There was the sting, there was the shame of it. All night long, between snatches of troubled sleep, he writhed and tossed in his berth, wishing that he were dead, wondering whether it were not the best thing he could do to throw himself overboard before daybreak and so make an end of these impotent regrets, this maddening reiteration of details, this perpetual representation of the hateful scene, for ever beginning and ending and beginning again in his tortured brain.

He would have decided upon suicide, perhaps, not having any strong religious convictions at this stage of his existence; but his life was not his own to fling away, however unpleasant he might have made it for himself.

He had a mother who adored him, and to whom he, for his part, was warmly attached. She was a widow, and he was the head of the house, sole master of the estate, and to him she looked for dignity and comfort. Were he to die the landed property would pass to his uncle, a dry old bachelor, and though his mother would still have her income, she would be banished from the house in which her wedded life had been spent, and she would be the loser in social status. He had an only sister, too, a fair, frivolous being, of whom, in a lesser degree, he was fond; a sister who had made her appearance in Society at the pre-Lenten Drawing-Room, and had been greatly admired, and who was warranted to make a good match.

Poor little Maud! What would become of Maud if he were to

throw himself off a P. and O. steamer? Think of the scandal of it. And yet, if he lived, and that brutal business in the Venetian caffè were to be brought home to him—murder, or manslaughter—it would be even worse for his sister. Society would look askance at a girl with such a ruffian for a brother—an Englishman who used the knife against his fellow-man. Daggers and stilettos might be common wear among Venetians; but the knife was not the less odious in the sight of an Englishman because he happened to be in a city where traditions of treachery and secret murder were interwoven with all her splendour and her beauty. It would be horrible, humiliating, disgraceful for his people if ever that story came to be known—a choice topic for the daily papers, with just that spice of romance and adventure which would justify exhaustive treatment.

Thinking over the question from the Society point of view—and in most of the great acts of life Society stands with the modern Christian in the place which the religious man gives his Creator—Vansittart told himself that every effort of his intelligence must be bent upon dissociating himself from that tragedy in the Venetian caffè. He had got clear of the city by a wonderful bit of luck; for had the steamer started five minutes earlier, or a quarter of an hour later, escape that way would have been impossible.

He had heard the men giving chase on the Piazzetta as he jumped from the quay; heard them shouting when he was in the water. Had the steamer been stationary those men would have boarded her, and the whole story would have been known. She had weighed anchor in the nick of time for him. But what then? A telegram to the police at Brindisi or Alexandria might stop him, as other fugitive felons are caught every month in the year—men who get clear off at Liverpool, to be arrested before they step ashore at New York.

He paid his passage on the morning after his flight, and gave his name as John Smith, of London. The captain scrutinized him rather suspiciously on hearing that name of Smith; but Vansittart did not look like a swindler or a blackguard. He was under a cloud, perhaps, the captain thought, and Smith was most likely an alias; but anyhow he was a gentleman, and the captain meant to stand his friend.

"Are you going to stay long in Cairo?" he asked Vansittart, when they were within sight of Alexandria.

"Not long. Perhaps only till I get my luggage. I shall go up the Nile."

"You'll find it rather hot before you've been a long way."

"Oh, I don't mind heat. I'm not a feverish subject," said Vansittart, lightly, having no more idea of going up the Nile than of going to the moon.

"You'll stop at Sheppard's, of course?"

"Yes, decidedly. I'm told it's a very good hotel."

While they were nearing their port he contrived to get a good deal of information about the steamers that touched there. He meant to get off on the first boat that sailed after he landed. All the interval he wanted was the time to buy some ready-made clothes and a valise, so that he might not appear on board the homeward-bound steamer in the miserable condition in which he had introduced himself to the captain of the P. and O.

He parted with that officer with every expression of friendliness.

"I shan't forget how good you've been to a traveller in distress," he said lightly; "you may not hear of me for a month or two, perhaps. I may be up the Nile——"

"Take care of the climate," interjected the captain.

"But as soon as I go back to London I shall write to you. Good-bye."

"Good-bye, Mr. Smith, and good luck to you for a fine swimmer wherever you go."

"Oh, I won a cup or two at Oxford," answered the other. "We rather prided ourselves on our swimming in my set."

He went to a restaurant where he could sit under an awning and read the latest papers that had found their way to Alexandria. There were plenty of Paris papers—*Galignani*, *Le Figaro*, *Le Temps*. There was a Turin paper, very stale—and there was a copy of the *Daily Telegraph* that had been left by some traveller, and which was a fortnight old. Nothing to fear there. Vansittart breathed more freely, and thought of going on to Cairo. But second thoughts warned him that Cairo was very English, and that he might meet some one he knew there. Better to stick to his first plan, and go back to England by the first steamer that would take him.

He had to think of his possessions at Danieli's, and whether the things he had left there would provide a clue to his identity. He thought not. He had not given his name to the hall porter.

The hotel was crowded, and he had—like a convict—been simply known as "150," the number of his room.

Clothes, portmanteau, dressing-bag, bore only his initials, J. V. He had been travelling in lightest marching order; carrying no books save those which he picked up on his way, no writing materials, except the compact little case in his dressing-bag. It was his habit to destroy all letters as soon as he had read them—even his mother's, after a second or third reading. His card-case, note-case, and purse were all in his pockets when he made the plunge. No, he had left nothing at Danieli's; nor had he left Danieli's deep in debt, for he had paid his account on Tuesday morning, with a half-formed intention of starting for Verona by the early train on Wednesday. He could resign himself to the loss of portmanteau and contents, and the plain pigskin bag, which had seen good service and had been scraped and battered upon many a platform.

Reflection told him that he had nothing to fear from the newspapers yet awhile, since no newspaper could have travelled faster than the steamer that had brought him, while the news of that homicide at Venice was hardly important enough to be telegraphed to any Egyptian journal. No, he was safe so far; but he told himself that the best thing he could do was to get back to England and the wilderness of London; while the *Berenice* and her good-natured captain went on to Bombay, where, no doubt, the captain would read of that fatal brawl in the Venetian caffè, and identify his passenger as the English tourist who had stabbed another man to death.

Vansittart pulled himself together, counted his money, and rejoiced at finding that he had enough for his voyage home, and a trifle over for incidental expenses and a small outfit. The greater part of his money was in English bank-notes, about which no questions would be asked.

He went to the steamboat office, and found that there was a P. and O. boat leaving that night for London, so he took his passage on board her, selected his berth, and then drove off to an outfitter's to get his kit, and a new cabin trunk, just big enough to hold his belongings. He bought a few French novels, and those small necessities of life without which the civilized man feels himself a savage.

His ship sailed at midnight. He was on board her early in the evening, pacing the deck in the balmy night, and looking at the lighted town, the massive quays, which testify to English enterprise, the Pharos sending out its long lines of bright white light seaward—the gigantic breakwater—all that makes the Egyptian port of to-day in some wise worthy of the Alexandria of old, when her twin obelisks stood out against the sky, and when her name meant all that was grandest in the splendour of the antique world.

Vansittart looked at the starlit sky and lamplit city with a dull unobservant gaze, while the burden upon his mind deadened his sense of all things fair and strange, and made him indifferent to scenes which would once have aroused his keenest interest. How often he had dreamed his summer daydream of Egypt, lying on a velvet lawn in Hampshire, with a volume of old Herodotus, or some modern traveller, flung upon the grass beside him, in the idlesse of a July afternoon! How often he had promised himself a long winter in that historic land! He had not much of the explorer's ardour in those boyish days, no bent towards undiscovered watersheds and unpleasant encounters with blackamoors, no ambition to be reckoned amongst the mighty marksmen of the world, or to be called the father of lions; though in some vague visions he had fancied himself wandering in that lone land where the Zambesi leaps headlong into the fathomless gorge, in blinding whiteness of foam and deafening thunder of sound, a beauty and a terror to eye and ear. The things he most wanted to see were the things that his fellow-men had made, the palaces and statues, and fortresses and tombs that mean history. He was not a naturalist or a scientific traveller, had no hope of making the world any richer by his discoveries, or of reading the smallest paper at the Geographical Society. He wanted to see men and cities, and all splendid memorials of past ages, for his own pleasure and amusement; and Egypt was one of the countries to which he had looked for delight, if ever satiety and weariness should overtake him amidst the nearer delights of his beloved Italy.

And, behold, to-day he had walked those Egyptian streets, and let those Egyptian faces pass by him, with eyes that saw not, and with a mind that felt no interest in the things the eyes looked at. The distress in his thoughts, the perpetual labouring of his troubled mind, would not allow of pleasure in anything. That aching agony of remorse had taken hold of him, and left room for no other feeling. To the end of his life all that was picturesque and individual in this Egyptian seaport would be part and parcel of his self-humiliation, associated for ever with the thought that he had slain a fellow-creature, under circumstances for which he could find no excuse.

Again and again, as he paced the deck in the starlight, the face of the man he had killed stood out against the deep azure of the sky and sea, as it had looked at him in that awful moment when one last ejaculation, "God!" broke from the parted lips, and the man fell as if struck by a thunderbolt. There was scarcely any change in his face as he fell—no ghastly pallor, no convulsion of the features. As he lay there looking up at the ceiling, one might hardly have thought him dead. No torrent of blood rushed from those parted lips. The stream ebbed slow and dull from the pierced heart. That savage thrust of the dagger had done its work well. How many daggers and what a gory butchery had been needed to make an end of Cæsar; and behold this man was done for with one movement of an angry hand. For John Vansittart murder had been made easy.

The homeward voyage seemed ever so much longer than the outward, and the gloom of his mind deepened as the summer days wore out; summer, for it was summer here on the Mediterranean, whatever season it might seem in London, summer at Genoa, summer all along the Riviera, where the mimosas flung their fairy gold across the villa gardens, and the lateen sails shone dazzling white in the vivid sun, and the berceaus were beginning to clothe themselves with young vine leaves, unfolding out of crumpled woolly greyness into tender, translucent green.

He thought of Fiordelisa, and his thoughts of her were bitterest of all. He could not doubt that he had robbed her of her protector, the man whose purse provided for the little household of which she and her aunt had talked so gaily. It might be that he had left her to starve—or worse. Was it likely she would ever go back to Burano, and her lace-work, and her threepence-halfpenny a day, and her slipshod shoes, and her polenta, after having tasted the flesh-pots of Venice, the pallid asparagus and fat cauliflowers from the market in the Rialto, the savoury messes at the sign of the Black Hat? Would she go back and be a peasant again, after trapesing the Piazzetta in her flashy black and yellow gown, and sitting in a lantern-lit gondola, and twanging on her mandoline?

His experience of her sex and degree inclined him to think that she would not return to the old laborious life, with its hardships and privations. The first step upon the broad high-road of sin having been taken, there would be but little scruple about the second; and those bold, beautiful eyes, that swan throat and graceful form, would belong to somebody else. The easy-going aunt would hardly stand in the way of a new settlement, when the last of their poor possessions had been carried to the Monte di Pietà, and hunger was at hand. Somebody else would pay the little old singing-master, and listen admiringly while Lisa sang to the wiry tinkling of her mandoline; and the lanterns would swing from the beak of the gondola in the festival evenings, and the rockets would shoot up through the purple night in front of Santa Maria della Salute, and all the palaces on the Grand Canal would shine rosy red, reflecting the Bengal fires, and Lisa would forget her murdered man, while those substantial feet of hers tripped gaily down the brimstone path.

If that tall, broad-shouldered, sandy-haired man had lived he might have kept his promise and married her. Who is to be sure that he would not? There are men in the world who will wed the girl they love, be she barmaid or ballet-dancer; and that this man was fond of Fiordelisa there could be little doubt. His savage jealousy indicated the passionate force of the civilized savage's love.

Alas for Fiordelisa, widowed in the very morning of life! He who had wrecked her fortune could do nothing to help her. He dared not stretch out his hand towards her. His interest, for the sake of others as well as for his own sake, lay in severing every link that could connect him with the catastrophe of that fatal night. No, he could do nothing for Fiordelisa. He would not have grudged her the half of his income; and he dared not send her so much as a ten-pound note! She must sink or swim.

The thought of her peril doubled the sum of his remorse.

He landed at Marseilles, and here, too, it was summer—summer at her brightest, with azure skies, and a sea deeper, bluer, more darkly glorious than the lapis lazuli in a jewelled châsse. The streets were full of traffic and abloom with flower-girls, noisily pressing their bunches of roses and pale Parma violets upon him as he walked up the Rue de la Cannebière on his way from the quay to the railway hotel. There had been a time when the sights and sounds of that southern port were like strong wine, exhilarating, delighting him, when he could not have too much of the animation and picturesqueness of the place, the Corniche road, the wide-stretching bay with rocks and lighthouses, the sea marks of every kind, and that glittering point where the waterways divide—to the left for Hindostan, China, Japan; to the right for the New World and the setting sun; two paths upon the trackless blue that seemed each to lead direct to fairyland.

And behold he had come from the land of glamour and mystery, from the tombs of the Pharaohs, from the ashes of Cleopatra, heart-weary, caring for nothing.

He went into one of the big caffès on his right hand, seated himself at a table in an obscure corner, and began to examine the papers, hastily turning them over one after another, worried by the sticks to which they were fastened. Yes, here it was, in the Paris *Figaro*.

"A fatal brawl occurred last Tuesday night in one of the caffès in the Piazza at Venice. Two Englishmen fought savagely about a Venetian girl who had entered the caffè in the company of one of them. Both men appeared to have been drinking, and after a desperate encounter with fists, in the English fashion, the younger and better-looking of the two snatched up a dagger and stabbed his antagonist to the heart. Death was almost instantaneous. The murderer managed to get away in the confusion caused by the unexpected catastrophe, the crowded state of the Piazzetta and the Riva favouring his escape. It is supposed that he jumped into the water, and either managed to scramble into a gondola and get himself conveyed to the railway station or was drowned—though the latter supposition seems unlikely when it is considered that the canal was crowded with boats. Every effort to discover traces of the missing man has been made by the Venetian police, but as yet without success. The name of the murdered man was John Smith. He had been some time resident in Venice, but did not bear a good character in the city, where he was in debt to several of the smaller tradespeople in the Rialto. Very little seems to have been known about his surroundings, even by the elderly woman who kept house for him, or the girl whose existence cost him his life."

John Smith. An assumed name, no doubt; just as false as that name of Smith which Vansittart had given to the captain and steward of the *Berenice*.

It did not seem to him, as he re-read this paragraph among the Faits Divers in the *Figaro*, that the fatal event had created so much stir as he had supposed it would create. It seemed to him that he was getting off cheaply, and that he might go down to the grave without being called upon to answer for that deadly stroke. The man's isolation saved him. Had his victim been the member of a respectable English family, had there been father and mother, brothers and sisters to bewail his loss, much more stringent efforts might have been made to find his murderer. But a reprobate Englishman, a man who had perhaps severed every link that bound him to kindred and country, a scampish individual, living under an assumed name and unable to pay his way, was not the kind of person whose death in a tavern brawl was likely to make a great stir.

Had he disappeared, had there been the attraction of mystery about his doom, a riddle to solve, a crime unexplained and seemingly unexplainable, French and English newspapers might have given columns or florid writing to the case. But here there was no mystery, no dark enigma of love and murder. In the full glare of the gas, in sight of the crowd, these two men had fought, and one had proved himself unworthy of his British birthright by using a dagger against an unarmed antagonist.

Vansittart found the same paragraph repeated in several papers, and amongst his researches, aided by a waiter who brought him the accumulation of the last ten days, he found an old *Daily Telegraph* in which his crime formed the basis for a spirited leader, full of vivacity and local colour, written by a journalist who evidently knew Venice by heart. In this article the picturesqueness of the city, the riot of Carnival time, the historical associations of Doge and Republic,

28

were more insisted upon than the brutality of the fight, or the unfair use of the dagger.

He felt a little easier in his mind after his examination of the papers. It seemed to him that by the time he arrived at Charing Cross most people would have forgotten all about an event which was already three weeks old, and it would hardly occur to any one to connect him with the fatal brawl in the Piazza di San Marco.

He dined in the crowded, bustling restaurant in the Station Hotel with a little better appetite than he had felt for a long time, and took his seat in a corner of a compartment of the Rapide—not affecting the stuffy luxury of the "Sleeping"—for the long night journey to Paris, with a calmer mind than he had known since Shrove Tuesday. He looked out into the darkness when the train stopped at Avignon, and it was winter again, the bleak March winter before the Easter Noon; and at Lyons the blasts from the two rivers blew colder still, and he felt that he was near home.

He was in Charles Street by afternoon teatime, sitting in the cosy drawing-room with his mother and sister, being petted and made much of in a manner calculated to stimulate any young man's self-love. His mother adored him, and he had been away from her nearly half a year. His sister was seven years his junior, a pretty, frivolous young creature, whose mind rarely dwelt upon any more serious question than the fashion of her next ball-dress or how she should wear her hair, or the newest toy on her silver table. Yet she, too, adored Jack Vansittart in her pretty frivolous way, and had not yet begun to adore anybody else.

The room was full of flowers and old china, and little tables crowded with silver, and enamels, and Dresden boxes, and ivory paper-knives; and there were books in every available corner; an old room with panelled walls and a low ceiling, in a somewhat shabby old house which had belonged to Mrs. Vansittart's grandfather, an East India director, in the days when the Pagoda tree was still worth shaking. The furniture was seventy years old, a quaint mixture of old-fashioned English things, before the influence of Sheraton and Chippendale had died out, and Indian things, really and intensely Indian, bought in the East, long before Oriental goods began to be manufactured wholesale for English buyers. Bombay blackwood, with its clumsy bulkiness enriched by elaborate carving, ivories, screens of black and gold, rainbow-hued embroideries which time had scarcely faded, porcelain jars and enamelled vases, relieved the stern simplicity of rosewood and pale chintz. A few choice water-colours on the walls, and an abundance of flowers harmonized everything, and made Mrs. Vansittart's drawing-room a fitting nest for a very elegant woman and her very pretty daughter.

The London house was Mrs. Vansittart's own property; the house in Hampshire belonged to her son, and she spoke of herself and her daughter laughingly as caretakers.

"When you marry," said Maud, tossing up her pretty head, with pale gold hair crisped and curled in the prevailing fashion, "mother and I will have to budge. Whatever slut you may choose to fall in love with will be mistress of Merewood."

"Why must you needs suppose I may fall in love with a slut?"

"Oh, by the doctrine of opposites. You are one of those orderly, superior persons who are foredoomed to admire some wild girl of the woods, some harum-scarum minx, with fine eyes and half an inch of mud on the edge of her gown."

"However fine the eyes were, I think the half-inch of mud would be a warning that I could hardly ignore. But I do not claim to be either orderly or superior. My father's Irish blood has infused a spice of disorder into my Anglo-Saxon character."

And now on this bright April afternoon Jack Vansittart was being petted and fed by these two loving women, who could not do too much to prove their devotion to him after the long severance. They had only given him time to wash his hands and brush the Kentish dust and chalk out of his hair and clothes before he sat down between them to a cup of tea. He had to assure them that he had lunched heartily at Calais, and wanted nothing but tea, or else a substantial meal would have been set out in the dining-room below.

"And you have come straight through from Marseilles?" said Mrs. Vansittart. "What a terrible journey!"

"Hot and dusty, mother; not very appalling to a traveller. But you are such a stay-at-home."

"To my cost," pouted Maud. "I haven't the least idea of what the world is like. I have to take other people's word that it is round."

"We found your telegram from Marseilles at two o'clock this morning when we came home from Mrs. Mountain's dance, and, rejoiced as I was to know you were coming back to us, I took it for granted you would loiter in Paris for a week," said Mrs. Vansittart.

"Paris is always delightful," replied her son; "but I was tired of wandering, and was honestly homesick. And here I am safe at home, and ever so much better off than poor old Odysseus. By the way, mother, your Italian spaniel did her level best to bite me as I came upstairs, and she and I were once such friends. Dogs have altered since the days of Argus."

"How silly of her! but she'll love you again after a day or two. And now tell me, Jack, all you have been doing and seeing since you left Merewood last October. You are such a bad correspondent that one knows nothing about your wanderings, and if I were not well broken to your neglect I should be miserable about you."

"See how wise my system is," he said, laughing; "were I a good correspondent an interval of a week without a letter would scare you. I have heard of men who write regularly once a week to their people, or who keep a journal of their travels and send it home every fortnight for family perusal. But since you and Maud both know that I detest letter-writing, you expect nothing of me, and are never anxious."

"Indeed you are wrong, Jack," said his mother, with a sigh. "I have had many an anxious hour about you. But I'm not going to be doleful now I have you at home again, and for a long time, I hope."

"Yes, for a long time," echoed Jack. "I am sick of travelling."

There was a weariness in his tone that sounded as if he meant what he said.

"And now tell me your adventures."

The word hurt him like the sharp edge of a knife.

"I have had none. No one has adventures nowadays," he said. "I had a fortnight on an American friend's yacht in the Mediterranean, and we had some rather dirty weather, but nothing to hurt. That's my nearest approach to an adventure. I had a month at Monte Carlo, shot a good many pigeons, and missed nearly as many as I shot; played a little, with varying luck, but am not ruined; came off on the whole a winner, though to no substantial amount, perhaps enough to buy a pair of solitaires for Maud's pretty little ears"—pinching the ear that was nearest him, as the girl sat on a low chair at his side. "No, I have had no adventures. I have only been in familiar places. Let me see, from where did I write last?"

"From Bologna, ages ago; a shabby little letter," answered Maud.

"Ah, I spent a few days in Bologna after I left Florence. I am rather fond of Bologna."

"And after that? Where did you go after Bologna? It must be nearly two months since you were there."

"Oh, I went to Padua and—and Verona," he answered carelessly, "and then back to Genoa, and then I dawdled along the Riviera, stopping a night or two here and there, to Marseilles; and here I am. That is my history—and I am ready for another cup of tea."

Maud filled his cup, and offered him dainty biscuits and tempting cakes, and hung about him fondly, touching the thick hair which made such a waving line across the broad forehead.

"Why, how tremendously sunburnt you are!" she exclaimed. "You look as if you had just come off a sea voyage."

"Do I? Well, I have basked in the sun that shines upon the Mediterranean; and a March sun on the Riviera is a blazer."

"And you were at Bologna and Padua, and did not go to your beloved Venice?" said his mother. "I thought you were so fond of Venice?"

"Yes, I delight in the place, but I wanted to go back to the Riviera, where I should be more secure of sunshine and balmy air."

"And you left Italy without revisiting Venice?" exclaimed Maud, who had often listened to his raptures about the City by the Sea.

There was no more to be said. For the first time in his life he had deliberately lied, and to his mother and sister, of all people—to those who in all the world most trusted and believed in him. He hated himself for what he had done; and yet he meant to maintain that false assertion doggedly. He had not been to Venice. Let no casual acquaintance come forward to allege that he had been seen there. In the very teeth of assertion he would declare that in this springtime of 1886 he had not been in Venice. He rejoiced in the thought that he had told his name to no one at Danieli's, and that he had entered the hotel as a stranger, having stopped at one of the hotels on the Grand Canal on his previous visits. He told himself that no one could convict him of having been in the fatal city last Shrove Tuesday—no one who knew him as Jack Vansittart.

"And now that you've had the history of my travels——"

"A sorry history, forsooth!" cried Maud. "You men have no capacity for description. When Lucy Calder came home from her Italian honeymoon she talked to me for hours about the places and things she had seen there."

"Pretty prattler! Would you like me to recite a few pages of Murray or Joanne? All travelling is alike nowadays, Maud, and pleasure and comfort are only a question of good railway service and well-found hotels. We have done with romance and adventure. Life is pretty much the same all over Europe. And now tell me what you have been doing; there is more interest in a girl's life in her first season than in all the cities of Europe."

"Well, Jack, to begin with, I was presented at the February Drawing-Room. I went out with mother a goodish bit last November, don't you know, but I was not actually out. That only began after the Drawing-Room."

"And had you a pretty frock, and did the Royalties look kindly at you when you made your curtsy?"

"The Royalties might all have been waxwork, from Her Majesty downwards, for anything I knew to the contrary," said Maud. "I saw no faces—only a cloud of feathers, and a splendour of jewels, and velvet, and satin, all vague and troubled, like the figures in a dream—but I got through the business somehow, and mother said I made no mistakes."

"And the frock?"

"Oh, the frock was just as pretty as a frock can be. It was mother's taste. She talked out every detail with Mdlle. Marie. She was not content to hear that Lady Lucille Plantagenet had worn this sort of thing, or Lady Gwendoline Tudor that sort of thing. She insisted on having just the frock she thought would suit me, Maud Vansittart. The train and petticoat were white satin—the satin you see in old pictures, satin in which there are masses of deep, steel-grey shadow and floods of white, silvery light—and then there was a cloud of aerophane arranged as only Marie can arrange a drapery, and in the cloud there were clusters of lilies of the valley and fluffy ostrich tips. The papers—the lady-papers mostly—went into raptures about my frock."

"And did the lady-papers say nothing of the wearer?"

"Oh, some of them were so good as to say I was not quite the most hideous débutante of the year, and that they liked the way I had my hair dressed—and now I find our French hair-dresser has the impertinence to advertise the style as the Vansittart Coiffure."

"What a frightful outrage! And having been presented, and being now actually out, I conclude you have found London a very pleasant place, under mother's wing?" said Jack.

"Oh, it is all very quiet so far, and will be till after Easter, no doubt; but we have been to a few friendly dinners and a good many luncheons, and we have a cloud of invitations and engagements for May, and some of our Hampshire friends are in town, so there is plenty to do."

"And have you seen anything of your Yorkshire friend, Sir Hubert Hartley?" asked Jack.

"Yes. Sir Hubert is in town."

"And did he see you in your débutante's finery?"

"Yes, mother had a tea-party that afternoon, and there were a good many people—and, yes, Sir Hubert dropped in."

"And didn't that finish him?"

"Finish him! oh, Jack, what a horrid expression! I don't understand you in the least!"

"Of course not. Well, I'll say no more about my old friend Hubert. I can look him up at the Devonshire to-morrow."

"The Devonshire," sighed Maud. "How sad to think that he is one of the few respectable people who can find it in their hearts to be Liberals!"

"Yes, he is on the wrong side, no doubt, but that doesn't matter to us," said Jack.

Mrs. Vansittart sighed slightly as she touched her daughter's fluffy hair, the girl sitting on her low chair between mother and brother.

"My Maud would like her friends to be of the same opinion as herself," she said, "and she is such an ardent Conservative, and knows so much about politics."

"At least, I know that I am not a Radical, and that I hate what people call Progress," protested Maud. "Progress means pulling down every historical house and widening every picturesque street, cutting railways through Arcadian valleys, and turning romantic lakes into reservoirs."

"And progress sometimes means feeding the hungry, and teaching the ignorant," said her mother, "and building healthy dwellings for people who are herding in poisonous slums. I think we are all agreed as to the necessity for reform, Maud, whether we are Whigs or Tories."

"Oh, of course I want people to be taken care of all over the world," replied Maud, "and I am prouder of our sound, roomy cottages than anything on our estate."

"Ah, that's the mother's work," said Vansittart. "One can see that a woman's eye watches over the parish."

"Sir Hubert tells me they have very good cottages at Hartley," pursued Maud, "but I cannot imagine either comfort or picturesqueness within twenty miles of Sheffield."

"Yet there are some romantic spots and some fine, bold scenery in that part of the world, I believe," said her brother.

* * * *

Later in the evening mother and son were alone together in the room which had always been John Vansittart's sanctum and tabagie, a snug little room on the ground floor; and here the conversation was more serious than it had been at teatime, for wherever Maud was frivolity reigned. She had not yet discovered that life is a troublesome business. For her life meant new frocks and new admirers.

"Dear Jack," sighed the mother, looking fondly at the young man's sunburnt face, as he sat silently enjoying his pipe, "I hope now we have you home again you are going really to settle down."

"Really to settle down," he repeated; "that sounds rather alarming. Settle down to what, mother? Not to matrimony, I hope!"

"To that in good time, dear; but at your own good time, not mine. That is a crisis I would be the last to hasten—not because I am afraid of being turned out of the big house at Merewood; this house will be more than enough for me—but because a hasty union is seldom a happy union."

"Ah, that's the old-fashioned way of looking at it. I believe in the love of a day, the happiness of a lifetime. I believe in elective affinities, and upon this teeming earth there is somewhere just the one woman who could make me happy. Don't be frightened, mother, the chances are against my meeting her; but till I do, till my heart goes tick-tack at the sight of her face, at the first sound of her voice, I shall not marry. I shall not marry because the wisdom of my elders says that it is good for a man to marry. I shall not marry just to place a handsome woman at the head of my table. I will be content with a round table, where there need be no headship."

"I was not thinking of marriage, Jack. I only want to see you settle down to the real business of life. I should be sorry to see you always an idler—sauntering through a London season, yachting a little in the Cowes week, shooting a little in September and October, hunting a little in November, and running away from the winter to amuse yourself at Nice or Monte Carlo. Independent as you are, you ought to do something better with your talents."

"My talents are an unknown quantity. I doubt if any one in this world, except my fond mother, gives me credit for being even moderately clever."

"I remember what you were as a boy, Jack, and how well you got on at Balliol."

"Oh, that was in the atmosphere, I think. I was in love with Greek because I worshipped Jowett. That was a boyish dream. All scholarly ambition is a thing of the past. I shall never do anything in that line."

"Perhaps not. You have too much energy and activity for a student's life. I should like to see you a power in the House."

"Dearest flatterer, you would like to see me Prime Minister. I have no doubt you think that it simply rests with myself to become First Lord of the Treasury at an earlier age than William Pitt."

"No, no, Jack, I am not a foolish mother, fondly as I love you.

But I know that you have good gifts, and I want the world to profit by them. I should like to see you in Parliament. There is so much to be done by good men in the shaping of our new England—the England of enlightenment and humanity—and I want to see my son's hand at the plough."

"The field to be ploughed is wide and the soil is stubborn; but I don't know that my hand would be strong enough to drive a furrow."

"You could help, Jack; every good man can help."

"Mother, I believe you are at heart a Radical."

"I don't think one need be a Radical to wish that the masses were better off and more thought of than they are. Some of the best and noblest things that have been done for the poor have been done by Conservatives. No, Jack, it is because I am not a Radical that I want to see you in Parliament. You are rich, well-born, well-educated. You could fill a place that might be filled by some Radical adventurer who would look to Parliamentary life as a means of pushing his own fortune."

"If I can find any constituency willing to elect Conservative me instead of that Radical adventurer—who would in all probability be a much better speaker than I am, and appeal to a larger electorate—well and good. I have no great aversion to Parliament, but oh, you artful woman, I know why you would have me write M.P. after my name. 'If I can pen him up with the other sheep in the House of Commons he can go no more a-roving.' That is what you say to yourself, mother mine."

"No, no, Jack. I sadly want you at home, but I am not a hypocrite. Most of all I want to see you with higher aims than those of a mere pleasure-seeker. I want to be proud of my son."

She drew her chair nearer his and took his strong, broad hand in both her own. In her eyes he was all that youth and manhood should be. She was proud of him already, though he had done nothing for fame. She was proud of his height and strength, proud of his good looks, courage, good temper, of all those qualities which go to make an English gentleman.

"Proud of me," he echoed. "Poor mother!" He drew his hand away, remembering that it was stained with the blood of his fellow-man.

CHAPTER III.

"FAIRIES!"

Nearly three years had gone by since that fatal night in Venice. It was mid-winter, only a few days after Christmas, and Mrs. Vansittart and her son were spending their Christmas holidays within twenty miles of Merewood.

Maud Vansittart had become Maud Hartley, but before bestowing herself upon her adoring lover she had insisted that he should buy a place within reasonable distance of the house in which she had been born and reared, the home in which she could so vividly recall the image of a beloved father, and where all her happy years of girlhood had been spent with the mother she fondly loved. Sir Hubert had a fine place in the wild Yorkshire hills, half an hour's journey from Sheffield, a solid red-brick manor house in the Georgian style, built by his great-grandfather; but to that house as a home Maud would not consent to go. Her lover being rich enough to buy a second country seat as easily as some men buy a second horse, there had only remained the trouble of choosing a home that Maud could approve.

A house was found, neither too old nor too new, upon the side of Blackdown, in that rich and picturesque country between Petworth and Haslemere—Redwold Towers, a roomy, well-built mansion, with just land enough to satisfy Hubert Hartley's idea of a home-farm, with out diverting his capital from that wider domain of Hartley Manor, where he had fields and pastures of a hundred acres each, and where he grew prize oxen and cart-horses worth their weight in gold, as it seemed to Maud, when she heard of six or seven hundred pounds being given for one of these creatures.

Merewood, John Vansittart's patrimonial estate, was near Liss, in Hampshire, a long, low, capacious house, on a ridge of pineclad hill, and fronting a wild valley, which grew very little of a profitable nature for man or beast, but where the perfume of the pine woods and the gold and purple of gorse and heather were worth all that the fattest soils can produce. Fertile pastures and spacious cornfields were not wanting to the estate, but those lay behind the crest of the hill.

Maud had been married nearly two years, and there was a short-coated baby in the nursery at Redwold, albeit Sir Hubert would rather the eyes of his firstborn had opened upon the light that shone into the family bed-chamber at Hartley Manor, the patriarchal bed-chamber with its patriarchal bed, birth chamber and death chamber, room in which the good old great-grandsire's eyes had closed peacefully, verily "falling on sleep," after a life of ninety years, and after having enriched the world with many useful inventions, and established a wealthy progeny. Unhappily, Maud hated Hartley Manor House, and only went there for a month in the shooting season as a concession to the best of husbands.

"Of course, I always meant to marry him," she told her brother, "and he is the only man for whom I ever cared a straw; but I wanted to have my fling in London; and I liked being talked about as the pretty Miss Vansittart. I was, you know, Jack. You needn't laugh at me. And I liked making other young men miserable, by leading them on a little, meaning nothing all the time."

"Had you many victims? Were there any suicides?"

"Don't talk nonsense. You know how little young men care nowadays. There were some of them who would have liked to marry me, had everything been made easy, settlements, and all that. And," with sudden solemnity, "I might have had a coronet if I had made the most of my chances."

"A hard-up coronet, do you mean? A coronet that wanted regilding."

"No, sir. All those go to America. My coronet was well provided for—but it was not to be," with a faint sigh. "I could not throw Hubert over. He was so ridiculously fond of me."

"Was? Is, I hope," said Jack, this retrospective survey of a girl's career being made one afternoon in the snowy Christmas week, as Jack and his sister tramped home with the shooters, after a day on the hills.

"Yes, he still adores me, poor fellow, though he has found me out ever so long ago."

"Found you out—how?"

"Oh, he has found that I am frivolous and selfish, and utterly worthless, from the socialist's point of view. He has found out that although I am fond of pretty cottages and cottage gardens, I don't care much about the cottagers, and that I never know what to say to them. He has found out that I haven't the interests of the poor really at heart. In short, he has found that I am a thorough-bred Tory instead of a hot-headed Radical, as he is. I'm afraid we ought never to have married. It is like trying to join fire and water."

"Oh, but I think you manage to get on capitally together, in spite of any difference in your political views. Indeed, I did not think you knew much about politics."

"I don't. I know hardly anything. I never read the debates, and my mind always wanders when people are talking politics; but my Conservatism and Hubert's Radicalism enter into everything—into our way with servants, into our treatment of our friends, into our ideas about dress, manners, church. I cannot even shake hands with a cottager as he does. I have tried to imitate him, but I can't achieve that unconscious air of equality which comes so natural to him. And do what I will I can't help feeling ashamed of that great-grandfather of his who began life in Sheffield as a poor lad, and who invented something—some quite small thing, it seems to me—and so laid the foundations of the Hartley wealth. That is a little bit of family history which I should so like everybody to forget, while poor Hubert is quite proud of it. At Hartley Manor he loves to show strangers the great-grandfather's portrait in his working clothes—just as he looked when he invented the thing, whatever it was."

"You would not have him ashamed of the founder of his fortune. I have heard of a house in which the portrait of the good man who made the family wealth has a looking-glass in front of it, so that the will which ordained that that portrait should hang on one particular panel in the dining-room as long as the family mansion stood may be kept to the letter, while it is broken in the spirit. But this was a particularly irksome case, for the good man had made his money out of tallow, and had been painted with a pound of mould candles in each hand. Think of that, Maud! Fustian and corduroy are paintable enough; but not even Herkomer could make anything out of two bunches of tallow candles."

"I wish Hubert would let me hang a fine Venetian glass in front of his worthy great-grandfather. However, since he himself is a gentleman, I suppose I ought to be satisfied," said Maud; "I don't believe there is a finer gentleman in England than my husband, Radical as he is."

Vansittart's sister was perfectly happy in her married life. She had a husband who petted and indulged her, with inexhaustible good humour, and who thought her the most enchanting of women, with infinite capacities for soaring to a higher level than she had yet attained. She had as much money as ever she cared to spend, and a house in which she was allowed to do what she liked, so long as she did not trample on the rights and privileges of the old servants from

Hartley Manor, who had been dominant there since Hubert's infancy; servants whose proud boast it was to have been associated with every circumstance of their master's life, from the cutting of his first tooth to the bringing home of his bride. It is strange what Conservative ways these Radicals sometimes have in the bosoms of their families.

Sir Hubert Hartley was not like David, ruddy and fair to see. He was a small, dark man, who looked as if some of the original Sheffield smoke, the smoke inhaled by the inventor day after day for half a century, had given its hue to his complexion. He was wiry, and well built, active, energetic, a good shot, a good horseman, a lover of field sports and wild animals, loving, after the sportsman's fashion, even the creatures he destroyed, curious about their habits, keen in his admiration of their strength and beauty. For the rest, he was a man of widest beneficence, charitable, hospitable, and he was a man whom the better-born Jack Vansittart loved and honoured.

They were about the same age, and had been at Eton and Oxford together, and Jack knew his friend by heart. He could have chosen no better husband for his sister; he could have chosen no man he would have preferred to call his brother-in-law. It seemed to him sometimes that he could have hardly liked a brother better than he liked Hubert Hartley.

Vansittart was still a gentleman at leisure. He had coquetted with politics, and had allowed himself to be spoken of as a young man who might prove an acquisition to the Conservative party, but he had not allowed himself to be nominated for any constituency. "The party is strong enough to get on without me," he said; "I'll wait till the General Election, and then I'll go in for all I know, and try to gain them a seat from the enemy. I should like to try my luck in Yorkshire, and win an election against Hubert and all his merry men. I might stand for Burtborough—attack Hartley in his own stronghold."

Burtborough was the small market town that supplied the necessities of Hartley Manor House. The Hartleys had represented Burtborough for two generations, but Hubert had withdrawn from the political arena, disgusted at the turn of events, and finding more pleasure in turnips and prize cattle than in the art of legislation. He had never been brilliant either as an orator or debater, and he thought he had done his duty by country and party when he had secured the election of a conscientious Liberal for Burtborough. Marriage had helped to make him lazy. He loved his home; stable and gardens; farm and woods; his pretty wife and cooing baby. His brother-in-law

40

thought him the most enviable among men.

"He has all the desires of his heart," thought Vansittart. "He has not an unsatisfied ambition. He has a clear conscience, can look his fellow-men straight in the face and say, 'I have injured no man:' as I cannot, God help me: as I never can so long as I live. At every turn of the road I expect to meet some one whom I have injured—a mother who may have loved that man as my mother loves me—a sister whose life has been made desolate by his death, reprobate though he was. No man stands alone in the world. Whoever he may be, when he falls, he will drag down some one."

And then he thought of Fiordelisa, with her sunny Italian eyes, and her light-hearted acceptance of such good things as Fate threw in her way—the lodgings on the Rialto, the mandoline lessons, the fine dress and good food. She had taken these things as if they were manna from heaven; and assuredly no rigid principle, no adherence to her Church Catechism, would restrain her from seeking manna from new sources. What had she become, he wondered, in the years that had made his crime an old memory? An artist's model, or something worse? In these days of photography that beautiful face of hers would have less value than in the golden age of Tintoret and Veronese.

He had done his best to forget that scene at Florian's; but the image of Fiordelisa returned to his memory very often, harden himself as he might against the pangs of remorse, and the thought of her always saddened him. He had the same kind of sorrow for having spoilt her life as he might have felt had he been cruel to a child. Her ignorance, her friendlessness appealed so strongly to his pity—and even the old aunt, who so placidly accepted the situation, did not appear to him as odious as a hard-headed Englishwoman would have appeared under the same conditions.

Nearly three years had passed, and he knew no more about the man he stabbed than he had known when the dagger dropped from his hand warm with the stranger's life-blood. The most watchful attention to the newspapers had resulted in no further knowledge. There had been an occasional paragraph about the fatal brawl in Venice. He was thankful to observe that no one had written of his crime as murder. The fact that the dagger had been bought within an hour of its fatal use—the accidental nature of the encounter—and the brutality of the unknown's attack had been discussed at length, and there had been a good deal of speculation as to his own character and social status. Had the event happened a few years later some keen-witted special correspondent would doubtless have contrived

41

to interview Fiordelisa; and the girl's artless prattle and her Venetian environment would have furnished material for a spirited article.

The interest in the death of a nameless Englishman soon died out, and the newspapers found no more to say about the fatal brawl in the Piazza, and as the years went by Vansittart told himself that this dark chapter in his life was closed for ever, that the mother who loved him would never know that his conscience was burdened with the death of a fellow-creature.

Looking backward he remembered an occasion in his boyhood when a sudden impulse of fury had brought disgrace upon him, and had caused his mother much distress of mind. It was at a time when he was reading hard at home with a private tutor, shortly before he went to Oxford. A groom had ill-used one of his horses, or Vansittart believed he had, and the young man had attacked and belaboured him severely. The lad had been able to defend himself, and the two had been fairly matched as to weight and size, but Vansittart had all the science on his side, and he felt afterwards that he had disgraced himself by the encounter. His mother's distress grieved him deeply; and he went so far as to apologize to the vanquished hireling, which apology raised him to the pinnacle of honour in the opinion of the stable generally.

"There's plenty of young masters as would chuck a sovereign to a lad he'd whacked, but it's only a thoroughbred one that would say, 'I beg your pardon, Bates; I ought to have known better,'" said the old family coachman, who had driven Master Jack to be christened.

The burden upon his conscience was an old burden by this time, and he was able to carry his load so that no one suspected evil under that pleasant, open-hearted aspect of a man who fulfilled all the social duties. He was a good son, a kind and affectionate brother, a generous landlord and master. As the world saw his life there was no flaw in it. He had troops of friends, an honourable status, plenty of money, everything that this world can give of good, in that moderate measure which the poet-philosopher has taught us to esteem as life's best.

"I suppose the sword is hanging by a hair somewhere, and will drop when I least expect it," he said to himself, in the hour of dark memories.

A chance allusion—some loving word of praise from his mother, the turn of a conversation, the plot of a play or a novel—would sometimes stir the dark waters of memory; but he did his best to forget, since there was nothing that he could do to atone; and he tried to convince himself that it was all the better for humanity at large that there was one reprobate less in the world.

This had been his temper for the last year or so, as memory lost something of its vivid colouring; and he had come to take that act of his in Venice as part and parcel of his life and character.

He bore himself gaily enough in this Christmas holiday at Redwold Towers, and Lady Hartley declared that he was the life and soul of her house-party.

"You have not such a passion for field-sports as the rest of the men," she said. "One may hope to be favoured with your society for an occasional hour between breakfast and dinner, while those other wretches troop off in their horrid thick boots before I come downstairs in the morning, and I hear no more of them till dinner, unless I go with the luncheon cart."

"I'm afraid my superiority must be put down to advancing years and growing laziness. I never was so good a shot as Hubert, and I have never been as keen a sportsman."

"Perhaps that is because you have spent so much of your holiday life on the Continent. Hubert would be miserable if he were asked to spend a winter out of the British Isles, unless he were pig-sticking in India, or fishing in Canada, or hunting lions in Africa. He cannot get on without killing things. You are not like that. You have no thirst for blood."

"No," answered Jack, with a laugh; "I am not great at killing things, though I am just English enough to think poorly of the straightest run if it doesn't end in blood."

"Oh, of course, I know you can ride, and that you have a proper English love of hunting and shooting, but you don't give your life up to sport and farming as Hubert does. You have only to look at his boots, and you can understand his life. Such an array of bluchers, tops, brogues, waterproof fishing boots and dreadful hobnailed, broad-toed things, that look like instruments of torture—as if they had been modelled upon the boot that one reads of under the Plantagenets and Tudors. People talk of writing as an index of character. I would rather see a man's boots than his penmanship if I wanted to know what kind of man he was."

"And you put me down as a single-soled, effeminate person?" said Jack; whereat there was a laugh from the house-party, sitting cosily round the morning-room fire, with the exception of one industrious matron who sat by the window, toiling at an early English counterpane which required to be worked upon a frame.

"No, no. I don't consider you womanish. You would never sink into the useful family friend, or the tame cat, even if you were to remain a bachelor all your life. But your boots are more human than Hubert's; and you are fond of art, and books, and music, for which I fear he cares very little."

"He cares for something much better," said Vansittart. "He cares for humanity, and is always thinking how he can improve the condition of the people who are dependent upon him. His cottages at Hartley are models of all that cottages should be, and there is not a good point about them that he has not thought out for himself."

"Yes, he is always his own architect, and he has really some very good notions, though he is not as picturesque as I should like him to be in his ideas. The cottages about here may not be as commodious as ours in Yorkshire, but they are ever so much prettier—dear old cottages, more than half roof, and with the quaintest casements."

"And very little light or air inside, I dare say; capital cottages for the landscape, but not so agreeable for the folks inside."

The party in the morning-room consisted of the three Miss Champernownes, daughters of a Cornish baronet, all three handsome, stylish, accomplished, everything in short that Mrs. Vansittart would have approved in a daughter-in-law; Mrs. Baddington, the lady of the counterpane, who was so completely absorbed in her needlework that she might as well have stopped at her own fireside; but as her husband, Major Baddington, was a good shot and a pleasant companion, the lady's inoffensive dulness was tolerated in country houses.

The other ladies present were Mrs. Vansittart and a Miss Green, a young lady who gave herself airs on the strength of her people being *the* Greens—the Greens of Peddlington—in whose particular case the name of Green was supposed to rank with Guelph or Ghibelline. Miss Green was plain, but clever, and was as boastful of her plainness as of her good old name. Her people were rich, and she had inherited an independent fortune from a bachelor uncle, who had bequeathed his wealth to her with an embargo against marriage with any man—less than a Peer—who should refuse to assume the name of Green. And even in the case of her marriage with a Peer, it was ordained that her second son should be called Green—by letters patent—and should inherit the Green wealth, strictly tied up in the case of the heiress.

Miss Green was economical to meanness—perhaps with some dim idea of enriching that hypothetical scion of nobility—and was proud of her economy. Her chief delight in the metropolis was to go long distances—generally in an omnibus—in quest of cheapness; and she was a scourge to all the young matrons of her acquaintance by her keen interest in their housekeeping, her knowledge of prices, and her outspoken condemnation of their extravagance. She had one original idea which had achieved a kind of distinction for her from the housekeeping point of view, and that was her non-belief in the Co-operative Stores.

Such was the feminine portion of the house-party at Redwold Towers, and it was to this party that John Vansittart had succeeded in making himself eminently agreeable. He had admired the artistic shading and Tudoresque scroll-work of Mrs. Baddington's counter-pane, and had surprised that lady by what seemed a profound knowledge of early Florentine needlework. He had tramped Blackdown in the wind and the weather with the Miss Champernownes, turn and turn about, and was no nearer falling in love with any of the three than when he began these rambles; he had discussed the art of dressing well upon fifty pounds a year with Miss Green, and had allowed her to convince him that the Greens of Peddlington were a purer race than the Plantagenets; and to-day he had given himself up to idleness in the gynæceum, otherwise morning-room, and had offered himself for two round dances apiece to the four young ladies, at the hunt ball in the little rustic town, to which they were all going that evening.

"It will be an awful drive," said Maud Hartley; "think what the hills will be like in this weather."

There had been an "old-fashioned Christmas," and the world outside the windows was for the most part a white world.

"The horses have been roughed, and your coachman tells me he has no fear of the hills," said Vansittart. "He is going to take four horses."

"I'm sure they'll be wanted, poor things, with that big omnibus and a herd of us to drag up those terrible hills," said his sister.

"If you have any feeling for the brute creation you can get out and walk up the hills," said Jack.

"What, in our satin slippers? How very delightful!"

There was no one heroic enough to propose walking up the hills at ten o'clock that evening, when the omnibus from Redwold went bowling merrily over the frost-bound roads, uphill and downhill, at a splendid even pace, and with a rhythmical jingle of bars and chains, as the four upstanding browns laid themselves out for their work, going as if it was a pleasure to go through the steel-blue night, with the quiet fields and pastures stretching round them, silvery in the moonshine, while in every dip and hollow the oak and chestnut copses lay wrapped in shadow, darkly mysterious.

They skirted Bexley Hill, they passed by sleeping villages and wind-swept commons.

"Are we nearly there?" asked Hilda Champernowne.

"Hardly halfway," answered Lady Hartley. "I told you it was a long drive."

There was a bright lamp inside the omnibus, a lamp which lit up the three Miss Champernownes in a cloud of gauze and satin, white as the snow-drifts in the valleys, a lamp which shone on three heads of glittering gold-brown hair, and three pairs of fine eyes, and three cherry mouths, and three swanlike throats rising out of ostrich plumage. It shone on Maud Hartley's cloak of scarlet and gold and blue-fox fur, and sparkled on the diamond solitaires in her ears, clear and white as dewdrops on a sunny morning.

They were a very merry party. Major Baddington and Sir Hubert were outside, wrapped to the ears in fur coats and caps, and enjoying their smoke in the frosty air. Vansittart and two other young men rode inside with the feminine contingent, who were glad of this leaven of masculine society, though they pretended to be in alarm at the crushing of their draperies.

"I feel a dark foreboding that all the dancing men will have engaged themselves for the evening before we arrive," said Claudia Champernowne.

"Not if they know the Miss Champernownes are going to be there," said Mr. Tivett, a young man with a small voice and a reputation for all the social talents.

"Who cares anything about us?" cried Claudia. "We are strangers in the land."

"I think that some of the dancing men will wait for my party," said Maud. "I am famous for taking pretty girls to our local dances."

They were steadily ascending the worst hill they had to climb; the omnibus was on an inclined plane, and Hilda Champernowne in her place at the back of the vehicle looked down upon Jack Vansittart seated in a hollow by the door. They were near the top, when the brake was put on suddenly, and the horses were pulled up. A ripple of silvery laughter rang out upon the frosty air.

"Fairies!" cried Vansittart.

"Who can it be, and why are we stopping?" asked Miss Champernowne, "when we are so late, too!"

There were voices, two or three feminine voices, all talking at once, and then Hubert was heard answering. Anon more laughter. Sir Hubert and a groom got off the 'bus, and the former came to the door.

"Can you make room for three girls?" he asked.

"Not for a mouse," replied his wife. "We are hideously crushed already. I believe all our gowns are spoilt."

"Then a little more squeezing won't hurt," said Sir Hubert. "Look here, you three men can come outside. It'll be a tight pack, but we'll manage it, and the three ladies can have your places. It's a lovely night. You're none of you bronchial, I hope."

"A chronic sufferer, from my cradle," said Mr. Tivett, in a meek, little voice.

"Oh, Tivett can stay inside. He is the nearest approach I know to Euclid's definition of a line—length without breadth."

Jack Vansittart was out by this time, and Reggie Hudson, a soldierly young man, slipped out after him. The women drew themselves together discontentedly. Each would have had an omnibus to herself if she could.

"I haven't the faintest idea whom we are making room for," grumbled Maud.

"I know we shall be dreadfully late," sighed Claudia.

"I say, you good folks out there, hurry up, please," cried the gallant Tivett. "It's getting on for eleven, and this isn't a picnic-party."

He was talking to the empty air. A ripple of that elfin laughter from the top of the hill was all that answered him. Sir Hubert, Vansittart, and Major Baddington were all standing round a most melancholy specimen of the genus fly, the very oldest and mouldiest of one-horse landaus, which had broken down hopelessly on the top of the hill.

"We knew that the springs were weak," said a silver-clear voice out of a swansdown hood. "They've been getting weaker and weaker ever since we've had anything to do with the fly; but we had no idea the shafts were all wrong."

"The shafts were right enough when we started, miss," growled a voice that was half muffled in a red comforter, such a comforter as denotes the rustic fly-man. "It was your weight coming up the hill as did it."

"My weight!" cried Swansdownhood, lifting herself up on her springy feet like a feminine Mercury. "Do I look such a Daniel Lambert?"

Her hood fell off with that arch toss of the head, and looking at her in the vivid moonlight it seemed to Jack Vansittart as if that jocular exclamation of his had been well founded, and that the woman who stood before him on the crest of the hill, her beauty and her whiteness shining out against the steel-blue sky—"like a finer light in light"—was enchanting enough to have stood for Titania.

47

She was very tall, but so slim and willowy of form that her height made her no less sylph-like—a queen of sylphs, perhaps, but assuredly of that aerial family. She was dazzlingly fair, and her small head was crowned with a nimbus of pale gold hair, in which there sparkled a galaxy of diamond starlets. Her small nose was tip-tilted, but with a tilt so archly delicate as to be more beautiful than the purest Grecian, or so Vansittart thought, seeing her thus for the first time in the glamour of night and moonshine, and with all the piquancy of the unexpected.

"The horse fell down, and the shafts went crash," said another young person, who presented to view only a nose and narrow slip of face between the folds of a red plaid shawl, just such a shawl as a well-to-do farmer's wife might have worn driving to market. "I thought we should all be killed."

"And so you would have been, if I hadn't put the brake on sharp, and got down and sat on 'is 'ed," said the fly-man. "That horse didn't ought to have been sent out on such roads as this, and if I'd been master he wouldn't have been."

"We won't trouble you for your opinions, my friend," said Sir Hubert, throwing a florin lightly into the man's hand. "You'd better take your beast home, and give yourself a hot drink. I'll take care of Miss Marchant and her sisters."

"Oh, but really," said Swansdownhood, "it is immensely good of you—only they had better send a fly for us after the dance. We can't encroach upon you for the home journey."

"Why not? Of course we shall take you home. Come along; I'm afraid you're catching cold while we're talking."

He marched the three girls—the spokeswoman and tallest all in white from top to toe, the second with a black lace frock showing below her Stuart shawl, the third muffled in a blue opera cloak and a blue Shetland scarf, commonly called a cloud.

"Here are the Miss Marchants, come to claim your hospitality," said Sir Hubert to his wife; whereupon Maud replied, graciously—

"Oh, how do you do, you poor things? Pray come in. How cold you must be! Did your carriage break down? How dreadful! I'm afraid there's not much heat left in our foot-warmers, but it is tolerably warm here still"—the atmosphere inside the 'bus was tropical—"and I hope you'll be able to make yourselves comfortable."

"Such a dreadful intrusion!"

"Such a herd of us!"

"How you must all detest us!" cried three fresh young voices all at once.

48

The three Champernownes and the Green maintained a stolid silence. Those four pairs of eyes were coldly appraising the intruders—their faces, their dress, their social status, everything about them.

The fair tall girl in the swansdown hood was very pretty. That fact the most unfriendly observer could not deny. Whether that dazzling fairness was in some part artificial remained to be proved under a more searching light than the omnibus lamp; but even if that alabaster complexion were due to blanc de something the girl's eyes were real—lovely dancing blue-grey eyes, softened by dark brown lashes. Her nose was the prettiest thing in that unrecognized order of noses; mouth and chin were in perfect harmony; and she looked round at the strange faces with the sweetest smile, as if she had never suffered from prejudice or undeserved disdain.

The other two girls were of the same type, but not so pretty. The blue girl was freckled and weather-beaten; the Stuart plaid girl was too pale. Titania had taken the lion's share of the family beauty.

But their dress—that at least afforded widest scope for the scorner. The swansdown hood was of the year one, or perhaps might have been fashionable in the historic winter of the Crimean war; the blue cloud and tawdry blue opera cloak suggested all that is commonest in cheap finery; and what manner of surroundings could a girl have whose people allowed her to go to a hunt ball with her head and shoulders skewered in a tartan shawl with a blanket pin?

"We are taking no chaperon," said Titania, brightly. "Mrs. Ponto is to chaperon us."

Mrs. Ponto was the wife of a solicitor at Mandelford, the little town where the ball was being given. It was the first hunt ball there had been at Mandelford within the memory of Sussex, and the fact that this ball was taking place at Mandelford was due to the enterprise of a local cabinet-maker, who had built a public hall or assembly room at the back of his shop, and had thus provided a place for festivity or culture; music, amateur theatricals, Oxford or Cambridge lectures, conjuring or Christy Minstrels.

After that little apologetic remark about the chaperon, there followed a silence, the Champernownes and Miss Green remaining figures of stone, and Maud Hartley feeling that she had done her duty as hostess. The carriage rolled merrily over the frost-bound road, and the hoofs of the four horses sounded like an advance of cavalry in the winter stillness. Perhaps the silence inside the omnibus would have lasted all the way to Mandelford had it not been for little Mr. Tivett, who sat between two Miss Champernownes, half hidden among billows of snowy gauze, peeping out at the three pretty faces on the other side of the 'bus, with bright, inquisitive eyes, like a squirrel out of his nest.

"I don't know what I have done to offend you, Lady Hartley, that you should not think me worthy to be introduced to these young ladies," said the good little man at last.

"My dear Mr. Tivett, it was an oversight on my part. I forgot that you and the Miss Marchants had not met before. Of course, you are dying to know them.—Miss Marchant, allow me to introduce Mr. Tivett, a devoted admirer of your sex—a gentleman who knows more about a lady's dress, and a lady's accomplishments and amusements, than one woman in a hundred."

"My dear Lady Hartley," remonstrated Tivett, in his piping voice, "Miss Marchant will run away with the idea that I am a horrible effeminate little person."

"She will very soon discover that you are the most obliging little person, and I dare say she will end by being as fond of you as I am."

"Dearest Lady Hartley, how delightful of you to say that!" exclaimed Mr. Tivett, with a coquettish giggle, darting out his little suède glove to give his hostess an affectionate pat on the shoulder; "and now you have heard my character, Miss Marchant, please will you give me a dance?"

"With pleasure," replied Eve, wondering whether she would look very ridiculous spinning round a public ball-room with this funny little man, who was small enough to be almost hidden in the Champernowne draperies; "which shall it be?"

"Oh, the first waltz after our arrival, and I hope your sisters will each give me one of the extras."

"I shall be very glad," said the girl in the tartan shawl. "I don't suppose I shall have too many partners."

Mr. Tivett looked at the three faces critically. The eldest girl was much the prettiest, but there was a family likeness. The faces were all of one type, and they were all pretty. It smote Mr. Tivett's gentle heart to think these nice girls should be so badly dressed, while the Champernownes, who always snubbed him, and whom he hated, were glorious in frocks fresh from Bond Street. Lady Hartley had not exaggerated Mr. Tivett's devotion to the fair sex. He loved the society of young matrons and girls in their teens, was never happier than when making himself useful to the ladies of the family, and especially rejoiced when consulted upon any question of etiquette or costume. He was reputed to have faultless taste in dress, and an exquisite tact in all social matters; and when two matrons of his acquaintance happened to quarrel, each was apt to impart the story of her wrongs to Mr. Tivett, whose only difficulty was to be the adviser of both, without seeming unfaithful to either. He was not a sportsman, and he pleaded a weak chest as a reason for loving easy-chairs, and cosy corners in boudoirs and morning-rooms, and a seat in a carriage when other men were walking. His Christian name was Augustus; but he was always known as Gus, or Gussie.

Having been introduced to the eldest sister, Mr. Tivett was on easy terms with the three girls in about five minutes, and for the rest of the journey the four were prattling gaily, Lady Hartley chiming in now and then, just for civility's sake, while the other women maintained their unfriendly silence.

"I knew we should be late," Claudia Champernowne exclaimed at last, as the omnibus drew up at a lighted door, and she saw the long line of carriages filling the rustic street from end to end.

Miss Green and the Champernownes marched at once to the cloak-room, an upper room over the shop, whither Lady Hartley followed. The Marchant girls fell back, and lingered in the vestibule—said vestibule being neither more nor less than the cabinet-maker's empty shop, transformed by scarlet and white draperies and evergreens in pots. The Marchants felt that Lady Hartley's hospitality came to an end at the door of the ball-room, and that they would do ill to attach themselves to her party.

"I think we had better wait here for our chaperon," said Eve, as Maud looked back at her from the stairs. "I'm sure we can never be too grateful to you for bringing us, Lady Hartley."

"Please don't speak of such a trifle. I am to take you home, remember. You must look out for us at three o'clock."

"At three o'clock," thought Jenny, of the tartan shawl; "that's as much as to say, 'In the mean time we don't know you.'"

They waited in a little group near the stairs, and saw the three Champernownes come sweeping down, swanlike, beautiful, "in gloss of satin and glimmer of pearls," and Miss Green in a very severe, tight-fitting yellow silk frock, with a shortish skirt, and round her homely-complexioned throat a collet necklace of emeralds without flaw or feather; and Lady Hartley in a fuss and flutter of palest blue, which seemed just the most telling background for her diamonds. She had diamonds everywhere, butterflies, stars, true lovers' knots, hearts, and horseshoes, dotted about bust and shoulders amongst the soft fluffiness of azure gauze; diamonds in her hair, in her ears, on her arms. And yet she did not look vulgarly fine. The slender elegance of her form, the delicate colouring of her face and neck harmonized the jewels.

While the Hartley party were composing themselves for their entrance to the dancing-room, a stout matron in red satin and black lace came sailing in, wrapped to the eyes in a white Shetland shawl, and at once made for the Marchants, whom she deliberately kissed, one after the other.

"I hope you haven't been waiting long, dears," she said, in a fat, good-natured voice. "Ponto had a business appointment at Haslemere, and didn't get back to his dinner till nine o'clock."

Mr. Ponto was grinning in the background, very red and puffy, as from a hurried toilet, and with a scarlet camelia in his button-hole; scarlet out of compliment to the hunt.

"Oh no, we have only just come," answered Eve, troubled by the supercilious stare of the youngest Miss Champernowne, who was looking back from the threshold of the ball-room while the others went in, looking at Mrs. Ponto as at some natural curiosity; and indeed to a young lady whose evening frock had been produced new and immaculate from a Bond Street carton Mrs. Ponto's crimson satin, lately "done up" with Nottingham lace, and obviously "let out" to accommodate Mrs. Ponto's increasing bulk, was a thing to wonder at.

The three Marchants and their chaperon entered the ball-room in a cluster. The Redwold Towers party was absorbed in the brilliant throng, had gone straight into the zenith, where the two local peeresses were holding a kind of court, a court splendid with family diamonds and hereditary *point d'Alençon*. Mrs. Ponto made a dash for a corner of the raised bench that went round the room, and established herself and her charges in this coign of vantage.

"If we don't get seats at once we mightn't have a chance of sitting down for an hour," said Mrs. Ponto. "Ain't the room full? Now, dears, I shall stay here till some one takes me in to supper, so you can leave your fans with me, and feel you've got some one to come to between your dances. I had my cup of tea before I came, so I shan't trouble about the tea-room. It's a pretty sight, ain't it?"

A waltz was just ending. The room was very full, but there was the usual surplus of nice-looking girls sitting down, with the usual sprinkling of men who wouldn't dance, and who were quite satisfied to stand about and get in the way of the dancers.

The peeresses and their court were on the opposite side of the room, in a central position, which commanded dancers, band, and the festooned archway leading to the tea-room. Lady Hartley had seated herself next old Lady Mandelford, a dowager with white hair, whose son was the well-known Lord Mandelford, a man of prodigious wealth and local importance, a rustic Royalty.

Eve had shaken out her well-worn white frock. It was made of some soft woollen stuff, which her old servant Nancy had washed, so it had at least the merit of purity. On that tall and perfectly balanced figure the cheap, simple gown looked exquisite, and the fair fluffy head, with its glitter of starlets, could not have looked more enchanting had the starlets been old Brazilian diamonds, like Lady Mandelford's, instead of cut glass mounted at Birmingham. The younger sisters had aimed higher than Eve. One in blue, the other in red, straining after Parisian fashion, in cheap silk and satin, had only achieved tawdriness. Eve, in her white frock, might challenge criticism.

There was some one on the other side of the room who thought her lovely as a dream, the same man whose eyes had gazed on her beauty in the moonlight an hour ago, and who had told himself that such a face belonged to fairyland rather than to this dull, everyday earth. He stood looking at her now, across the dancers and the crowd, as she sat demurely in her corner, her alabaster fairness set off by the scarlet background. He put his arm through Sir Hubert's. "When you've done talking to Miss Champernowne I want you to introduce me to Miss Marchant," he said.

"With all my heart. But there are three Miss Marchants. Which of the three are you dying to know?"

"The fair girl, in white."

"Oh, she's the eldest. They are all fair, but I suppose she's the fairest. Come along, then. I'm to dance the Lancers, Maud tells me," he added, lowering his voice, "and with Lady Mandelford. I'm to steer the dowager through that complicated performance."

Sir Hubert wore the hunt colours, a scarlet coat with black velvet collar and white satin facings, and he felt that it behoved him to make some sacrifice in honour of a dance that was called the hunt ball.

"Don't forget that you have engaged yourself to us, Mr. Vansittart," said Miss Green, severely. "You are bespoken for eight dances out of eighteen. Three of the eighteen are gone already. You will have to make the most of the seven that remain to you after you have done your duty to us."

He had forgotten all about those pledges given in the morning-room. Eight dances with young women for whom he cared not a straw, about whom familiarity had bred something not very far from contempt. Eight dances, a veritable bondage; while Eve Marchant was sitting meekly in her corner, partnerless. No, not partnerless; even as he looked little Mr. Tivett marched up to her with an all-conquering air, and led her in among the dancers, just beginning a waltz.

Vansittart took Miss Green's programme out of her hand with a desperate air.

"Let's begin at once—if you are disengaged," he said.

"That makes one off," she answered, laughing, as she rose and took his arm. "How dreadfully sorry for yourself you look!"

"Then my looks belie me. I was never gladder for myself. I see you have ever so many engagements already. Shall I put myself down for number eighteen?"

"Certainly. You are sure we shall have left before that number arrives."

They were moving slowly among the dancers by this time, and a minute later they spun off with a fine rhythmical swing. Miss Green was what the hunting men called a splendid mover. She had taken trouble to excel in her paces, knowing that her appearance was against ball-room triumphs. Men liked to dance with her—for three reasons. She was rich; she waltzed well; and she had a malevolent tongue, which amused her partners.

It was her delight to criticize her fairer sisters—the flaws in their beauty; the tricks which helped them to be beautiful; their affectations; their vanities; their bad taste.

"Did you ever see three young women 'fagotées' like those Marchant girls?" she murmured, in a low, clear voice, which she had cultivated for speaking evil of people near at hand. "That blue girl—that red girl! I don't know which is worse! The blue frock is an inch and a half shorter on one side than on the other—an advantage, as it shows off the blue slipper, which doesn't match the frock, and the blue stocking, which doesn't match the slipper. But the red girl! Please notice the lacing of the red bodice. I assure you the girl isn't humpbacked, though that bodice certainly suggests deformity."

"How observant you are, Miss Green; and with what a keen eye for the infinitesimal!"

"I am looking at their chaperon now—the enormous person in dyed crimson satin. It must have been her wedding-gown ages ago—a sweet silver-grey. You don't call that lady infinitesimal, I hope?"

"Physically large, perhaps—but, from your mental standpoint, microscopic. Now, confess, Miss Green, don't you think these people infinitely insignificant, simply because they happen not to be rich?"

"I think them immensely amusing. One sees such people only at public balls in the heart of the country. That is why public balls are such fun. Do look at the glass stars in the tallest Miss Marchant's hair! Did you ever see anything so absurd?"

"What does it matter whether they are glass or diamonds of the purest water? All the gems that were ever ground at Amsterdam could not make her more like a beautiful sylph—Undine—Titania—what you will."

"Your comparisons are not flattering to the young lady's intellect. Undine was mindless and soulless; Titania—if Shakespeare knew anything about her—was a silly little person who fell desperately in love with a donkey."

Their waltz was over, but Miss Green wanted tea, or an ice, or a change of atmosphere—anything which would retain Vansittart in attendance upon her as long as possible. She kept him sitting by her side while she sipped her tea, and ridiculed the people who came in and out of the tea-room. She kept him in bondage while Mr. Tivett conducted Eve Marchant to the buffet, and talked and laughed with her gaily as she ate her ice. How prettily she ate that pink ice—with such a graceful turn of the delicate wrist! Vansittart had leisure to study every line of head and figure, while Miss Green prattled in his ear. He gave a little automatic laugh now and then, feeling that the lady meant him to be amused. Miss Marchant was a long time eating her ice, and was evidently interested in Mr. Tivett's conversation. Vansittart watched her dreamily, not more jealous of Tivett than if he had seen her a few years earlier, playing with her doll; but just as she had resigned the empty ice-plate, and was moving towards the door, a man in a hunt coat met and stopped her with a semi-authoritative air that made Vansittart's blood rush angrily to his brow, almost as if the man had insulted him.

"You are saving some dances for me, I hope, Miss Marchant?" said the unknown, with an easy, off-hand manner.

"I don't know," faltered Eve. "I mean I think I am engaged for a good many waltzes—as many as I shall care to dance."

"Let me see," taking her programme out of her hand. "Oh, you fair deceiver! Why, you might answer about this programme as Olivia did about her history—'A blank, my Lord.' I shall write myself against number seven—the dear old Manola—and eleven—a Waldteufel waltz—and, let me see, shall we say fifteen?"

The man was good-looking, dark-haired and dark-eyed, well set up, showing to advantage in the hunt coat—a man likely to be in request at a dance; yet it was evident that Eve Marchant wanted to avoid him. She looked pained and even angry at his persistence.

"My engagements are not upon that card," she said; "and I am sure you must have a great many people with whom you ought to dance—sooner than with me."

"That's my business. I have set my heart upon at least three dances with you."

"Then I am sorry to disappoint you; I am engaged for all those numbers."

"But you are free for others? Tell me which."

"That is Mr. Sefton, of Chadleigh," said Miss Green, confidentially. "Rather handsome, ain't he? But not good form. He is not a favourite in his own neighbourhood; but he and Miss Marchant are evidently upon very friendly terms."

Eve had left the tea-room with Mr. Tivett, closely followed by Mr. Sefton, and Vansittart sat looking after the three retreating figures till they were absorbed in the crowd that filled the dancing-room.

"Did you think so?" he said coldly. "It seemed to me that the gentleman was not a favourite with the young lady."

"If you had seen them on Christmas Eve on the ice you would have a very different opinion. He was teaching her the outside edge. He was devoted, and she seemed delighted. He would be a great catch for her; but I'm afraid he's too much a man of the world to be trapped by a pretty face. He will look higher than Miss Marchant."

"What and who is he?"

"Oh, he belongs to an old Sussex family, and has a fine place on the other side of Blackdown. I am told he is clever; but he is not nice, somehow. People don't seem to trust him. And there are ugly stories about him, I believe, stories that are not told to ladies, but which have made him unpopular in his own neighbourhood, especially among his own tenant-farmers and cottagers. There are the Lancers, and I am engaged to a callow youth who came with the Mandelford party."

She rose hurriedly, relinquishing her teacup, which Vansittart had been wearily waiting for, with an air of having been detained by his assiduity. The callow youth, looking very fair and pretty in his brand-new pink coat, appeared in the doorway.

"Oh, Mith Gween, I have been looking for you evewywha'," he murmured; and they went off to take their places.

Their vis-à-vis were Mr. Sefton and Miss Marchant.

"So she is dancing with him, after all," thought Vansittart, curiously vexed. "Varium et mutabile semper femina!"

CHAPTER IV.

"THE PRELUDE TO SOME BRIGHTER WORLD"

While the Lancers were being danced to the good old hilarious tunes, which always give an air of boisterous gaiety to a public ballroom, Vansittart, ignoring all further obligations to his home party, went in search of little Mr. Tivett, so that by impounding that gentleman he should make sure of an introduction to Miss Marchant before the next dance.

He found the agreeable Tivett in an anteroom, an apartment much affected by sitters out, and peculiarly congenial to flirtation, where the good little man had found agreeable occupation in pinning up the lace flounce of a portly matron in yellow satin, not too portly to indulge in round dances, which imparted an alarmingly purple shade to the pearly whiteness of her complexion. "Only mother-of-pearl," as Mr. Tivett said afterwards. "You may be quite happy about your Mechlin, dear lady," said Tivett, after planting the last pin; "nothing but the stitches gone. No harm done to your lovely lace, I assure you."

"He was a clumsy bear all the same. How sweet of you, dear Mr. Tivett! Ten thousand thanks. And now I'll run back to my party, or my young man will be looking for me for the next waltz;" and the lady waddled away pantingly, to be steered carefully round the room by-and-by, in the protecting arm of a tall youth, who had an eye to free luncheons and dinners in the best part of Belgravia.

"You lucky little man," cried Vansittart, when the lady was gone, "in favour with both youth and age. You save Mrs. Fotheringay's priceless Mechlin, and you secure your first waltz with the belle of the ball."

Tivett gave a little conscious laugh, and shook his suède glove at Vansittart airily.

"Pretty girl, that Miss Marchant, ain't she?" said he, "and not a bit of nonsense about her; naïveté itself. You should have heard her and the sisters prattle in the 'bus, while the Champernownes sat looking thunder."

"You dog, I believe that bronchitis of yours was all humbug. Come along with me, Tivett; I am going to waylay Miss Marchant, and you must introduce me to her."

"She'll be parading about with that black-muzzled man, most likely. I don't like to shoot another fellow's bird."

"Nonsense. She doesn't like the black man. She didn't want to dance with him. I am going to be Ivanhoe and rescue her from that black-bearded Templar."

"I couldn't quite make her out," said Tivett. "She seemed not to want to dance with him, and yet she let him march her off. I fancy there's an understanding between them. No doubt the puss is an arrant flirt," said Tivett, with his little coquettish shrug, as if he were flirting himself.

Miss Marchant and Sefton, the black-bearded, came into the anteroom at the head of a procession of youths and maidens, and in the confusion made by so many couples pouring out of the big room into the small room, Vansittart contrived to waylay the lady. She dropped Sefton's arm and turned smilingly to Tivett, and in the next moment the introduction was made, while Sefton was captured by the eldest Miss Champernowne, to whom he was engaged for the next dance.

Miss Marchant's programme was still a blank, and she allowed Vansittart to write down his name for a couple of waltzes. There was no question now of unwritten engagements blocking the way. He gave her his arm, and they walked slowly to the ball-room, talking those commonplaces with which even the most fateful acquaintance must needs begin.

Vansittart talked of the long, cold drive; of the rooms, with their red and white panels, and vizards and other emblems of the chase; of the heat and the draughts; of the people, the faces, the frocks. Easily as she had prattled with the lively Tivett, Vansittart found her somewhat reticent, and even shy. But she waltzed delightfully, and he had never enjoyed a dance better than this dance, in which his arm was round that slender waist, and that pretty, fair head with its crystal starlets was almost level with his own, so tall and straight was she.

The waltz ended, these two dancing till the final chord, he took her for the conventional scamper through anteroom and tea-room, which communicated with each other by a canvas corridor, delightfully cool and dangerously draughty, and so back to the ball-room, where he restored her to the worthy lady in the red gown, with whom sat the younger Marchant girls, who were glad to dance one dance out of three; like those hunting men of modest pretensions who were satisfied with a day a week. They were quite aware that although tolerated by the county, and invited to garden-parties, they were not in society, and must not expect that the fine flower of the hunt, greatly in request among a majority of the fair sex, would indulge them with more than an occasional dance. Secure of an after-supper waltz with Eve, Vansittart remembered his home engagements, tore himself away from Miss Marchant, and went across the room to that galaxy of the best people in which his sister had her place. The Champernownes were wandering with their partners, but Miss Green was sitting by Lady Mandelford, and entertaining that mild old lady with the cheap cynicism which passes current for wit.

Vansittart booked himself for his second dance with Miss Green, and then went to look for the Champernownes. He found Claudia enjoying a confidential chat with Mr. Sefton in a corner of the ante-room, and avoided them both as if they had been plague-stricken.

He discovered a younger Champernowne in the tea-room, and offered himself for those dances so lightly promised in the morning. She had kept some numbers open for him. He went to the other sister and wrote his name on her programme for other two waltzes, and this, with his number on Miss Green's programme, and the two still owing to Claudia, left him a very poor chance of sitting out a dance or two with Miss Marchant. He pined for one quiet quarter of an hour of confidential talk with her. He wanted to make friends with her; so that she should prattle to him as freely as she had prattled to little Tivett.

That golden opportunity did not come till late in the evening. His dance with Claudia Champernowne came at just the hour when all the best people were pouring into the supper-room. When their waltz was over he could not avoid asking her to go in to supper, and she promptly accepted.

"There will be a crowd," she said, "but we shall get the first of the oysters, and the scrimmage will be more fun than a half-empty room."

It was an hour later when he danced his extra with Eve Marchant. The next dance was the Caledonians.

"Surely you are not going to dance the Caledonians?" he said. "It is a cruelty to keep the floor from all those portly matrons in fine raiment who are sighing for a square dance."

"I am happy to say I am not engaged for the Caledonians."

"Then let us go into that little talking-room. Of course you have been in to supper?"

Miss Marchant owned blushingly that she had not supped.

"Poor dear Mrs. Ponto had been sitting so long in her corner," she said, "so I asked my last partner to take her in."

"Poor dear partner, I think. What a sacrifice for him! Why, you must be famishing. And I'm afraid all the oysters must have been eaten by this time."

"I can be quite happy without oysters."

"Can you? The youngest Miss Champernowne was inclined to scold the waiters because of the poor supply of natives."

"The Miss Champernownes are used to such luxuries as oysters, and can't do without them," laughed Eve. "My sisters and I have been brought up in a harder manner."

"Curious, isn't it, how fashion changes?" said Vansittart, taking her to a little table in the furthest corner of the room—a tiny table that would only just accommodate two people. "When Byron was in society it was considered odious for a young woman to care what she eat, or to have a healthy appetite. Nowadays, it is rather chic for a girl to be a gourmet. We have bread-and-butter Misses affecting a fine taste in dry champagne and a passion for quails. And now what can I get you—mayonnaise lobster, truffled turkey, boar's head, chicken?"

She decided for chicken, and trifled with a wing while Vansittart sipped a glass of champagne, enchanted to have her all to himself in this corner, wishing that the Caledonians might last for ever, and inclined to be reckless about his engagement for the waltz that was to follow.

"You have been dancing every dance, I think," he said.

"No; not all. I sat in my corner with Mrs. Ponto all through a most exquisite waltz."

"Was it possible you had no partner?"

"Mr. Sefton asked me to dance—and I told him I was tired."

"I have an idea you don't much like Mr. Sefton?"

"No, he's not a favourite of mine; but he has always been very kind, and he has given my father some shooting; so I don't want to be rude to him."

"Was that why you danced the Lancers with him, after refusing him a dance?"

"How did you know I refused him? Ah, I remember, you were sitting in the tea-room. You must have heard all we said."

"Every syllable."

"How flattering to the lady who was talking to you!"

"Dear Miss Green! Oh, she would not mind. She is so pleased with her own conversation that it does not matter whether people listen or not. She is a lady who shakes hands with herself every morning, and says, 'My dear soul, you are really the cleverest, wittiest, brightest creature I know—not exactly beautiful, but infinitely charming,' and in that humour she comes smiling down to breakfast, and lets us all see what poor creatures she thinks us."

"I find you can be ill-natured, Mr. Vansittart. You are not like Lady Hartley, who has always a kind word to say of every one."

"That is my sister's little way. She pays most of her debts with kind words."

"Ah, but she has given us more than words. She asks us to her delightful summer parties, and seems always glad to see us."

"She is very lucky to have such young ladies at her parties. What would a garden-party be if there were not faces in the crowd worth following and asking questions about? But what of Mr. Sefton? I am interested in Mr. Sefton."

"Why?" she asked, with innocent wonder.

"Oh, for various reasons. My father and his father were once friends. And then he is a landowner, a great man in these parts, and one always wants to know about such people."

"Yes, he has a fine estate, and he is said to be rich; but he is not as popular as his father was. I remember old Mr. Sefton, a splendid gentleman. But this Mr. Sefton and my father get on very well together."

"You say he has been kind. How kind?"

"He asks my father to shooting parties, and he sends us game, and grapes, and pines. I would rather for my own part that he didn't, for we can give him nothing in return. Sophy wanted to work him a pair of slippers—preposterous—as if he were a curate! My two nursery sisters offered to make him a set of mats in Russian cross-stitch. Imagine sending Mr. Sefton mats for his toilet table."

"He scarcely looks the kind of man to appreciate that particular form of attention. Tivett, now, would be delighted with such a gift. There is nothing too microscopic or too feminine to interest that dear little man."

"He is a dear little man. It is quite delightful to hear him talk about London people and London parties."

"Did he set you longing to be in the whirl of a London season?"

"I don't know. It would be very nice, for once in one's life; but I am quite happy in our country home, as long as—as," she faltered a little, "father is well and contented."

He felt that in this faltering phrase there was a hint of domestic cares. Hubert Hartley had told him, during a few minutes' talk on the omnibus, that Colonel Marchant was something of a Bohemian, and a difficult man to get on with.

"I always feel sorry for those five girls of his," Sir Hubert concluded.

"You are wise in liking your country life," said Vansittart. "It is the happier life. All my best days are at Merewood—our place near Liss. Do you know Liss, by-the-by?"

"No, indeed. I know there is such a place somewhere between here and Portsmouth."

"You must have passed it, I think. I dare say you sometimes go to Southsea or to the Isle of Wight for your summer holidays."

"You dare to say too much," she answered, with her frank, girlish laugh. "We never go anywhere for our summer holidays. We live in the same house all the year round. When a poor man has five daughters he can't afford to carry them about to seaside lodgings, which are always dreadfully dear in the season, I am told. I think we ought to go back to the ball-room. I am engaged for the next waltz."

"And I, to a most exacting partner."

The waltz was half over when they entered the dancing-room, and Hilda Champernowne, who saw them enter side by side, looking very happy, was evidently offended.

"It is hardly worth while standing up," she said; "the waltz is just over."

"I thought it had only just begun."

"That shows how engrossed you must have been."

"I was giving a young lady some supper, and a young lady who might have starved but for me."

"Impossible! The young lady was Miss Marchant, whom you yourself pronounced the belle of the ball. Mr. Tivett told me so."

"In such an assembly as this—where there is some of the best blood in England—there are many belles," said Vansittart. "Will you come for a turn round the rooms, if you won't dance?"

The lady rose, and took his arm, somewhat mollified, and in the course of that turn—which could not, from the limited space, last very long—she questioned Vansittart sharply about Miss Marchant. Did he think her good style? Had he found her bright and clever in conversation, or was she very dull?

"The poor things go nowhere, I am told, except to garden-parties, where they are lost in a crowd of nobodies. It has been too sad to see them sitting with that awful woman in the red gown. Why do girls go to dances to endure such purgatory? I would as soon sit in the pillory, like Daniel Defoe, as in that corner with the crimson lady."

"Oh, but they have been dancing a good deal. Theirs is not quite such a piteous case as you make out."

"Have they really?" asked Miss Champernowne, with a disparaging drawl; "I'm glad some one has taken compassion upon them. They've always been sittin' when I happened to look their way."

The Champernownes and the Marchants met an hour later in the cloak-room, and this time Lady Hartley formally introduced the Miss Marchants to the haughty Devonians, in the hope that this might make the return journey a little more sociable; a vain hope, for the Champernownes and Miss Green affected to be overcome by sleep as soon as they had settled themselves in the omnibus. So Mr. Tivett and the Marchants had all the talk to themselves, as before, with an occasional kindly word from the hostess, who was genuinely sleepy, and who dreamt that she and the Marchant girls were travelling in Italy, and that their carriage was stopped by brigands.

The brigand-in-chief was her own groom, who came to open the door, and assist the young ladies to alight at their garden gate. But he was not allowed to do more than hold the door open, for Vansittart was standing on the whitened road ready to hand his partner and her sisters to the ground. They alighted as airily as Mercury on the heaven-kissing hill.

"Dear Lady Hartley, we have no words to express our gratitude," said Sophy, as Maud shook hands with her at parting.

Eve was less demonstrative, but not less grateful, and the youngest of the three only murmured something unintelligible from between the folds of her tartan shawl.

Vansittart opened a low wooden gate. The house stood boldly out against the clear moonlit sky; but he had no time to look at it, for he was absorbed in guiding Eve Marchant's footsteps on the slippery garden path, while the groom followed in attendance on her sisters. The path was smooth as glass, and he almost held her in his arms as they went slowly up the sharp little hill that led to the rustic porch.

An old woman opened the door, and the three girls were speedily absorbed into a dark vestibule, a single candle glimmering in the distance.

"Are we very late, Nancy?" asked Eve.

"Not later than I thowt you'd be," answered the woman, with a north-country accent; and then there was nothing for Vansittart to do except to wish the three sisters good night, and go back to the 'bus, where Sir Hubert was beginning to be uneasy about his horses waiting in the frosty air.

"Cuts into them like knives," said Sir Hubert, as his brother-in-law clambered on to the box. "You might have made shorter work of seeing Miss Marchant to her door."

"I might have let her fall on that inclined plane," growled Vansittart. "Capital for tobogganing, but very dangerous for a young lady in satin shoes."

"Poor girl, I wonder where her next satin shoes will come from," said Hubert.

"Is the Colonel so very hard up?"

"Very, I should think, since he is always in debt to the little tradespeople about here."

"And on the strength of that you all talk about those three girls as if they were lepers," retorted Vansittart. "I have no patience with the pettiness of village society."

CHAPTER V.

TEATIME IN ARCADIA

It was long since Vansittart had been haunted by the face of a woman as he was haunted by the face of Eve Marchant. He had not come to nine and twenty years of age without one or two *grandes passions*, which had begun out of a mere fancy, a glance—like one of those once fashionable toys called Pharaoh's Serpents—had swollen to colossal dimensions, and had ended, like the serpent, in a puff of smoke. This time he wondered at his own feelings when he found himself so deeply interested in the girl he always thought of as Titania. He was inclined to ascribe this sudden interest to the eccentric manner of their first meeting, the three pretty faces springing out of a turn in the wooded road, like sylphs in fairyland, the light, silvery laughter, and the something of sadness in the fate of this bright, light-hearted girl which appealed to his deeper feelings.

To whatever cause he might ascribe his interest, the fact remained that he was interested; for he found himself thinking about Eve Marchant a great deal more than he had ever thought of any one subject, except that one fatal subject of his misadventure at Venice; and he found himself very bad company for other people in consequence.

For ten days after the ball at Mandelford he lived in expectation of seeing Miss Marchant again, somewhere, somehow; and to further that desire of his heart he lived in a state of perpetual locomotion; now driving one of the Hartley dog-carts to Mandelford or Midhurst, Fernhurst or Haslemere, as the case might be; and anon patrolling those towns and villages on foot, in the ardent expectation of meeting Colonel Marchant's daughters upon some shopping or visiting expedition.

Go where he would he drew blank. Could it be that the Colonel was so deep in debt to the local tradespeople that his daughters dared not show themselves in those rural streets, where, after all, as the local gentry said condescendingly, one could really get almost everything one wanted?

He walked, he drove, he haunted the great pond in Redwold Park, which was thrown open to the public for skating, and where the men and maidens of the neighbourhood came daily to disport themselves: but vainly did he look for the Marchants.

"I thought the Miss Marchants were skaters," he said to Miss Green, on the third morning, as he helped her to put on her Mount Charles skates.

"So they are. They almost lived on this pond before Christmas. Perhaps they have worn out their boots, and are obliged to stay at home."

Those ten days of expectancy and disappointment made Jack Vansittart desperate. It seemed to him ages since the night of the ball. He began to think he should never see Eve Marchant again, and panic-stricken at this idea, he started after a morning's pheasant shooting to walk to the Homestead, Fernhurst, to make a formal call upon the sisters. Surely he had the right to call and inquire how they had survived the fatigue of the dances, the perils of the cold drive home. He was quick to make up his mind that he had such a right, and no walk taken for pleasure or for health had ever been more exhilarating than that tramp from the westward shoulder of Blackdown to the further side of Fernhurst. The roads were hard and dry, the wind was north-west, and the sun was going down in wintry splendour. It was late in the afternoon to make a ceremonious visit, but there was all the better hope that he would find Colonel Marchant's daughters within doors.

The house stood high above the road, on a ridge of meadow-land which had been encroached upon for half an acre of garden. It was a long, low house, with steep gable ends, and a high slanting roof, red tiled and lichen grown. Originally only a farm labourer's cottage, it had been expanded and improved by more than one tenant, the last addition being made by Colonel Marchant, who at the beginning of his tenancy had built a comfortable covered porch, which served as vestibule, and a large room on the ground floor, which had been first known as the nursery, then as the schoolroom, and which was now simply the parlour, or general living-room for the whole family. The resident governess, that element of respectability, had shaken the dust of Colonel Marchant's Bohemian dwelling-place off her feet a year ago, and had vanished into space, leaving a long arrear of salary behind her.

It was twilight, the grey twilight of a frosty winter day. Vansittart noted the snowdrops peeping over the box border as he walked up the steep gravel path that made the only approach to the Marchant dwelling. Carriage approach there was none. The Marchant girls' cheap satin slippers had to trip along that gravel path, in fine weather or foul, when they went to a party, and the poor little feet inside the slippers had to dance away any feeling of chilly dampness which the sodden gravel might occasion.

Vansittart looked about him in the evening grey as he waited for the opening of the door. He had rung a bell that sounded twice too loud for the size of the house, and had set up much barking of indoor and outdoor dogs.

There were two long strips of grass sloping down to the holly-hedge that shut off the road, and a long flower border on either side of the gravel path. This was the garden, so far as ornamental garden went, but beyond the grass strip on one side of the house there were cabbage rows, and the usual features of a vegetable garden. Beyond, right and left, stretched meadow-land, away to the dark background of copse and hillside.

The house, even after all its improvements, had a humble and homely aspect; walls roughly plastered, small lattice windows, and that steep slant of the roof, which Vansittart could have touched with his hand. The porch was a square enclosure, with a sloping thatch, and two little windows, right and left. An old woman, in a blue stuff gown and white cap and apron, opened the door, and even as it opened Vansittart heard again that ripple of silver-clear laughter which he had heard on the hilltop in the snowy night, nearly ten days ago.

Ten days. Only ten! Until ten days ago he had lived in happy ignorance that there was such a woman as Eve Marchant in the world. It seemed to him now as strange not to have known of her as it would be not to know of her namesake—the universal mother.

The same sweet laughter, not loud or boisterous, but soft and clear! Her laugh! He would have known it amidst a chorus of laughing girls.

Miss Marchant was at home, the old woman told him, and thereupon led him through a small, dark room—the original cottage parlour—through another room, faintly lit by a low fire, into a third and much larger room, which was bright with fire and lamp light.

Here the whole Marchant family, except the Colonel, were assembled at afternoon tea, which in this establishment had come to be the most enjoyable meal of the day.

Happily Vansittart had lunched lightly in the woods with the shooters, so was hungry enough to find the odour of toasting bread rather a comfortable addition to the atmosphere; or, at any rate, he was in a humour to be pleased with everything, even the sprawling attitude of a tall overgrown girl in a yellow cotton pinafore, sitting on the hearthrug, and making toast, watched and assisted by a smaller sister.

The three grown-up Miss Marchants sat at the table, two of them with their elbows on the board, where a large home-made cake—in north-country phraseology, a plum-loaf—a glass dish of marmalade and another of jam, and a pile of thick bread and butter, testified to the serious purpose of the meal.

Eve, the tea-maker and mistress of the feast, rose as Mr. Vansittart was announced, and came forward two or three steps to greet him, half in firelight, half in lamplight, brilliant and full of colour as an early Italian picture. Her gown was bright red merino, which set off the fairness of her complexion, and the pale gold in her brown hair; such a cheap gown, if he had only known, bought at one of the sales for half its value, timid beauty being afraid of the strong colour.

The other two girls were in somewhat tawdry attire, skirts of one colour, bodices of another; but they were fond of colour at the Homestead, and girls with scanty purses cannot bend to the iron rule of fashion.

To Vansittart's admiring eyes, Eve's red gown was the most exquisite and artistic of garments. He who was generally so much at his ease in all kinds of company found himself hesitating a little as he said that he had come to ask them if they had quite recovered from the fatigue of the dance; and, if so, how it was they had not been on the ice in Redwold Park.

"But perhaps you are tired of skating."

"Tired? Why, we all adore it," cried Eve. "But we have been dreadfully busy, making our winter gowns."

The second week in January seemed to Mr. Vansittart a late date at which to set about the making of winter raiment. He did not know that for many young women with slender purses the January and July sales are the only periods for the purchase of drapery. Twice a year the Marchant girls treated themselves to third-class tickets from Haslemere to Waterloo, and spent a long day going from shop to shop to secure the utmost value for their poor little stock of cash.

"Yes; it's really dreadful to lose a week of this delicious hard frost, ain't it?" exclaimed Sophy, much readier of speech this evening than her elder sister.

"Run to the kitchen and get me another teapot, Peggy," whispered Eve; whereupon the youngest girl started up from the rug and bounded off on her errand.

"Just as we were all improving in our skating," said Jenny. "We had conquered the outside edge, and Sophy and I were beginning to grasp the right idea of the Dutch roll, and were even aspiring to the grape vine."

"And then the hockey," interjected Sophy; "the hockey was too delightful."

Again the fair head bent itself towards the hearthrug. There was another whisper, and the elder girl bounced up and ran off.

"She has gone for a cup and saucer, and I am going to give you some fresh tea," said Eve, smiling at the visitor as he sat in the Colonel's chair, in that corner of the room which bore no traces of girlish litter. "I hope you don't mind our waiting upon ourselves. We have only our old Yorkshire Nancy, and a little parlour-maid; and as it is the little maid's afternoon out, here we are, five intelligent young people, ready to help each other."

"I cannot conceive a more delightful spectacle. But why make fresh tea, Miss Marchant? I am sure there is some of your last brew which would do capitally for me."

"If I did not know you are saying that for kindness, I might think you one of those unsympathetic people who don't care for tea."

"Do tea and sympathy go together?"

"I think most nice people are tea-drinkers. Indeed, it seems to me that tea is the link that holds society together. Oh, what should we do with our afternoons—however could we go and call upon people—if it were not for afternoon tea?"

"And I see that afternoon tea, with you young ladies, is a somewhat serious function," said Vansittart, with a glance across the well-spread table to the pile of toast which Sophy was buttering.

The younger girls had come back, one with a china teapot, the other with a cup and saucer, and Eve was busy with her second brew.

"Please don't laugh at us. We are a very irregular family in the matter of luncheon, and this is our hungriest meal."

The youngest girl, who had resumed her seat on the hearthrug, was at this juncture seized with a giggling fit, which she vainly endeavoured to suppress, and which speedily communicated itself to the youngest but one, also seated on the rug.

"Those children are too absurd," exclaimed Sophy, after trying to frown them into propriety. "They are always laughing at nothing."

"Happy age," said Vansittart; "the time so soon comes when we can't laugh at anything."

"She said it was our hungriest meal!" gasped Hetty, of the yellow pinafore, in convulsions of undisguised laughter; "I should rather think it was."

"I suppose these young ladies are not yet promoted to late dinners?" hazarded Vansittart, wondering a little why this question of afternoon tea could afford such scope for mirth.

"No, we don't dine late," protested Hetty, more and more hilarious. "*We* don't, do we, Peggy?"

Peggy, the white-pinafored youngest, was speechless with laughter.

Vansittart began to divine the mystery. In this household of narrow means there was no late dinner for the ladies of the family. There was doubtless a dinner for the Colonel. Man cannot long support life without the regulation evening meal; but for this household of girls bread and jam and plum-loaves were an all-sufficient repast. Was low living—this diet of innocent bread and butter—one of the causes of Eve's peerless complexion, he wondered? All the girls were more or less pretty. It might be that this Arcadian fare had something to do with their prettiness.

Never had he enjoyed a meal so much as that afternoon tea in the Marchants' parlour. As he sat looking at the room in the lamplight he began to think he had never seen a prettier room for a family to live in. The fireplace was wide and spacious, an open hearth, with a high projecting mantelpiece, and narrow shelves over that, slanting upward to the ceiling, and dotted about with trumpery blue teacups, and yellow and red vases from the Riviera. The Colonel had begun with the intention of making an ingle nook, but being told, in the rustic builder's phraseology, that an ingle nook would run into money, he had contented himself with a wide fireplace and a projecting chimney. There was only black and white on the walls, a few etchings, and a good many photographs of pictures, against a dark red paper. There was a cottage piano in a corner, draped with a Bellagio rug of vivid amber, and there were other Bellagio rugs on the sofa, and on the Colonel's armchair. For the rest the furniture was of the shabbiest; clumsy substantial old chairs and tables that suggested the hindermost dens of the second-hand furniture dealer, those yards and back premises in which he keeps his least attractive goods. The room was uncarpeted, but crudely coloured Indian rugs of the cheaper kind brightened the oak-stained floor here and there, and gave a suggestion of luxury. The lamp in the middle of the round table was subdued by a large shade of art muslin, daintily frilled and ribboned, evidently a home production; the German tablecloth was of white and red damask, the crockery was white, cheap but pretty, and there were a few winter flowers and bright berries in brown glass vases. Altogether that tea-table had a delightful aspect to John Vansittart. The room, the firelight, the fresh young faces, with that one fairest face shining like a star among the others, the hoydens upon the hearthrug giggling at the idea of a dinnerless household, made up a scene of homely enchantment. Even a white fox-terrier which had begun by snapping at him, and which was now at his knee begging for toast, seemed part and parcel of the pleasant homeliness. It was teatime in a domestic fairyland; a fairyland where people eat slices of buttered plum-loaf and hot frizzling toast; a fairyland odorous of strawberry jam; a land where young women put their elbows on the table, and had no need of a chaperon to keep them in countenance during the visit of a young man; in a word, the fairyland of Bohemia. To Vansittart, who in England had known only the respectabilities, the everlasting laws and conventionalities of smart people, differing in detail with the fashion of the hour, but fundamentally the same—to Vansittart, the young man of property and position, this glimpse of an unconventional household was as novel as it was fascinating. Pretty as Eve Marchant was, he would not have admired her half so much at a ball in Grosvenor Square. It was the touch of pathos, the touch of comedy in the girl's history and surroundings which interested him.

He sat long at the tea-table, and eat more buttered toast than he had eaten at a sitting since he was an undergraduate. He forgot even to ask if Colonel Marchant were at home, and had almost forgotten the existence of that gentleman when Hetty, the youngest but one, on being reproved for noisy utterance, replied, "It don't matter, father can't hear me at the Rag."

"Colonel Marchant is in town, I conclude," said Vansittart.

"He went up by the afternoon train," Eve answered with a stately air. "He is dining with some old chums to-night, and I don't think he'll be home before Saturday."

"I have not been fortunate enough to meet him yet."

"I'm afraid he's rather unsociable," answered Eve, suddenly serious, while over all the young faces there spread a shadow of seriousness. "He lets us accept invitations—and I'm sure people are very kind to go on asking us when we can't pay them the proper respect of new frocks."

"What do people care about frocks?" exclaimed Jenny, the third daughter, with a Republican air. "If we are asked out it is because we are liked, in spite of our old frocks."

"Or because people are sorry for us," said Eve, gravely.

"I don't think people are ever sorry for youth and beauty," said Vansittart. "Both are objects of envy rather than of compassion."

"Oh, I can't follow you there," answered Eve; "everybody is young once. Youth is as common as chickweed or groundsel, and it lasts such a short time; and if one has to spend that one bright little bit of life in a state of perpetual hard-uppishness, I am sure one deserves to be pitied."

She talked of her poverty with an alarming frankness. Most people hide their indigence as if it were an ugly sore, or if they speak of it, speak softly, apologetically, or with an assumed lightness, as if their poverty were not really poverty, but only a genteel limitation of means, implying none of the shortcomings of actual want. But this girl talked of her old frock and her father's poverty, without a blush.

"Father won't visit anywhere now," she said. "He can't forget that he once lived in a big house, and had a thousand acres of shooting, and bred his own pheasants. He can hardly bring himself to shoot other people's birds, even when they ask him to their big shoots."

"Your old home was in the North, I think?" said Vansittart, delighted at being let into the family secrets.

"In Yorkshire—within ten miles of Beverley. Do you know Beverley?"

"Yes; I was there once—a queer sleepy old place, once renowned for its corruption; now from a political point of view *nil*. A town with a Bar—a Bar which did something to Charles the First, I believe. Did Beverley shut him out, or did Beverley let him in after Hull had shut him out? My common or Gardiner history is at fault there."

"Beverley is a dear old town," asserted Eve. "I haven't seen it since I was twelve years old, but I can remember the countenance of every house in the market-place, and the colouring of every window in the Minster. Father won a cup at the races when I was eleven, and I took it home in the carriage with me. I remember having it in my lap, a great gilt cup. I thought it was gold till my governess told me it was only silver-gilt. Heaven knows what became of that cup! Father despised it. The race was a paltry affair, I believe, and his horse was a poor creature. He had won ever so many better cups at bigger races; but I only remember the cup I carried home, and the broad, bright common, and the blazing July day, and the happy-looking people. It was my last summer in Yorkshire, my last summer in the house where I was born. Before the next summer we all came here. Mother, and the governess, and the rest of us. Peggy was a baby in long clothes, and mother was only just beginning to be seriously ill."

"And if you could have seen this place when we first came to it you would have pitied us," said Sophy. "A parson's family had been

72

living in it, an overgrown family like us, but without the faintest idea of the beautiful. The parson's wife kept poultry, and there were horrid wired enclosures close to the parlour window, and there was no porch, and no possibility of saying 'Not at home' to callers. There were only vegetables in the garden, potatoes and scarlet-runners, where we have made lawns."

"She calls those long strips of grass lawns," interjected Peggy, irreverently disposed towards a dictatorial grown-up sister who was not the eldest. Against Eve no one rebelled.

"And think how squeezed we all must have been till father built this room, and picture to yourself the mess and muddle we had to endure all the time it was being built. It didn't matter to him, for he was out of the worst of it."

"He had to take mother to the South that winter," explained Eve. "She had been in weak health for ever so long before we left Yorkshire. A weakly plant can't bear being torn up by the roots, can it? I think that change in our fortunes broke her heart—added to—to other things."

She did not say what the other things were, and he could not ask her; nor would he ask her what had brought about the Colonel's ruin. He could make a shrewd guess upon the latter point. The value of landed property had gone down, and the man had kept a racing stud. Between those two facts there was ample room for change of fortune.

"Mother never came back to us," said Eve, with a gentle sigh. "She is lying in the cemetery at Cannes. People have told me about her grave, and that it is in a lovely spot. There is some comfort in being able to think of that, after all these years."

"I know that resting-place well," said Vansittart. "There is no lovelier home for the dead."

There was a brief silence. Even the children on the hearthrug were dumb, and there was no sound but the contented purring of Hetty's colossal cat, a brindled grey, with a fluffy white breast, a cat that was satiated with the worship of pretty girls, and gave himself as many airs as if he had been kittened in Egypt, and ranked among gods.

"Dear as Beverley was, I hope you all like your Sussex home," said Vansittart.

"Sussex is well enough, but when one is used to a big stone house, with a picture-gallery, and one of the finest Jacobean staircases in the East Riding, it is rather hard to come down to a labourer's cottage that has been dodged and expanded into the most inconvenient house in the neighbourhood," said Sophy, with a grand air, and tilting her retroussé nose a little higher than usual.

Again the girls on the hearthrug burst into inextinguishable laughter.

"What a snob you are, Sophy!" cried the outspoken Hetty. "You say all that as if you had learnt it by heart; and as for coming down, you came down to the labourer's cottage when you were eleven years old. You ought to be used to it now you are twenty."

Twenty. Sophy, the second, was twenty—and there was only a year between her and Vansittart's incomparable she, who had migrated to Sussex when she was twelve. One and twenty, in the fair majority of her girlish charms. He thought it the most delightful period in woman's life—fair as in her teens, but wiser: mature for love and wisdom.

All earthly blisses must end. The blissfullest five o'clock tea cannot last for ever; but Vansittart was determined to make this endure as long as he could. The meal was finished. Even those long, lean hands of the youngsters had ceased to be stretched harpy-like towards the table for more bread and jam, or another slice of cake, which an elder sister dispensed with somewhat offensive comments upon the ravenous maw of youth.

"Oh, come now," cried the offended Peggy. "Suppose I do eat a lot; I haven't stopped growing yet. You have, yet I've heard you say you could sit and eat one of Nancy's plum-loaves all the evening. But that was when there was no one here but ourselves."

Sophy blushed furiously, and Vansittart came laughingly to the rescue.

"I can vouch for the seductiveness of Nancy's plum-loaf," he said. "I think I must coax her to impart the recipe to my mother's cook. Is your Nancy a coaxable person?"

"Not very. She adores us, but she is rather gruff and grim to the outside world. She was in father's service as kitchen-maid when she was fourteen, at the time of his marriage, ages before I was born," said Eve.

Ages. Yet she was the eldest. What did that word ages mean? Three years, perhaps, in a young lady's vocabulary.

"And she followed your fortunes from the old house, and she is as faithful as Caleb Balderstone, I dare say," said Vansittart, and felt in the next moment that it was precisely one of those things he had better have left unsaid.

"She is just like Caleb," replied Eve, frankly accepting the suggestion, "just as faithful and true. I feel sure that if it were suddenly put upon us to give a dinner, and there were a saddle of mutton or a fore-quarter of lamb hanging conveniently before a neighbour's fire, Nancy would elope with it just as audaciously as Caleb made off with the cooper's spit—all for the credit of the family. She works like a slave for us from morning till night. She is a splendid manager, and she makes tea-cakes as only a Yorkshirewoman can."

"And in cooking she could give points to many of your professed cooks," said Jenny. "Father is a difficult man in the matter of dinner."

"And dinner is a difficult matter for poor people," laughed Eve, to the annoyance of Sophy, who had not yet taken to heart the foolishness of the ostrich family, and who was always anxious to slur over an impecuniousness which was visible to the naked eye. It was only Eve who had learnt to grasp the nettle. Perhaps it was her country life, among green fields and blackthorn hedgerows, and chestnut copses, and the barren heather-clad hills, which had kept her free from the age's worst fever, the sickly longing for wealth. Had she been reared in Pimlico or Brompton, she too might have been spoilt, her nature warped, her mind tainted with the sordid thirst for gold, the desire for finery and fine living, the aching envy of rich men's daughters. The people she knew and mixed with were county people, who wore their old gowns, and lived simple, old-fashioned lives when they were in the country, and left their modern vices behind them in London ready for use next season.

Vansittart glanced at a cheap little American clock ticking among the cups and vases on the chimney-piece. A quarter past six, and his watch had told him that it was a quarter before five as he approached the Homestead.

"I don't know how to apologize for staying so long," he faltered, as he rose from the Colonel's comfortable chair and extricated his hat from the reluctant paws of the grey cat.

"Don't apologize," said Jenny, who was the pertest of the sisters; "there is nothing so unflattering to one's amour propre as a short visit. And then there are so many of us. A visitor must stay a longish time in order to give each of us a civil word."

Vansittart's conscience smote him at this remark. He feared that he had addressed his conversation exclusively to Eve. He had no consciousness of having spoken to any one else. For him the room had held only Eve; only that one salient figure. The others were faintly sketched in the background. She was the picture.

He got out of the room somehow, after shaking hands all round, and even in his deep trance of love he was conscious that the two youngest hands were sticky with traces of strawberry jam. There being no one else to show him out—for who could disturb Nancy, remote in the kitchen, with futile ringing of a ceremonial bell?—the whole bevy of sisters accompanied him to the outer door, the youngest carrying a tall candle, which threatened to topple over and sprinkle her with a shower of ozokerit. He had time to notice the rooms through which they went—one shabbily furnished as a dining-room, with an old harpsichord for sideboard; the other evidently the Colonel's den for books, boots, and tobacco. He had time to note the porch or vestibule, where there hung much outer apparel, feminine and masculine, hats, scarves, fishing basket, sticks of all shapes and thicknesses, mostly from native woods and hedgerows. He had time to note everything during that lingering departure, protracted by idle talk about the roads and the weather: and yet while his eye took in the shabbiness and smallness of those two rooms, the rustiness of the Colonel's overcoats, mind and eye both were filled with but one image—the figure of a tall, fair girl, whose fluffy head overtopped her sisters, and shone conspicuous among them all (as it would have shone, he thought, amidst a thousand), by its fresh and innocent beauty.

"And that is the girl I love; and that is the girl I mean to marry," he said to himself, as he walked briskly along the footpath towards Blackdown.

After such dawdling in Armida's parlour he would have to walk his fastest to be in time to dress for the eight o'clock dinner.

CHAPTER VI.

WHY SHOULD HE REFRAIN?

Why should he not marry Colonel Marchant's daughter? Vansittart asked himself, in the quiet of those night watches which are said to bring counsel.

Why should he not marry Eve Marchant? asked Jack Vansittart of Counsellor Night. He was lord not only of himself but of a handsome income and a desirable estate. He had nobody to please but himself, and—well, yes, he wanted to please his mother, even in a matter so entirely personal as his choice of a wife. She had been so devoted a mother, and they had loved each other so dearly! In all his life he had kept only one secret from her—the secret of that night at Venice. In all his life he had only once told her a lie; when he told her he had not been in Venice during that last Italian tour. He wanted to please her, if it were possible, in this most serious question of his marriage. He knew that she loved him too unselfishly to be sorry that he should marry, albeit marriage must in some wise lessen their companionship as mother and son. The major half of his existence must needs belong to the woman he chose for his wife. His mother was resigned to take her lesser place in his life, she had often told him, provided that the wife were worthy.

"Pure as well as beautiful, sprung from an honourable race, reared by a good mother."

These were the conditions she had laid upon his choice. What would she think of Colonel Marchant's daughter, motherless, the child of a disreputable father, a girl reared under every social disadvantage; a girl who had dragged herself up anyhow, according to village gossips; a girl who had neither accomplishments nor education, and who had shown herself an audacious flirt, said the village—for Eve's frank freedom of speech and manner was the rustic idea of audacity in flirtation? To talk easily with a man under forty was to be an outrageous flirt. The rustic idea of a well-conducted young woman was simpering silence.

What would his mother think of such a choice; his mother, who had been born and bred in just that stratum of English respectability which is narrowest in its sociology and strongest in its prejudices;

his mother, who belonged to the county families, those deeply rooted children of the soil to whom the word trade is an abomination; who think that the Church and the Army were established for the maintenance of their younger sons, who consider they make a concession when they send a son to the Bar, and who shudder at the notion of a doctor or a solicitor issuing from their superior circles? What would Mrs. Vansittart think of an alliance with the daughter of a man whose name was dishonoured, who, albeit he too had been born of that elect race, and was indisputably "county," had made himself a pauper and an outcast by his misconduct, and who had lived for the last nine years in a Bohemian and utterly intolerable manner, spending his time mysteriously in London, letting his daughters run wild, and having to be summoned for his rates and taxes?

The charges against Colonel Marchant, as Vansittart had heard them, were manifold. He had begun life in a marching regiment, without expectations, had married a lovely girl of low birth, or supposed to be of low birth, since her pedigree was unknown to Sussex, and her antecedents and uprising had never been explained or expounded to the curious in the neighbourhood of the Colonel's present abode. Within two years of this marriage he had succeeded, most unexpectedly, by the death of a young cousin, to a fine estate in Yorkshire, considerably dipped by previous owners, but still a fine estate, and had immediately begun a career of extravagance, horse-racing, betting, and disreputable company, which had ultimately forced him to sell mansion and manor, farms and homesteads, that had belonged to his family since the Commonwealth, when the lands of East Grinley were bestowed by Cromwell on one of his finest soldiers, Major Fear-the-Lord Marchant, an officer who had helped to turn the fortunes of the day at Marston Moor, and who had been left for dead on the field of Dunbar.

Colonel Marchant had kept race-horses, and in his latter and worst days—when ruin was close at hand—had been suspected of shady dealings in the management of his stud, and had been the subject of a Jockey Club inquiry, which, albeit not important enough to become a *cause célèbre*, had left the Colonel with a tarnished reputation on the Turf, and the dark suspicion of having made a good deal of money by in and out running. He withdrew from the racing world under a cloud, not quite cleaned out, for the money he had won in the previous autumn served to buy the cottage near Fernhurst, and to carry his family from Yorkshire to Sussex. Here he began life anew, a ruined man, with five young daughters and an invalid wife.

Of Colonel Marchant's existence at the Homestead local society had very little to say, except in a general way that he was not "nice." He neglected his daughters, he never went to church, and he was always in debt. Maiden ladies and old women of the masculine gender used to speculate upon how long he would be able to go on before his creditors took desperate measures. How long would Midhurst and Haslemere bear and forbear with a man who was known to be deep in debt in both towns? All this and much more had John Vansittart heard from various people since the night of the hunt ball, for he had laid himself out with considerable artfulness to hear all he could about the Marchant family. In the beginning of things, albeit Eve appeared to him in all the innocent loveliness of Titania, he had told himself that he could not marry into such a family. Such an alliance would blight his life. He would have those four sisters upon his shoulders. He would be disgraced by a disreputable father-in-law.

And now in the night watches he told himself a very different story. He told himself that he should be a craven and a cur if he allowed Eve Marchant to suffer for her father's sins. What was it to him that the Colonel had squandered his money on third-rate racers, and had been suspected of in and out running on second-rate racecourses? He loved the Colonel's daughter; and as an honest man it was his duty to take her away from unworthy surroundings. Inclination and honesty pointing the same way, he was determined to do his duty—yes, even at the risk of disappointing the mother he loved.

So much for the night watches. He saw before him a fierce battle between love and prejudice, but he was determined to fight that battle.

The war began while this resolve was yet a new thing.

"So you have been calling at the Homestead, Jack," said his sister at luncheon next day.

"Who told you that?" he asked curtly, reddening a little.

"One of those little birds of which we have a whole aviary. I drove into Midhurst this morning to talk to the fishmonger, and met the two Miss Etheringtons. They saw you going in at Colonel Marchant's gate yesterday afternoon."

"I wonder they didn't wait outside to see when I came out again," said Vansittart.

"I dare say they would have waited if it had been warmer weather. What could have induced you to call upon Colonel Marchant? Colonel, indeed! Colonel of a Yorkshire Volunteer regiment! I don't believe he was ever any higher than ensign in the 107th."

"Very likely not. But I didn't call upon the Colonel; I called upon my partners at the hunt ball."

"And no doubt they received you with open arms!"

"They received me with true Yorkshire hospitality, and gave me some excellent tea, to say nothing of buttered plum-loaf."

"And I dare say they were not in the least embarrassed at doing the honours to a strange young man, without mother, or aunt, or so much as a governess to keep them in countenance."

"Why should they require to be kept in countenance? Surely five girls ought to be chaperon enough for each other?"

"They are the most unconventional young women I ever met with," said the eldest Miss Champernowne, who was a good judge of the conventional.

"They are very pretty, poor things," said Mrs. Vansittart. "It is sad for them to belong to such a father."

"You might spare your pity, mother," exclaimed her son, growing angry. "I don't know anything about Colonel Marchant; but I haven't the slightest doubt that the things that are said about him in this neighbourhood are the usual exaggerations and distortions of the truth. As for his daughters, I never made the acquaintance of five brighter, healthier, merrier girls. The household is full of interest for me; and I want you to call at the Homestead with me, mother, and see with your own eyes what manner of girls Eve Marchant and her sisters are."

"I call upon them, Jack!" exclaimed his mother. "I, who am only a visitor here! What good could that do?"

"Plenty of good, if you like. You don't live quite at the other end of England. From Haslemere to Liss is not half an hour's journey; and if you happen to like Miss Marchant—as I think you will—you might ask her to visit you at Merewood."

A light dawned upon the hitherto unsuspecting mother, a light which was far from welcome. She sat looking at her son dumbly.

"Why not ask the whole five, while you are about it, Mrs. Vansittart?" said Claudia Champernowne, her thin lips contracting a little, as if she, too, saw cause for offence in Vansittart's suggestion.

"My dear Jack, you must know I am the last person in the world to invite strange young women to my house—young women whose Bohemian ways would make me miserable," remonstrated Mrs. Vansittart, severely. "I can't think what can have put such an idea into your head."

"Christian charity, no doubt," sneered Claudia.

"Well, after all, these girls are not actually disreputable," pleaded Lady Hartley, who was always good-natured; "one sees them at all the omnium gatherums in the neighbourhood, and they don't behave worse than the general run of girls. If you had asked me to take notice of them, Jack, I could understand you—but to bother mother—mother who lives in another county, and who can't be supposed to care about taking up strange girls."

"So be it, Maud. You shall go with me the next time I call at the Homestead."

"What, you are actually going to keep up a calling acquaintance with the Marchant girls? How very eccentric!"

"Yes, I am going to keep up my acquaintance with the Miss Marchants. I am going to make myself acquainted with their father. I am going to see with my own eyes whether Lucifer is quite as black as he is painted," answered Vansittart, doggedly.

"You won't like the Colonel. I am positive upon that point," said Maud. "Hubert is an excellent judge of character, and he couldn't stand the Colonel; although he felt sorry for the man and tried to be civil to him. Colonel Marchant is an impossible person."

"What has he done that makes him impossible?"

"Oh, I really can't give you the exact details; but they say all sorts of unpleasant things about him."

"'They say.' We know who 'they' are—an unknown quantity, which, when inquired into, resolves itself into half a dozen old women of both sexes."

"Unhappily everybody knows that he is in debt all over the neighbourhood."

"He must be a remarkable man to have found a neighbourhood so trustful."

"Oh, I suppose he pays a little on account from time to time, or he would not be able to go on anyhow; but really, now, Jack, you can't expect me to be on intimate terms with a household of that kind. I am very glad to have those poor girls at my garden-parties, for they are pretty and tolerably well-behaved, though their frocks and hats are too dreadful. What did I tell you Lady Corisande Hawberk called those poor girls when she saw them here last summer, Claudia?"

"Lady Hartley's burlesque troupe."

"Yes, that was it—Lady Hartley's burlesque troupe! They were all three dressed differently—and so fine—especially the two younger. The eldest is a shade more enlightened. One wore cheap black lace over apricot silk—you are a man, so you don't know what cheap black lace means—and a Gainsborough hat. Another was in peach-coloured cotton—that papery, shiny cotton, which is meant to look like silk, with a straw sailor hat all over nodding peach-coloured poppies—and her parasol!—heavens, her parasol! bright scarlet cotton, and six feet high! Lady Corisande was immensely amused."

"Is poverty so good a joke?" asked Vansittart, black as thunder.

"Oh, it wasn't their poverty one laughed at. It was their childlike ignorance of our world and its ways. If they had all three worn clean white frocks and neat straw hats they would have looked charming. It was the effort to be in the height of fashion——"

"With colours and materials three years old," put in Claudia.

"I tell you it is poverty you laugh at—poverty alone that is ridiculous. We have arrived at a state of things in which there is nothing respected or respectable except money. We pretend to honour rank and ancient lineage, but in our secret hearts we set no value on either unless sustained by wealth."

"What a tirade!" cried Lady Hartley, "and all because of a little good-natured laughter at those girls' frocks. To think that a pretty face, which you have seen only twice, should exercise such dominion over you!"

The ladies left the dining-room in a cluster to put on their hats for a walk to the ice. Skating was the rage at Redwold Towers, and even Mrs. Vansittart went to look on. She liked to see her son and daughter disporting themselves, each an adept in the art; and then there was the off-chance of meeting the German nurse with the year-old baby somewhere in the grounds before sunset. The baby had already taken a strong grip upon the grandmother's heart.

John Vansittart did not go with the skaters, as it had been his wont to go. Nor did he offer to keep his mother company in her afternoon walk. He was in a sullen and resentful mood, resentful of he knew not what; so he started on a solitary ramble in the Redwold copses, where he would have only robins and jays and chaffinches, and the infinite variety of living things whose names he knew not, for his companions.

He was angry with all those talking women, his sister first and foremost; but most of all was he angry with himself.

Yes, it was her beauty that had caught him, that picture of Titania delicately fair against the darkly purple night, her pale gold hair, her sapphire eyes shining in the starlight. Yes, his sister's flippant tongue had hit upon the humiliating truth. It was only because this girl appealed to his fancy that he was so eager and so angry, this girl whom he had seen the other night for the first time, of whose heart, character, antecedents, kindred, he knew absolutely nothing. It was only because she was so lovely in his eyes that he was prepared to champion her, ready to marry her if she would have him.

"I am a fool," he told himself, "an arrant fool, a fool so foolish that even shallow-brained Maud can see my folly. I know nothing of this girl, absolutely nothing except that surface frankness which passes for innocence—and which might be assumed by Becky Sharp herself. Indeed, we are told that it was Becky's guilelessness which always impressed people in her favour. May not this girl, daughter of a shady father, be every bit as clever and far-seeing as Becky Sharp? I dare say she is laughing at my infatuation already, and wondering how far it will lead me. Sefton, too! Miss Green said there was an understanding between them. His manner was certainly a thought too easy. No doubt she is trying to hook Sefton, a landowner, one of the best matches in the neighbourhood. And she puts on that stand-offish manner of malice aforethought, to lead him on by keeping him off. I should be an idiot if I were to commit myself, without knowing a great deal more about the young lady. I have been getting absolutely maudlin about the girl. This is how half the unhappy marriages are made."

He stopped in his swinging walk, after tramping along the narrow muddy track at five miles an hour. The ring of the skates, the shouts of boys playing hockey, sounded clear upon the frosty air. He was not more than a mile from the pond as the crow flies.

"Sophy said their gowns would be finished this morning," he mused. "I wonder whether they will be on the ice this afternoon."

He tramped the narrow track between the thick growth of oak and fir, emerged from the copse, and struck out a path across some low-lying pastures to the lake, which lay in the lowest part of Redwold Park, and only five minutes' walk from one of the lodges, where some of the skaters kept their skates. There were a good many skaters this fine bright afternoon—an afternoon in which there was no consciousness of cold, though the atmosphere was twelve degrees below freezing point, just such a calm, clear atmosphere as Vansittart had often enjoyed in the Upper Engadine. There were a good many people on the ice—the villagers at one end of the long irregular-shaped piece of water, the gentry at the other—a rustic bridge dividing the classes from the masses. About twenty girls were playing hockey, the three Champernownes conspicuous among the rest by their fine carriage and sober attire. Those girls had certainly mastered the art of dress, Vansittart admitted to himself. They wore black serge gowns, cut to perfection by a fashionable tailor, black cloth jackets, tight-fitting, severe, with narrow collar and cuffs of Astrakhan, at a time when Astrakhan was not everybody's wear. Their hats were the neatest on the ice—black felt hats, with the least touch of scarlet in the loose knot of corded ribbon which was their only trimming. No wings, claws, or beaks; no anchors, arrows, crescents, or buckles of jet, gilt or steel; none of those tawdry accessories which sometimes convert a young lady's headgear into a museum of curiosities. Long tan gloves, fresh and perfectly fitting, completed the toilet of the three sisters, who had early realized the effect that is made in any public assembly by three handsome girls dressed alike.

Jack Vansittart paced the bank, stopping now and then to watch the skating, but with no inclination to join the revellers. The walk along the side of the lake was a pleasant walk, in some parts open to the water, in other places screened by hazel and alder. Here and there in a bend of the lake there was a hillock, on which the skaters sat to take off or adjust their skates, and on which the spectators sometimes stood to watch the sport.

From this point of vantage Vansittart surveyed the scene, and as he did so became conscious of a man standing on the opposite side of the lake, also surveying the scene. A second glance assured him that the man was Sefton. He had only seen Sefton at the ball, but he could not be mistaken in that sharp, hooked nose, sallow complexion, and black beard. It was Sefton, lightly clad, as if prepared for skating, but holding himself aloof from the throng.

There was a fascination for Vansittart in this solitary spectator, and it was while watching him that he became aware of a new arrival. Sefton, whose hawk-like eyes had been looking up and down the lake, suddenly concentrated his attention on one spot at the end near the lodge, and as suddenly walked off in that direction. Vansittart imitated him on his side of the lake, and was speedily enlightened as to the cause of Sefton's movements. As he neared the lodge gate he saw three young women approaching—three young women in blue gowns, widely different in shade.

Now, the Champernownes and his sister—who talked of chiffons for an hour at a stretch—had dinned into his brain the fact that blue was not worn that winter. The colour might be a beautiful colour in the abstract, the colour of sky and sea, of sapphires and forget-me-nots, of children's eyes and running brooks, but it was a colour which no woman who respected herself would wear. It was "out," and that monosyllable meant that it was anathema maranatha.

And behold here came the three girls in their new winter frocks, a blaze of blue; Sophy splendid in peacock cloth, trimmed with plush that *almost* matched; Jenny in uncompromising azure, the blue of Reckitt's and the British laundress; Eve less startling in a dark Oxford cloth, very plainly made, with a little home-made toque of the same stuff.

The fact was that the fashionable drapers were almost giving away their blue stuffs that January, and the prudent Marchants had been able to get the best materials at a third of their value.

"And after all it isn't the colour, but the style of a gown that makes it fashionable or otherwise," Sophy had said philosophically, as she pored over a fashion plate, trying to realize a creation which nobody ever saw out of that fashion plate.

The girls seemed quite happy in their blue raiment, or at least the two younger girls, who greeted Vansittart with frank cordiality. Eve had a somewhat absent air as she shook hands, he thought, though her sudden blush thrilled him with the fancy that he might not be quite indifferent to her. He saw her glance away from him while they were talking, and look right and left, as if expecting to see some one. Could it be Sefton? Mr. Sefton came across the ice while Vansittart was asking himself that question, shook hands with the three girls, and then walked away with Eve along the path, where the hazels and alders soon hid them from the jealous eyes that followed their steps. "Miss Green was right," thought Vansittart; "there is an understanding between them."

The two younger girls skipped off to an adjacent bank to put on their skates, and were soon provided with a pair of youthful admirers, both clerical, to assist them in the operation. Vansittart stood looking idly at the hockey-playing for some minutes, quite long enough to allow Eve and her companion to get a good way towards the further end of the pond, and then he turned and strolled in the same direction. As he sauntered on, disgusted with life and the world, which seemed just now made up of disillusions, he heard slow footsteps approaching him, just where the path made a sudden bend, footsteps and voices.

They were coming back, those two. They had not prolonged their *tête-à-tête*. The aspect of affairs was not quite so black as it had seemed ten minutes ago. He did not purposely listen to what they were saying. The sharp bend of the path, screened at this point by a clump of hazels, divided him from them. Short of calling out to them to warn them of his vicinity he could not have avoided hearing what he did hear: only five short sentences.

"I am very sorry. It was a false scent," said Mr. Sefton.

"And we are no nearer knowing anything?"

"No nearer. I sincerely regret your disappointment."

There was a lingering tenderness in his tone that made Vansittart feel a touch of the original savage that lives in all of us—a rush of boiling blood to brain and heart which hints at the hereditary taint transmitted by bloodthirsty ancestors. A few more steps and he and Miss Marchant were face to face, as she and her companion turned the corner of the hazel clump. She looked at him piteously through a veil of tears as they passed each other. Sefton had power to make her cry. Surely that implied something more than common acquaintance, nay, even more than friendship. All the tragedy of an unhappy love affair might be in those tears.

He looked back. She and Sefton had parted company. He was talking to some men on the bank. She had joined her sisters on the ice, and was standing with her skates in her hand, as if debating whether to put them on or not.

Should he go and entreat to be allowed to kneel at her feet, and do her knightly service by buckling stiff buckles and battling with difficult straps? No, he would not be such a slave. Let Sefton wait upon her; Sefton, who had all her confidence; Sefton, who could bring tears to those lovely eyes.

Vansittart rambled off across the frozen pasture, turning his back resolutely upon the noise of many voices, the ringing of many skates.

"It was a false scent." What could that possibly mean? How in the language of lovers could that phrase come in? A false scent. "I deeply regret your disappointment." What disappointment? Why should she be disappointed, and Sefton regretful? In any love affair between those two there could seem no reason for disappointment. The man was free to marry whom he pleased. Did he mean honourably by this girl; or was he only fooling her with attentions which were to end in unworthy trifling? Was he taking a base advantage of her dubious position to essay the seducer's part? From all that he had heard of Sefton's character Vansittart doubted much that he was capable of a generous love, or that he was the kind of man to marry a girl whose father was under a cloud.

And she?—was she weak and foolish, innocently yielding her heart to a man who meant evil? or was she her father's daughter, a schemer by instinct and inclination, like Becky Sharp? Vansittart tried to put himself in Joe Sedley's place, tried to realize how a man may see honesty and sweet simplicity where there are only craft and finished acting. To poor vain Josh Becky had seemed all truth and girlish innocence. Only one man of all Becky's admirers had ever thoroughly understood her, and that man was Lord Steyne.

Vansittart walked a long way, engrossed by such speculations as these—at one time inclined to believe that this girl whom he so ardently admired was all that girlhood should be—inclined to trust her even in the face of all strange seeming, to trust her and to follow her footsteps with his reverent love, and if he found her responsive to that love to take her for his wife, in the teeth of all opposition.

"Why should my mother be made unhappy by such a marriage?" he asked himself. "If I can prove that Eve Marchant is in no wise injured by her surroundings, what more do we want? What are the surroundings to my mother or to me? Even if I had to pension the Colonel for the rest of his life I should think little of the cost—if it brought me the girl I love."

After all, he told himself time was the only test—time must decide everything. His duty to himself was to possess his soul with patience, to see as much as he could of the Marchant family without committing himself to a matrimonial engagement, and without being guilty of anything that could be deemed flirtation. No, he would trifle with no woman's feelings; he would not love and ride away. He would put a bridle upon his tongue; but he would make it his business to pluck out the heart of the Marchant mystery. Surely among five girls he could manage to be kind and friendly without entangling himself with any one of the five.

Having made out for himself a line of conduct, he walked back to the lake. The shadows of twilight were creeping over the grass. There were very few people on the ice. The Marchants had taken off their skates, and were saying good-bye to the two curates who had been their attendant swains.

"We have such an awful way to walk if we go by the high-road, and we must go that way, for the footpath will be snowed up," said Sophy. "It will be dark long before we are home."

The curates had, one an evening school, the other a penny reading, coming on at half-past seven, so they were fain to say goodnight. Vansittart came up as they parted.

"Let me walk home with you," he said; "I haven't had nearly enough walking."

"Then what a tremendous walker you must be!" said Jenny; "I saw you marching over the grass just now as if you were walking for a wager."

His attendance was accepted tacitly, and presently he and Eve were walking side by side, in the rear, while the two younger girls walked on in front, turning round every now and then to join in the conversation, so that the four made one party.

Eve's eyes were bright enough now, but she was more silent than she had been at their tea-drinking, and she was evidently out of spirits.

"I'm afraid you didn't enjoy the skating this afternoon."

"Not much. The mornings are pleasanter. We came too late."

"Shall you come to-morrow morning?"

"Yes; I have promised my young sisters to bring them for a long morning. They won't let me off."

"Do they skate?"

"Hetty skates. The little one only slides. She is a most determined slider."

"Does Colonel Marchant never come with you?"

"Never. He does not care about walking with girls."

"Perhaps it is presumptuous in a bachelor to speculate on domestic feelings, but I think if I were a widower with five nice daughters my chief delight would be in going about with them."

"If you look round among your friends I fancy you will find that kind of father the exception rather than the rule," Eve answered, with a touch of bitterness.

They walked on in silence for a little while after this, she looking straight before her into the cool grey evening, he stealing an occasional glance at her profile.

How pretty she was! The pearly complexion was so delicate, and yet so fresh and glowing in its youthful health. Hygeia herself might have had just such a complexion. The features, too, so neatly cut, the nose as clear in its chiselling as if it were pure Grecian, but with just that little tilt at the tip which gave piquancy to the face. The mouth was more thoughtful than he cared to see the lips of girlhood, for those pensive lines suggested domestic anxieties; but when she smiled or laughed the thoughtfulness vanished, lost in a radiant gaiety that shone like sunlight over all her countenance. He could not doubt that a happy disposition, a power of rising superior to small sordid cares, was a leading characteristic of her nature.

She had natural cheerfulness, the richest dowry a wife can bring to husband and home. Presently, as he swung his stick against the light tracery of hawthorn and blackberry, a happy thought occurred to him. His sister had pledged herself to be kind to these motherless girls. Her kindness could not begin too soon.

"You are to bring your sisters to the ice to-morrow morning, Miss Marchant," he said presently. "What do you call morning?"

"I hope we shall be there before eleven. The mornings are so lovely in this frosty weather."

"The mornings are delicious. Come as early as you possibly can. After two hours' skating you will be tolerably tired, I should think—though you walk with the air of a person who does not know what it is to be tired—so you must all come to lunch with my sister."

"You are very kind," said Eve, blushing, and suddenly radiant with her happiest smile, "but we could not think of such a thing."

"I understand. You would not come at my invitation. You think I have no rights in the case. Yet it would be hard if a brother couldn't ask his friends to his sister's house."

"Friends, perhaps, yes; but we are mere acquaintance."

"Please don't say anything so unkind. I felt that we were friends from the first, you and your sisters and I, from the hour we found you on the top of the hill, when I mistook you for fairies. However, all the exigencies of the situation shall be complied with. My sister shall write to you this evening."

"Pray, pray don't suggest such a thing," entreated Eve, very much in earnest. "Lady Hartley will think us vulgar, pushing girls."

"Lady Hartley will think nothing of the kind. She was saying, only a few hours ago, that she would like to see more of you all. You must all come, remember—all five. The Champernownes leave by an early train to-morrow morning," he added cheerfully; "there will be plenty of room for you."

"Are the Miss Champernownes going away?"

"Yes, they go on to a much smarter house, where baccarat is played of an evening, instead of our modest billiards and whist. My brother-in-law is a very sober personage. He is not in the movement. It is my private opinion that those three handsome young ladies have been unspeakably bored at Redwold Towers."

"I am very glad they are going," answered Eve, frankly. "We don't know them, so their going or coming ought not to make any difference to us. But there is something oppressive about them. They are so handsome, they dress so well, and they seem so thoroughly pleased with themselves."

"Yes, there's where the offence comes in. Isn't it odd that from the moment a man or woman lets other people see that he or she is thoroughly delighted with his or her individuality, talents, beauty, or worldly position, everybody else begins to detest that person? A Shakespeare or a Scott must go through life with a seeming unconsciousness of his own powers, if he would have his fellow-men love him."

"I think both Shakespeare and Scott contrived to do so, and that is one of the reasons why all the world worships them," said Eve, and on this slight ground they founded a long conversation upon their favourite books and authors. He did not find her "cultured." Of the learning which pervades modern drawing-rooms—the learning of the *Fortnightly*, and the *Contemporary*, the *Nineteenth Century* and *Macmillan*—he found her sorely deficient. She had read no new books, she knew nothing of recent theories in art, science, or religion. She knew her Shakespeare and Scott, her Dickens, Thackeray, and Bulwer-Lytton, and had read the poets whom everybody reads. She had never heard of Marlow, and Beaumont and Fletcher were to her only names. She revelled in fiction, the old, familiar fiction of the great masters; but history was a blank. She had not read Froude; she had never heard of Green, Gardiner, Freeman, or Maine.

"You will find us woefully ignorant," she explained, when she had answered in the negative about several books, which to him were of the best. "We have only had a nursery governess. She was a dear old thing, but I don't think you could imagine a more ignorant person. She came to us when I was six, and she only left us when Peggy was nine, and she would have stayed on as a kind of Duenna, only she had a poor, old, infirm mother, and she was the only spinster daughter left, and so had to go home and nurse the mother. She was very strong upon the multiplication table, and she was pretty good at French. She knew La Grammaire des Grammaires by heart, I believe. But as to history or literature! Even the little we contrived to pick up for ourselves was enough to enable us to make fun of her. We used to ask her why Charles the Second didn't make Erasmus a bishop, or whether Eleanor of Aquitaine was the daughter or only the niece of Charlemagne. She always tumbled into any trap we set for her."

"A lax idea of chronology, that was all," said Vansittart.

He walked very nearly to the Homestead, and was dead beat by the time he got back to Redwold Towers. He had been tramping about ever since luncheon. He and Eve Marchant had done a good deal of talking in that four-mile walk, but not once had he mentioned Sefton's name, nor had he made the faintest attempt to discover the drift of that confidential conversation of which a few brief sentences had reached his ear. Yet those sentences haunted his memory, and the thought of them came between him and all happier thoughts of Eve Marchant.

His sister was considerably his junior, and he had been accustomed to order her to do this or that from her babyhood upward, she deeming herself honoured in obeying his caprices. It was a small thing, then, for him to request her to invite Miss Marchant and all her sisters to luncheon next day.

"Do you really mean me to ask all three?" questioned Maud, arching her delicate eyebrows in mild wonder.

"I mean you to ask all five. The little girls are coming to skate on your pond. Give them a good lunch, Maud. Let there be game and kickshaws, such as girls like—and plenty of puddings."

"All five! How absurd!"

"You said you would be kind to them."

"But five! Well, I don't suppose the number need make any difference. What alarms me is the idea of getting too friendly with them—a dropping in to lunch or tea acquaintance, don't you know. The girls are as good as gold, I have no doubt; but they lead such an impossible life with that impossible father—he almost always away, no chaperon, no nice aunts to look after them—only an old Yorkshire servant and a bit of a girl to open the door. It is all too dreadful."

"From your point of view, no doubt; but lives as dreadful are being led by a good many families all over England, and out of lives as dreadful has come a good deal of the intellectual power of the country. Come, Maud, don't prattle, but write your letter—just a friendly little letter to say that I have told you they are coming to skate, and that you must insist upon their stopping to lunch."

He had found her in her boudoir just before dressing for dinner, and in the very act of sealing the last of a batch of letters. She took up her pen at his bidding, and dashed off an invitation, almost in his own words, with a thick stroke of the J pen under "insist."

"Will that do?" she asked.

"Admirably," said Vansittart, with his hand on the bell. "All you have to do is to order a groom to ride to the Homestead with it."

"Hadn't I better invite Mr. Sefton to meet them?" inquired Maud, with a malicious little laugh.

"Why?"

"Because he is said to be running after Miss Marchant. I only hope *pour le bon motif.*"

"However shady a customer Colonel Marchant may be, I shouldn't think any man would dare to approach his daughter with a bad motive," said Vansittart, sternly.

"The Colonel encourages him, I am told; so I suppose it is all right."

"You are told," cried Vansittart, scornfully. "What is this cloud of unseen witnesses which compasses about village life so that what a man owes, what a man eats, what a man thinks and purposes are common topics of conversation for people who never enter his house? It is petty to childishness, all this twaddle about Colonel Marchant and his daughters."

"Jack, Jack!" cried Maud, shaking her head. "I can only say I am sorry for you. And now run away, for goodness' sake. We shall both be late for dinner. I shall only have time to throw on a tea-gown."

A footman brought Lady Hartley a letter at half-past nine that evening. Vansittart crossed the drawing-room to hear the result of the invitation.

"DEAR LADY HARTLEY,

"It is too good of you to ask us to luncheon after skating, and I know it will be a treat for my young sisters to see your beautiful house, so I am pleased to accept your kind invitation for the two youngest and myself. Sophy and Jenny beg to thank you for including them, but they cannot think of inflicting so large a party as five upon you.

"Very sincerely yours,

"EVE MARCHANT."

"She has more discretion than you have, at any rate, Jack," said Maud, as he read the letter over her shoulder.

"She writes a fine bold hand," said he, longing to ask for the letter, the first letter of hers that his eyes had looked upon.

"I'm very sorry the five are not coming," he went on. "Those two poor girls will have a scurvy luncheon at home, I dare say—dismal martyrs to conventionality. You must ask them another day."

"We'll see how to-morrow's selection behave," answered Maud, with her light laugh.

* * * *

Vansittart was on the pathway by the lake before eleven o'clock, and he had a bad half-hour of waiting before Eve and her two young sisters appeared at the lodge. He met them near the gates, and they set off for the ice together.

"I hear you only slide," he said to the little one, who was red as a rose after the long walk through the nipping air. "That won't do. You must turn over a new leaf to-day, and learn to skate. I'm going to teach you."

"That would be lovely," answered Peggy; "but I've got no

skates."

"Oh, but we must borrow a pair or steal a pair. Skates shall be found somehow."

"Won't that be jolly?" cried Peggy.

The skates were found at the lodge, where Vansittart coolly appropriated a pair belonging to one of the little girls at the nearest parsonage, and the lesson was given. A lesson was also given to Eve, who skated fairly well, but not so well as Vansittart after one winter's experience in Norway and another in Vienna. Sefton came strolling on to the ice while they were skating, and tried to monopolize Miss Marchant; but the young lady treated him in rather an offhand manner, greatly to Vansittart's delight. He hung about the lake for some time talking to one or another of his neighbours, most of the young people of the neighbourhood and a good many of the middle-aged being assembled this fine morning. Towards one o'clock he came up to Eve, who was playing hockey with a number of girls. "Is the Colonel at home?" he asked.

"Yes, father came home last night."

"Then I'll walk over and see him. It's a splendid day for a good long tramp. Let me know when you and your sisters are leaving, that I may walk with you. That road is uncommonly lonely for girls."

"You are very kind; but we are never afraid of the road. And to-day we are not going home for ever so long," added Eve, joyously. "We are going to lunch with Lady Hartley."

"That alters the case," said Sefton, prodigiously surprised. "Then I'll look your father up another day, when I can be of some use as an escort. I dare say Mr. Vansittart will see you home."

"Haven't I told you that we want no escort?" exclaimed Eve, impatiently. "One would think there were lions between here and Fernhurst."

"There are frozen-out gardeners and such-like, I dare say. Quite as bad as lions," he answered, as he turned on his heel, jealous and angry.

This fellow was evidently pursuing her with some kind of suit, Vansittart thought. Could he mean to marry her? Could any man with an established position in the county mean to ally himself with Colonel Marchant?

Vansittart had seen the two talking, but had not been near enough to hear what they said. He rejoiced at seeing Sefton walk away discomfited. There was anger in the carriage of his head as he turned away from her. He had been snubbed evidently. But if she snubbed him to-day, must she not have sometimes encouraged his attentions?

He had all the manner of a man to whom certain rights have been given.

They walked up to the house merrily, over the grey, frosty grass, Hetty and Peggy running on in front and racing and wheeling like fox-terriers, so elated by the day's delights. Peggy had distinguished herself on her borrowed skates. Her teacher declared she was a born skater.

Lady Hartley was sunning herself in the broad portico, waiting to receive her guests. Miss Green had gone out shooting with Sir Hubert and his party. There were only Mrs. Vansittart, Mrs. Baddington, and Mr. Tivett at home.

"Only us two men among all you ladies," said Tivett, cheerily, as they assembled before the huge wood fire in the drawing-room.

"Hadn't you better say us one and a half, Gussie?" asked Mrs. Baddington, laughing. "It seems rather absurd to talk of yourself and Mr. Vansittart as if you were of the same weight and substance."

Mr. Tivett, who was half hidden between Hetty and Peggy, received this attack with his usual amiability. "Never mind weight and substance," he said; "in moral influence I feel myself a giant."

"Not without justification," said Vansittart. "If you were to compare Tivett's reception at a West End tea-party with mine you would see what a poor thing mere brute force is in an intellectual environment."

"Oh, they like me," replied Tivett, modestly, "because I can talk chiffons. I can tell them of the newest ladies' tailor—some little man who lives in an alley, but has found out the way to cut a habit or a coat, and is going to take the town by storm next season. I can put them up to the newest shade of bronze or auburn hair—the Princess's shade. I can tell them lots of things, and the dear souls know that I am interested in all that interests them."

"I never talk to Gussie Tivett without thinking how much nicer a womanly man is than a manly woman," said Mrs. Baddington, meditatively.

"Ah, that is because the former imitates the superior sex, the latter the inferior," answered Lady Hartley.

Eve sat in the snug armchair where Vansittart had placed her, silent, but happy, looking about the room and admiring the wonderful mixture of old and new things; furniture that was really old, furniture that cleverly reproduced the antique; trifles and modern inventions of all kinds which make a rich woman's drawing-room a wonderland for the dwellers in shabby houses; the tall standard lamps of copper or brass or wrought iron, with their fantastical shades; the abundance of flowers and flowering plants and palms, in a season when for the commonalty flowers are not; all those things made an atmosphere of luxury which Colonel Marchant's daughter needs must feel in sharpest contrast with her own surroundings.

She admired without a pang of envy. She had taken her surroundings for granted a long time ago; and so long as her father was able to pacify his creditors by occasional payments, and so long as rates and taxes got themselves settled without desperate measures, Eve Marchant was at peace with destiny.

While her senses of sight and scent were absorbing the beauty and perfume of the room, Mrs. Vansittart came in from a walk with the nurse and baby, and her son made haste to introduce his sister's guest.

"Mother, this is Miss Marchant," he said briefly, and Eve rose blushing to acknowledge the elder woman's greeting.

He would not commit himself, forsooth. Why, in the look he gave her as she rose shyly to take his mother's hand, in the tenderness of his tone as he spoke her name, he was committing himself almost as deeply as if he had said outright, "Mother, this is the woman I love, and I want you to love her."

Mrs. Vansittart, prejudiced by much that she had heard of the Marchant household, could but acknowledge to herself that the Colonel's eldest daughter was passing fair, and that this sensitive countenance in which the bloom came and went at a breath, had as candid and innocent an outlook as even a mother's searching eye could desire in the countenance of her son's beloved. But then, unhappily, Mrs. Vansittart had seen enough of the world and its ways to know that appearances are deceitful, and that many a blushing bride whose drooping head and gentle bashfulness suggested the innocence that might ride on lions and not be afraid, has afterwards made a shameful figure in the Divorce Court.

CHAPTER VII.

HE WOULD TAKE HIS TIME

The luncheon at Redwold Towers was a very sociable meal. Lady Hartley was at all times a gracious hostess, and she was perhaps a little more attentive to Colonel Marchant's daughters than she would have been to guests of more assured position.

The meal was abundant, and served with the quiet undemonstrative luxury which steals over the senses like the atmosphere of the Lotos Island, with its suggestion of a world in which there is neither labour nor care, no half-empty mustard-pots, or stale bread, or flat beer, or unreplenished pickle-jars.

There was plenty of game, and there were those appetising kickshaws, Russian salads, and such-like, which Vansittart had bargained for, and cold and hot sweets in profusion. Hetty and Peggy eat enormously, urged thereto by Mr. Tivett, who sat between them; but Eve had no more appetite than might have been expected in a sensitive girl who finds herself suddenly in a new atmosphere—an atmosphere of unspoken love, which wraps her round like a perfume. Vansittart remonstrated with her for eating so little after a long walk and a morning on the ice; but she could but see that he eat very little himself, and that all his time and thoughts were given to her.

The cup of coffee after lunch was the most fragrant she had ever tasted.

"If I could only make such coffee as that father wouldn't grumble as he does at his after-dinner cup," she said.

"The still-room maid always uses freshly roasted coffee," said Lady Hartley. "I believe that is the only secret of success."

She felt in the next moment how foolish it was to talk of still-room maids to this girl, whose household consisted of two faithful drudges, and who no doubt had to do a good deal of housework herself.

Miss Marchant had enough savoir faire to depart very soon after luncheon. She only lingered long enough to look at the flowers which Mrs. Vansittart showed her, during which brief inspection the elder lady spoke to her very kindly.

"You are the head of the family, I am told," she said. "Isn't that rather an onerous position for one so young?"

"I was twenty-one last November, and I begin to feel quite old," answered Eve; "and then our family is not a difficult one to manage. My sisters are very good, and accommodate themselves to circumstances. We live very simply. We have none of those difficulties with servants which I hear rich people talk about."

"You and your sisters look wonderfully well and happy," said Mrs. Vansittart, interested in spite of herself.

"Yes, I think we are as happy as people can be in a world where everybody must have a certain amount of trouble," Eve answered, with the faintest sigh. "We are very fond of each other, and we have great fun out of trifles. We contrive to be merry at very little cost. Peggy and Hetty are very amusing. Oh, how they have eaten to-day! It will be a long time before they forget Lady Hartley's banquet."

"It does children good to go out now and then. They must come again very soon. I know my daughter will like to have them; but my son and I are going home almost immediately."

"Home." Eve looked a little crestfallen as she echoed the word. "You don't live very far off, I think, Mrs. Vansittart?"

"No. Only an hour's journey. We live in a region of pine and heather; and I have a garden and an arboretum, which are my delight. But our country is not any prettier than yours, so I mustn't boast of it."

"This is not my country," said Eve. "I feel like a foreigner here, though we have lived at the Homestead a good many years. Yorkshire is my country."

"But surely you must prefer Sussex. Yorkshire is so far away from everything."

The two girls came to Eve and hung about her. They had put on their gloves and little fur tippets—spoil of rabbit or cat—and were ready for the start. Mrs. Vansittart noticed their coarse serge frocks, their homely woollen stockings and village-made boots. They were tidily clad, and that was all that could be said of them. A village tradesman's children would have been smarter; and yet they looked like young ladies.

"These are your two youngest sisters, and you have two older—five daughters in all," said Mrs. Vansittart. "Colonel Marchant ought to be very proud of such a family. And have you no brothers?"

"None in England," Eve answered, with a touch of sadness, and then without another moment's delay she began to make her adieux.

"I am going to see you home, if you will let me," said Vansittart, in the hall; "I heard you say that Colonel Marchant is at home, and I should like to seize the opportunity of making his acquaintance."

A faint cloud spread itself over Eve's happy face, and she was somewhat slow in replying. "I am sure father will be very pleased to see you."

"And I'm sure you won't like father when you see him," cried Peggy, the irrepressible.

"Peggy, how dare you?" exclaimed Eve.

"Well, but people don't like him," urged the resolute damsel. "He ain't civil to people, and then we have to suffer for it; for, of course, people think we're just as bad. He keeps all his good manners for London."

"Peggy, Peggy!"

"Don't Peggy me. It's the truth," protested this dreadful child; and then she challenged Vansittart boldly, "You like us, Mr. Vansittart, I know you do; but you'll never be kind to us any more after you've seen father."

This gush of childish candour was discouraging, and Vansittart's heart sank as he asked himself what manner of man this might be whom he was thinking of as a father-in-law. Other people had spoken ill of Colonel Marchant, and he had made light of their disparagement; but this denunciation from the lips of the eleven-year-old daughter was far more serious.

"Perhaps the Colonel and I may get on better than you expect, Madam Peggy," he said, with a forced laugh; "and allow me at the same time to suggest that you have forgotten a certain commandment which tells us to honour our fathers and mothers."

"Are we to honour any kind of father?" asked Peggy; but Vansittart was not called upon to answer, for Hetty at that moment descrying a squirrel, both little girls rushed off to watch his ascent of a tall beech that grew on the grassy waste by which they were walking.

The walk was a long one, but though there was time for Vansittart and Eve to talk about many things, time for the two younger girls to afford many distractions, an undercurrent of thought about the man he was going to see ran beneath all that light surface talk, and made Vansittart's spirit heavy.

"You must not think anything of what Peggy says," Eve apologized, directly after that little outbreak of the youngest born. "Father is irritable sometimes. He can't endure noise, and Hetty and Peggy are dreadfully noisy. And our house is so small—I mean from his point of view. And then he snubs them, poor young things, and they think him unkind."

"It is a way we have when we are young," answered Vansittart gently, "to take snubs too seriously. If our parents and guardians could only put themselves inside those small skins of ours they would know what pain their preachings and snubbings inflict."

"Father is much to be pitied," pursued Eve, in a low voice. "His life has been full of disappointments."

"Ah, that is a saddening experience," answered Vansittart, tenderly sympathetic.

His heart thrilled at the thought that she was beginning to confide in him, to treat him as a friend.

"His property in Yorkshire was so disappointing. I suppose land has gone down in value everywhere," said Eve, rather vaguely; "but in father's case it was dreadful. He was forced to sell the estate just when land in our part of the country was a drug in the market."

Vansittart had never heard of this cheapness of land in the East Riding, but he felt that if this account of things were not actual truth, Eve Marchant fully believed what she was telling him.

"And then his horses, they all turned out so badly."

"Ungrateful beasts."

"You can understand that the life we lead at Fernhurst is not a very happy life for such a man as my father—a sportsman—a man whose youth was spent in the best society. It is hard for him to be mewed up with a family of girls. Everything we say and do must jar upon him."

"Surely not everything. There must be times in which he can take delight in your society."

"Oh, I'm afraid not. There are so many of us; and we seem so shallow and silly to a man of the world."

"A man of the world. Ah, there's the difficulty," said Vansittart, slightly cynical. "That kind of man is apt to be miserable without the world."

After this they talked of other things; lightly, joyously; of the country through which they were walking; its beasts, and birds, and flowers, and humble cottage folk; of the places he had seen and the books she had read, those fictions of the great masters which create a populace and a world for the dwellers in lonely homes, and provide companions for the livers of solitary lives. They were at no loss for subjects, though that well-spring of polite conversation, a common circle of smart acquaintance, was denied to them. Their talk was as vivacious as if they had had all London society to dissect.

It was teatime again by the time they arrived at the Homestead. The lamp was lighted in the family parlour; the round table was spread; the kettle was hissing on the hob; Sophy and Jenny were sitting on one side of the fire; and on the other side, in that armchair which Vansittart had occupied on a previous occasion, sat a man of about fifty, a man with clear-cut features, silver-grey hair and moustache, and a querulous expression of countenance.

"What in the name of all that's reasonable made you stay so late, Eve?" he grumbled, as his daughters entered. "Both those children will be laid up with influenza, I dare say, in consequence of your folly."

Only at this moment did he observe the masculine figure in the rear. He rose hastily to receive a visitor.

"Mr. Vansittart, father," explained Eve.

The two men shook hands.

"Girls are so foolish," said the Colonel, by way of apology for his lecture. "It was very kind of you to take care of my daughters on the dark road; but Eve ought not to have stayed so long."

"We left very soon after luncheon, father; but the days are so short."

"Not any shorter than they were last week. You have had time to become familiar with their shortness, and to make your calculations accordingly."

"I am sure you didn't want us, father," said the sturdy Peggy; "so you needn't make a fuss."

Colonel Marchant gave his youngest born a withering scowl, but took no further notice of her contumacy.

"Pray sit down, Mr. Vansittart, and take a cup of tea before you tramp home again. You must be a good walker to make so light of that long road—for I suppose you came by the road."

"I am country bred, Colonel Marchant, and am pretty well used to tramping about, on foot or on horseback."

"Ah, you live near Liss, Eve told me. Have you good hunting thereabouts?"

Vansittart mentioned three or four packs of hounds accessible from his part of the country.

"Ah," sighed the Colonel, "you young men think nothing of prodigious rides to cover, and long railway journeys. You hunt with the Vine from Basingstoke—with the Hambledon from Bishop's Waltham! You are tearing about the country all November and December, I have no doubt?"

"Indeed, Colonel, I am not so keen a sportsman as you appear to think. A couple of days a week content me, while there are any birds to shoot in my covers."

"Ah, two days' hunting and four days' shooting. I understand. That is what an Englishman's life should be, if he lives on his estate. Sir Hubert tells me you have travelled a good deal?"

"I have wandered about the Continent, on the beaten paths. I cannot call myself a traveller, in the modern acceptation of the word. I have never shot lions in Africa, nor have I ever bivouacked among the hill-tribes in Upper India, nor risked my life, like Burton, in a pilgrimage to Mecca."

"Ah, the men who do that kind of thing are fools," grumbled the Colonel. "Providence is too good to them when they are allowed to come home with a whole skin. I have no sympathy with any explorer since Columbus and Raleigh. After the discovery of America, tobacco, and potatoes, the rest is leather and prunella."

"The Australian and Californian gold-fields were surely a good find," suggested Vansittart.

"Has all the gold ever found there made you or me a shilling the richer, Mr. Vansittart? It has reduced the purchasing value of a sovereign by more than a third, and for men of fixed incomes all the world over those gold-fields have been a source of calamity. When I was a lad, a family man who was hard up could take his wife and children to France or Belgium, and live comfortably on the income he had been starving on in London. Now, life is dear everywhere—even in an out-of-the-way hole like this," concluded the Colonel, savagely.

Vansittart observed him closely as he talked, and was all the better able to do so, as the Colonel was not given to looking at the person he addressed. He had a way of looking at the fire or at his boots while he talked. His enemies called it a hang-dog air.

He had not a pleasant face. It was a face wasted by dissolute habits, a face in which the lines were premature and deep, lines that told of discontent and sullen thought. Vansittart could but agree with Hubert Hartley's estimate of Colonel Marchant. He was not a nice man. He was not a man to whom open-hearted men could take kindly.

But he was Eve's father.

Vansittart had been sorry for her yesterday; sorry for her because of those narrow means which cut her off from the pleasures and privileges of youth and beauty. He was sorrier for her to-day, now that he had seen her father.

He took his tea by the family hearth, which had lost its air of rollicking happiness and Bohemian liberty. The five girls were all seated primly at the round table, silent for the most part, while the Colonel rambled on with his egotistical complaining, in the tones of a man maltreated alike by his Creator and by society.

"Sir Hubert Hartley has a fine place at Redwold," he said, "and he got it dog-cheap. He is a very lucky man."

"He's an uncommonly good fellow," said Vansittart, "and he ought to be an acquisition to the neighbourhood."

"Oh, the neighbours take to him kindly," retorted the Colonel. "He's rich—gives good dinners and good wine. That is the kind of thing country people want. They don't ask too many questions about a man's pedigree when his cellar and his cook are good."

"My brother-in-law's pedigree is not one to be ashamed of, Colonel Marchant."

"Of course not, my dear fellow. Honest labour, talent, patience, invention, the virtues of which Englishmen are supposed to be proud. But you don't mean to tell me that the Hartleys date from the Heptarchy, or even came over with the Conqueror. There was a day—when I was a lad, unless my memory of social matters plays me false—when county people clung to the traditions of caste, and didn't bow down to the golden calf quite so readily as they do now."

Vansittart could but agree with Peggy as to her father's demerits. He stole a glance at the child on the opposite side of the table, but she was too much absorbed in bread and jam to notice her father's speech, or the impression he was making. Eve had a pained look. He felt very sorry for her as he watched her restless fingers smoothing out the gloves which lay on the table before her, with a movement that told of irritated nerves.

He finished his cup of tea, and rose to go; yet lingered weakly, intent on resolving certain jealous doubts of his, if it were possible.

"I see you are a stickler for blue blood, Colonel Marchant," he said. "I conclude that is one of the reasons you like Mr. Sefton, who, as I hear in the neighbourhood, is by no means a general favourite."

"Did you ever hear of a man worth anything who was a general favourite?" grumbled the Colonel. "Yes, I like Sefton. Sefton is a gentleman to the marrow of his bones—the son and grandson and great-grandson of gentlemen. His ancestors were gentlemen before Magna Charta. If you want to know what good blood is, you have a fine example in Sefton—a staunch friend, a bitter enemy, stand-offish to strangers, frank and free with the people he likes. He's the only man in this part of the country that I can get on with; and I am not ashamed to confess my liking for him."

Vansittart watched Eve's face while her father was praising his friend. It was a very grave face, almost to pain; but there was no confusion or embarrassment in countenance or manner. She stood silent, serious, waiting for her father to say his say, and for the guest to leave. And then, without a word, she shook hands with Vansittart, who made the round of the sisters before he was solemnly escorted to the porch by Colonel Marchant.

He walked home through the fine, clear night, by hedgerows powdered with snow, through a landscape which was somewhat monotonous in its black and white, past woods and hills, above which the frosty stars shone out in almost southern brilliancy.

No, he did not believe that Eve Marchant cared for Wilfred Sefton. There had been no emotional changes from white to red in the fair face he studied, only a serious and somewhat anxious expression, as if the subject were painful to her. No, he had no rival to fear in Sefton; and yet—and yet—there was some lurking mysteriousness in their relations, some secret understanding, or why those tears? Why that confidential conversation, and those stray sentences, which seemed to mean a great deal? "I sincerely regret your disappointment." "It was a false scent." There must be some meaning deeper than the trivialities of everyday life in such words as these.

He thought, and gloomily, of Colonel Marchant as a possible father-in-law. A most unpleasant person to contemplate in that connection—a soured, disappointed man, at war with society, and quick to sneer at men whom he disliked only because they were more fortunate than himself. That he should sneer at Hubert Hartley, a universal favourite, who from boyhood to manhood had been known to all his friends and neighbours as "Bertie," a familiar style which testified to his popularity! Would Bertie take the hounds on an emergency? Would Bertie do this or that for the common weal?—Bertie being always relied on for liberality and good-fellowship. It was intolerable that this out-at-elbows Colonel should presume to sneer at Bertie Hartley because the wealth which he dispensed so nobly had been earned in trade.

* * * *

That second visit to the Homestead had a dispiriting effect, and again Vansittart told himself that he would take his time; that having breathed no word of love in Eve Marchant's ear, he was free to carry her image away in his heart, and brood over it, and find out in the course of much sober meditation whether he really loved her well enough to sacrifice all worldly advantages, and to disappoint his mother and sister in the great act of marriage, that act upon which hangs the happiness or misery of all the after life.

A man who has few belongings, and who has been to those belongings as a hero, has need to give some consideration to his people's prejudices before he lead his bride home to the family hearth, where she is to take her place for ever in the family history, either as an ornament or a blot upon a fair record.

No, he would go no further. He would not be the slave of a foolish passion for a lovely face. He was free to come to Redwold Towers whenever he pleased. He might see Eve Marchant as often as he pleased in the year that was so young. He would take his time.

And if, while he hesitated and meditated, some bolder wooer were to appear and snatch the prize—what then? Well, that was a risk which he must run; but he told himself that the chances were against any suitor for the daughter's hand while the father was to the fore. Colonel Marchant's children were heavily handicapped in the race of life.

CHAPTER VIII.

A FACE IN THE CROWD

Vansittart spent five weeks at Merewood, hunting a good deal, dining with some of his neighbours once a week or so, and occasionally entertaining them at dinner or luncheon; tiring himself prodigiously with long rides to cover, or railway journeys before and after the chase, and falling asleep of an evening by the drawing-room fire, lulled by the monotonous click of his mother's knitting needles, or the flutter of the turning leaves as she read.

Those fireside evenings after the chase in January and February were delightful to Mrs. Vansittart. She rejoiced with an exceeding joy at having brought her son safe and sound out of the cave of the syren, having no suspicion of those serious thoughts of the syren which occupied his mind. There were half a dozen girls in the neighbourhood, two of them heiresses, any one of whom would be welcome to her as a daughter-in-law, for any one of whom she would have resigned her place in that household without a murmur, almost without a regret. But she shuddered at the idea of a girl brought up in a Bohemian fashion; a girl who had suffered all the disadvantages which poverty carries with it; the skimped education; the vulgarizing influence of petty household cares; a girl whose father never went to church. Such a girl would be unspeakably distasteful to her. If Eve Marchant were to reign at Merewood, Mrs. Vansittart's grey hairs must go down in sorrow to the grave.

She rejoiced in her son's company, and was even reconciled to the perils of the hunting field, since hunting occupied his days, and prevented his running after Eve Marchant. If he was unusually silent and thoughtful by the fireside, she ascribed silence and thoughtfulness to physical exhaustion. He was there, safe within her ken; and that was enough. She took infinite pains to bring the girls she liked about her, and in her son's way, which was not easy, since Vansittart was far afield nearly every day. She would invite one of her favourites to a friendly dinner, escorted by a young brother, perhaps—a proceeding which bored her son infinitely, since instead of sleeping or brooding by the fire he must needs play billiards with the cub, or put himself out of the way to amuse the young lady.

He was very fond of music of a broad dramatic style—loved grand opera, from Gluck to Meyerbeer and Verdi; but he had no passion for Grieg or Rubinstein, as expounded, neatly, elegantly, with lady-like inexpressiveness, by his mother's protégées; and it seemed to his ignorant ear that all his mother's protégées played exactly the same pieces in precisely the same manner.

* * * *

If perchance he spent an afternoon at home, he invariably found one of those selected vestals in morning-room or drawing-room when he went to five o'clock tea, that meal being one which his mother loved to share with him, and at which dutiful affection constrained his presence whenever he was on the premises. All the charm of that unconstrained half-hour of chat between mother and son was scared away by the presence of a young lady, albeit the most admirable of her sex. His mother's favourites were very nice girls, every one of them, and only two out of the six were painfully religious. He liked them all well enough, in the beaten way of friendship; but the handsomest and most attractive of them left him cold as marble. He had gone beyond the season of easily kindled fires. He had passed the age at which a man falls in love once in six weeks. His heart was no longer touch-paper. A few months ago he had believed that he would spend his days as a bachelor, had calculated the manifold advantages of remaining single, with an estate which for a single man meant wealth, but which for a man with wife and family would only mean a modest competence.

He grew so weary at last of those social tea-drinkings and those eminently domestic evenings, that before the hunting season was over he suddenly announced his intention of going to London. It was an understood thing between his mother and himself that the house in Charles Street was always ready for him. The housekeeper left in charge had been his nurse, and administered to his comfort with unwearying devotion. She was an excellent cook, by force of native talent rather than by training and experience, and, with a housemaid under her, kept the house in exquisite order. These two women, with Vansittart's valet, an Italian, able to turn his hand to anything, made up an efficient bachelor establishment.

To Charles Street, therefore, Vansittart repaired, in the Lenten month of March. He had been at some trouble to resist the inclination which would have taken him to Redwold Towers, rather than to London. It would have been so easy to offer himself to his sister for a week; and at Redwold it would have been so easy to see Eve Marchant; so difficult, perhaps, to avoid seeing her, since Lady Hartley, who was, above all things, cordial and impulsive, had told him in one of her letters that she had taken a fancy to Miss Marchant, and had invited her and one of the sisters to Redwold very often.

"As a wife for you, she is impossible," wrote Maud Hartley. "Pray remember that, Jack. Mother and I are ambitious about your future. We want you to look high, to improve your position from that of a small country gentleman, to make your mark in the world. But, although quite impossible as your wife, as a human being Miss Marchant is charming, and I mean to do all I can in a neighbourly way to make things pleasanter for her. The father is shockingly neglectful, spends the greater part of his life in London; but that is perhaps an advantage for his daughters, for when he is at home Eve is a slave to him, has to worry about his dinners, and fetch and carry for him, and try to amuse the unamusable, as Madame de Maintenon said. I gather this not from any murmurings of Eve's, but from the young sisters, who are appallingly outspoken."

Vansittart had pledged himself to spend the Easter holidays at Redwold; so he resisted the promptings of inclination, and swore to himself that he would not try to see Eve Marchant before Easter. The interval would then have been long enough to test his feelings, to give him time for thought, before he took any fateful step, and perhaps to throw him in the way of hearing some more specific account of Colonel Marchant's character and antecedents. There is no place, perhaps, in which it is more difficult to get a faithful description of a man than in the village where he lives. There, everything is exaggerated—his income, if he is rich; his debts, if he is poor; his vices, eccentricities, and shortcomings, in any case.

Although it was the Lenten season, and although the churches of London were filled with Lenten worshippers, the town looked bright and animated, and there were plenty of votaries in the temples of pleasure—theatres, picture galleries, concert halls—and plenty of snug little dinner-parties to which a man in Vansittart's position was likely to be bidden. He had a wide circle of acquaintance, and was popular with men and women, accounted a clubbable man by the former, and an eligible parti by the latter. Even the women who had no matrimonial views for daughters, or sisters, or bosom friends, still affected Jack Vansittart's society. He had plenty to say to them, was always cheery and cordial, and never seemed to think himself too good for the particular circle in which he found himself.

He was dining one evening en petit comité with an old college chum and his young wife; the husband a rising barrister; the wife an accomplished woman, and a marvellous manager, able to maintain a pretty little house in Mayfair on an income which a stupid woman would have found hardly enough for Notting Hill or Putney, and to give an appetizing dinner, daintily served, and unhackneyed as to menu, for the cost of the average housekeeper's leg of mutton and trimmings.

While the cheery little meal was being discussed, a servant brought in a coroneted envelope for the hostess, which being opened, contained a box for Covent Garden, where there was an early season of Italian Opera.

"For to-night," said Mrs. Pembroke. And then she read aloud from the letter, "'I find at the last moment that I can't use my box. Do go if you are free. The opera is *Faust*, with a new "Margherita."' That's rather a pity," sighed the lady, folding up the letter.

"Why a pity?" asked Vansittart. "Why shouldn't you go? I dare say your box will hold me as well as Tom, so you need have no conscientious scruples on the ground of inhospitality."

"Oh, there will be plenty of room. It is Lady Davenant's box, on the grand tier. But Tom asked you for a quiet evening, a long talk and smoke, and perhaps an adjournment to the Turf for a rubber. I'm afraid you'll be dreadfully bored if I take you to the opera instead."

"Pray don't think so badly of me. If it were Wagner perhaps I might be less sure of myself. There are bits I enjoy in his operas, but I confess myself a tyro in that advanced school. Gounod's *Faust* I adore. We shall be in time for the Kermess scene, and the new Gretchen. Pray let us be off."

A cab was sent for, and the trio packed themselves into it, Mrs. Pembroke sparkling with pleasure. She was passionately fond of music, and she had been looking forward to a solitary evening by the drawing-room fire, while her husband and his friend sat smoking and prosing together in the barrister's ground-floor den.

* * * *

The house was thin, this premature opera season not having been a marked success. Lady Davenant's box was near the proscenium, a spacious box, which would have accommodated six people as easily as three. Vansittart sat in the middle, between his host and hostess. Tom Pembroke, who was no music lover, dozed in the shadow of the curtain, agreeably lulled by melodies which were pleasant from their familiarity.

The cast was not strong, but the Margherita was very young, rather pretty, and sang well. Vansittart and Mrs. Pembroke were both interested.

It was near the close of the Kermess scene that the lady asked her companion, "Do you ever look at the chorus? Such poor old things, some of them! I can't help thinking how weary they must be of singing the same music season after season, and tramping in and out of the same scenes—banquets where there is nothing to eat, too, and then going home to bread and cheese."

"Yes, it must be a hard life," assented Vansittart; "all the trouble of the show, and none of the glory."

And then he took a sweeping survey of the gay crowd, peasants, soldiers, citizens, feasting and rejoicing in friendly German fashion under the open sky. Yes, Mrs. Pembroke was right; most of the chorus were middle-aged, some were elderly—withered old faces, dark skins which even bismuth could not transform to fairness. Italian eyes, dark and glowing, shone out of worn faces where all other beauty was lacking.

Suddenly among all those homely countenances he saw a young face, young and beautiful, a face that flashed upon him first with a rapid thrill of recognition, and then with an aspect that struck into his heart like a dagger, and when that sharp pang was over left a heaviness as of lead.

It was Fiordelisa's face. He could not be mistaken. Nay, the fact was made certainty as he looked, for he saw that the girl recognized him. She was gazing upward to the spot where he sat; she was talking about him to the woman who stood next her, indicating him with too expressive gesticulation.

Was she telling that stolid listener that the man yonder had slain his fellow-creature in a tavern row; that he was a murderer? She would put it so, no doubt—she whose lover he had killed.

If she were saying this the stolid woman received the statement very placidly. She only nodded, and shrugged her shoulders, and then nodded again, while Fiordelisa talked to her more and more excitedly, with dramatic emphasis. Surely no woman would stand and shrug and nod as this woman shrugged and nodded, at a tale of murder.

Then Lisa looked up again at him, beaming with smiles, her dark eyes sparkling in the gaslight; and then her turn came to swell the chorus; and then the curtain fell, and he saw her no more.

It was as much as he could do to get through the interval before that curtain rose again. Tom Pembroke wanted him to go out for a stroll in the foyer, for a drink of some kind. "I would rather stay with Mrs. Pembroke," he said, full of wild surmises, prepared for a mysterious knock at the box door, and the appearance of a police-man from over the way to take him in custody at Lisa's instigation; prepared for anything tragic that might happen to him. What might not happen when the hot-blooded Southern nature was in question? What bounds would there be for the revengeful passion of such a girl as Fiordelisa, who had been robbed by his act of her lover and protector, her possible husband? She had talked of her Englishman's promise of marriage with an air of innocent security, the remem-brance of which smote him sharply, recalling her light-hearted gai-ety at the restaurant and at the opera, her grief as she flung herself upon her lover's corpse. And he, who had thought never to see her again, never even to know her fate, found himself face to face with her, recognized by her, having to answer to her and to society for the deed which he had done.

With these thoughts in his mind, with his ear strained for the knocking at the door, he had to talk small talk to Mrs. Pembroke, to counterfeit amusement at her criticism of the people in the stalls—the man with two strips of hair combed in streaks over a bald head, the woman with corpulent arms bared to the shoulder, the country cousins. He had to laugh at her little jokes, and even to at-tempt one or two smart sayings on his own account.

The knocking came, and he almost started out of his seat.

"It can't be Tom," said Mrs. Pembroke. "He never comes back until after the curtain is up, and sometimes not till the act is nearly over."

Vansittart opened the box door, and a treble voice questioned, "Ices, sir?"

He made way for the young woman with the tray of ices, and in-sisted upon Mrs. Pembroke taking one of those parti-coloured slabs which have superseded the old-fashioned rose-pink strawberry ice. He sat down again, ashamed of his overstrained nerves, and looked at the great curtain, wondering whether in all that wide expanse there were any gimlet holes through which Fiordelisa's ardent eyes might be watching him. The curtain rose, and the act began; but Vansittart had no longer any ear for the music he loved. His whole attention was concentrated upon the chorus singers. He watched and waited for their coming and going, searched out Lisa's famil-iar figure amidst the throng that watched Valentine's death-throes and Margherita's despair. He singled her out again and again as the troupe moved about the spacious stage—now on one side, now on the other, in the foreground or the background, according to the exigencies of the scene. He watched the stage till the green curtain fell; and then he woke as from a dream, and began to wonder what he must do next. Something he must do assuredly, he told himself, as he helped Mrs. Pembroke with her wraps, and heard her chatter about the performance, which she denounced as second-rate, declaring further that she had been taken in by Lady Davenant's gift of the box. Something he must do; first to ascertain what Fiordelisa's intentions might be—whether she would denounce him to the police; next to make whatever atonement he could make to her for the loss of her lover. He was not going to run away this time, as he had done at Venice. He had been seen and recognized. He would be watched, no doubt as he left the theatre. This girl would make it her business to find out his name and residence. Even if he wanted to elude her, the thing would be impossible. He had been sitting there all the evening in a conspicuous box on the grand tier, and he had to get away from a sparsely filled theatre.

Again there was a knock at the box door. It came while he was putting on his overcoat, and before Mrs. Pembroke had begun to move off.

It was a boxkeeper this time, with a letter.

"For you, sir," he said, handing it to Vansittart, after looking at the two men.

"An unaddressed envelope," chirruped Mrs. Pembroke; "this savours of mystery."

Vansittart put the letter into his pocket without a word. His most ardent desire at that moment was to get rid of the Pembrokes.

"Can I be of any use in fetching a cab?" he said in the hall.

"You can stop with my wife while I get one, if you don't mind," said Pembroke.

Happily there were plenty of cabs that night, and it was only the carriage people who had to wait. Mr. Pembroke came back for his wife in two or three minutes.

"I've got a four-wheeler," he said. "You'll come home with us for a smoke and a drink, won't you, Van?"

"Not to-night, thanks; it's late—and—and—I've some letters to write."

"Good night, then. I'm afraid you've been bored."

"On the contrary. I was never more interested in my life."

CHAPTER IX.

"THOUGH LOVE, AND LIFE,
AND DEATH SHOULD COME AND GO."

Vansittart tore open the blank envelope under one of the lamps at the back of the vestibule, while the crowd about the doors was gradually melting away, and the question "Cab or carriage?" was being asked, often with a sad want of discrimination on the part of the questioners. The letter was from Lisa.

It was in English, mixed with little phrases in Italian, badly spelt and badly written, but quite plain enough for him to read.

> "I knew you directly," she wrote, "and your face brought back the past—that dreadful night, and all I suffered after the of him death. Come to see me, I pray you. It must that we talk together. Come soon, soon. I live with la Zia, in Stone Court, Bow Street, No. 24B, quite near the Opera House. Come to-night if she can.—Her humble servant,
>
> > "Fiordelisa."

He stood with the letter in his hand, pondering.

Should he do what the letter asked him? Yes, assuredly; although to obey that summons was to place himself unreservedly in Lisa's power. He was in her power already, perhaps. She might have made her arrangements promptly, so that he should be watched and followed when he left the theatre, and his name and address discovered.

In any case, whatever risk there might be in going to Fiordelisa's lodging, he did not for a moment hesitate. In his remorseful thoughts of the man he had killed, the bitterest pang of all had been the thought of Fiordelisa and her shattered life, her dream of happiness darkened for ever, her prosperity changed to desolation and bitter want. Again and again he had told himself that the memory of his sin would sit more easily upon him could he but secure Lisa's comfort, dry her tears for the lover who was to have been her husband, shelter her from the chances of the downward road which the feet that have once turned astray are but too ready to tread.

112

He had found her, which was more than he had hoped, and had found her earning her bread in a legitimate manner, and living with the aunt who was in some wise a protector, although, remembering that lady's easy manner of regarding her niece's former position, there was perhaps not overmuch security in such a duenna.

He walked across Bow Street, and speedily found Stone Court, which seemed a quiet haven from the roar and roll of carriages in the street outside; a highly respectable retreat, consisting for the most part of private houses, one of which—wedged into an obscure corner, where a narrow alley, like the neck of a bottle, cut through into another street—proved to be 24B.

La Zia herself opened the door in answer to Vansittart's knock, and welcomed him with a cordiality which took his breath away.

"Welcome, Signor. She said you would come, but I was doubtful that you would trouble about her or me," she said, in Italian, and then, in very tolerable English: "Do me the favour to walk upstairs; it is rather high—il secondo piano. She knew you again in an instant. She has such eyes."

They ascended the narrow staircase, lighted only by the Zia's candle. The door of the front room on the second floor was open, and Fiordelisa stood on the threshold, in the light of a paraffin lamp, dressed in a shabby black gown, and with her splendid hair rolled up on the top of her head in a roughened mass.

She held out both her hands to Vansittart, and welcomed him as if he had been her dearest friend. The aunt had fairly astonished him, but the niece was even more astounding.

"I knew you would come," she exclaimed. "I knew you would not turn your back upon the poor girl whose life you made desolate."

And then she burst into a tempest of sobs. She flung herself on to the little horsehair sofa, and sobbed as if her heart would break; whereupon la Zia tumbled into an armchair, and sobbed in concert.

What could Vansittart do between two fountains of tears? He could only patiently abide till this passionate grief should abate, so that he might speak with the hope of being heard.

"I am deeply distressed," he said at last, when these lamentations had subsided. "I have never ceased to repent the act that bereaved you—both—of a friend and protector. I dared not go back to Venice—lest—lest the law should weigh heavily upon me. I had no means of communicating with you. I knew neither your names nor your address, remember. I had no means of helping you. I could do nothing to lighten the load upon my conscience—nothing. You must have thought me an arrant coward for running away and leaving you

113

to suffer for my sin?"

"If you had stopped you would have been put in prison—perhaps for ever so many years," said la Zia, with a philosophical air.

Fiordelisa had dried her tears, and was looking at him graciously, with almost a smile in the soft Italian eyes.

"Your going to prison would not have brought him back to life," she said. "I am glad you got away. Poor fellow! he was so fond of me—and so jealous! Ah, how jealous he was! It was foolish. I had done no harm. A little pleasure at Carnival time, while he was away! What a pity that he should come back to Venice that night, and find me at the Florian with you! We ought not to have gone to that caffè. He always went there—it was just the likeliest place for him to find us. But then I did not know he was coming back to Venice so soon."

The lightness of her tone, thus easily accepting the tragic past, surprised him, so strangely did her speech contrast with her passionate sobs of a few minutes ago. That she should threaten him with no vengeance, that she should welcome him as a friend, was stranger still; and he had to remember that this lightness was characteristic of the Italian nature; he had to remember that in Rome a noble lady and her daughter will go out to dine at a restaurant because it is so dull at home where the husband and father lies dead, or a mother will take her daughters to the opera to revive their spirits after a brother's untimely death.

It was a relief to him, naturally, to find a philosophical submission to Fate where he had expected to find a thirst for his blood, a stern resolve that the law should claim from him the uttermost atonement it could exact. It was a tremendous relief to find himself sitting between aunt and niece—while they eat their frugal supper from a tin box of mortadello, a bundle of radishes, and a half quartern loaf—listening to their account of their lives after his victim's death.

"He was buried next day," said la Zia; "a very pretty funeral. It was a lovely day, and the gondola was full of flowers, though flowers are dear in Venice. Lisa and I, and the Padrona from the house where we lived, went with him to the cemetery, where it was all so still and happy-looking in the sunlight. Lisa tried to throw herself into his grave, but we would not let her. Poor child, she was so miserable, and we thought of the day before when we were returning from the Lido in your gondola——"

"And when the lagoons looked enchanted in the sunset," said Lisa; "and our dinner at the Cappello Nero, and the champagne, and the pastiti, and the opera afterwards, and the beads you gave me. I have the beads still. I wore the blue necklace to-night. Did you notice it?"

"Indeed, no, Poverina. I was too full of thoughts of you to notice your necklace."

"Ah, you were surprised to see me, weren't you—after so long? And was not I surprised to see you? I was looking at all the faces, the pretty dresses, the jewels, like faces in a dream, for they are there every night, and they never come any nearer, or seem any more real; and then in an instant, out of the unreality, your face flashed upon me—your face and the memory of that happy day and evening, that dreadful midnight. Are you sorry to see us again?" she asked, naively, in conclusion.

"Sorry, Lisa? no. I am glad, very glad; for now I hope I may be able to make some atonement to you and your aunt."

"Atonement! but how? You cannot bring him back to life. While we sit here, he is lying in San Michele, where the gondolas with the black flags are his only visitors, where nothing but sorrow and death ever enters. You cannot bring him back to life."

"Alas, no, Fiordelisa; but I may do much to make your life easier. I can make sure that you and your aunt shall know no more poverty and deprivation."

"Ah," sighed la Zia: "we knew both after that good Signor Smitz was carried to San Michele. He had never been rich, mark you; but while he lived there was always enough for the coffee and macaroni, and for a stufato on Sundays, and a flask of Chiante that lasted all the week. We did not waste his money, and he used to praise his little Lisa as the cleverest manager and best wife a man ever had. And she would have been his wife, mark you, had he lived. Oh, he had promised her again and again, and he meant to keep his word. She would have been an English gentleman's wife—all in good time."

"All in good time," echoed Lisa; "and my son would not have been fatherless."

"Your son!" exclaimed Vansittart.

"Ah, you do not know," said la Zia; "her baby was born half a year after his father's death. It was the late autumn when the bambino came. The leaves were all dying off the vines, the strangers were all leaving Venice, the boats were bringing in the winter fuel, and the cold winds were creeping up from the Adriatic and blowing round all the corners of the Calle. We were very poor. There was a little money in the house when he died—and there was more than enough in his purse when he fell to pay for his funeral—but when the last lira was gone there was nothing but to go back to the lace-making, both of us, and work for the dish of polenta and the garret that lodged

115

us. We did not want to go back to Burano, to see the old faces and hear the old comrades talk about us, after we had lived like ladies and worn velvet gowns, so we went to work at the factory in Venice, and we lived in one little room in the Rialto, right up in the roof of an old, old house, where we could see nothing but the sky; and there Lisa's baby was born, a beautiful boy. Ah, how proud Signor Smitz would have been had he lived to see that lovely infant!"

"Is the boy living?" asked Vansittart, gently.

"Living! Yes, he is in the next room; he is the joy of our lives," answered the aunt.

Lisa started up from the supper table, with her finger on her lips, and went across the room, beckoning to Vansittart to follow. She opened a door, cautiously, noiselessly, and led him into a bedroom, where, by the faint glimmer of a night-light, he saw a boy lying in a little cot beside the ancient four-post bed, a boy who was the image of one of Guido's child-angels—full round cheeks, with a crimson glow upon their olive clearness, lips like Cupid's bow, long dark lashes fringing blue-veined eyelids, and dark brown hair waving in loose curls about the broad forehead. Truly a beautiful boy! Vansittart could not withhold his praises of that childish sleeper.

"You are very fond of him," he said gently, as Lisa stooped to rearrange the blanket over the child's round and dimpled arm, pressing a kiss upon the fat little hand before she covered it.

"Oh, I adore him. He is all in the world I have to love, except la Zia."

"And you have had a hard time of it, through my fault," said Vansittart, gravely, as they went back to the sitting-room.

It was one o'clock by the little American clock on the chimney-piece—one by the clock of the church in Covent Garden, which pealed its single stroke with solemn sound as they resumed their seats by the shabby round table, in the light of the paraffin lamp; but, late as it was, neither Lisa nor her aunt seemed in any hurry to get rid of their visitor, nor did he mean to go until he had made a compact with them—a compact which should set his mind at rest as to the future.

"How did you come from the lace factory at Venice to the stage of Covent Garden?" he asked. "This is a long way for you to have travelled, without a friend to help you along."

"We had a friend," answered Lisa. "My good old music-master. We lost sight of him when our troubles began; but he met me one day as I was leaving the factory—it was when my baby was three months old—and he stopped to talk to me. He was shocked to see me so thin and pale, and when I told him how poor we were—la Zia and I—he asked me why I did not turn my voice to account. He always used to praise my voice when Signor Smitz asked him how I got on with my education. I had a voice that was worth money, he said. And now in our poverty he was very good to us. He gave me more lessons, without a sous, to be paid for only when I should be earning plenty of money; and after he had taught me a good many choruses in Verdi's operas, he gave me a letter to the Impresario at Milan, and he lent us the money for the journey to Milan, and once there all went well with us. I was engaged to sing in the chorus, and I sang there for two seasons, and la Zia and I were able to live comfortably and to save money, until one day, when the Scala was closed, an English Impresario came to Milan, to engage singers for the London season, and I, who had always wanted to go to London, went to him, and asked him to engage me, and it was all settled in a few minutes. We have been a year and a half in England, la Zia and I, sometimes travelling with the opera company, but mostly in London."

"And you have made wonderful progress in our language, Signora."

"Don't call me Signora," she said softly. "Call me Fiordelisa, as you did that day at Venice."

"Tell me how you both like our England."

The elder woman shrugged her shoulders, elevated her eyebrows, and flung up her hands in boundless admiration.

"Wonderfullissimo!" she exclaimed. "The streets, the long, broad streets, and splendid, splendid shops; the carriages, the fine-dressed people, the smoke, the roar of wheels, the everlasting noise. When I look back, and think of Burano, it is like a dream of quiet; a tranquil world set in the bosom of the waters; a cradle for sleep; life that is half slumber. Here every one is awake."

"But your London is not beautiful," said Lisa. "This court is not like Venice. It is liker than your big, noisy streets; but when one looks up the sky is murky and grey—not like the strip of blue above the Calle. If I could live where I could see water from my window—even your dull, dark river—I should be happier; but to be away from the sound and the sight of waters! That was hard even at Milan, which was still Italy."

"There are places in London where you might live in sight and sound of the river," said Vansittart. "We cannot offer you anything like your lagoons; we have no mountains like the Friuli range for our sunsets to glorify; but we have a river by which people can live if they like."

"Not if they like, but if they are rich enough," argued Lisa. "We asked if we could have a lodging near the river; but the people at the theatre told us such lodgings are dear—they are not for such as us."

"We will see about that," said Vansittart; and then he went on more seriously, "I want to make a compact with you and your aunt. I want to come to a clear understanding of what we are to be to each other in the future. Are we to be friends, Lisa?"

"Yes, yes, friends, true friends," she answered eagerly.

"And you forgive me for—what was done that night?"

"Yes, I forgive you. The fault was not all yours. He insulted you—he struck you—and you were maddened—and the dagger was there. It was a fatality. Let us think of it no more. We cannot bring him back. It is best to forget."

"You know, Lisa, that you have it in your power to blight my life—to tell the world what I did that night—to give me up to the strong arm of the law to answer for the life I destroyed. You could do that if you liked. Do you mean to do it?"

"No," she said resolutely.

"And you, Signora," to the aunt, "are you of the same mind as your niece?"

"In all things. Lisa is much cleverer than her poor old aunt. I do as she does."

"But some day, Fiordelisa, you might change your mind," urged Vansittart. "Women are capricious. You might take it into your head to betray me—to tell people of that tragedy in Venice, and that I was the chief actor in it."

"Not for the world would I tell anything that would injure you," she said.

"Do you mean that, Lisa?"

"A thousand times yes."

"Promise then, thus, with your hand in mine," taking her hand as he spoke, "promise by the Mother of God and by His Saints that, come what may, you will never tell how I stabbed an unarmed man in the Caffè Florian. Promise that as I am frank and true with you, so you will deal frankly and fairly by me, and will do no act and will say no word to my injury."

"I promise," she said, "by the Mother of God and by His Saints. I promise to be loyal and true to you all the days of my life."

"And you, Signora?" to the aunt.

"What she promises I promise."

"Why, then, thank God for the chance that brought us three together again," said Vansittart, earnestly, "for now I can make my atonement to you both with an easy mind. There is nothing I will not do, Lisa, to prove that my remorse is a reality, and not a pretence. You would like to live by the river, child? Well, it shall be my business to find you a home from which you shall look upon running water, and hear the splash of the tide. Your voice is your fortune. Well, it shall be my business to find you a master who can train you for something better than singing in a chorus. As you are loyal to me, Lisa, so, by the heaven above us, will I be loyal to you. All that a brother could do for a sister will I do for you, and deem it nothing more than my duty when it is done."

"Ah, what a noble gentleman," cried la Zia, wiping her tearful eyes, "and how gracious of the blessed Mary to give us so generous a friend! Little did I expect such fortune when I rose from my bed this morning."

"And now, ladies, I must bid you good night," said Vansittart. "I hope to call on you to-morrow afternoon with some news of your future home. You will not mind living two or three miles from your theatre. There are trams and omnibuses, and a railway to carry you backwards and forwards," he added.

"We should not mind even if we had to walk to and fro. We are good walkers," answered Lisa. "We lived a long way from la Scala. Ever so far off, on the other side of Milan."

"To-morrow, then. A rivederci."

Two o'clock struck while he was walking to Charles Street, happier than he had felt for a long time. It seemed to him that his burden was lightened almost to a feather-weight now that he knew the fate of these women. They were not destitute, as he had often pictured them. They had suffered a little poverty, but no more than was the common lot of the class from which they had sprung. And it was in his power to make ample reparation to them. He would do more for Lisa than that dead man would ever have done. He would put her in the way of an honourable career. Whatever talents she had should be cultivated at his cost. He would not degrade her by foolish gifts—but he would spend money freely to further her interests, and he would keep her feet from straying any further upon that broad road she had entered so recklessly.

He could but wonder at the lightness with which she accepted her lover's fate, and forewent every idea of retribution. Not so, he told himself, would an Englishwoman bow to the stroke of destiny, if her best-beloved were slain. And then he wondered whether, in all this world, near or far, there was any one, besides Fiordelisa, who had loved John Smith, and who was now mourning for him.

CHAPTER X.

"AS THINGS THAT ARE NOT
SHALL THESE THINGS BE"

Before two o'clock next day Vansittart had been up and down more stairs than he ever remembered to have mounted and descended in a single day. He had inspected flats in the neighbourhood of the Strand, and flats at Millbank, and flats at Chelsea; and finally, after much driving to and fro in a hansom, and interviews with several house-agents, he had discovered a third floor in a newly erected house near Cheyne Walk which seemed to him the ideal home for Fiordelisa and her aunt. The house stood at a corner, and the windows and balcony of this upper story commanded a fine view of the river and Battersea Park; while to the eastward appeared the Abbey and the Houses of Parliament, and southward rose the Kentish hills and the Crystal Palace. The flat contained three good rooms, with a tiny kitchen at the back. The balcony was architectural, and looked solid and secure. There was a fascinating oriel window at the corner of the principal room, which projected so as to command the west. Nothing could have been brighter or more airy, and the agent who took Vansittart over the rooms assured him that the house was substantially built, and altogether satisfactory. No doubt most agents would say as much about most houses, but the appearance of this house, the thickness of the walls, and the solidity of the woodwork went far to justify the agent's praises.

The rent was eighty-five pounds a year, all told; and this was a rent which came well within the amount that Vansittart was prepared to pay. He was thoroughly in earnest in his desire to be of substantial service to Lisa and her aunt. He was not a rich man; but he told himself that he could spare two hundred a year for the solace of his conscience; and he was prepared to impoverish himself to that amount for the rest of his life. Yes, even in that dim future when he should have sons at the University and daughters to marry, and when hundreds would be of much more consequence to him than they were now. Two hundred a year would he forfeit for his sin; and he contemplated the sacrifice with so much the more satisfaction because of his cordial liking for the impulsive peasant girl whose fate had become interwoven with his own.

He found aunt and niece at home, and expectant of his arrival. He had exchanged his hansom for a brougham from a livery stable, which would accommodate three people.

"I am going to take you to see the home I have chosen for you, Lisa," he said; "that is to say, if you would rather make your home in London than in Italy."

"Yes, yes; ever so much rather," she answered eagerly. "London is a grand city. You live in London, don't you?"

"Not always. I am seldom here more than a month or two at a time. I am not a lover of cities."

She looked disappointed at this reply.

"You will come and see us sometimes, when you are in London?" she asked.

"Certainly. I shall look in upon you now and then to see how you and la Zia are getting on in your new surroundings. And now let us go and look at the apartments I have chosen. Perhaps you will not like my choice."

La Zia protested that this was out of the question. His choice must be perfection. It was not possible for so noble a gentleman to err in taste or judgment.

Fiordelisa was dressed for going out. She was poorly clad in her well-worn black gown and a little cheap black net bonnet, with pale pink roses in it, but her dress was neater than usual. La Zia had also dressed herself tidily, and looked more reputable than he would have thought possible, remembering the flaunting ruby plush and coppery gold chain in Venice. The little boy had been committed to the care of the landlady, who was prodigiously fond of him, Lisa told Vansittart.

The drive by St. James's Park, Buckingham Palace, and Eton Square was a delight to the Venetians. They exclaimed at every new feature of the way. The houses, the soldiers, the trees, the palace, and even the long, solemn, unbeautiful square impressed them. The magnitude of everything was so astounding after Venice. The wide expanses and seemingly illimitable distances filled them with wonder. They had been surprised at the extent of Milan; but this London looked as if it could swallow twenty Milans.

The brougham drove along the King's Road, turned into Oakley Street, and brought them suddenly face to face with the Thames in one of its pleasantest aspects. The sun was shining on the river, the trees were purple with swelling leaf-buds, the old houses of Cheyne Walk looked bright and gay in the sunlight.

"Oh, how pretty!" cried Lisa, and Lisa's aunt was quite as enthusiastic.

"There is one thing I must ask you," said Vansittart, "before we come to business with the house-agent. I don't know the surname of either of you ladies."

"My name is Vivanti," said the aunt, "and Lisa's is the same. She is my brother's daughter."

"Then Lisa shall be Madame Vivanti, and you—shall we say Mademoiselle?"

"As you will. I have never been married. The man I loved and was to have married was a fisherman, and his boat was wrecked one stormy night between Venice and Chioggia. I never cared for any one else; so I lived with my brother and his wife, and worked for them and with them. He has a swarm of children, of whom Lisa is the eldest."

"Then you have a number of brothers and sisters, Lisa," said Vansittart. "Can you reconcile your mind to living in England and seeing them no more?"

Lisa shrugged her shoulders.

"There are too many of us," she said; "each of us felt what it was to be one mouth too many. The mother died six years ago, worn out like an old shoe that has tramped over the stones through all weathers. My father would beat us for a word or a look. It was a hard life at Burano. I don't want to go back there—ever. And your name, Signor; you have not told us that."

"My name! Ah, true!"

He hesitated for an instant or so. Could he trust them with the knowledge of his name and surroundings? He thought not. They were women, impulsive, uneducated, therefore uninstructed in the higher law of honour.

"My name is Smith," he said.

"How strange! The same as his," exclaimed Lisa.

"It is a common English name."

The carriage stopped at a street corner, and Vansittart led the way up the brand-new staircase to the brand-new third story. Lisa and her aunt were in raptures. Everything was so pretty, the paint, the paper, the ceilings, the windows and balconies, the fireplaces, with their tasteful wooden mantelpieces, and shining flowery tiles, and artistic little grates, warranted to consume a minimum of coals and give a maximum of heat.

There was a somewhat spacious sitting-room, with five windows, including the oriel in the western corner. Opening out of this were two small bedrooms; and on the other side of the landing there was the doll's-house kitchen, furnished with many shelves and conveniences for cooking and washing up, a kitchen as ingenious in its arrangements, and almost as small as the steward's cabin on a Jersey steamer.

"Now, Madame Vivanti," said Vansittart, when the inspection had been made, addressing Lisa with some ceremony, "if you and your aunt are pleased with these rooms, and if you would like to make your permanent home in London, turning your musical gifts to as much account as you can, I shall be happy to furnish them for you, and to pay the rent always, or at any rate as long as you remain unmarried—and"—in a graver tone, "lead a virtuous and reputable life, making no hasty acquaintances, and keeping yourself to yourself until you know this country well enough to make a wise choice of friends. Would you like me to do this?"

"How can you ask such a question? Ah, you are too good and generous to me. I shall be as happy as a queen—to live in rooms like these, with that lovely view over the river. It will be like living in a palace. But pray don't call me Madame Vivanti. I feel as if you were angry with me."

"Foolish child! you know better than that," he said, smiling at her. "I am full of friendliest feelings towards you and your aunt. But I must not call you by your Christian name. Men and women do not do that in England, unless they are blood relations or affianced lovers. You must be Madame Vivanti in future."

Lisa pouted and looked distressed, but said nothing. La Zia expressed her heartfelt gratitude, for her niece chiefly, for herself in a lesser degree. The kitchen seemed to impress her most of all. There was a hot plate, on which she could cook a risotto or a stufato, or a dish of macaroni, and all those messes which are savoury to the Italian palate.

"You will keep house for your niece, and take care of her boy"—Vansittart approached this subject with a certain hesitation totally unshared by the boy's mother—"until he is old enough to go to school. Lisa—Madame Vivanti—will have to work hard at her musical education if she means to rise from the ranks of the chorus. I will look about for a respectable singing-master, who is not too famous to teach on moderate terms, and I will pay him for a course of lessons—to last, say, six months. By that time we shall know what Madame's voice is made of."

"Call me Si'ora, if you won't call me Lisa," said the young woman, impetuously. "I won't be called by that formal Frenchified

123

Madame."

"It shall be Si'ora, then, if that will content you. And now, Si'ora, and la Zia, tell me that you are satisfied with me, and that what I am glad to do for you will be in some sense an atonement for—what I did that night."

Lisa burst into a flood of tears.

"You are too generous; you do too much," she cried. "He would never have done so much, not even if he had been rich. He thought anything good enough for us—after, after he began to get tired of us. You are a hundred times better than he was——"

"Lisa, Lisa," remonstrated the elder woman, "that is a hard thing to say."

"Oh, I know; I loved him once—passionately, passionately. I prayed the Holy Mother every night and morning to make him keep his word and marry me. He gave me my velvet gown. Yes, I loved him passionately. He gave me lessons on the mandoline, and promised he would have me trained to be a lady. Yes, I loved him. I shall never forget the day he first came into the factory at Burano, and looked at us all as we sat at our work, and began to talk to me in Italian. There are so few Englishmen who can speak a single sentence of Italian, and his voice was so soft and kind, and he asked me questions about my work. But afterwards, when we were in Venice, he was not always kind; not as kind or as gentle as you are."

She cried a little more after these simple utterances; and then she dried her tears, and la Zia comforted her, and they all three went downstairs and drove to the house-agent's office, where Vansittart introduced Signora Vivanti, of the Royal Italian Opera, Covent Garden, as a tenant for the third floor of Saltero's Mansion, he himself, Mr. John Smith, vouching for the respectability of the ladies, and paying a year's rent in advance with some bank-notes he had ready for the transaction. This handsome payment, and the fact that the flat was unfurnished, reconciled the agent to the vagueness of a referee who only described himself as John Smith, of London.

This done, and the key of the third-floor flat having been handed over to him by the agent, Vansittart put Lisa and her aunt into the carriage and bade them good-bye.

"You will be driven back to Stone Court," he said, "in plenty of time for your work at the theatre. I will see about furnishing the new rooms to-morrow, and everything ought to be ready for you in a week. You had better give your landlady a week's notice."

"She will be sorry to part with Paolo," said la Zia. "She is as fond of him as if she were his grandmother."

"You will come to see us in a week?" said Lisa, earnestly, as he shut the carriage door.

"In a week your new home will be ready," he answered; "I will come or write. Good-bye."

He waved his hand to the driver, whom he had instructed to take the ladies back to the entrance of Stone Court. The carriage moved off, Lisa looking at him earnestly, with something of a disappointed air, to the last.

"Poor child! Did she think I was going to give them a dinner at a restaurant, as I did that day in Venice?" he asked himself, as he walked towards Piccadilly. "What a curious, impulsive, infantine nature it is; made up of laughter and of tears; taking the ghastliest things lightly, and yet with the capacity for passion and grief. Well, it is a good thing, it is a happy thing for me to be able to mend the broken life, and to give happiness where I had brought misery."

He devoted the best part of the following day to the business of furnishing. It was his first experience in that line since he had taken over his predecessor's sticks at Balliol, adding such luxuries and artistic embellishments as his youthful fancy prompted. He had been interested then with the undergraduate's pleasure in his emancipation from the Etonian's dependence. He was interested now. He felt as if he had been furnishing a doll's house for the occupation of a talking doll, so childishly simple did Lisa's intellect seem to him. He took a pleasure in the task, and exercised taste and common sense in every detail.

The rooms were furnished in less than a week, for the furniture was of the simplest, and all ready to his hand at a West End upholsterer's. He had but to make his selection from a variety of styles, all graceful, artistic, and inexpensive. At the end of the week he sent the livery brougham to carry aunt and niece and boy to their new home. He sent Fiordelisa a little note by the coachman.

"Your house is ready. I shall call at four o'clock to-morrow afternoon to take a cup of tea in your drawing-room, and to hear if you approve of my furnishing."

He received one of Lisa's ill-written letters by the next morning's post:—

"The rooms are lovely; everything is as pretty as a picture or a dream; but why did you not come this afternoon to let us thank you? To-morrow is so far off."

This little letter induced punctuality. He was at Lisa's door on the stroke of the hour. The afternoon light was shining in at the south windows. The sun shone golden over the western river. There were daffodils in a glass vase on the little white-wood table in the oriel, and the new cups and saucers that he had chosen were set out upon a bamboo table with many shelves. Aunt and niece were neatly dressed in their black merino gowns, and the little boy was playing with a set of bricks in a corner of the room, silently happy. Aunt and niece poured out their gratitude in a gush of Italian and English, curiously intermixed. Never was anything so pretty as this house of theirs; never so noble a benefactor as Vansittart. He could but feel happy in seeing their happiness. He had never been so near forgetting that scene of blood in the Venetian caffè.

He stayed for an hour or so, sipped half a cup of straw-coloured tea which Lisa fondly believed was made in the English manner, and then departed, promising to call again when he had found a singing-master.

"I shall be very particular in my choice, Signora," he said gaily. "First and foremost, the Maestro must be old and ugly, lest you should fall in love with him; next, he must be a genius, for he is to teach you in a year what most people take three years to learn; and he must be a neglected genius, because we want to get him cheap."

"I wish the good little man who taught me the mandoline were in London," said Lisa.

Vansittart could not echo that wish, since the good little man must needs know the story of that midnight in the caffè, and he wanted no such Venetian in London.

"We shall find some one better than your professor," he answered; "and that reminds me I have never heard you play on your mandoline."

"Would you like?" asked Lisa, sparkling with almost as happy a smile as he remembered when she sat at the little table in the crowded Black Hat, before the beginning of trouble.

The mandoline was hanging against the wall, decked with a bunch of ribbons, red, white, and green. She took it down, and seated herself by the window, in the sunlight, and began to tinkle out "Batti, batti," in thin, wiry tones, while the boy left his bricks on the floor and came and stood at her knee, open-mouthed, open-eyed, intently listening.

"Sing, Lisa, sing," said la Zia.

Lisa laughed, blushed, looked shyly at Vansittart, as if she feared his critical powers, and then began that tenderest melody in a fresh young voice, whose every note was round and ripe and full of power. Nor was the singer lacking in expression; the tender legato passages were given with a pleading pathos that touched the listener almost to tears.

"Brava, Signora mia!" he cried, at the end of the song. "Your voice is worlds too good to be drowned in a middle-aged chorus. To my ear you sing 'Batti, batti,' as well as the most famous Zerlina I ever heard. Two years hence, or sooner perhaps, we shall have the new Venetian prima donna, Signora Vivanti, taking the town by storm. But we must make haste, and find our Maestro, able to coach you in all the great operas."

He had to explain that word coach to Lisa, whose knowledge of English had made rapid progress during her residence in the country, and who had a quick apprehension of every new word or phrase.

He left her, charmed at the discovery that she could sing so well, and that her future was therefore so full of hope. He was pleased with her gentleness, her simplicity, her frank acceptance of his friendly services, pleased most of all by the thought that by his protection of these two lonely women he was in some measure atoning for his crime. Yet there were points upon which his conscience remained unsatisfied—questions that he wanted to ask—and to this end he dropped in upon the little family on the third floor three or four times before the Easter holidays.

He was not long in finding the ideal singing-master. An application to one of the chief music publishers and concert-givers brought him in relation with a Milanese musician, who played the 'cello at the Apollo, the new opera-house on the Embankment—the very man Vansittart wanted, ugly enough to satisfy the most jealous husband, elderly, but not old enough to fall asleep in the middle of a lesson; a man of character and talent, but not one of Fortune's favourites, and therefore willing to give lessons on moderate terms.

This gentleman's opinion of Signora Vivanti's voice was most encouraging, and his manner of expressing that opinion seemed so modest and conscientious that Vansittart was fain to believe him.

"La Signora is absolutely ignorant of music," said the Professor, "but if she is industrious and persevering she has a fortune in her throat."

Lisa took very kindly to the Professor, and showed no lack of industry. She was an obedient pupil, and worked very patiently at her piano, which was a much harder ordeal for the untrained fingers than the solfeggi were for the birdlike voice. All her hours unclaimed by the theatre were free for study, since la Zia bore the whole burden of household cares, the marketing and cooking, and the looking after the little boy.

One afternoon, shortly before Easter, Vansittart, calling after a week's interval, was admitted by Lisa instead of by her aunt, who usually opened the door.

La Zia had gone into London in quest of certain Italian comestibles, only procurable in the foreign settlements of Soho, and Fiordelisa was alone with her boy. It was an opportunity that Vansittart had been hoping for, the chance of questioning her about the dead man, whose manes, though in some wise propitiated as he thought, had a trick of haunting him now and again.

"Lisa," he began gently, forgetting that he had forbidden himself that familiar address, "there is something that I want to talk about—if—if I were sure it would not grieve you too much. I want you to tell me—more—about the man you loved—the man I killed. I know what sorrow his death brought upon you; but, tell me, was there no one else to grieve for him? Had he no kindred in England—father, mother, brothers, sisters?"

"I think not," she answered gravely. "He never spoke of any one in England, never at least as if he cared for any one. His mother was dead. I know as much as that. For the rest, he told me hardly anything about himself; except that he had been away from England for a good many years, and that he was not fond of England or English people."

"He was called John Smith. Do you think that was his real name?"

"I don't know. I never heard of any other."

"And in all the time you were associated with him did he write no letters to English friends, nor receive letters from England?"

"None that I ever saw."

"And after his lamentable death were there no inquiries made about him? Did no one come to Venice in search of a missing friend or relative?"

"No one. Except la Zia and me there was no one who cared—no one who was any the worse for his death. He had only us in all the world, I think."

"But when he came first to Burano he came with people—friends—you told me."

"He came with a party of Americans who were staying at the Hô-tel de Rome. They were nothing to him. They had left Venice when he came to Burano the second time."

"Do you know where he had been living before he came to Venice?"

"Living nowhere—wandering about the earth, he told me, like Satan. That is what he said of himself. He had been in Africa—in

America. He called himself a rolling stone. He told me that it was only for my sake he was content to live six months in the same place."

"Had he no friends in Venice?"

"None, except the people with whom he used to play cards at the caffès of an evening. Sometimes he would bring two or three strangers to our salon, and they would sit playing cards half the night, while la Zia and I used to fall asleep in a corner, and wake to find the morning light creeping in through the shutters. Sometimes he won a heap of gold in a single night, and then he was so kind, so kind, and he would give us presents, la Zia and me, and we had champagne for dinner next day. Sometimes, but not often, he had bad luck for a whole night, and that used to make him angry."

"Did he never tell you where he was born and reared, or what kind of life he led before he took to wandering over the face of the earth?"

"Never. He did not like to talk about England or his early life."

Never! There was no more to be heard. There was infinite relief to Vansittart's mind in this blank history. The life he had taken was an isolated life—a bubble on the stream of time, that burst, and vanished. He had broken no mother's heart; he had desolated no home; he had made no gap in a family circle. The man had been a worthless nomad; and his death had brought sorrow upon no one but this peasant and her kinswoman.

Their wounds were healed; their lives were made happy; and so there was an end of his crime and its consequences. Fate had been very good to him. He walked back to Charles Street with his burden so far lightened that he thought he might come eventually to forget that he had ever taken a fellow-creature's life, that he had ever carried about with him any guilty secret.

Easter was close at hand, and he was to spend Easter at Redwold Towers, within walking distance of Eve Marchant's cottage. Easter was to decide his fate, perhaps.

CHAPTER XI.

"ONE THREAD IN LIFE WORTH SPINNING."

Vansittart's heart was lighter than it had been for a long time, the day he left Charles Street for Waterloo on his way to Haslemere. He longed to see Eve Marchant, with all a lover's longing, and he told himself that he had tested his own heart severely enough by an absence of three months, and that he had now only to discover whether the lady's heart was in any way responsive to his own. He knew now that his love for Eve Marchant was no passing fancy, no fever of the moment; and he also told himself that if he could be fairly assured of her worthiness to be his wife, he would lose no time in offering himself as her husband. Of her father's character, whatever it might be, of her present surroundings, however sordid and shabby, he would take no heed. He would ask only if she were pure and true and frank and honest enough for an honest man's wife. Convinced on that point, he would ask no more.

An honest man's wife? Was he an honest man? Was he going to give her truth in exchange for truth? Was there nothing that he must needs hold back; no secret in his past life that he must keep till his life's end? Yes, there was one secret. He was not going to tell her of his Venetian adventure. It would grieve her woman's heart too much to know that the man she loved had to bear the burden of another man's blood. Nay, more, with a woman's want of logic she might deem that impulse of a moment murder, and might refuse to give herself to a man who bore that stain upon his past.

He meant to keep his secret. He could trust Lisa not to betray him. She and her kinswoman had pledged themselves to silence; and over and above the obligation of that promise he had bound them both to him by his services, had made their lives in some wise dependent on his own welfare. No, he had no fear of treachery from them. Nor had he any fear of what the chances of time and change might bring upon him from any other belongings of the dead man—so evidently had his been one of those isolated existences which drop out of life unlamented and unremembered. He was safe on all sides; and the one lie in his life, the lie which he began when he told his mother that he had not been to Venice, must be maintained steadily, whatever conscience might urge against it.

Easter came late this year, and April, the sunny, the showery, the capricious, was flinging her restless lights and shadows over the meadows and copses as he drove from the station. He had to pass Fernhurst on his way to Redwold Towers, and it was yet early in the afternoon as he drove past the quaint little cottage post-office in the dip of the hill, the tiny graveyard on the higher ground, the church and parsonage. It was early enough for afternoon-tea, and he had no need to hurry to Redwold. His sister had sent a groom with a dog-cart instead of coming to meet him in her capacious landau, a lack of attention for which he was grateful, since it left him his own master. He would have been less than human if he had not stopped at the Homestead, and being in his present frame of mind very human, he pulled up the eager homeward-going horse at the little wooden gate, and flung the reins to the groom.

"I am going to make a call here; wait five minutes, and if I am not out by that time take the horse to the inn and put him up for an hour."

"Yes, sir."

How lightly his feet mounted the steep garden path between the trim box borders! There were plenty of flowers in the garden now—sweet-smelling hyacinths, vivid scarlet tulips with wide open chalices, half full of rain; a snowy mesphilus flinging about its frail white blooms in the soft west wind; a crimson rhododendron making a blaze of colour.

The long, low cottage, with its massive porch, was covered with flowering creepers, yellow jasmine, pale pink japonica, scented white honeysuckle. The cottage looked like a bower, and seemed to smile at him as he went up the path. He had a childish fancy that he would rather live in that cottage with Eve for his wife than at Merewood, which was one of the prettiest and most convenient houses of moderate size in all Hampshire. What dwelling could ever be so dear as this quaint old cottage, bent under the burden of its disproportionate thatch, with lattice windows peeping out at odd levels, and with dormers like gigantic eyes under penthouse lids?

She was at home; everybody was at home, even that undomestic bird, the Colonel. They were all at tea in their one spacious parlour—windows open, and all the perfume of flowers and growing

131

hedgerows and budding trees blowing into the room.

Colonel Marchant welcomed him with marked cordiality. The girls were evidently pleased at his coming.

"How good of you to call on us on your way from the station!" said Sophy. "Lady Hartley told us you were to be met by the afternoon train."

Lo, a miracle! The five Miss Marchants were all dressed alike—severely, in darkest blue serge. The red Garibaldis, the yellow and brown stripes, the scarlet, the magenta, the Reckitt's blue, which had made their sitting-room a battle-field of crude colours, had all vanished. In darkest serge, with neat white linen collars, the Miss Marchants stood before him, a family to whose attire the severest taste could not object.

Eve was the most silent of the sisters, but she had blushed vividly at his advent, and she was blushing still. She blushed at every word he addressed to her, and seemed to find a painful difficulty in handling the teapot and cups and saucers when she resumed her post at the tea-tray.

Vansittart asked them for the news of the neighbourhood. How had they managed to amuse themselves after the frost, when there was no more skating?

"We were awfully sorry," said Sophy, "but the hunting men were awfully glad."

"And had you any more balls?"

"No public ball—but there were a good many dances," with half a sigh. "Lady Hartley gave one just before Lent, the only one to which we were invited, and I am happy to say it was out and away the best."

"Lady Hartley has been more than kind to us," said Eve, finding speech at last. "She is the most charming woman I ever met. You must be very proud of such a sister."

"I am proud to know that you like her," answered Vansittart, in a low voice.

He was sitting at her elbow, helping her by handing the cups and saucers, and very conscious that her hand trembled when it touched his.

"My daughter is right," said the Colonel, with a majestic air; "Lady Hartley is the one lady in this neighbourhood—the one womanly woman. She saw my girls ignored, and she has made it her business to convince her neighbours that they are a little too good for such treatment. Other people have been prompt to follow her lead."

"Oh, but it's not for that we care. It is Lady Hartley's friendship

132

we value, not her influence on other people," protested Eve eagerly.

"We are going to Redwold to-morrow afternoon," said Jenny; "but I don't suppose we shall see you, Mr. Vansittart. You will be shooting, or fishing, or something."

"Shooting there is none, Miss Vansittart. The pheasants are a free and unfettered company in the copses, among the primroses and dog-violets. Man is no longer their enemy. And I never felt the angler's passion since I fished for sticklebacks in the shrubbery at home."

The Colonel chimed in at this point, as if thinking the conversation too childish.

He began to discuss the political situation—the chances of a by-election which was to come on directly after Easter. He expressed himself with the ferocity of an old-fashioned Tory. He would give no quarter to the enemy. He had just returned from Paris, he told Vansittart, and had seen what it was to live under a mobocracy.

"They have been obliged to shut up one of their theatres—cut short the run of the finest play that has been produced in the last decade, simply because their sans culottes object to any disparagement of Robespierre. There are a dozen incipient Robespierres in Paris at this day, I believe, only waiting for opportunity to burst into full bloom."

He had been to Paris, then, thought Vansittart. He could afford to take his pleasure in that holiday capital, while his daughters were on short commons at Fernhurst.

"Was Paris very full?" asked Vansittart.

"I hardly know. I met a good many people I know. One meets more Englishmen than Parisians on the boulevards at this season. April is the Englishman's month. Your neighbour, Mr. Sefton, was at the Continental—in point of fact, he and I went to Paris together."

This explained matters to Vansittart. No doubt Sefton paid the bills for both travellers.

"Mr. Sefton is not a neighbour of mine, but of my sister's," he said. "My father and his father were good friends before I was born, but I know nothing of this gentleman."

"A mutual loss," replied the Colonel. "Sefton is a very fine fellow, as I told you the last time you were here. You can hardly fail to get on with him when you do make his acquaintance."

"I saw him at the hunt ball, and I must confess that I was not favourably impressed by his manner."

"Sefton's manner is the worst part of him," conceded Colonel Marchant. "He has been spoilt by Dame Fortune, and is inclined to be arrogant. An only child, brought up in the expectation of wealth, and taught by a foolish mother to believe that a landed estate and a fine income constitute a kind of royalty. Sefton might easily be a worse fellow than he is. For my own part, I cannot speak too warmly of him. He has been a capital neighbour, the best neighbour we had, until Lady Hartley was good enough to take a fancy to my girls."

"I hope you don't compare Lady Hartley with Mr. Sefton, father," cried the impulsive Hetty. "There is more kindness in a cup of tea from Lady Hartley than in all the game, and fruit, and trout, and things with which Mr. Sefton loads us."

"They are enthusiasts, these girls of mine," said the Colonel, blandly. "Lady Hartley has made them her creatures."

"Her name reminds me that I must be moving on," said Vansittart. "I hope you will all forgive this invasion. I was anxious to learn how you all were. It seems a long time since I was in this part of the world."

"It is a long time," said Eve, almost involuntarily.

Those few words rejoiced his heart. They sounded like a confession that she had missed him and regretted him, since those long friendly walks and talks in the clear cold January afternoons. He had never in all their conversation spoken to her in the words of a lover, but he had shown her that he liked her society, and it might be that she had thought him cold and cowardly when he left her without any token of warmer feeling than this casual friendship of the roads, lanes, and family tea-table. To go away, and stay away for three months, and make no sign! A cruel treatment, if, if, in those few familiar hours, he had touched her girlish heart by the magnetic power of unspoken love.

He left the Homestead happy in the thought that she was not indifferent to the fact of his existence; that he was something more to her than a casual acquaintance.

He was to see her next day; and it would be his own fault if he did not see her the day after that; and the next, and the next; until the solemn question had been asked, and the low-breathed answer had been given, and she was his for ever. All was in his own hand now. He had but to satisfy himself upon one point—her acquaintance with Sefton, what it meant, and how far it had gone—and then the rest was peace, the perfect peace of happy and confiding love.

He was unfilial enough to be glad that his mother was not at Redwold. There would be no restraining influence, no maternal arm stretched out to pluck him from his fate. He would be free to fulfil his destiny; and when the fair young bride was won, it would be easy for her to win her own way into that motherly heart. Mrs. Vansittart was not a woman to withhold her affection from her son's wife.

Lady Hartley appeared in the portico as the cart drove up to the door.

"What a fright you have given me!" she said. "Did anything happen to the train?"

"Nothing but what usually happens to trains."

"But you are an hour late."

"I called on Colonel Marchant. It never occurred to me that you could be uneasy on my account, or I should not have stopped on the way. I am very sorry, my dear Maud," he concluded, as he kissed her in the hall.

"You are not cured of your infatuation, Jack."

"Not cured, or likely to be cured, in your way. I have heard nothing but your praises, Maud. You seem to have been a fairy godmother to those motherless girls."

"Have I not? How did you like their appearance? Did you see any improvement?"

"A monstrous improvement. They were all neatly dressed, and in one colour."

"That was my doing, Jack."

"Really! But how did you manage it, without wounding their feelings?"

"My tact, Jack, my exquisite tact," cried Maud, gaily.

They were in her morning-room by this time, and Vansittart sank into a low armchair, prepared to hear all she had to tell. Maud had generally a great deal to say to her brother after an interval of severance.

"I'll tell you all about it," she began. "It grieved me to see those poor girls in their coats of many colours, or rather in their assemblage of colours among the five sisters, so I felt I must do something. I was always looking at them, and thinking how much better I could dress them than they dressed themselves, and quite as economically, mark you. So one day I said casually that I thought sisters—youthful sisters understood—looked to particular advantage when they were all dressed exactly alike, whereupon Eve, who is candour itself"—Vansittart's heart thrilled at this praise—"declared herself entirely of my opinion, but she explained that she and her sisters had very little money to dress upon, and they were all great bargain-hunters, and could get most wonderful bargains at the great drapery sales, if they were not particular in their choice of colours. 'And that is how we always look like a ragged regiment,' said Eve, 'but we certainly get good value for our poor little scraps of money.'"

"A girl who ought to be dressed like a duchess," sighed Vansittart.

"Well, on this I read her one of my lay sermons. I told her that so far from getting good value for her money, she got very bad value for her money; that she and her sisters, in their thirst for stuff at a shilling a yard, reduced from three and sixpence, made themselves in a manner queens of shreds and patches. She was very ready to admit the force of my reasoning, poor child. And then she pleaded that her sisters were so young—they had no control over their feelings when they found themselves in a great drapery show. It seemed a kind of fairyland, where things were being given away. And then such a scramble, she tells me, women almost fighting with each other for eligible bits of stuff and last season's finery. I told her that I had hardly ever seen the inside of a big shop, and that I hated shopping. 'What,' she cried, 'you who are rich! I thought you would enjoy it above all things.' I told her no; that Lewis and Allanby sent me one of their people, and I chose my gown from a pattern-book, and the fitter came and tried it on, and I had no more trouble about it; or that I went to my dressmaker, and just looked over her newest things in a quiet drawing-room, without any of the distracting bustle of a great shop."

"My sweetest Maud, what a dear little snob she must have thought you!"

"I don't think she did. She seemed pleased to know my ways. And then I told her that I should like to see her and her sisters all dressed alike, in one of my favourite colours; and then I told her that I knew of a most meritorious family—invented that moment—who were going to Australia, and whom I wanted to help. 'In a colony, those bright colours your sisters wear would be most suitable,' I said. 'Will you make an exchange with me—just in a friendly way—give me as many of your bright gowns as you can spare, and I will give you a piece of good serge and a piece of the very best cloth in exchange?'"

"Did she stand that?" asked Vansittart.

"Not very well. She looked at me for a moment or two, blushed furiously, and then got up and walked to the window, and stood there with her back towards me. I knew that she was crying. I went over to her and put my arm round her neck and kissed her as if she had been my first cousin. I begged her to forgive me if I had offended. 'I really want to help those poor girls who are going to Melbourne,' I said;

'and your bargains would be just the thing for them. They could get nothing half as good for the same money.' I felt ashamed of myself the next moment. I had lied so well that she believed me."

"Never mind, Maud; the motive was virtuous."

"'No, they couldn't,' she said; 'not till next July. The sales are all over.' And then, after a little more argument, she yielded, and it was agreed that I should drive over to the Homestead next morning, and we would hold a review of the frocks and furbelows, and whatever was suitable for my Australian emigrants I should take, giving the sisters fair value in exchange. Eve stipulated that it should be only fair value. Well, the review was capital fun. The girls were charming—evidently proud of their finery, expatiating upon the miraculous cheapness of this and that, and the genuineness of the sales at the best houses. They had sales on the brain, I think. Of course I left them all the gay frocks suitable for home evenings; but I swooped like a vulture on their outdoor finery. I had taken a large portmanteau over with me, and we crammed it with frocks and fichus and Zouave jackets for my Australians. I am sorry to say the portmanteau is still upstairs in the box-room. And now, Jack, you know the history of the serge frocks."

"You are a dear little diplomatist; but I'm afraid you must have made Miss Marchant suffer a good deal before your transmutation was accomplished."

"My dear Jack, that girl is destined for suffering—of that kind; small social stings, the sense of the contrast between her surroundings and those of other girls no better born, only better off."

"She will marry and forget these evil days," said Vansittart.

"Let us hope so; but let us hope that she will not marry you."

"Why should you—or any one—hope that?"

"Because it ain't good enough, Jack; believe me, it ain't. She is a sweet girl—but her father's character is the opposite of sweet. Hubert has made inquiries, and has been told, by men on whose good faith he can rely, that the Colonel is a black-leg; that there is hardly any dishonourable act that a man can do, short of felony, which Colonel Marchant has not done. He is well known in London, where he spends the greater part of his time. He is a hanger-on of rich young men. He shows them life. He wins their money—and like that other hanger-on, the leech, he drops away from them when he is gorged and they are empty. Can you choose the daughter of such a man for your wife?"

"I can, and do choose her, above all other women; and if she is as pure and true as I believe her to be, I shall ask her to be my wife.

The more disreputable her father, the gladder I shall be to take her away from him——"

"And when her father is your father-in-law how will you deal with him?"

"Leave that problem to me. I am not an idiot, or a youth fresh from the University. I shall know how to meet the difficulty."

"You will not have that man at Merewood, Jack," cried Maud, excitedly, "to loaf about my mother's garden—the garden that is hers now—and to play cards in my mother's drawing-room?"

"You are running on very fast, Maud. No; if I marry Eve Marchant be assured I shall not keep open house for her father. He has not been so good a parent as to make his claim indisputable."

"Such a marriage will break mother's heart," sighed Maud.

"You know better than that, Maud! You know that only a disreputable marriage would seriously distress my mother, and there can be nothing disreputable in a marriage with a good and pure-minded girl. I promise you that I will not offer myself to Eve Marchant until I feel assured of her perfect truth. There is only one point upon which I have the shadow of a doubt. It seemed to me, from certain trifling indications, that there had been some kind of flirtation between her and Sefton."

"I cannot quite make that out, Jack," answered Maud, thoughtfully. "I have seen them together several times since you left. There is certainly something, on his side. He pursues her in a manner—contrives to place himself near her at every opportunity, and puts on a confidential air when he talks to her. I have watched them closely in her interest, for I really like her. I don't think she encourages him. Indeed I believe she detests him; but she is not as stand-offish as she might be; and I have seen her occasionally talking very confidentially with him—as if they had a secret understanding."

"That's it," cried Vansittart, inwardly raging. "There is a secret, and I must be possessed of that secret before I confess my love."

"And how do you propose to pluck out the heart of the mystery?"

"In the simplest manner—by questioning Eve herself. If she is the woman I think her she will answer me truthfully. If she is false and shifty—why then—I whistle her down the wind, and you will never hear more of this fond dream of mine."

"Well, Jack, you must go your own way. You were always my master, and I can't pretend to master you now. You'll have an opportunity of seeing Eve and Mr. Sefton to-morrow. He is coming to my afternoon. I hope you'll be civil to him."

"As civil as I can. I'll break no bounds, Maud; but I believe the

man to be a scoundrel. If he were pursuing Eve with any good motive he would have spoken out before now."

"Precisely my view of the case. It is shameful to compromise her
by motiveless attentions. There goes the gong. I am glad we have
had this quiet talk. You will not act precipitately, will you, Jack?"
concluded his sister, appealingly, as she moved towards the door.

"I will act as I have said, Maud, not otherwise."

"Well," with a sigh, "I believe she will come through the ordeal,
and that I am destined to have her for my sister."

"You have made her love you already. That leaves less work for
you in the future."

"Poor mother! She will be woefully disappointed."

"True," said Vansittart; "but as I couldn't marry all her protégées, perhaps it is just as well I should marry none of them; and be
assured I should not love Eve Marchant if I didn't believe that she
would be a good and loving daughter to my mother."

"Every lover believes as much. It is all nonsense," said Maud, as
she ran off to her dressing-room.

Mr. Sefton made an early appearance at Lady Hartley's afternoon. He arrived before the Marchants, and when there were only
about a dozen people in the long drawing-room, and Vansittart
guessed by the way he loitered near a window overlooking the drive
that he was on the watch for the sisters.

Lady Hartley introduced her brother to Mr. Sefton, with the respect due to the owner of one of the finest estates in the county,
a man of old family and aristocratic connections. Sefton was particularly cordial, and began to make conversation in the most amiable way, a man not renowned for amiability to his equals. The Miss
Marchants were announced while he and Vansittart were talking, and
Sefton's attention began to wander immediately, although he continued the discussion of hopes and fears about that by-election which
was disturbing every politician's mind; or which at any rate served
as a topic among people who had nothing to say to each other.

Only two out of the three grown-up sisters appeared, Eve and
Jenny. The more diplomatic Sophy thought she improved her social
status by occasional absence.

Sefton broke away from the conversation at the first opening,
and went straight to Eve, who was talking to little Mr. Tivett, arrived
that afternoon, no holidays being complete in a country house without such a man as Tivett, with his little thin voice, good nature, and
willing to fetch and carry for the weaker sex.

Vansittart stood aloof for a little while, talking to a comfortable

139

matron, who was evidently attached to the landed interest, as her conversation dwelt upon the weather in its relation to agriculture and the lambing season. He could see that Eve received Sefton's advances with coldest politeness. On her part there was no touch of the earnest and confidential air which had so distressed him that afternoon by the lake. She talked with Sefton for a few minutes, and then turned away, and walked into the adjoining room, where the wide French window stood open to the garden. Vansittart seized his opportunity and followed her. He found her with her sister, looking at a pile of new books on a large table in a corner, and he speedily persuaded them that the flower-beds outside were better worth looking at than magazines and books which were no less ephemeral than the tulips and hyacinths.

He walked up and down the terrace with them for nearly half an hour, but never a hint of anything more than lightest society talk gave he in all that time. He had made up his mind to speak only after gravest deliberation, only in the calmest hour, when they two should be alone together under God's quiet sky; but he so managed matters that Mr. Sefton had no further opportunity of offering his invidious attentions to Eve Marchant that afternoon. It was Vansittart who found seats for her and her sister in the drawing-room; it was Vansittart who carried their teacups, assisted only by Mr. Tivett, who tripped about with plates of chocolate biscuits, and buttered buns, with such activity as to appear ubiquitous.

The next day was Good Friday, a day of long church services and no visitors. On Saturday Vansittart went to Liss to spend the day with his mother, and to make a tour of grounds and home farm, a round of grave inspection which the mother and son took together, and during which they talked of many things, but not of Eve Marchant. If Mrs. Vansittart wondered that her son should have chosen to spend the recess at Redwold rather than at Merewood, she was too discreet to express either wonder or dissatisfaction. She was going to Charles Street directly after Easter, and Jack was to join her there for the London season; so she had no ground for dolefulness in being deprived of his society for just this one week.

She found him looking well, and, to her fancy, happier than he had looked for a long time. There was a ring of gaiety in his voice and laugh which she had missed of late years, and which she heard again to-day. They lunched together, and she drove him to the station in the late afternoon.

"It delights me to see you looking so well and so happy, Jack," she said, as they walked up and down the platform.

"Does it, mother?" he asked earnestly. "Is my happiness really enough to gladden you? Are you content that I should be happy in my own way?"

There were some moments of silence, and then she said gravely, "Yes, Jack, I am content, for I cannot believe that your way would be a foolish way. You have seen enough of the world to judge between gold and dross, and you are not the kind of man to plunge wilfully into a morass, led by false lights."

"No, no, mother, you may be sure of that. My star shall be a true star—no Jack o' Lantern."

The train steamed in opportunely, and cut short the conversation; but enough had been said, Vansittart thought, to break the ice; and it was evident to him that his mother had an inkling of the course which events were taking.

The next day was Easter Sunday, a day when the morning sun is said to dance upon the waters; a day when the dawn seems more glorious, when the flowers that deck the churches seem fairer than mere earthly flowers, when the swelling chords of the organ and the voices even of the village choir have a sweetness that suggests the heavenly chorus. To John Vansittart, at least, among those who worshipped in the village church that Easter Day, there seemed a gladness in all things—a pure and thrilling gladness as of minds attuned to holiness and ready to believe. He had read much of that new and widening school of thought which is gradually sapping the old foundations and pulling down the old bulwarks; but there was no remembrance of that modern school in his mind to-day as he stood up in the village church to join in the Easter hymn. His thoughts had resumed the simplicity of early years. He was able to believe and to pray like a little child.

He prayed to be forgiven for that unpremeditated sin of which the world knew not. He prostrated himself in heart and mind at the feet of the Christ who died for sinners. But he did not go to the Altar. The Easter Communion was not for him whose hands were stained with blood.

The Marchants were at the morning service, all five of them, fresh and blooming after their long walk, a bunch of English roses, redder or paler as Nature had painted each. Eve, tallest, fairest, loveliest, was conspicuous among the sisters.

"By Jove! how handsome that girl is!" whispered little Tivett, as he ducked to put away his hat.

He and Vansittart were sitting apart from the rest, the Redwold pew being full without them.

"I want to walk home with them after church," whispered Vansittart, also intent upon the disposal of the Sunday cylinder. "Will you come too?"

"With pleasure."

This was before the service began, before the priest and choir had come into the chancel.

The service was brief, a service of jubilant hymns and anthem and short flowery sermon, flowery as the chancel and altar, and pulpit and font, in all their glory of arums, azaleas, spireas, and lilies of the valley. The church clock was striking twelve as the major part of the congregation poured out. There was a row of carriages in the road, two of them from Redwold Towers; but Vansittart and Tivett declined the accommodation of landau or waggonette.

"We are going for a long walk," said Mr. Tivett. "It's such a perfect day."

"But you will lose your lunch, if you go too far."

"We must risk that, and make amends at afternoon-tea."

"Tivett," said Vansittart, when the carriages had driven off, "I am going to make a martyr of you. It will be three o'clock at the earliest when we get back to Redwold, and I know you enjoy your luncheon. It's really too bad."

"Do you think I regret the sacrifice in the cause of friendship? There go the Marchant girls, steaming on ahead. We had better overhaul them at once. Don't mind me, Vansittart. I have been doing gooseberry ever since I wore Eton jackets. Only one word—Is it serious?"

"Very serious—sink or swim—Heaven or Hades."

"And all in honour?"

"All in honour."

"Then I am with you to the death. You want a long walk and a long talk with Miss Marchant; and you want me to take the whole bunch of sisters off your hands."

"Just so, my best of friends."

"Consider it done."

They overtook the young ladies in the dip of the road, where a lane branches off to Bexley Hill. Here they stopped to shake hands all round, and to talk of the church, and the weather—quite the most exquisite Easter Sunday that any of them could remember, or could remember that they remembered, for no doubt memory severely interrogated would have recalled Easter Days as fair.

"Mr. Tivett and I are pining for a long walk," said Vansittart, "so we are going to see you home—if you will let us—or, if you are not tied for time, will you join us in a ramble on Bexley Hill? It is just the day for the hill—the views will be splendid—and I know that you young ladies are like Atalanta. Distance cannot tire you!"

"We could hardly help being good walkers," said Sophy, rather discontentedly. "Walking is our only amusement."

Hetty and Peggy clapped their hands. "Bexley Hill, Bexley Hill," they cried; "hands up for Bexley Hill."

There were no hands lifted, but they all turned into the lane.

"We can go a little way just to look at the view," assented Eve; and the younger girls went skipping off in their short petticoats, and the two elder girls were speedily absorbed in Mr. Tivett's animated conversation, and Eve and Vansittart were walking alone.

"A little way." Who could measure distance or count the minutes in such an exhilarating atmosphere as breathed around that wooded hillside in the balmy April morning? Every step seemed to take them into a finer air, and to lift their hearts with an increasing gladness. All around them rippled the sea of furze and heather, broken by patches of woodland, and grassy glades that were like bits stolen out of the New Forest, and flung down here upon this swelling hillside. Here and there a squatter's cottage, with low cob wall and steep tiled roof, stood snug and sheltered in its bit of garden, under the shadow of a venerable beech or oak—here and there a little knot of children sprawled and sunned themselves in front of a cottage door. The rest was silence and solitude, save for the voices of those rare birds which inhabit forest and common land.

"Gussie," whispered Vansittart, when they had passed one of these humble homesteads, and were ascending the crest of the hill, "do you think you could contrive to lose yourself—and the girls—for half an hour?"

"Of course I can. You will have to cooey for us when you want to see our faces again."

This little conversation occurred in the rear of the five girls, who had scattered themselves over the hillside, every one believing in her own particular track as the briefest and best ascent.

Eve had climbed highest of all the sisters, by a path so narrow, and so hemmed in by bramble and hawthorn, that only one, and that one a dexterous climber, could mount at a time.

Vansittart followed her desperately, pushing aside the brambles with his stick. He was breathless when he reached the top, where she stood lightly poised, like Mercury. The ascent, since he stopped to speak to Tivett, had taken only ten minutes or so, but when he looked round him and downward over the billowy furze and rugged hillside there was not one vestige of Augustus Tivett or the four Miss Marchants in view.

"What can have become of them all?" questioned Eve, gazing wonderingly around. "I thought they were only just behind me—I heard them laughing a few minutes ago. Have they sunk into the earth, or are they hiding behind the bushes?"

"Neither. They are only going round the other side of the hill. They will meet us on the top."

"It's very silly of them," said Eve, obviously distressed. "There is always some folly or mischief when Hetty is one of our party. Peggy is ever so much more sensible."

"Don't blame poor Hetty till you are assured she is in fault. I shouldn't wonder if it were all Tivett's doing. You must scold good little Tivett. I hope you don't mind being alone with me for a quarter of an hour. I have been longing for the chance of a little serious talk with you. Shall we sit down for a few minutes on this fine old beech trunk? You are out of breath after mounting the hill."

She was out of breath, but the hill was not the cause. Her colour came and went, her heart beat furiously. She was speechless with conflicting emotions—fear, joy, wonder, self-abasement.

They were on the ridge of the hill. In front of them, far away towards the south stretched the Sussex Downs, purple in the distance, save for one pale shimmering streak of light which meant the sea. Below them lay the Sussex Weald, rippling meadows, and the vivid green of spacious fields where the young corn showed emerald bright in the sun—pools and winding streamlets, copses and grey fallows, cottage roofs and village spires, a world lovely enough for Satan to use as a lure for the tempted.

But for Vansittart that world hardly existed. He had eyes, thoughts, comprehension for nothing but this girl who sat mutely at his side, the graceful throat bending a little, the shy violet eyes looking at the ground.

So far there had been no word of love between them, not one word, not one silent indication, such as the tender pressure of hands, or even the looks that tell love's story. But love was in the air they breathed, love held them and bound them each to each, and each knew the other's secret.

"Miss Marchant," begun Vansittart with ceremonious gravity, "will you forgive me if I ask you a few questions which may seem somewhat impertinent on my part?"

This was so different from what her trembling heart had expected that she paled as at a sudden danger. He was watching her intently, and was quick to perceive that pallor.

"I don't think you would ask me anything really impertinent," she faltered.

"Not with an impertinent motive, be assured. Well, I must even risk offending you. I want you to tell me frankly what you think of Mr. Sefton."

At this the pale cheeks flushed, and she looked angry.

"I don't like him, though he is my father's friend, and though he is always very kind—obtrusively kind. He has even offered Sophy and me his horses to ride—to have the exclusive use of two of his best hacks, if father would let us ride them; but of course that was out of the question. We could not have accepted such a favour from any one."

"Not from any one but an affianced lover," said Vansittart. "Do you know, Miss Marchant, when I first saw you and Mr. Sefton together at the ball I thought you must be engaged."

"How very foolish of you!"

"He had such an air of taking possession of you, as if he had a superior claim to your attentions."

"Oh, that is only Mr. Sefton's masterful way. He cannot forget the extent of his acres or the length of his pedigree."

"But he seems—always—on such confidential terms with you."

"I have known him a long time."

"Yes, but his manner—to a looker-on—implies something more than friendship. Oh, Miss Marchant, forgive me if I presume to question you. My motive is no light one. Last January by the lake I saw you and that man meet, with a look on both sides of a preconcerted meeting. I heard, accidentally, some few words which Mr. Sefton spoke to you, while you were walking with him by the lake; and those words implied a secret understanding between you and him—something of deep interest of which the outer world knew nothing. Be frank with me, for pity's sake. Speak openly to me today, from heart to heart, if you never speak to me again. Is not there something more between you and Wilfred Sefton than an everyday friendship?"

"Yes," she answered, "there is something more. There *is* a secret understanding—not much of a secret, but Mr. Sefton has taken advantage of it to offer me meaningless attentions which I detest, and which, I dare say, ill-natured people may talk about. They would be sure to think that Mr. Sefton could have no serious intentions about me, that he was only carrying on an idle flirtation."

"And if he were serious—if he asked you to be his wife?"

145

"To live in that grand house; to rule over all those acres; to have a wafer-space on that long pedigree! Could Colonel Marchant's daughter refuse such a chance?"

"Would Colonel Marchant's daughter accept it?"

"Not this daughter," answered Eve, gaily. "I might hand him on to Sophy, perhaps. Poor Sophy hankers after the pomps and vanities of this wicked world."

Her gaiety delighted her lover. It told of an unburdened conscience—a heart at peace with itself.

"Tell me what it was you overheard, Mr. Eavesdropper, that afternoon by the lake?" she asked.

"I heard him say to you, very earnestly, 'It was a false scent, you see;' and then he expressed his sorrow for your disappointment."

"You have a good memory. I, too, remember those words, 'It was a false scent.' It was. He had need to be sorry for my disappointment, for he had cheated me with false hopes."

"About what? About whom?"

"About my brother."

"Your brother? I did not know you had a brother."

"We don't talk about him in a general way. He has been a wanderer over the earth for many years. He was never with us at Fernhurst. He and my father had a terrible quarrel before we left Yorkshire—chiefly about his college debts, I believe. There seemed to be dreadful difficulties at Cambridge. My father used all his influence to get poor Harold out of the country, and succeeded in getting him a berth in the Cape Mounted Police. Parting with him perhaps went nearer to break my mother's heart than our loss of home and fortune."

"It must have been a hard parting."

"It was indeed hard. He went away in disgrace. My father would not speak to him or look at him. He lived at the Vicarage during those last weeks before the ship sailed away with him to Africa. The Vicar and his wife were very good to him, but everybody felt that he was under a cloud. I fear—I fear that he had done something very wrong at Cambridge—something for which he might have been arrested—for he seemed to be in hiding at the Vicarage. And he left one night, and was driven over to Hull, where he went on board a boat bound for Hamburg, and he was to sail from Hamburg for the Cape. My mother and I went to say good-bye to him that last evening, after dark; the others were too young to be told anything; they hardly remember him. He kissed us, and cried over us, and promised mother that for her sake he would try to do well—that he would bear the hardest life in order to redeem his character. He promised that he would write to her by every mail. The dog-cart was at the door while he was saying this. The Vicar came into the room to hurry him away. I have never seen my brother since that night."

CHAPTER XII.

"ONE BORN TO LOVE YOU, SWEET"

"And Mr. Sefton," asked Vansittart, "what has he to do with this?"

"He was with my brother at Cambridge—in the same year, at the same college, Trinity. It was not till the year before last that he ever spoke to me about Harold, or that I knew they had been friends. But one summer afternoon when he called and happened to find me in the garden, alone—a thing that seldom happens in our family—he began to talk to me, very kindly, with a great deal of good feeling, about Harold. He said he had been slow to speak about him, as he knew that he must be in some measure under a cloud. And then I told him how unhappy I was about my poor brother; and how it was four or five years since anything had been heard of him directly or indirectly. His last letter had told us that he was going to join a party of young men who were just setting out upon an exploring tour in the Mashona country. They were willing to take him with them on very easy terms, as he was a fine shot, and strong and active. He would be little better than a servant in the expedition, he told me."

"It was to you he wrote, then?"

"Yes, after my mother's death, only to me. He never wrote to his father. I told Mr. Sefton how unhappy I was about Harold, and my fear—a growing fear—that he must be dead. He argued me out of this terror, and told me that when a man who was leading a wild life far away from home once let a long time slip without writing to his relations, the probabilities were that he would leave off writing altogether. His experience had shown him that this was almost a certainty. And then, seeing how distressed I was, he promised that he would try and find out Harold's whereabouts. He told me that the newspaper press and the electric cable had made the world a very small world, and that he certainly ought to be able to trace my brother's wanderings, and bring me some information about him."

"And did he succeed?"

"No; he failed always in getting any certain knowledge of Harold's wanderings, though he did bring me some scraps of information about his adventures in Mashonaland; but that was all news of past years—ever so long ago. He could hear nothing about Harold in the present—not within the last four years—so there was very little comfort in his discoveries. Last November he told me that he had heard of a man at the diamond fields whose description seemed exactly to fit my brother, and he thought this time he was on the right track. He wrote to an agent at Cape Town, and took every means of putting himself in communication with this man—both through the agent and by advertisements in the local papers—and the result was disappointment. There was no Harold Marchant among the diamond-seekers. That was what he had to tell me the afternoon you overheard our conversation. He had received the final letter which assured him he had been mistaken."

"And that was all—and verily all?" inquired Vansittart, taking her hand in his.

"That was all, and verily all."

"And beyond that association, Mr. Sefton is nothing in the world to you?"

"Nothing in the world."

"And if there were some one else, quite as willing as Mr. Sefton, to hunt for this wandering brother of yours, some one else who loves you fondly"—his arm was round her now, and he was drawing her towards him, drawing the blushing cheek against his own, drawing the slender form so near that he could hear the beating of her heart—"some one else who longs to have you for his wife, would you listen to him, Eve? And if that some one else were I, would you say 'Yes'?"

She turned to answer him, but her lips trembled and were mute. There was no need of speech between lovers whose very life breathed love. His lips met hers, and took his answer there.

"Dearest, dearest, dearest," he sighed, when that long kiss had sealed the bond; and then they sat in silence, hand clasped in hand, in the face of the Sussex Weald, and the far-reaching Sussex Downs, and the silvery shimmer of the distant sea.

Oh, Easter Day of deep content! Would either of these two souls ever know such perfect bliss again—the bliss of loving and being loved, while love was still a new thing?

A shrill long cooey broke the silent spell, and they both started up as if awakened out of deepest slumber.

"They are looking for us," cried Eve, as she walked swiftly towards the other side of the ridge.

Tivett and the four girls came toiling towards her.

"Mr. Tivett has taken us a most awful round," cried Hetty. "He pretended to know the way, and he doesn't know it one little bit."

"My dear young lady," apologized the gentle Tivett, "the truth of the matter is that I trusted to my natural genius for topography, for I have never been on Bexley Hill before."

"And you pretended to pilot us, and have only led us astray."

"Alas! sweet child, the world is full of such pilots."

"Shall I tell them?" whispered Vansittart, at Eve's ear.

"If you like. They will make a dreadful fuss. Can you ever put up with so many sisters-in-law?"

"I would put up with them if you had as many sisters as Hypermnestra;" and then, laughing happily, he told these four girls that they were soon to have a sister less and a brother more.

Hetty and Peggy received the news with whooping and clapping of hands, Sophy and Jenny with polite surprise. Was there ever anything so wonderful? Nothing could have been further from their thoughts. Little Mr. Tivett skipped and frisked like a young lamb in a meadow. Had Eve Marchant been his sister he could hardly have shown more delight.

The descent of the hill for Eve and Vansittart was a progress through pure ether. They knew not that their feet touched the earth. They were like the greater gods and goddesses in the Homeric Olympus. They started and they arrived. The labour of common mortals was not for them.

"Do you remember the legend of the blue flower of happiness which grows upon the mountain peak, and is said to fade and wither in the lower air?" asked Vansittart, close at his fiancée's ear. "We have found the blue flower on the hilltop, Eve. God grant that for us the heaven-born blossom will keep its bloom even on the dull level of daily life."

"Will our life be dull?" she questioned, in her shy sweet voice, as if she scarcely dared speak of her love louder than in a whisper. "I don't think I can ever find life dull so long as you really care for me."

"No, Eve, life shall not be dull. It shall be as bright and varied, and as full of change and gladness, as devoted love can make it. Your youth has not been free from care, dearest; and you have missed many of the pleasures which girls of your age demand as a right. But the arrears shall be made up. There shall be full measure of gladness in your married life, if I can make you glad. I am not what the modern world calls a rich man; but I am very far from poverty. I have enough for all the real pleasures of life—for travel, and books, and music, and the drama, and gracious surroundings, and kindly charities. The sting of narrow means can never touch my wife."

"It can be a very sharp sting sometimes," said Eve; and then, dropping again into that shy undertone, "But if you were ever so poor, and if you were a working man, and we had to live in that cottage under the beech tree, squatters, with only a key-holding, I think I could be perfectly happy."

"Ah, that is what love always thinks, while the blue flower blooms; but when that mystic flower begins to fade there is some virtue in pleasant surroundings. Years hence, when you begin to be tired of me, and the blue flower takes a greyish shade, why, we can change the scene of our lives, wander far away, and in a new world I shall seem almost a new lover."

"Will you ever take me to Italy?" she asked. "Italy has been the dream of my life, but I never thought it would be realized."

"Ah, that is just a girl's fancy, fed by old-fashioned poets—Byron, for instance. The Italy of to-day is very disappointing, and just like everywhere else."

"Oh, Mr. Vansittart!"

"Mr.!" he echoed. "Henceforward I am John, or Jack; very soon, my husband. Never again Mr., except in your letters to tradespeople or your orders to servants."

"Am I really to call you Jack?"

"Really. It is the name by which I best know myself. But if you think it is too vulgar——"

"Vulgar; it is a lovely name. Jack! Jack!"

She repeated the monosyllable as if it were a sound of exquisite music, a sound on which to dwell lingeringly and lovingly for its very sweetness. To Vansittart also the name was sweet, spoken by those lips.

* * * *

Colonel Marchant received Mr. Vansittart's offer for his eldest daughter politely, but with no excess of cordiality. He had set his hope upon a richer marriage, had encouraged Sefton's visit to the Homestead, with the idea that he would eventually propose to Eve. He might not mean matrimony in the first instance, perhaps, though he obviously admired the young lady, but he would be led on and caught before he was aware. Colonel Marchant had implicit faith in his daughter's power to ward off any evil purpose of her admirer; and although he knew Sefton's character well enough to know that he would not willingly marry a penniless girl, he trusted to the power of Eve's beauty and personal charm to bring him to the right frame of mind.

He was too shrewd a campaigner, however, to refuse the humble sparrow in the hand for the goldfinch in the bush. Sefton had been dangling about the family for nearly two years, and had scrupulously abstained from any serious declaration; and here was a young man of good birth and breeding, with a very fair estate, who between January and April had made up his mind in the manliest fashion, and was willing to take Eve for his wife without a sixpence, and to settle three hundred a year upon her for pin-money. Vansittart had offered himself in a frank and business-like manner, had declared the amount of his income, and his anxiety to marry as soon as possible.

"We have nothing in this world to wait for," he said.

"Except a young lady's caprice," answered the Colonel. "Eve will be too happy in the pleasures of courtship to be anxious for the final step. And then there will be her trousseau to prepare. That will take time."

"My mother can help her in all those details," said Vansittart, thinking that in all probability his mother would have to pay for as well as to choose the wedding finery. "We can take all that trouble off your hands, Colonel Marchant."

He wrote to his mother on Sunday night, when his sister's household and guests were hushed in their first sleep; wrote at fullest length, dwelling fondly upon the graces and perfections of her whom he had chosen.

"She will love you dearly, if you will let her," he wrote; "she will be to you as a second daughter—nearer to you, perhaps, than Maud can now be; for, if you will have it so, our lives may be spent mostly together, in a triple bond of love. I know not what your inclination may be, but for my own part I see no reason why we should not live as one household. Merewood is large enough for a much larger family than ours could be for years to come. Eve has been so long motherless that she would the more gladly welcome motherly love and solicitude. Think of it all, mother, and act in all things as may be most congenial to yourself. I would ask no sacrifices, but I do ask you to love my wife."

This letter written, he could lay himself down to rest with an unburdened spirit, could fearlessly enter dreamland, knowing that his love would be with him in the land of shadows.

Strange, cruel irony, that the scene of his dreams should be Venice, where he and Eve were wandering confusedly, now on land, now on sea, greatly troubled by petty disturbances, and continually losing each other in labyrinthine streets and on slippery sea-washed stairs. Stranger still that Venice should be unlike Venice, and indeed unlike any place he had ever seen in his life.

The dream was but a natural sequence of Eve's talk about Italy. It had hurt him that one of her first utterances after their betrothal should express her desire to visit a land whose frontier he would never willingly cross again. He had loved Italy with all his heart; but now the image of Venice burnt and festered in his mind like a plague-spot on the breast of a man in full health. All except that one accursed memory was peace.

CHAPTER XIII.

"THE TIME OF LOVERS IS BRIEF"

When a man is sole master of his estate and thoroughly independent of his kindred, his choice of a wife, if not altogether outrageous and unpardonable, must needs be accepted by his belongings. Vansittart lost not an hour in telling his sister and her husband that henceforth they must look upon Eve Marchant as a very close connection.

"We shall be married at midsummer," he said, "so you may as well begin to think of her as a sister-in-law."

Sir Hubert, who was the essence of good nature, received the announcement with unalloyed cordiality.

"She is a bright, frank girl, very pretty, very winning, and very intelligent," he said. "I congratulate you, Jack—though naturally one would have wished——"

"That she were the daughter of a duke, or that she had half a million of money," interjected Vansittart. "I understand you. It is a bad match from a worldly point of view. I, who have between three and four thousand a year, should have stood out for other three or four thousand with a wife, and thus solidified my income. I ought at least to have tried America; seen if the heiress market there would have supplied the proper article. Well, you see, Hubert, I am of too impatient a temper for that kind of thing. I have found the woman I can love with all my heart and mind, and I have lost no time in winning her."

"You are a paladin, Jack—a troubadour—all that there is of the most romantic and chivalrous," laughed Sir Hubert.

"She is a dear, dear girl," sighed Maud, "and I could hardly be fonder of her if she were my sister—but it certainly is the most disappointing choice you could have made."

"Is it? Why, I might have chosen a barmaid."

"Not you. You are not that kind of man. But except a bar-

154

maid—or"—with the tips of her lips—"a chorus girl, you could scarcely have done worse than this. Now, don't rage and fume, Jack. I tell you I think the girl herself adorable—but four sisters and an impossible father! *Quelle corvée!*"

"It is a *corvée* that need never trouble you," cried Vansittart, indignantly.

"You are extremely ungrateful. Haven't I been forming her for you?"

"She needed no forming. She has never been less than a lady—simple and straightforward—never affecting to be rich when she was poor—or to be smarter than her surroundings warranted."

"Yes, yes, she is perfect, that is understood. She is the betrothed of yesterday, a stage of being which touches the seraphic. But what will you do with her father, and what will you do with her sisters?"

"Her sisters are very good girls, and I hope to treat them in a not unbrotherly fashion. As for her father—there, though the obligation is small, I grant the difficulty may be great. However, I shall know how to cope with it. No miner ever thought to get gold without some intermixture of quartz. The Colonel shall be to me as the gold-digger's quartz. I shall get rid of him as speedily as I can."

* * * *

Through all that Easter week Vansittart lived in the blissful dream which beginneth every man's betrothal. At such a time as this the dumpiest damsel of the milkmaid type is as fair as she who brought slaughter and burning upon Troy; but for Vansittart's abject condition there was the excuse of undeniable beauty, and a charm of manner which even village gossip had never disputed. The young ladies who condemned the Miss Marchants en bloc as "bad style" had been fain to confess that Eve had winning ways, which made one almost forgive her cheap boots and mended gloves.

Vansittart was happy. He had promised to join his mother in Charles Street on the Wednesday after Easter; but he wrote to her apologetically on Tuesday, deferring his arrival till the beginning of the following week—and the beginning of a week is a term so lax that it is sometimes made to mean Wednesday.

He was utterly happy. His mother's letter received on Tuesday morning was grave and kindly, and in no way damped his ardour.

"You have been so good a son to me, my dear Jack, that I should be hard and ungrateful if I murmured at your choice, although that choice has serious drawbacks in surrounding circumstances. You are too honest and frank and true yourself not to be able to distinguish the difference between realities and semblances. I do not doubt, therefore, that your pretty Eve is all you think her. She certainly is a graceful and gracious creature, with a delicate prettiness of the wild rose type, which I prefer greatly to the azalea or the camellia order of beauty. She cannot fail to love you—nor can she fail to be deeply grateful to you for having rescued her from shabby surroundings and a neglectful father. God grant that this step which you have taken—the most solemn act in a man's life—may bring you the happiness which the marriage of true minds must always bring."

There was much more, the outpouring of a mother's love, which ran away with the mother's pen, and covered three sheets of paper; but even this long letter did not suffice without a postscript.

"P.S.—Miss Marchant spoke to me—incidentally—of a brother, and from her evident embarrassment I fear that the brother is as undesirable a connection as the father. It would be well that you should know all that is to be known about him before he becomes your brother-in-law; so as to avoid unpleasant surprises in the future."

Happily the idea of this brother's existence was already familiar. In their first ramble together as engaged lovers Eve had told Vansittart a great deal about her brother. She dwelt with the younger sister's fond admiration upon his youthful gifts, which seemed to be chiefly of the athletic order; his riding, his shooting, his rowing, his running: in all which exercises he appeared to have excelled. At Cambridge his chief sins, as Eve knew them, had been tandem driving, riding in steeplechases, with frequent absences at Newmarket. Whatever darker sins had distinguished his college career were but dimly suspected by Eve.

"My father was very proud of him while he was a boy," Eve told her lover, "but when he grew up, and began to spend money, they were always quarrelling. Poor mother! It was so sad to see her between them—loving them both, and trying to be loyal to both; her poor heart torn asunder in the struggle."

"And he was fond of you, this brother of yours?" questioned Vansittart, to whom such fondness seemed a redeeming virtue.

"Yes, he was very fond of me; he was always good to me. When there was unhappiness in the dining-room and drawing-room—when Harold was what father called sulky—he used to come to the schoolroom, and sit over the fire roasting chestnuts all the evening. He would go without his dinner rather than sit down with father, and would have some supper brought to the schoolroom at ten o'clock, and my good old governess and I used to share his supper and wait upon him. What merry suppers they were! I was too thoughtless to consider that his being with us meant bad blood between him and father, and unhappiness for my poor mother. She used to look in at the schoolroom door sometimes, and shake her head, and call us naughty children; but I know it was a relief to her to see him eating and drinking and laughing and talking with dear little Mütterchen and me. But I am tiring you with these childish reminiscences."

"No, love; there is no detail in your past life so trifling that I would not care to know it. I want to feel as if I had known you from your cradle. We will go to see the old place near Beverley some day, if you like, and you shall show me the gardens where you played, the rooms in which you lived. One can always get into another man's house by a little management."

* * * *

That Easter week was a time of loveliest weather. Even the sun and the winds were gracious to these happy lovers, and for them April put on the bloom of May. Vansittart spent almost all his days at the Homestead, or rambling with the sisters, Eve and he walking side by side, engrossed in each other's company, as if the world held no one else—the sisters ahead of them or in the rear, as caprice dictated.

Every lane and thicket and hillside between Fernhurst and Blackdown was explored in those happy wanderings; every pathway in Verdley Copse was trodden by those light footsteps; and Henley Hill and its old Roman village grew as familiar to Vansittart as Pall Mall and the clubs. They revelled in the primroses which carpeted all those woodland ways; they found the earliest bluebells, and many a hollow whitened with the fairy cups of the wood-anemone.

One morning, as they were walking over the soft brown carpet of fir needles and withered oak leaves in Verdley Copse, Vansittart opened a little dark-blue velvet box, and showed Eve a ring—a half-hoop of sapphires set with brilliants.

"I chose the colour in memory of the blue flower of happiness that you and I found on the hilltop," he said, as he put the ring on the third finger of his sweetheart's slender hand. "If ever you are inclined to be angry with me, or to care for me a little less than you do now, let the memory of the mystical blue flower plead for me, Eve, and the thought of how dearly we loved each other that Easter Sunday years and years ago."

She gave a faint, shuddering sigh at the image those words evoked.

"Years and years ago! Will this day when we are young and happy ever be years and years ago? It seems so strange!"

"Age is strange and death is stranger; but they must come, Eve. All we have to hope for is that we may go on loving each other to the end."

After those ramblings in the coppices and over the hill, there was afternoon tea at the Homestead—a feast for the gods. Colonel Marchant, well content with the progress of affairs, had gone to Brighton for the volunteer review, and was not expected home again till the end of the week; so the sisters were sovereign rulers of the house, and afternoon tea was the order of the day. It is doubtful whether dinner had any part in the scheme of their existence at this time. The short-petticoated youngsters generally carried some hunks of currant cake in a basket, and these hunks were occasionally shared with the elder sisters, and even with Vansittart, who went without his luncheon day after day, scarcely knowing that he had missed a meal. Then they all tramped home in their muddy boots—for however blue the sky and however dry the roads there was always plenty of mud in the copses—and then they all sat round the big loo table to what Hetty called a stodgy tea. Stodgy being interpreted meant a meal of cake and toast, and eggs, and bread and jam, and a succession of teapots. Vansittart only left the Homestead in time to hurry back to Redwold and dress for dinner.

On the Thursday evening the Miss Marchants who were "out" were all bidden to dinner at Redwold, and were to be driven thither by that very fly which had broken down on the crest of the snowy hill. It was a grand occasion, for an invitation to dinner rarely found its way to the Homestead. Cards for garden-parties were the highest form of courtesy to which the Miss Marchants had hitherto been accustomed. And this dinner was to be a solemn affair, for Eve was to appear at it in all the importance of her position as Vansittart's future wife. Mrs. Vansittart was coming from London for a night or two in order to be present at the festivity, which would be in a manner Eve's formal acceptance as a member of the family.

It was only on Thursday morning that Vansittart discovered with some vexation that Sefton had been asked to this family dinner. Sir Hubert had met him, and had invited him in a casual way, having not the faintest idea that his society would be displeasing either to Eve or her lover. The first person Eve's eyes lighted on when she and her sisters entered the drawing-room was Mr. Sefton. He was standing near the door, and she had to pass him on her way to her hostess. He stood waiting until Lady Hartley turned to greet the younger sisters, and then at once took possession of Eve.

"As an old friend I venture to congratulate you most warmly," he said, holding her hand, after the inevitable shake-hands of old acquaintances. "You have done wonderfully well for yourself. It is really a brilliant match."

"For me, you mean," she said, looking at him with an angry light in her eyes. "Why don't you finish your sentence, Mr. Sefton, and say, 'for you, Miss Marchant, with your disadvantages'?"

"I am sorry I have offended you."

"I don't like to be told I have done well for myself. God has given me the love of a good man. If he were not Mr. Vansittart, but Mr. Smith with only a hundred a year, I should be just as happy."

Vansittart, that moment approaching, overheard the familiar British patronymic. "What are you saying about Mr. Smith?" he said, remembering how two men, one the slain and the other the slayer, had hidden their identity under that name.

"I was only talking of an imaginary Smith," she answered, her face lighting up as she turned to her lover. "There is no such person."

"Come and look at the azaleas," said Vansittart; "they are worth a visit;" and so, after the lover's fashion, he who had only parted from her at six o'clock took her away to the conservatory at the other end of the room, and absorbed her into a solitude of azaleas and orange trees.

Mr. Sefton in the mean while was talking to Mrs. Vansittart, and not having done over well with his congratulation of the future bride, now occupied himself in congratulating the elder lady upon the advantage of having secured so charming a daughter-in-law.

"I quite agree with you," replied Mrs. Vansittart. "She is very pretty, and altogether charming. The match is not of my making, but I am pleased to see my son happy, and pleased to welcome so fair a daughter. You talk as if you were an old friend of the family. Have you known Colonel Marchant long?"

"Ever since he came to this neighbourhood, nine years ago. He has been good enough to accept any little shooting I have had to offer—and he and I have seen a good deal of each other. I knew his son before I knew him. Harold Marchant and I were at Trinity together."

"Harold Marchant is dead, I conclude?"

"That is more than I or any of his friends can tell you. He is one of that numerous family—the lost tribe of society—the men who have dropped through."

159

"I don't quite follow you."

"My dear Mrs. Vansittart, the less said about Harold Marchant the better. If he is dead the good old saying comes in—*de mortuis*. If he is alive I think the less you, or your son, or your daughter-in-law have to do with him the happier it will be for you."

"Mr. Sefton, it is not fair to talk to me in this way. I am personally interested in Eve's brother. What do you mean?"

"Only what I might mean about a good many young men who have lived within the walls that sheltered Bacon and Newton, Whewell and Macaulay. Harold Marchant's career at Cambridge was a foolish career. Instead of devoting himself to the higher mathematics he gave himself up to hunting, horse-racing, and other amusement of a more dangerous order. He had to leave the University hurriedly—he had to leave the country still more hastily. He has never within my knowledge come back to England. Eve is, or was, passionately attached to him, and to gratify her I have taken a good deal of trouble in trying to find out his present whereabouts and mode of life; but without avail. It is nearly ten years since he left this country. He was then two and twenty years of age. He was last heard of more than five years ago with an exploring party in Mashonaland. He is exactly the kind of young man one would like to hear of in Central Africa, and intending to stay there!"

"Poor Eve; how sad for her!"

"But that is all over now. She has a new love, and will soon forget her brother."

"I do not think she is so shallow as that."

"Not shallow, but intense."

Dinner was announced at this moment, and Sir Hubert came to offer Mrs. Vansittart his arm. He was to have his mother-in-law on his right hand and Eve on his left, and Mr. Sefton was to sit by his hostess on the other side of the table. This ended the conversation about Harold Marchant, and it was not renewed after dinner.

CHAPTER XIV.

AS A SPIRIT FROM DREAM TO DREAM

Lady Hartley, once being reconciled to the inevitable, was full of kindness for her brother's future wife. Eve had seen nothing of London and its gaieties, and as the Hartleys had taken a house in Bruton Street for the season, it seemed only a natural thing to take her up to town with them, and initiate her into some of the pleasures to which her future position would entitle her.

"And when you are married I can present you," she told Eve. "It isn't worth while going through that ordeal till next year. You will have plenty to do between now and midsummer in getting your trousseau ready."

Eve blushed, and was silent for a few minutes, and then, as she was alone with Lady Hartley in the morning-room at Redwold, she took courage, and said—

"I'm afraid my trousseau will be a very small one. I asked my father last night what he could do for me, and he said fifty pounds would be the utmost he could give me. It wouldn't be overmuch if I were going to marry a curate, would it?"

"My dearest Eve, fifty pounds will go a long way, as I shall manage things. Remember I am going to be your sister, a real sister, not a sham one, and while we are buying the trousseau your purse and mine shall be one."

"Oh, I couldn't allow that. I couldn't let myself sponge upon you. I would rather be married in white alpaca."

"My child, you shall not be married in alpaca. And as for sponging upon me, well, if you are so mightily proud you can pay me back every shilling I spend for you, a year or so hence, out of your pin-money."

"My pin-money," repeated Eve. "Father told me how generously Mr. Vansittart had offered to settle an income upon me—upon me who bring him nothing, not even a respectable trousseau."

"Now, Eve, I won't hear a word more about the trousseau, until we are going about shopping together."

"You are too kind, yet I can't help feeling it hard to begin by taxing your generosity. Isn't it the custom for the bride to bring the house linen in her trousseau?"

"Oh, in bourgeois families no doubt, and with young people just setting up in the world; but Merewood is provided with linen. You can't suppose mother and Jack have lived there without tablecloths or dusters. There is nothing for you to think about, Eve, but your own frocks, and we will think about them together. I adore shopping, and all the frivolities of life."

* * * *

Ten days later Eve was in London, a petted guest in one of the prettiest houses in Bruton Street. Lady Hartley had the knack of beautifying any house she lived in, even a furnished house, a tent that was to be shifted at the end of the season. Huge boxes of flowers were sent up from Redwold every other day to decorate those London rooms, and not content with this floral decoration, Maud Hartley was always buying things—china, lamps, baskets, elegant frivolities of all kinds, to make the hired house homelike.

She would apologize to her husband in an airy way for each fresh extravagance. "That pretty china plaque caught my eye at Howell and James's while Eve and I were looking at their silks," she would say.

Sir Hubert complained laughingly that if the Kohinoor were for sale at a London jeweller's it would inevitably catch Maud's eye.

"And her eye once caught she is hypnotized," said Sir Hubert. "She must buy."

Charles Street and Bruton Street are very near. Vansittart could run over, as his sister called it, at any and every hour of the day; and the result of this vicinity was that he lived more in his sister's house than in his mother's. But Mrs. Vansittart was kind, and seemed really pleased with her future daughter-in-law; so when Jack was not in Bruton Street Eve was in Charles Street, at luncheon sometimes, but oftener at afternoon tea, and at cosy little dinners, in the arrangement of which Mrs. Vansittart excelled. She knew a great many people in London, military, clerical, legal, literary, and artistic, and she knew how to blend her society and bring people together who really liked to meet each other.

This world of London in the season was a new world to Eve Marchant; these homes in which the pinch of poverty, the burden of debt, had never been felt, had a new atmosphere. Her spirits, gay even in the midst of household care, rose in these happier circles, and she charmed all who met her by her spontaneous graces of mind and manner, her quickness to perceive, her ready appreciation of wit and sense in others.

For Vansittart that month of May in the great city was a period of consummate happiness. The freshness of Eve's feelings gave a new flavour to the commonest things. Parks and gardens, picture-galleries, concerts and theatres, were all new to her. Only on the rarest occasions had she been gratified by an evening in London and the sight of a famous actor. Her father had always excused himself from taking his daughters to any public amusements on the plea of poverty.

All the Marchant girls had known of London began and ended in the drapers' shops and the after-season sales. To travel to town by an early train, third class, to tramp about all day in mud or dust, as the case might be, snatching a skimped luncheon at some homely pastry-cook's, was the utmost they had known of metropolitan plea-sures; and even days so unluxurious had been holidays for them. To see the shop windows, to have the spending of a little money, ever so little, meant happiness. It was only when they had emptied their purses that the shadow of care descended upon them, and they began to doubt whether they had invested their pittance wisely.

Now Eve moved about like a queen, among people who never had to think of money. She was taken to see everything that was worth seeing; to hear everything that was worth hearing. She saw all the picture-galleries, and learnt to discriminate between all the schools of modern art. She heard Sarasate, and Hollmann, and Menter, and all the great instrumentalists of her epoch. She never heard of cabs or omnibuses, or fares, or money given for tickets. She was carried hither and thither in a luxurious barouche or a snug brougham, and her place at concert and play was always ready for her—one of the best places in the hall or the theatre. The dressmak-ers, and bootmakers, and milliners to whom Lady Hartley took her never talked of money; indeed they seemed almost to shudder at any allusion to that vulgar drudge 'twixt man and man. The people at the tailor's were as interested in the gowns and coats they were to make for her as if they had been works of art for which fame would be the sole recompense. The Frenchwoman who was to make her wedding-gown poohpoohed the question of cost. Expensive, this frisé velvet for the train—yes, that might be, but she would rather make Made-moiselle a present of the fabric than that, with her tall and graceful figure, she should wear anything commonplace or insignificant. Art for art's sake was ostensibly the motto for all Bond Street.

And Eve had so much to think of that she could not think very seriously about her trousseau. She let Lady Hartley order what she pleased. She, Eve, had her lover to think about; and that was an absorbing theme. She knew his footstep on the pavement below the open window; she knew the sound of the bell when he rang it. If the weather were wet, and he came from Charles Street in a hansom, she knew his way of throwing back the cab doors before the wheels stopped. When he was absent, all her life was made up of thinking about him and listening for his coming. In that morning hour in the drawing-room before he arrived she might have sat to Sir Frederick Leighton for "Waiting" or "Expectancy."

* * * *

It was scarcely strange that while John Vansittart was so absorbed in the new delight of his life, John Smith was just a little neglectful of his protégées in Saltero's Mansion, Chelsea. John Smith had, indeed, no consciousness of being neglectful. If the image of Lisa flashed across his mind in any moment of his full and happy day, it came and went together with the comfortable thought that he had done his duty to that young woman. She had her aunt, her bright and pretty home, her singing-master, and all the delightful hopes and ambitions of an artist who has discovered that she has fortune within her reach. Had he thought of Lisa all day long, he could never have pictured her otherwise than happy and contented.

He was at Covent Garden one evening with his sister and his betrothed, and he saw the Venetian amidst her troops of companions. The opera was *William Tell*, and Lisa was in short petticoats and Swiss bodice, with gold chains about her neck and arms, and gold daggers in her hair. She looked very pretty, amidst that heterogeneous crew of young, middle-aged, and elderly. He was in the stalls, and at a considerable distance from the stage, and those dark eyes did not find him out and fasten upon him as they had done that other night when he was in Lady Davenant's box. The sight of her reminded him that it was nearly a month since he had called upon the aunt and niece, and that she ought to have made some progress with her musical training in the interval, progress enough, at any rate, to make the childish creature anxious to report herself to him.

Eve was to be engaged at her dressmaker's on the following afternoon, in a solemn ordeal described as "trying on;" and Vansittart had been warned by his sister that he must not expect to be favoured with her society until the evening, when they were all to dine in Charles Street. It seemed to him that he could hardly employ this afternoon better than in visiting Fiordelisa and her aunt, whose warm southern hearts would be wounded perhaps if he should seem to have lost all interest in their welfare.

The day was delightful—one of those brilliant afternoons in May which give to West End London the air of an earthly paradise; a paradise of smart shops and smart people, thorough-bred horses and newly built carriages, liveries spick and span from the tailor's; flowers everywhere—in the carriages, in the shops, on the kerb-stone—flowers and fine clothes and spring sunshine. Vansittart walked to Chelsea, glad of an excuse for a walk after the habitual carriage or hansom. He had promised to look at some pictures in Tite Street upon this very afternoon—pictures of that advanced Belgian school whose work he would scarcely care to show to Miss Marchant without a previous inspection—so he availed himself of the opportunity, and called at the painter's house on his way to Saltero's Mansion.

He found a room full of people, looking at pictures set round on easels draped with terra-cotta silk, criticizing freely and talking prodigiously. He found himself in the midst of an artistic tea-party. There was a copper kettle singing over a spirit-lamp on a table crowded with Spanish irises, and there was the painter's young English wife, in an orange-coloured Liberty gown, pouring out tea, and smiling at the praises of her husband.

The painter was no phlegmatic Fleming, but a fiery son of French Flanders. He came from the red country between Namur and Liege, and had been reared and educated in the latter city.

He was standing by the largest of his pictures—a scene from "Manon Lescaut"—and listening to the criticisms of a little knot of people, all ecstatic, and among these élite of the art-loving world Vansittart was surprised to see Mr. Sefton.

Sefton turned at the sound of Vansittart's voice. They had met a good many times since Easter, and in a good many houses, for it was one of Sefton's attributes to be seen everywhere; but Vansittart had not expected to find him at a comparatively unknown painter's tea-party.

"Delightful picture, ain't it?" he asked carelessly. "Full of truth and feeling. How is Miss Marchant to-day? I thought she looked a little pale and fagged at Lady Heavyside's last night, as if her first season were taking it out of her."

"I don't think my sister would let her do too much." They had drifted towards the tea-table, and the crowd had stranded them in a corner, where they could talk at their ease. "I did not know you were by way of being an art critic."

"I am by way of being everything. I give myself up to sport—body and bones—all the winter. I let my poor little intellect hibernate from the first of September till I have been at the killing of a May fox; and then I turn my back upon rusticity, put on my frock-coat and cylinder hat, and see as much as I can of the world of art and letters. To that end I have chosen this street for my summer habitation."

"You live here—in Tite Street?"

"Is that so surprising? Tite Street is not a despicable locality. We consider ourselves rather smart."

"I should have looked for you nearer the clubs."

"I am by no means devoted to the clubs. I like my own nest and my own newspapers. Is not this charming?"

He turned to admire a cabinet picture on a draped easel—"Esmeralda and the Captain of the Guard;" one of those pictures which Vansittart would have preferred Eve Marchant not to see, but over which æsthetic maids and matrons were expatiating rapturously.

Vansittart did not stop to take tea, meaning to gratify Lisa by allowing her to entertain him with the mild infusion she called by that name. He spoke to the two or three people he knew, praised the pictures in very good French to the artist, who knew no English, and slipped out of the sultry room, redolent of violets and tea-cake, into the fresh air blowing up the river from the woods and pastures of Bucks and Berks.

He had not walked above half a dozen yards upon the Embankment when he heard the sound of hurrying footsteps behind him, and an ungloved hand was thrust through his arm, and a joyous voice exclaimed breathlessly, "At last! You were going to see me? I thought you had forgotten us altogether."

"That was very wrong of you, Signora," he answered, gently disengaging himself from the olive-complexioned hand, plump and tapering, albeit somewhat broad—such a hand as Titian painted by the score, perhaps, before he began to paint Cardinal Princes and great ladies.

He did not want to walk along the Chelsea Embankment, in the broad glare of day, with the Venetian hanging affectionately upon him. That kind of thing might pass on the Lido, or in the Royal Garden by the canal, but here the local colour was wanting.

"It is ages since you have been near us," protested Fiordelisa, poutingly. "I am sure you must have forgotten us."

"Not I, Signora. Englishmen don't forget their friends so easily.

I have been in the country till—till quite lately. And you—tell me how you have been getting on with your singing-master."

"He shall tell you," cried Fiordelisa, flashing one of her brightest looks upon him. "He pretends to be monstrously pleased with me. He declares that in a few months, perhaps even sooner, he will get me an engagement at one of the small theatres, to sing in a comic opera. They will give me ever so much more money than I am earning at Coveny Gardeny."

The Venetian often put a superfluous vowel at the end of a word, not yet having mastered our severe terminal consonants. "The maestro is to have some of the money for his trouble, but that is fair, is it not?"

"Fair that he should take a small percentage, perhaps, but not more."

"A percentage? What is that?"

Vansittart explained.

"But to sing in your English comic opera I must speak English ever so much better than I do now," pursued Lisa, "and for that I am working, oh, so hard. I learn grammar. I read story-books; 'Bootle's Baby;' the 'Vicar of Wakefield.' Oh, how I have laughed and cried over that Vicar and his troubles—and Olivia—Olivia who was so deceived—and so happy at last."

"Happy, with a scoundrel," exclaimed Vansittart.

"Ah, but she loved him. One does not mind how much scoundrel if one loves a man."

"A bad principle, Signorina. It is better to love a good man ever so little than a scoundrel ever so much."

"No, no, no. It is the loving much that means happiness," argued Lisa, and then she expatiated upon her English studies. "La Zia and I go to the theatre when there is no performance at Coveny Gardeny. We sit in the pit, where the people are kind, and make room for us because we are foreigners. Signor Zinco says there is no better way of learning English than in listening to the actors in good plays. Oh, how I listen! In three months from this day people will take me for an Englishwoman," she said finally.

"Never, Lisa, never," he said, laughingly contemplative of the sparkling olive face, the great dark eyes with golden lights in them, the careless arrangement of the coarse black hair, the supple figure in its plain black gown, and the essentially foreign air which years of residence in England would hardly obliterate. "Never, Si'ora! Your every glance is eloquent of Venice and her sister isles. It seems almost a crime to keep you captive in this sunless city of ours."

167

"Oh, but I adore London," she exclaimed, "and your London is not sunless. See how the sun is shining on the river this afternoon; not as it shines on the lagunes in May, I grant you, but it is a very pretty piccolo sole."

"And la Zia," asked Vansittart; "she is well, I hope?"

"She is more than well. She is getting fat. Oh, so fat. She is as happy as the day is long. She loves your London, the King's Road most of all. At night there are barrows, fish, vegetables, everything. She can do her marketing by lamplight, and the streets are almost as full and as gay as the Merceria. La Zia was never so happy in all her life as she is in London. She never had so much to eat."

They were near Saltero's Mansion by this time.

"You will come in and let me make you some tea, won't you?" pleaded Lisa.

"Not this afternoon, Si'ora. I wanted to see you, to know that all was going well with you. Having done that, I must go back to the West End to—to keep an appointment."

He was thinking that possibly Eve's "trying on" would be finished in time for him to snatch half an hour's tête-à-tête in one of the Bruton Street drawing-rooms, before she dressed for dinner. There were three drawing-rooms, in a diminishing perspective, dwindling almost to a point, the third and inner room too small to serve any purpose but flirtation, and here the lovers could usually find seclusion.

Lisa pouted and looked unhappy.

"You might stay and take tea with me," she said; "la Zia will be home soon."

"La Zia is out, then?"

"Yes; she has taken Paolo to Battersea Park for the afternoon. The rehearsal for the new opera keeps me all day long, and la Zia takes the boy for his daily walk; but it is past five, and they will be home as soon as I am, I dare say."

"I will come this way again in a week or so, Si'ora."

"You are very unkind," protested Lisa, in her impulsive way; and then, with one of those sudden changes which so well became her childish beauty, she exclaimed, "No, no; forgive me; you are always kind—kind, kindest of men. Promise you will come again soon."

"I promise," he said, stopping short and offering his hand.

"Then I'll walk back just a little piece of way with you—only as far as the big house with the swans."

Lisa's company on Cheyne Walk was an honour which Vansittart would have gladly escaped. She was too pretty and too peculiar-looking not to attract notice; and there was the tea-party in Tite Street, with its little crowd of worldlings, any of whom would be curious as to his companion, should he by chance be seen in this society. He did not want to be rude, for the lace-girl from Burano was a creature of strong feelings, and was easily wounded.

"I am in a desperate hurry, Si'ora."

"You were not in a hurry when I overtook you just now. You were walking slowly. You cannot walk faster than I. At Burano I never used to walk. I always ran."

"Poverina! How quickly you must have used up your island."

"Yes; it was like a prison. I used to watch the painted sails of the fishing-boats, and long for them to carry me away to any place different from that island, where I knew every face and every paving-stone. That is why I love your London, in spite of fogs and grey skies. It is so big, so big."

She stopped, with clasped hands and flashing eyes. A street boy wheeled round to look at her, and gave a low whistle of admiring surprise; and at the same instant Sefton turned a street corner, came across the road, and passed close to Vansittart and his companion.

Of all men living, this man was the last whom Vansittart would have cared to meet under such conditions.

CHAPTER XV.

"LOVE SHOULD BE ABSOLUTE LOVE"

Sefton lifted his hat and passed quickly. Vansittart stood mutely watching his retreating figure, till it was lost among other figures moving to and fro along the Embankment. An empty hansom came creeping by the curb while he stood watching.

"Here is a cab which will just do for me, Signorina," he said. "Good-bye. I'll see you on one of your maestro's days, so that I may hear his opinion of your chances."

"He comes on Tuesdays and Saturdays, from three to four. Who is that gentleman who bowed to you? A friend?"

"No; only an acquaintance. Good-bye."

"How vexed you look! Are you ashamed of being seen with me?"

"No, child, no; only that man happens to be one of my particular aversions. A rivederci. Stay! I will take you to your door. The cab can follow."

It had occurred to him in a moment that Sefton was capable of turning and pursuing Lisa if he left her unprotected. He was just the kind of man, Vansittart thought, who, out of sheer devilry, would try to discover the name and antecedents of this lovely stranger. He had a deep-rooted distrust of Wilfred Sefton, which led him to anticipate evil.

He walked with Lisa to Saltero's Mansion, and saw her vanish under the lofty Queen Anne portico, and then he turned and walked slowly back as far as Tite Street, with the cab following him. So far there was no sign of Sefton, who might, therefore, be supposed to have continued his way Londonwards; but the rencontre had been a shock to Vansittart's nerves, and had set him thinking seriously upon the danger of his relations with Fiordelisa and her aunt, and more especially of the peril which must always attach to the use of an alias.

Was it well, or wise, or safe that he, Eve Marchant's promised husband, should be the guardian angel of this wild, impulsive peasant girl—a guardian angel under the borrowed name of Smith, liable at any hour to be confronted with people who knew his real name and surroundings? He considered his position very seriously during the drive to Bruton Street, and he resolved to do all in his power to narrow his relations with the Venetians, while fulfilling every promise and every obligation to the uttermost.

* * * *

Colonel Marchant was at the family dinner in Charles Street. It had been agreed between Mrs. Vansittart and her son that he should be invited to this one gathering, so that he should not have any ground for considering himself left out in the cold, albeit his future son-in-law's intention was to hold as little communion with him as possible. Eve's neglected girlhood had not fostered filial affection. The parental name had been a name of fear in the Marchant household, and the sisters had been happiest when their father was amusing himself in London, careless of whether the angry baker had stopped the daily supply, or the long-suffering butcher had refused to deliver another joint. Such a man had but little claim upon a daughter's love, and Eve had confessed to Vansittart that her father was not beloved by his children, and that it would not grieve her if in her future life she and that father met but rarely.

"You are going to be so generous to me," she said, "that I shall be able to help my sisters—in ever so many ways—with their clothes, and with their housekeeping; for I can never spend a third part of the income you are settling upon me."

"My frugal Eve! Why, there are women with half your charms who would not be able to dress themselves upon such a pittance."

"I have no patience with such women. They should be condemned to three gowns a year of their own making, as my sisters and I have been ever since we were old enough to handle needles and scissors. I am horrified at the extravagance I have seen at the dressmaker's—the reckless way some of your sister's friends spend money."

"And my sister herself, no doubt. She has a rich husband, and I dare say is one of the worst offenders in this line?"

"Not she! Lady Hartley dresses exquisitely, but she is not extravagant like the others. She is too generous to other people to be lavish upon herself. She is always thinking of doing a kindness to somebody."

"Poor little Maud! I remember when she was in the schoolroom all her pocket-money used to be spent upon dolls for the hospital children. She used to come and beg of me when she was insolvent."

* * * *

Vansittart met Wilfred Sefton at an evening party within a few days of that rencontre at Chelsea; and at the same party Vansittart was disturbed by seeing Sefton and his mother in close confabulation in one of those remote and luxurious corners where people are not obliged to listen to the music that is being performed in the principal room.

He questioned his mother about Sefton at breakfast next morning. "You and he seemed uncommonly thick," he said. "What were you talking about?"

"About you, and your approaching marriage."

"I am sure you said nothing that was not kind, but I wish to Heaven you would not discuss my affairs with a stranger," said Vansittart, with some warmth.

"Mr. Sefton is not a stranger. Your father and his father were very good friends. He is your sister's most influential neighbour, and they are on the friendliest terms. Why should you call him a stranger?"

"Because I don't like him, mother; and because I wish never to feel myself on any other footing with him."

"And yet he likes you."

"Does he? I am a very bad judge of humanity if my dislike of Sefton is not heartily reciprocated by Sefton's dislike of me. And no doubt the more he dislikes me the more he will assure other people—my kindred especially—that he likes me. You are too straight yourself, mother, in every thought and purpose, to understand the Seftonian mind. It is the kind of intellect which always works crookedly. He admired Eve Marchant, allowed his admiration to be patent to everybody, and yet was not man enough to try to win her for his wife."

"He had not your courage, Jack, in facing unpleasant surroundings and disagreeable antecedents."

"He had not manhood enough to marry for love. That is what you mean, mother. He was quite willing to compromise an innocent and pure-minded girl, by attentions which he would not have dared to offer to a girl with a watchful father or mother."

"My dear Jack, you exaggerate Mr. Sefton's attentions. He assured me that his chief interest in Eve arose from his old compan-

172

ionship with her brother, with whom he was on very intimate terms until the unhappy young man turned out an irretrievable scamp."

Vansittart winced at the phrase. It is not an agreeable thing for a man to be told that his future brother-in-law, the brother whom his future wife adores, is irretrievable.

"Mr. Sefton has taken a great deal of trouble to trace Harold Marchant's career since he was last heard of," continued Mrs. Vansittart, "and would hold out a friendly hand to him if there were anything to be done."

"He has no need to hold out a friendly hand. If there is anything to be done for my brother-in-law I can do it."

"How ready you are to take new burdens!"

"I think nothing a burden which comes to me with the woman I love."

Mrs. Vansittart sighed, and was silent. The idea of these disreputable connections which her son was to take to himself in marrying Eve was full of pain for the well-born matron, whose people on every side were of unblemished respectability. Never had there been any doubtful characters in her father's family, or among that branch of the Vansittarts to which her husband belonged. She had been born in just that upper middle class which feels disgrace most keenly. There is no section of society so self-conscious as your county gentry, so fixed in the idea that the eyes of Europe are upon them. The duke or the millionaire can live down anything—sons convicted of felony, daughters divorced—but the country gentleman who has lived all his life in one place, and knows every face within a radius of twenty miles from the family seat, to him, or still more to his wife or widow, the slightest smirch upon a relative's character means agony.

Mrs. Vansittart liked and admired Eve Marchant; but she did not let her heart go out to her as it ought to have gone to the girl who was so soon to be to her as a daughter. Colonel Marchant's existence was a rock of offence which even maternal love could not surmount. She had talked to her family lawyer, an old and trusted ally, and from him she had heard all that was to be said for and against Eve's father. He was not quite so black, perhaps, as his neighbours in the country had painted him; but his career had been altogether disreputable, and his present associations were among the most disreputable men, calling themselves gentlemen, about town. He was a familiar figure in the card-room at clubs where play was high, and was looked upon with unmitigated terror by the parents and guardians of young men of fortune or expectations. A youth who affected Colonel Marchant's society was known to be in a bad way.

And now the question was not only of Colonel Marchant, but of his son, who was even a darker character than the father, and whose darkness might at any time overshadow his sister's name. It was easy enough to say that the sister was blameless, that it was no fault of hers that her father was a Bohemian, and her brother a swindler and a forger. Society does not easily forgive sisters or daughters for such relationships, and now that the pseudo-scientific craze of heredity has taken hold of the English mind, society is less inclined even than of yore to ignore the black sheep in the fold. Every one who heard of Eve Marchant's antecedents would anticipate evil for her husband. The bad strain would show itself somehow before long. The duskiness in the parental wool would crop up in the fleece of the lamb.

It was hard for the mother who doated on her only son to feel ashamed of his wife's relations and up-bringing; and Mrs. Vansittart feared that to the end of her life she must needs feel this shame. Already her neighbours at Merewood had tortured her by their keen interest in her son's betrothed, their eagerness to know every detail, their searching questions about her people, all veiled under that affectionate friendliness which excuses the most tormenting curiosity.

Mrs. Vansittart was a good woman and a devoted mother, but she had the temperament which easily yields to worrying ideas, to apprehensions of potential evils, and her love of her son had just that alloy of jealousy which is apt to cause trouble. While Vansittart was going about with his betrothed from one scene of amusement to another, utterly happy in her company, enchanted to show her places and people which were as new to her as if they had been in fairyland, his mother was brooding over her fears and fostering her forebodings, and affording Wilfred Sefton every opportunity of improving his acquaintance with her. It was a shock to Vansittart to find that Sefton had established himself on the most familiar footing in Charles Street, a privileged dropper-in, who might call six days out of the seven if he chose, since Mrs. Vansittart had no allotted day for receiving, but was always at home to her friends between four and five during the summer season, when the pleasantest hour for driving was after five.

Sefton was clever, lived entirely in society and for society, during the brief London season, frequented the studios of artists and the tea-parties of litterateurs, knew, or pretended to know, everything that was going to happen in the world of art and letters, and would have been welcome on his own merits in the circles of the frivolous. He contrived to amuse Mrs. Vansittart, and to impress her with an

174

exaggerated idea of his talent and versatility.

"He can talk well upon every subject," she told her son.

"My dear mother, you mean that he is an adept in the season's jargon, and can talk of those subjects which came into fashion last month; like the new cut of our coat collars, and the new colour of our neckties. A man of that kind always impresses people with his cleverness in May and the first half of June. Talk with him later, and you'll find him flat, stale, and unprofitable. By July he will have emptied his bag."

* * * *

It was scarcely a surprise to Vansittart, knowing his mother's liking for Mr. Sefton, to find that gentleman seated in her drawing-room one Saturday evening when he returned rather late from a polo match at Hurlingham. It was to be Eve's last Saturday in London. June was at hand, and she was to go back to Fernhurst on the first of the month, to spend the small remnant of her single life with her sisters. She was to be married on St. John's Day.

They had lingered at the tea-table on the lawn, sighing sentimentally over the idea that this was positively the last Saturday: that not again for nearly a year could they sit together drinking tea out of the homely little brown teapot, and watching the careless crowd come and go in the sunshine and the summery air.

In Charles Street, the cups and saucers had not been cleared away, although it was past seven. A side window in the front drawing-room looked westward, up the old-fashioned street, towards the Park, and the low sunlight was pouring in through the Madras-muslin curtain, shining on the jardinière of golden lilies and over the glittering toys on the silver table.

Vansittart opened the drawing-room door, but changed his mind about going in when he saw Sefton established on the sofa, half hidden in a sea of pillows.

"I'm very late," he said. "How do you do, Sefton?" with a curt nod. "I'm to dine in Bruton Street, mother. Good night, if I don't see you again."

"Pray come in, Jack. I have something very serious to tell you—or at least Mr. Sefton has. He has been waiting for you ever since five o'clock. I wanted him to tell you at once. It is too serious for delay."

"If I hadn't left Miss Marchant and my sister five minutes ago I should think, by your solemnity, that one of them had been killed," exclaimed Vansittart, scornfully, crossing the room with leisurely step, and seating himself with his back to the yellow brightness of that western window. "And now, my dear mother, may I inquire the nature of the mountain which you and Mr. Sefton have conjured out of some innocent molehill? Please don't be very slow and solemn, as I have only half an hour to dress and get to Bruton Street. Boïto's *Mephistopheles* will begin at half-past eight."

"This is no trivial matter, Jack. Perhaps when you have heard what Mr. Sefton has to tell you may hardly care about the opera—or about seeing Miss Marchant, before you have had time for serious thought."

"There is nothing that Mr. Sefton—or the four Evangelists—could tell me that would alter my feelings about Miss Marchant by one jot or one tittle," cried Vansittart, furiously, his angry feeling about this man leaping out of him like a sudden flame.

"Wait," said the mother, gravely—"wait till you have heard."

"Begin, Mr. Sefton. My mother's preamble is eminently calculated to give importance to your communication."

"I am hardly surprised that you should take the matter somewhat angrily, Vansittart," said Sefton, in his smooth, persuasive voice. "I dare say I shall appear an officious beast in this business—and, had it not been for Mrs. Vansittart's express desire, I should not be here to tell you the facts which have come to my knowledge within the last two days. I considered it my duty to tell your mother, because in our previous conversations she has been good enough to allude to old ties of friendship between your father and my father—and this made a claim upon me."

"Proem the second," cried Vansittart, impatiently. "When are we coming to facts?"

"The facts are so uncommonly disagreeable that I may be pardoned for approaching them diffidently. You know, I believe, that Miss Marchant has a brother——"

"Who disappeared some years ago, and about whose fate you have busied yourself," interrupted Vansittart, with ever-growing impatience.

"All my efforts to trace Harold Marchant's movements after his departure from Mashonaland resulted in failure, until the day before yesterday, when one of the two men whom I employed to make inquiries turned up at my house in Tite Street as suddenly as if he had dropped from the moon. This man is a courier and jack-of-all-trades, as clever and handy a dog as ever lived, a man who has travelled in all the quarters of the globe, a Venetian. When I began the search for Miss Marchant's brother, I put the business in the first place into the hands of a highly respectable private detective; but as a second string to my bow it occurred to me to send a full statement of the circumstances, and a careful description of the missing man, to my old acquaintance, Ferrari, the courier, who travelled with my poor father on the sea-board of Italy for several months, and who helped to nurse him on his sick-bed."

Vansittart bridled his tongue, but could not keep himself from drumming with his fingers on the dainty silver table and setting all the toy harpsichords, and sofas, and bird-cages, and watering-pots, and tiny tables rattling.

"I had half forgotten that I had employed this man in Harold Marchant's business when the fellow turned up in Tite Street, irrepressibly cheerful, with the most unpleasant information."

"What information? For God's sake, come to the point!"

"He had traced Marchant's career—from Mashonaland to the diamond fields, where he picked up a good bit of money; from the diamond fields to New York, from New York to Venice. For God's sake, leave those bibelots alone," as the silver toys leapt and rattled on the fragile table. "Do you think no one has nerves except yourself?"

"Your man traced Marchant to Venice," said Vansittart, the restless hand suddenly motionless; "and what of him at Venice?"

"At Venice Marchant lived with a girl whom he had taken out of a factory. Pardon me, Mrs. Vansittart, for repeating these unpleasant facts—lived, gambled, drank, and enjoyed life after his own inclination, which always leaned to low company even when he was an undergraduate. From Venice he vanished suddenly, more than three years ago."

Vansittart fancied they must needs hear that heavily beating heart of his thumping against his ribs. He fancied that, even in that dimly lighted room, they must needs see the ashen hue of his face, the beads of sweat upon his forehead. All he could do was to hold his tongue, and wait for that which was to come.

"Do you happen to remember a murder, or, I will rather say, a scuffle ending in homicide, which occurred at Venice three years ago in Carnival time—an English tourist stabbed to death by another Englishman, who got away so cleverly that he was never brought to book for what he had done? The row was about a woman, and the woman was Harold Marchant's mistress. Marchant was jealous of the stranger's attentions to the lady—he had lived long enough in Italy to have learnt the use of the knife—and after a free fight of a few moments he stabbed his man to the heart. Ferrari heard the story from a Venetian, who was present in the Caffè Florian when the thing happened."

"Did the Venetian know Marchant?"

The words came slowly from dry lips, the voice was husky; but neither Mrs. Vansittart nor Mr. Sefton wondered that Eve Marchant's lover should be deeply moved.

"I don't know; but there were people in Venice who knew him, and from whom Ferrari heard his mode of life."

"But you said that Marchant was living under an assumed name."

"Did I?" asked Sefton, surprised. "I don't remember saying it, but it is the fact all the same. At Venice Harold Marchant called himself Smith; and Smith was the name he gave on board the P. and O. steamer which took him to Alexandria."

"Why did he go to Alexandria?"

"Why? To get away from Venice in the quickest and completest manner he could. When he saw that the knife had been fatal, he grasped the situation in an instant, made a dash for the door, ran through the crowd along the Piazzetta, jumped into the water, and swam to the steamer, which was getting up steam for departure. No one guessed that he would make for the steamer. It was a longish swim; and while his pursuers were groping about among the gondolas the steamer was moving off with Harold on board her. Just like him—always quick at expedients; ready at every point where his own interests were at stake; tricky, shifty, dishonest to the core; but a devil for pluck, and as strong as a young lion."

"I begin to remember the story, now you recall the details," said Vansittart, who had by this time mastered every sign of agitation, and was firm as iron. "But in all that you have said I see nothing to fix Harold Marchant as the homicide. He might as easily have been the man who was killed."

"No, no; the man who was killed was a stranger—a Cook's tourist, a nobody, about whose fate there were no inquiries. It was Marchant who was the Venetian girl's protector. It was Marchant who was jealous. The whole story is in perfect accord with Marchant's character. I have seen his temper in a row—seen him when, if he had had a knife handy, by Heaven! he would have used it."

"But where is the link between Marchant—Marchant at the diamond fields, Marchant at New York—and the man at Venice calling himself Smith? You don't even pretend to show me that."

"Ferrari shall show you that. The story is a long one, but there is no solution of continuity. Ferrari shall take you over the ground, step by step, till he brings you from Marchant in Mashonaland to Marchant landing at Alexandria."

"And after the landing at Alexandria? What then? The thing happened more than three years ago, you say. Did the earth open and swallow Harold Marchant after he landed at Alexandria? Or, if not, what has he been doing since? Why has not your Ferrari—this courier-guide who is so clever at tracing people—traced him a little further? Why should the last link of the chain be the landing at Alexandria?"

"Because, as I have been telling you, Harold Marchant is an uncommonly clever fellow; and having got off with a whole skin—escaping the penalty of a crime which at the least was manslaughter—he would take very good care to sink his identity ever afterwards, and in all probability would bid a long farewell to the old world."

"But your genius—your heaven-born detective—would track him down in the new world. My dear Sefton, the whole story is a farrago of nonsense; and I wonder that you, as a man of the world, can be taken in by so vulgar a trickster as your incomparable Ferrari."

"He is not a trickster. I have the strongest reasons, from past experience, for believing in his honesty. Will you see him, Vansittart? Will you hear his story, calmly and dispassionately?"

"I will not see him. I will not hear his story. I will see no man who trumps up a sensational charge against my future wife's brother. I can quite understand that you believe in this man—that you have brought this absurd story to my mother and me in all good faith."

"Why absurd? You admit that there was such a catastrophe—an English traveller killed by an English resident in a Venetian caffè in Carnival time."

"Yes; but plain fact degenerates into nonsense when your courier tries to fasten the crime upon Eve Marchant's brother."

"Hear his statement before you pronounce judgment. He had his facts from people who knew this young man in New York as Harold Marchant, who met him afterwards in Venice, and visited him at his Venetian lodgings, and played cards with him, when he was calling himself Smith—respectable American citizens, whose names and addresses are set down in Ferrari's note-book. I am not utterly wanting in logic, Mr. Vansittart, and if the circumstantial evidence in this matter had been obviously weak I should never have troubled Mrs.

179

Vansittart or you with the story."

The mother spoke now for the first time since Sefton had begun his revelation. Her voice was low and sympathetic. Her son might doubt her wisdom, but he could not doubt her love.

"I am deeply sorry for you, Jack," she said, "deeply sorry for poor Eve, who is a blameless victim of evil surroundings, but I cannot think that you will obstinately adhere to your engagement in the face of these dreadful facts. It would have been bad enough to be Colonel Marchant's son-in-law; but you cannot seriously mean to marry a girl whose brother has committed murder."

"It was not murder," cried Vansittart, furiously. "Even Mr. Sefton acknowledges that the crime at worst was manslaughter—a fatal blow, struck in a moment of blind passion."

"With a dagger against an unarmed man," interjected Sefton. "You are inclined to minimize the crime when you call it manslaughter at the worst. I said that at the least—taking the most indulgent view of the case—the crime was manslaughter; and I doubt if an Italian tribunal would have dealt very leniently with that kind of manslaughter. I take it that rapid run and long swim of his saved Harold Marchant some years of captivity in an Italian prison."

"It is too horrible," said Mrs. Vansittart. "My dear, dear son, for God's sake don't underrate the horror of it all because of your love for this poor girl. You cannot marry a girl whose brother is an unconvicted murderer."

How she harped upon the word murder! Vansittart ground his nails into the palms of his clasped hands, as he stood up, frowning darkly, in an agony of indignant feeling. His mother to be so womanish, so illogical, so foolish in her exaggeration of evil.

"I say again, the man who struck that unlucky blow was no murderer. The word is a lying word applied to him," he protested. "The story you have told me—the crime you try to fix upon Harold Marchant—can make no shadow of difference in my love for Harold Marchant's sister. Had she ten brothers, and every one of the ten were a felon, I would marry her. It is she whom I love, mother—not her surroundings. And as for your modern fad of heredity, I believe in it no more than I do in table-turning. God made my Eve—as pure, and single, and primitive a being as that other Eve in His Garden of Eden; and over the morning of her fair life no act of her kindred can cast a shadow."

There was a silence. Sefton had risen when Vansittart rose. He took up his hat, and came through the flickering lights and shadows towards Mrs. Vansittart, who sat with drooping head and clasped hands, betwixt sorrow and anger—sorrow for her son's suffering, anger at his obstinate adherence to the girl he loved. She gave Sefton her hand mechanically, without looking up.

"Good night, Vansittart," said Sefton, as he moved towards the door. "I can only admire your loyalty to Miss Marchant, though I may question your wisdom. She is a very charming person, I grant you; but, after all"—with a little laugh—"she is not the only woman in the world."

"She is the only woman in my world."

"Really?"

The intonation of this one word, the slight shrug of the shoulders, were full of meaning. Vansittart perceived the covert sneer in that parting speech, and saw in it an allusion to that lovely foreigner whom Sefton had seen hanging affectionately upon his arm a few days ago on the Chelsea Embankment.

"One word, Mr. Sefton," said Vansittart, in a peremptory tone. "I take it that your employment of detectives and couriers—that all you have done in this business—has been done out of regard for a college chum, who was once your friend, and from a kindly desire to relieve Miss Marchant's anxiety about a brother whom—whom she appears to have dearly loved. I think, under these circumstances, I need not suggest the wisdom of keeping this unhappy business to yourself—so far as she is concerned."

"You are right. I shall say nothing to Miss Marchant."

"Remember that, clever as your courier may be, he is not infallible. The case is only a case of suspicion. The Smith, of Venice, may be anybody. One missing link in your amateur detective's chain of evidence, and the whole fabrication would drop to pieces. Don't let Miss Marchant be tortured needlessly. Promise me that you will never tell her this story."

"On my honour, I will not."

"I thank you for that promise, and I beg you to forgive any undue vehemence upon my part just now."

"There is nothing to forgive—I can sympathize with your feelings. Good night."

"Good night."

Vansittart dined in Bruton Street, as he had promised, sat by his betrothed, and listened to her happy talk of the things they had seen and the people they had met, sat behind her chair all through Boïto's opera, unhearing, unseeing, his mind for ever and for ever travelling over the same ground, acting over and over again the same scene—the row at Florian's, the scuffle, the fall—his own fall—the knife; and then that fatal fall of his adversary, that one gasping, surprised cry of the unarmed man, slain unawares.

Her brother! His victim, and her brother. The nearest, dearest kin of this girl on whose milk-white shoulder his breath came and went, as he sat with bent head in the shadow of the velvet curtain, and heard the strange harmonies of Pandemonium, almost as if voices and orchestra had been interpreting his own dark thoughts.

Charmed as she was with the music, Eve Marchant was far too sensitive to be unconscious of her lover's altered spirits. Once during the applause that followed that lovely duet at the beginning of the last act, and while Lady Hartley's attention was fixed upon the stage, Eve's hand crept stealthily into the hand of her lover, while she whispered, "What has happened, Jack? I know there is something wrong. Why won't you trust me?"

Trust her? Trust her with a secret that must part them for ever—let her suffer the agony of knowing that this strong right hand which her slim fingers were caressing had stabbed her brother to the heart?

"There can be nothing wrong, dearest, while I have you," he answered, grasping her hand as if he would never let it go.

"But outside me, you have been worried about something. You have quite changed from your gay spirits at Hurlingham."

"My love, I exhausted myself at Hurlingham. You and I were laughing like children. That can't last. But for me there is no outside world. Be sure of that. My world begins and ends where you are."

"My own dear love," she whispered softly.

And so hand in hand they listened to the last act, while Lady Hartley amused herself now with the stage, and now with the audience, and left these plighted lovers alone in their fool's paradise.

Sunday was given up to church and church parade, looking at people and gowns and bonnets in Hyde Park. Vansittart had to be observant and ready, amusing and amused, as he walked beside his sister and his betrothed. He had to say smart things about the people and the bonnets, to give brief biographies of the men whom he saluted, or with whom he spoke. He had to do this, and to be gay and light-hearted in the drive to Richmond, and at the late luncheon in the pretty upstairs room at the Star and Garter, where the balcony hung high over the smiling valley, over the river that meanders in gracious curves through wooded meadows and past the townlet of "Twicks." Happiness is the dominant in the scale of prosperous love. Why or how should he fail to be happy, adored by this sweet girl, who in less than six weeks was to be his, to have and to hold till death?

He played his part admirably, was really happy during some of those frivolous hours, telling himself that the thing which had happened at Venice was a casualty for which Fate would not too cruelly punish him.

"Even Œdipus Rex had a good time of it after he killed his father at the cross roads," he told himself mockingly. "It was not till his daughters were grown up that troubles began. He had a long run of prosperity. And so, Dame Fortune, give me my darling, and let her not know for the next twenty years that this right hand is red with her kindred's blood. Let her not know! And after twenty years of bliss—well, let the volcano explode, and bury me in the ashes. I shall have lived my life."

He parted with Eve in Bruton Street after tea. She was going to an evening service with Lady Hartley. They were to hear a famous preacher, while the mundane Sir Hubert dined at Greenwich with some men. Eve was to leave Waterloo Station early next morning, and as Lady Hartley was sending her maid to see the young lady and her luggage safely lodged at the Homestead, Vansittart was told he would not be wanted.

"This is a free country," he said. "You will find me at the station to say good-bye."

He went home to dine with his mother, a very melancholy dinner. Mrs. Vansittart's pale cheeks bore traces of tears, and she was obviously unhappy, although she struggled to keep up appearances, talked about the weather, the sermon she had heard in the morning, the dinner, anything to make conversation while the servants were in the room.

Vansittart followed her to the drawing-room directly after dinner, and seated himself by her side in the lamplight, and laid his hand on hers as it turned the pages of the book upon her knee.

"Canon Liddon is a delightful writer, mother; logical, clear-headed, and eloquent, and you could hardly have a better book than his Bampton Lectures for Sunday evening; but you might spare a few minutes for your son."

"As many minutes or as many hours as you like, Jack," answered his mother, as she closed the book. "My thoughts are too full of you to give themselves to any book that was ever written. My dear son, what can I say to you? Do you really mean to persist in this miserable alliance?"

"Oh, mother, how cruel you are even in your kindness! How cruel a mother's love can be! It is not a miserable alliance—it is the marriage of true minds. Remember what your Shakespeare says, 'Let me not to the marriage of true minds admit impediments.' Will you, mother, admit impediments here, where practically there is none?"

"Jack, Jack, love has made you blind. Is the existence of that wicked young man no impediment—a man who may at any day be tried for his life as a murderer?"

"Again, mother, I say he was no murderer. The utmost that can be urged against this wicked young man is that he was a hot-tempered athlete who killed a man in a scuffle. Let us forget his existence, if we can. There is nothing in this life more unlikely than that we shall ever hear of him again. From that night in the Venetian caffè he ceased to exist—at any rate for England and his kindred. Be sure, mother, that Harold Marchant will never be heard of again."

"You believe what you wish to believe, Jack, and you forget the French proverb that nothing is so likely to happen as the unexpected."

"No, I don't, mother. That useful adage has been borne in upon me of late. But now, dearest and best, let us be at peace for ever upon this question. I mean to marry my beloved, and I mean you to love her, second only to Maud and me. She is ready to love you with all her heart—with all the stored-up feeling of those motherless years in which she has grown from child to woman, without the help of a mother's love. You are not going to shut your heart against her, are you, mother?"

"No, Jack, not if she is to be your wife. I love you too well to withhold my love from your wife."

"That's my own true mother."

On this mother and son, between whom there had hung a faint cloud of displeasure, kissed, not without tears; and it was agreed that for these two henceforward the name of Harold Marchant should be a dead letter.

CHAPTER XVI.

TO LIVE FORGOTTEN AND LOVE FORLORN

Vansittart had made up his mind. Were that which he accounted but a dark suspicion to be made absolute certainty he meant still to cleave to the girl whom he had chosen for his wife, and who had given him her whole heart. He would marry her, even although his hand had shed her brother's blood, that brother whom of all her kindred she loved best, with the romantic affection which clings round the image of a friend lost in childhood, when the feelings are warmest, and when love asks no questions.

Once, in the little room in Bruton Street, between two stolen kisses, he said to her, "You pretend to be very fond of me, Eve. I wonder whom you love next best?"

"Harold," she answered quickly. "I used to think I should never give any one his place in my heart. But you have stolen the first place. He is only second now, poor dear—dead or living, only second."

The tears welled up in her eyes as she spoke of him. A brother is not often loved so fondly; hardly ever, unless he is a scamp.

And would she marry him, Jack Vansittart, if she knew that he had killed her brother? Alas, no! That dark story would make an impassable gulf between them. Loving him with all her heart, dependent upon him for all the happiness and prosperity of her future life, she would sacrifice herself and him to the manes of that worthless youth, slain by the man his brutality had provoked to responsive violence.

"There was not much to choose between us," Vansittart told himself; "ruffians both. And are two lives to be blighted because of those few moments of fury, in which the brute got the upper hand of the man? No, a thousand times no. I will marry her, and let Fate do the worst to us both. Fate can but part us. Why should I anticipate evil by taking the initiative? A man who has happiness in his hand and lets it go, for any question of conscience, may be a fine moral character, but he is not the less a fool. Life is not long enough for scruples that part faithful lovers."

He looked the situation full in the face. He told himself that it

185

was for Eve's welfare as well as for his own that he should keep from her the knowledge of his wrong-doing. Would she be happier, would mankind be any the better off for his self-abnegation, if he should tell her the truth, and accept his dismissal? Knowing what he knew she could scarcely lay her hand in his and take him for her husband; but once the vow spoken, once his wife, he thought that she might forgive him even her brother's blood.

She must never know! He had blustered and raged in that troubled scene with Sefton; but sober reflection taught him that if he were to be safe in the future he must conciliate the man he hated. A word from Sefton could spoil his happiness; and he could not afford to be ill friends with the man who had power to speak that word; nor could he afford to arouse that man's suspicions by any eccentricity of conduct. He had refused to hear the story of Harold Marchant's life from the courier's lips, as Sefton suggested, had refused with scornful vehemence. But reflection told him that he ought to examine the courier's chain of evidence, and to discover for himself if the links were strong enough to make Harold Marchant's identity with Fiordelisa's lover an absolute certainty. He wanted to know the worst, not to be deluded by the illogical imaginings of an amateur detective. Again, it was natural that a man in his position should look closely into this story, testing its accuracy by the severest scrutiny; and he wanted to act naturally, to act as Sefton would expect him to act.

Influenced by these considerations, he called in Tite Street on Monday afternoon, and found Sefton at home, in a room which occupied the entire first floor of a small house, but which could be made into two rooms by drawing a curtain.

It was the most luxurious room that Vansittart had seen for a long time, but there was a studied sobriety in its luxury which marked the man of sense as well as the sybarite. The colouring was subdued—dull olive—without relief save from a few pieces of old Italian ebony and ivory work, a writing-table, a coffer, a book-case. Every inch of the floor was carpeted with dark-brown velvet pile. No slippery parquetry or sham oak here, no gaudy variety of Oriental prayer-rugs or furry trophies of the chase. Capacious armchairs tempted to idleness; a choice selection of the newest and oldest books invited to study; two large windows looking east and west flooded the room with light; and a fireplace wide enough for a baronial hall promised heat and cheerfulness when frosts and fogs combine to make London odious.

"You like my den," said Sefton, when Vansittart murmured his

186

surprise at finding so good a room in so small a house. "Comfortable, ain't it? The house is small, but I've reduced the number of rooms to three. Below I have only a dining-room; above, only my bedroom. There is a rabbit-hutch at the back of the landing for my valet, and a garret in the roof for the women. Living in a colony of artists, I have taken pains to keep clear of everything artistic. I have neither stained glass nor tapestry, neither Raffaelle ware nor bronze idols; but I can offer my friends a comfortable chair and a decently cooked dinner. I hope you'll put my professions to the test some evening, when I can get one or two of my clever neighbours to meet you."

Vansittart professed himself ready to dine with Mr. Sefton on any occasion, and straightway proceeded to the business of his visit.

"You were good enough to suggest that I should see the courier, Ferrari," he said, "and I was impolite enough to refuse—rather roughly, I fear."

"You were certainly a little rough," answered Sefton, with his suave smile, "but I could make allowances for a man in your position. I honour the warmth of your feelings; and I admire the chivalry which makes you indifferent to the belongings of the woman you love."

"That which you are pleased to call chivalry, I take to be the natural conduct of any man in such circumstances. Honestly, now, Mr. Sefton, would you give up the girl you love if you found her brother had been the—the chief actor in such a scene as that row in the Venetian caffè?"

"Well, I suppose not; if I were tremendously in love. But life would be considerably embittered, to my mind, by the apprehension of such a brother-in-law's reappearance, or by any unlooked-for concatenation which might bring his personality into the foreground."

"I am willing to risk such a concatenation. In the mean time it has occurred to me that I ought to see Ferrari, and look into his story dispassionately. If you will kindly give me his address I will write and ask him to call upon me."

"You will find him a very good fellow—a splendid animal, with a fair intelligence," said Sefton, writing an address. "And now I hope you have forgiven me for bringing an unpleasant train of circumstances under your notice. You must remember that the facts in question came to my knowledge solely from my wish to oblige Miss Marchant. It would not have been fair to you to leave you in ignorance of what so nearly concerned your future wife."

"Certainly not; but it would have been kinder, or wiser, on your part to have kept this knowledge from my mother."

"Mrs. Vansittart had won my warmest regard by her kindness to the son of an old friend. I felt my first duty was to her."

"That was unwise; and your unwisdom has caused much pain. However, I thank you for having spared Miss Marchant the knowledge that would make her miserable. I may rely upon you to keep the secret always—may I not?" asked Vansittart, earnestly.

"Always. You have my promise."

"Thank you. That sets my mind at rest. I know how to deal with my mother's prejudices; and I know that her affection for Eve will overcome those prejudices—in good time."

* * * *

Ferrari called at Charles Street at eleven o'clock next morning, in accordance with Vansittart's request. As the clock struck the hour a tall, good-looking man, with reddish-brown hair, reddish-brown eyes, and a cheerful, self-satisfied smile, was ushered into Vansittart's study.

"You are punctual, Signor Ferrari. Sit down, please, and come to business at once. Mr. Sefton tells me that you are the most business-like of men, as well as the best of fellows."

"Mr. Sefton have know me many years, sir. I have had the honour to nurse the of him father in his last illness. Ten years ago we was at Venice, at the Grand Hotel—Mr. Sefton's father threw himself out of the window in a paroxis of pain—I pick him out of the canal at risk of to drown. The son does not forget what Ferrari did for the father."

Those who knew Ferrari intimately discovered that this rescuing of would-be suicides from the Grand Canal was an idiosyncrasy of his. He affected to have saved half the distinguished travellers of Europe in this manner.

"Now, Signor Ferrari, you have no doubt considered that the charge you have brought against Mr. Harold Marchant is a very serious one——"

"Scusatemi, illustrissimo gentleman, I bring no charge," protested Ferrari, in his curious English, which he spoke with an American accent, having improved his knowledge of the language in the society of American travellers, few of whom condescended to Italian or even French. "I bring no charge. Mr. Sefton tell me, trace for me the movements of a young man called 'Arol Marchant. Find him for me. He was last heard of with a party of explorers in Mashonaland. He good shot. Kill big game. With these bare facts I set to work. I am one who never stop. I am like the devil in Job, always going to and fro over the earth. I know men in all parts; couriers, interpreters, servants of every class, money-changers, shipping agents. From among these I get my information, and here it is tabulated. It is for the illustrissimo to judge for herself, having seen my facts."

He opened a neat little book, where, upon ruled paper, appeared a record of the movements of Harold Marchant from the hour of his appearing at the diamond fields to his return from New York with a party of Americans, in whose company he put up at the Hotel di Roma, Pension Suisse, on the Grand Canal.

When he was at the Hotel di Roma he was known as Marchant. His signature was in the visitors' book at the hotel. Ferrari had seen it, and had recorded the date, which was in the September preceding that February in which Vansittart had shared in the gaieties of the Carnival at Venice. A fortnight later Mr. Marchant took a second floor in the Campo Goldoni, under the name of Smith. There was no doubt in the courier's mind as to the identity of the man in the Campo Goldoni with the man at the Hotel di Roma. He had talked with a New Yorker who had known Marchant under both names, and who knew of his relations with the pretty lace-maker. But there was nothing in Ferrari's statement which could be called proof positive of this identity. The facts rested on information obtained at second hand. It was open to Vansittart to doubt—since error was not impossible—error as complete as that mistake which had put the man who was killed in the place of the man who killed him.

Ferrari tracked the fugitive on his voyage to Alexandria: recorded the name of Smith given to the captain of the P. and O. After Alexandria there was nothing.

"Do you think he came back to Europe by another steamer?" asked Vansittart, testing the all-knowing Venetian.

"Not he, Altissimo. Having once set his foot upon the soil of Africa he would be too wise to return to Europe. He might go to India, to America—north or south—but he would not come to England, to answer for the English life which he had taken. You Englishmen set great store upon life."

Vansittart dismissed the man with a present, but before he went Ferrari laid his card upon the table, and begged that if ever the illustrissimo required a travelling servant, he, Ferrari, might be remembered.

When he was gone Vansittart took up his pen and wrote hastily to Sefton.

"DEAR MR. SEFTON,

"Your excellent Ferrari has been here, and I have gone carefully through his statement. It is plausible, but by no means convincing; and I see ample room for error in a chain of facts which rest upon hearsay. Under these conditions I am more than ever desirous that no hint of Ferrari's story should reach Miss Marchant. Forgive me for reminding you of your promise. It would be a deplorable business if this dear girl were made unhappy about a chimera.

"I go to Redwold to-morrow, and shall stay over Whitsuntide. We are to be married before the end of June, very quietly, at Fernhurst Church.

"Yours sincerely,

"J. VANSITTART."

He rather despised himself for writing in this friendly strain to a man for whom he had an instinctive dislike; but he tried to believe that his dislike was mere prejudice, and that Sefton's manner with Eve, to which he had taken such violent objection, was only Sefton's manner to young women in general; a bad manner, but without any sinister feeling underlying it—only a bad manner.

To-morrow he was to go to Redwold, to be his sister's guest till after Whitsuntide, or until the wedding, if he pleased. And before June was pushed aside by her sultrier sister July, he was to be Eve Marchant's husband. Every day of his life brought that union a day nearer. It had come now to the counting of days. It seemed to him as if time and the calendar were no more—as if he and his love were being swept along on the strong current of their happiness. He could think of nothing, care for nothing but Eve. His bailiff's letters, his lawyer's letters, remained unanswered. He could not bring himself even to consider his mother's suggestions as to this or that improvement at Merewood, whither Mrs. Vansittart was going at Whitsuntide, to prepare all things for the coming of the bride, and to arrange for her own removal.

"Do as much or as little as you like, mother," Vansittart said. "You need alter nothing. Eve will be pleased with things as they are."

"It will be a great change from a cottage," sighed Mrs. Vansittart. "I'm afraid she will be bewildered and overpowered by a large household. She can have no idea of managing servants."

"The servants can manage themselves, mother. I don't want a managing wife. Yet from what I have seen of Eve in her own home I take her to be well up in domestic matters. Everything at the Homestead seemed the essence of comfort."

He remembered his wintry tea-drinking, the tea and toast, the cake and jam-pots, and Eve's radiant face; the firelight on Eve's hair; the sense of quiet happiness which pervaded the place where his love was queen. It seemed to him that there could not have been one inharmonious note in that picture. Order and beauty and domestic peace were there. Should Fate reduce him to poverty he could be utterly happy with his love in just such a home. He wanted neither splendid surroundings nor brilliant society.

Having heard all that Ferrari could tell him, he felt easier in his mind than he had felt since that unpleasant hour with his mother and Sefton on Saturday evening. The more he thought of the courier's chain of evidence, the weaker it seemed to him. No, he could not think that the man he had killed was the brother of the woman he was going to marry. He tried to recall the man's face; but the suddenness and fury of that deadly encounter had afforded no time for minute observation. The man's face had flashed upon him out of the crowd—fair-haired, fair-skinned, amidst all those olive complexions—a face and figure that bore down upon him with the impression of physical power; handsome only as the typical gladiator is handsome. What more could he remember? Irregular features, strongly marked; a low forehead; and light blue eyes. The Marchants were a blue-eyed race; but that went for little in a country where the majority of eyes are blue or grey.

Vansittart remembered his promise to visit Fiordelisa and her aunt; and as this was his last day in London, perhaps, for some time, he gave up his afternoon to the performance of that promise. Tuesday was one of the Professor's days; and he had promised to hear the Professor's opinion of Signora Vivanti's progress.

Since that painful hour on Saturday he had thought seriously of the impulsive Venetian, and of his relations with her—relations which he felt to be full of peril. It had occurred to him that there was only one way to secure Fiordelisa's future welfare, while strictly maintaining his own incognito, and that was by the purchase of an annuity. It would cost him some thousands to capitalize that income of two hundred a year, which he had resolved to allow Lisa; but he had reserves which he could afford to draw upon, the accumulations of his minority, invested in railway stock. Any lesser sacrifice would appear to him too poor an atonement; for after all, it was possible that, but for him, Fiordelisa's Englishman might have kept his promise and married her. No, Vansittart did not think he would be doing too much in securing these two women against poverty for the rest of their lives—and the annuity once bought he would be justified in disappearing out of Fiordelisa's life, and leaving her in ignorance of his name and belongings.

He spent an hour with his lawyer before going to Chelsea, and from that gentleman obtained all needful information as to the proper manner of purchasing an annuity, and the best people with whom to invest his money.

* * * *

This done, he walked across the Park, and arrived at Saltero's Mansion on the stroke of four. Lisa had told him that her lesson lasted from three to four, so he had timed himself to meet the maestro.

The ripe round notes of Lisa's mezzo soprano rose full and strong in one of Conconi's exercises as la Zia opened the door. She attacked a florid passage with force and precision, ran rapidly up the scale to A sharp, and held the high note long and clear as the call of a bird.

"Brava, brava!" cried Signor Zinco, banging down a chord and rising from the piano as Vansittart entered.

Lisa flew to meet him. She was in her black frock, with a bit of scarlet ribbon tied round her throat, and another bit of scarlet tying up her great untidy knot of blue-black hair. The rusty black gown, the scarlet ribbons, the olive face, with its carnation flush and starlike eyes, made a brilliant picture after the school of Murillo. Vansittart could but see that she was strikingly handsome—just the kind of woman to take the town by storm, if she were once seen and heard in opera bouffe.

Zinco was a little old man, with no more figure than an eighteen-gallon cask. He had a large bald head, and benevolent eyes. He was very shabby. His coat, which might once have been black, was now a dull green—his old grey trousers were kneed and frayed, his old fat hands were dirty.

"Ah, I thought you had forgotten me again," said Lisa. "But you are here at last; and now ask the master if he is pleased with me."

"I am more than pleased," began Zinco, bowing and smiling at Vansittart as one who would fain have prostrated himself at the feet of so exalted a patron.

"Stay," cried Lisa. "You shall not talk of me before my face. I

192

will go and make the tea—and then Zinco will tell you the truth, Si'or mio, the very truth about me. He will not be obliged to praise."

She dashed out of the room, as if blown out on a strong wind, so impetuous were her movements. La Zia began to clear a table for tea, a table heaped with sheets of music and play-books. Fiordelisa had been learning English out of Gilbert's librettos, which were harder work for her than Metastasio for an English student.

"Well, Signor Zinco, what do you think of your pupil?" asked Vansittart.

"Sir, she is of a marvellous natural. She has an enormous talent, and with that talent an enormous energy. She is destined to a prodigious success upon the English scene."

"I am delighted to hear it."

"She has all the qualities which succeed with your English people—a fine voice, a fine person, and—that that may not displease you—a vulgarity which will command applause. Were I more diplomatist I should say genius—where I say vulgarity—but this divine creature is adorably vulgar. She has no nerves. I say to her sing, and she sings. 'Attack me the A sharp,' and she attacks, and the note rings out like a bell. She is without nerves, and she is without self-consciousness, and she has the courage of a lion. She has worked as no pupil of mine ever worked before. She is mastering your difficult language in as many months as it cost me years. She has laboured at the theory of music, and though she is in most things of a surprising ignorance, she has made no mean progress in that difficult science. She has worked as Garcia's gifted daughter worked; and were this age worthy of a second Malibran, she has in her the stuff to make a Malibran."

The fat little maestro stopped for breath, not for words. He stood mopping his forehead and smiling at Vansittart, who was inclined to believe in his sincerity, for that *roulade* he had heard at the door just now displayed a voice of brilliant quality.

"You are enthusiastic, Signor Zinco," he said quietly. "And pray when you have trained this fine voice to the uttermost what do you intend to do with it?"

"I hope to place the Signora in the way of making her fortune. Were you English a nation of music-lovers, I should say to this dear lady, give yourself up to hard study of classical opera for the next three years, before you allow yourself to be heard in public; but pardon me if I say, Signor, you English are not connoisseurs. You are taken with show and brilliancy. You think more of youth and beauty in the *prima donna* than of finish or science. Before your winter season of opera bouffe shall begin the Signora will have learnt enough to ensure her a *succes fou*. I count upon getting her engaged at the Apollo in November. There is a new opera being written for the Apollo—an opera in which I am told there are several female characters, and there will be a chance for a new singer. I have already spoken to the manager, and he has promised to hear the Signora sing before concluding his autumn engagements."

"Festina lente, Signor Zinco. You are going at railroad pace. Do not spoil the Signora's future by a hasty *début*."

"Have no fear, sir. She will have all the summer for practice, and for further progress in English. A foreign accent will be no disadvantage. It takes with an English audience. You have had so many sham Italians in opera that it will be well to have a real one."

The maestro bowed himself out, as Fiordelisa came in with the tea-tray, beaming with smiles, happy and important. She placed a chair for Vansittart by the open window. She arranged the light bamboo table in front of him, and began to pour out the tea, while la Zia seated herself at a little distance.

"I have learnt to make tea in your English fashion," Lisa said gaily, as she handed the teacups. "Strong, oh, so strong. No xe vero? Our neighbour on the upper floor taught me. She laughed at my tea one day when she came to see me. And now, what did little Zinco say? He always pretends to be satisfied with me."

"He praised you to the skies. He says you will make your fortune in opera."

"And do you like operas?" Lisa asked, after a thoughtful pause.

"I adore music of all kinds, except hurdy-gurdies and banjos."

"And will you come sometimes to hear me sing?"

"Assuredly! With the greatest pleasure."

"I shall owe fame and fortune to you, if ever I am famous or rich," said Lisa, seating herself on a low stool by the window, in the full afternoon sunlight, basking in the brightness and warmth.

"What has become of Paolo?" asked Vansittart, looking round the room, where some scattered toys reminded him of the child's existence.

"Paolo has gone to tea with the lady on the top floor. She has three little girls and a boy, and they all love *el puttelo*. They let him play with their toys and pull their hair. Hark! there they go."

A wild gallop of little feet across the ceiling testified to the animation of the party.

"He has been there all the afternoon. He is a bold, bad boy, and so full of mischief," said Lisa, with evident pride. "He is very big for his age, people say, and as active as a monkey. You must go and fetch him directly you have had your tea, Carina mia," she added to her aunt. "He has been with those children nearly two hours. He will be awake all night with excitement."

"Is he excitable?" asked Vansittart, who felt a new and painful interest in this child of a nameless parent.

"Oh, he is terrible. He is ready to jump out of the window when he is happy. He throws himself down on the floor, and kicks and screams till he is black in the face, when he is not allowed to do what he likes. He is only a baby, and yet he is our master. That is because he is a man, I suppose. We were created to be your slaves, were we not, Si'or mio? La Zia spoils him."

La Zia protested that the boy was a cherub, an angel. He wanted nothing in life but his own way. And he was so strong, so big, and so beautiful that people turned in the streets to look at him.

"Among all the children in Battersea Park I have never seen his equal. And he is not yet three years old. He fought with a boy of six, and sent him away howling. He is a marvel."

"When he is old enough I shall send him to a gymnasium," said Lisa. "I want him to be an athlete, like his father. He told me once that he won cups and prizes at the University by his strength. Oh, how white you have turned!" she cried, distressed at the ghastly change in Vansittart's face. "I forgot. I forgot. I ought not to have spoken of him. I never will speak of him again. We will forget that he ever existed."

She hung over his chair. She took up his hand and kissed it.

"Forgive me! Forgive me!" she murmured, with tears.

Unmoved by this little scene, la Zia emptied her teacup, rose, and left the room; and they two—Vansittart and Fiordelisa—were alone.

"You know that I would not pain you for the world," she sighed. "You have been so good to me, my true and only friend."

"No, no, Si'ora; I know that you would not willingly recall that memory which is branded upon my heart and brain. I can never forget. Do not believe even that I wish to forget. I sinned; and I must suffer for my sin. My friendship for you and for your good aunt arose out of that sin. I want to atone to you as far as I can for that fatal act. You understand that, I am sure."

"Yes, yes; I understand. But you like us, don't you?" she pleaded. "You are really our friend?"

"I am really your friend. And I want to prove my friendship by settling an income upon you, in such a manner that you will not be

195

dependent upon my forethought for the payment of that income. It will be paid to you as regularly as the quarter-day comes round. I am going to buy you an annuity, Lisa; that is to say, an income which will be paid to you till the end of your life; so that whether you make your fortune as a singer or not, you can never know extreme poverty."

"But who will give me the money when quarter-day comes?"

"It will be sent to you from an office. You will have no trouble about it."

"I should hate that. I would rather have the money from your hand. It is you who give it me—not the man at the office. I want to kiss my benefactor's hand. You are my benefactor. That was one of the first words I taught myself after I came to this house. Bén-é-factor!" she repeated, with her Italian accent; "it is easier than most of your English words."

"Cara Si'ora, I may be far away. It would be a bad thing for you to depend on my memory for the means of living. Let us be reasonable and business-like. I shall see to this matter to-morrow. And now, good-bye."

He rose, and took up his hat. Lisa hung about him, very pale, and with her full lower lip quivering like the lip of a child that is trying not to cry.

"Why are you doing this? why are you changing to me?" she asked piteously.

"I am not changing, Lisa. There is no thought of change in me. Only you must be reasonable. There is a dark secret between us—the memory of that fatal night in Venice. It is not well that we should meet often. We cannot see each other without remembering——"

"I remember nothing when I am with you—gnente, gnente!" she cried passionately. "Nothing except that I love you—love you with all my heart and soul."

She tried to throw herself upon his breast, but as he recoiled, astonished and infinitely pained, she fell on her knees at his feet, and clasped his hand in both of hers, and kissed and cried over it.

"I love you," she repeated; "and you—you have loved me—you must have loved me—a little. No man was ever so kind as you have been, except for love's sake. You must have cared for me. You cared for me that day in Venice—the happiest day in my life. Your heart turned to me as my heart turned to you, in the sunshine on the lagune, in the evening at the theatre. Every day that I have lived since then has strengthened my love. For God's sake, don't tell me that I am nothing to you."

"You are very much to me, Lisa. You are a friend for whom I desire all good things that this world and the world that comes after death can give. Get off your knees, child. This is childish folly; no wiser than Paolo's anger when you won't let him have all his own way. Come, Si'ora mia, let us laugh and be friends."

He tried to make light of her feelings; but she gave him a look that frightened him, a look of unmitigated despair.

"I thought you loved me; that by-and-by, when I was a famous singer, you would marry me. I should be good enough then to be your wife. You would forget that I was once a poor working girl at Burano. But I was foolish; yes, foolish. I could never be good enough to be your wife—I, the mother of Paolo. Let me go on loving you. Only come to see me sometimes—once a week, perhaps! The weeks are so long when you don't come. Only care for me a little, just a little, and I shall be happy. See how little I am asking. Don't forsake me, don't abandon me."

"There is nothing further from my thoughts than to forsake you; but if you make scenes of this kind I can never trust myself to come here again," he answered sternly.

"You will never come here again!" she cried, looking at him with wild eyes. "Then I will not live without you; I cannot, I will not."

The window stood open with its balcony and flowers, and the sunlit river, and the sunlit park and dim blue horizon of house-tops and chimneys stretching away to the hills of Sydenham. The girl looked at him for a moment, clenched her teeth, clenched her hands, and made a rush for the balcony. Happily he was quick enough and strong enough to stop her with one outstretched arm. He took her by the shoulder, savagely almost, with something of the brutal roughness of her old lover it might be, but with no love. Beautiful as she was in her passionate self-abandonment, he felt nothing for her in that moment but an angry contempt, which he was at little pains to conceal.

The revulsion of feeling upon that wild impulse towards self-destruction came quickly enough. The tears rolled down her flushed cheeks, she sank into the chair towards which Vansittart led her, and sat, helpless and unresisting, with her hands hanging loose across the arms of the chair, her head drooping on her breast, the picture of helpless grief.

He could but pity her, seeing her so childlike, so unreasoning, swayed by passion as a lily is bent by the wind. He shut the window, and bolted it, against any second outbreak; and then he seated himself at Lisa's side and took one of those listless hands in his.

"Let us be reasonable, Si'ora," he said, "and let us be good friends always. If I were not in love with a young English lady whom I hope very shortly to make my wife I might have fallen in love with you."

She gave a melancholy smile, and then a deep sigh.

"No, no, impossible! You would never have cared. I am too low—the mother of Paolo—only fit to be your servant."

"Love pardons much, Lisa; and if my heart had not been given to another your beauty and your generous nature might have won me. Only my heart was gone before that night at Covent Garden. It belonged for ever and for ever to my dear English love."

"Your English love! I should like to see her"—with a moody look. "Is she handsome, much handsomer than I?"

"There are some people who would think you the lovelier. Beauty is not all in all, Lisa. We love because we love."

"'We love because we love,'" she repeated slowly. "Ah, that is what makes it so hard. We cannot help ourselves. Love is destiny."

"Your destiny was in the past, Lisa. It came to you at Burano."

"No, no, no. I never cared for him as I have cared for you. I was happier in that one day on the Lido, and that one evening in Venice, than in all my life with him. There was more music in your voice when you spoke to me, ever so lightly, than in all he ever said to me of love. You are my destiny."

"You will think the same about some one else by-and-by, Si'ora—some one whose heart will be free to love you as you deserve to be loved. You are so young and so pretty and so clever that you must needs win a love worth the winning by-and-by, if you will only be reasonable and live a tranquil, self-respecting life in the meanwhile."

She shook her head hopelessly.

"I shall never care for any one again," she said. "No other voice would ever sound sweet in my ears. Don't despise me; don't think of me as a shameless creature. I was mad just now. I should never have spoken as I did; but I thought you cared for me. You were so kind; you did so much for us."

"I have tried to do my duty, that was all."

"Only duty! Well, it was a dream, a lovely dream—and it is over."

"Let it go with a smile, Lisa. You have so much to make life pleasant—a face that will charm every one; a voice that may make your fortune."

"I don't care about fortune."

"Ah, but you will find it very pleasant when it comes—carriages and horses, a fine house, jewels, laurel wreaths, applause, all that is most intoxicating in life. It is for that you have been working so hard."

"No, it is not for that. I have been working only to please you; so that you should say by-and-by, 'This poor little Lisa, for whom I have taken so much trouble, is something more than a common lace-worker, after all.'"

"This poor little Lisa is a genius, I believe, and will have the world at her feet, by-and-by. And now, Si'ora, I must say good-bye. I am going into the country to-morrow."

"For long?"

"Till after my marriage, perhaps."

"Till after your marriage! And when you are married will you ever come and see me?"

"Perhaps; if you will promise never again to talk as foolishly as you have talked to-day."

"I promise. I promise anything in this world rather than not see you."

"If I come, be sure I shall come as your true and loyal friend. Ah, here is your son," as a babyish prattle made itself heard in the little vestibule.

First came a rattling of the handle, and then the door was burst open, and Paolo rushed in—a sturdy block of a boy, with flaxen hair and great black eyes—a curious compromise between the Saxon father and the Venetian mother; square-shouldered, sturdy, stolid, yet with flashes of southern impetuousness. He was big for his age, very big, standing straight and strong upon the legs of an infant Hercules. He excelled in everything but speech.

Vansittart lifted him in his arms, and looked long and earnestly into the cherubic countenance, which first smiled and then frowned at him. He was trying, in this living picture of the dead, to see whether he could discover any trace of the Marchant lineaments.

It might be that a foregone conclusion prompted the fancy—that the fear of seeing made him see—but in the turn of the eyebrow and the contour of cheek and chin he thought he recognized lines which were familiar to him in the faces of Eve and her sisters—lines which were not in Fiordelisa's face.

He set the boy down with a sigh.

"Don't spoil him, Signora," he said to la Zia. "He looks like a boy with a good disposition, but a strong temper. He will want judicious training by-and-by."

Lisa followed him to the vestibule, and opened the door for him.

"Tell me that you are not angry before you go," she said imploringly.

"Angry? No, no; how could I be angry? I am only sorry that you should waste so much warmth of feeling on a man whose heart belongs to some one else."

"What is she like—that some one else? Tell me that—I want to know."

"Very lovely, very good, very gentle and tender and dear. How can I describe her? She is the only woman in the world for me."

"Shall I ever see her?"

"I think not, Si'ora. It would do no good. There is that sad secret which you and I know, but which she does not know. I could not tell her about you without making her wonder how you and I had come to be such friends; and then——"

"You do not think that I would tell her?" exclaimed Lisa, with a wounded air.

"No, no; I know you would not. Only secrets come to light, sometimes, unawares. Let the future take care of itself. Once more, good-bye."

"Once more, good-bye," she echoed, in tones of deepest melancholy.

CHAPTER XVII.

"SHE WAS MORE FAIR THAN WORDS CAN SAY"

If Easter had been a time of happiness for Vansittart and Eve, bringing with it the revelation of mutual love, Whitsuntide was no less happy; happier, perhaps, in its serene security, and in the familiarity of a love which seemed to have lasted for a long time.

"Only seven weeks!" exclaimed Eve, in one of their wanderings among the many cattle-tracks on Bexley Hill, no sound of life or movement in all the world around them save the hum of insects and the chime of cow bells. "To think that we have been engaged only seven weeks! It seems a lifetime."

"Because you are so weary of me?" asked Vansittart, with a lover's fatuous smile.

"No; because our love is so colossal. How can it have grown so tremendous in so short a time?"

"Romeo and Juliet's love grew in a single night."

"Ah, that was in Italy—and for stage effect. I don't think much of a passion that springs up in a night, like one of those great red fungi which one sees in this wood on an October morning. I should like our love to be as strong and as deep-rooted as that old oak over there, with its rugged grey roots cleaving the ground."

"Why, so it is; or it will be by the time we celebrate our golden wedding."

"Our golden wedding! Yes, if we go on living we must be old and grey some day. It seems hard, doesn't it? How happy those Greek gods and goddesses were, to be for ever young! It seems hard that we must change from what we are now. I cannot think of myself as an old woman, in a black silk gown and a cap. A cap!" she interjected, with ineffable disgust, and an involuntary movement of her ungloved hand to the coils of bright hair which were shining uncovered in the sun. "And you with grey hair and wrinkles! Wrinkles in *your* face! That is what your favourite Spencer calls 'Unthinkable.'

Stay"—looking at him searchingly in the merciless summer light. "Why, I declare there is just one wrinkle already. Just one perpendicular wrinkle! That means care, does it not?"

"What care can I have when I have you, except the fear of losing you?"

"Ah, you can have no such fear. I think, like Juliet, 'I should have had more cunning to be strange.' I let you see too soon that I adored you. I made myself too cheap."

"No more than the stars are cheap. We may all see them and worship them."

"But that deep perpendicular line, Jack. It must mean something. I have been reading Darwin on Expression, remember."

"Spencer—Darwin. You are getting far too learned. I liked you better in your ignorance."

"How ignorant I was"—with a long-drawn sigh—"till you began to educate me! Poor dear Mütterchen never taught us anything but the multiplication table and a little French grammar. We used to devour Scott, and Dickens, and Bulwer, and Thackeray. The books on our shelves will tell you how they have been read. They have been done to rags with reading. They are dropping to pieces like over-boiled fowls. And we know our Shakespeare—we have learnt him by heart. We used to make our winter nights merry acting Shakesperean scenes to Nancy and the parlour-maid. They were our only audience. But, except those dear novelists and Shakespeare, we read nothing. History was a blank; philosophy a word without meaning. You introduced me to the world of learned authors."

"Was I wise? Was it not something like Satan's introduction of Eve to the apple?"

"Wise or foolish, you gave me Darwin. And now I want to know what kind of trouble it was that made that line upon your forehead. Some foolish love affair, perhaps. You were in love—ever so much deeper in love than you are with me."

"No, my dearest. All my earlier loves were lighter than vanity—no more than Romeo's boyish passion for Rosaline."

"What other care, then? You, who are so rich, can have no money cares."

"Can I not? Imprimis, I am not rich; and then what income I have is derived chiefly from agricultural land cut up into smallish farms, with homesteads, and barns, and cowhouses, that seem always ready to tumble about the tenant's ears, unless I spend half a year's rent in repairs."

"Dear, picturesque old homesteads, I've no doubt."

"Eminently picturesque, but very troublesome to own."

"And did repairs—the cost of roofs and drainpipes—write that deep line on your brow?"

"Perhaps. Or it may be only a habit of frowning, and of trying to emulate the eagles in looking at the sun."

"Ah, you have been a wanderer in sunny lands—in Italy! And now we had better go and look for the girls."

They roamed over Bexley Hill or Blackdown during that happy Whitsuntide, favoured with weather that made these Sussex hills a paradise. It was the season of hawthorn blossom, and an undulating line of white may bushes came dancing down the hill like a bridal procession. It was the season of bluebells; and all the woodland hollows trembled with azure bloom, luminous in sunlight, darkly purple in shadow; the season of blossoming trees in cottage gardens, of the laburnum's golden rain, the acacia's perfumed whiteness, the tossing balls of the guelder rose, the mauve blossoms of wistaria glorifying the humblest walls, the small white woodbine scenting the warm air. It was a season that seemed especially invented for youth and love; for the young foals sporting in the meadow; for the young lambs on the grassy hills; and for Eve and Vansittart.

They almost lived out of doors in this delicious weather. The four sisters were always ready to bear them company, and were always discreet enough to leave them alone for the greater part of every rambling expedition. Mr. Tivett had reappeared on the scene. He had been particularly useful in London, where he was full of information about the very best places for buying everything, from a diamond bracelet to a tooth-brush, and had insisted upon taking Eve and Lady Hartley to some of his favourite shops, and upon having a voice in a great many of their purchases. He took as much interest in Eve's trousseau as if he had been her maiden aunt.

The wedding was to be the simplest ceremonial possible. Neither Vansittart nor Eve wished to parade their bliss before a light-minded multitude. The Homestead was not a house in which to entertain a large assembly; and Colonel Marchant was not a man to make a fuss about anything in life except his own comfort. He ordered a frock-coat and a new hat for the occasion; and the faithful Nancy, cook, housekeeper, and general manager, toiled for a week of industrious days in order that the house might be in faultless order, and the light collation worthy of the chosen few who were invited to the wedding. There were to be no hired waiters, no stereotyped banquet from the confectioner's, only tea and coffee, champagne of a famous brand—upon this the Colonel insisted—and such cakes and biscuits and delicate sandwiches as Nancy knew well how to prepare. For bridesmaids, Eve had her four sisters, all in white frocks, and carrying big bunches of Maréchal Niel roses. Hetty and Peggy had been in ecstatic expectation of the day for a month, and full of speculation as to what manner of present the bridegroom would give them. They squabbled about this question almost every night at bedtime, under the sloping roof of the attic which they occupied together, close to the overhanging thatch where there was such a humming and buzzing of summer insects in the June mornings.

"He is bound to give us a present," said Peggy. "It's etiquette"—accentuating the first syllable.

"You should say eti*quette*," reproved Hetty. "Lady Hartley lays a stress upon the kett."

"Don't bother about pronounciation," muttered Peggy; "one can never get on with one's talk when you're so fine-ladyfied."

"Pronounciation!" cried Hetty. "You pick up your language from Susan. No wonder Sophy is horrified at you."

"Sophy is too fine for anything. Mr. Vansittart said so yesterday when she gave herself airs at the picnic, because there were no table napkins. I wonder what the present will be! He's so rich, he's sure to give us something pretty. Suppose he gives us watches?"

A watch was the dream of Peggy's life. She thought the difference between no watch and watch was the difference between a humdrum existence and a life of exquisite bliss.

"Suppose he doesn't," exclaimed her sister, contemptuously. "Did you ever hear of a bridegroom giving watches? Of course, the bridesmaids are supposed to have watches. Their fathers give them watches directly they are in their teens, unless they are hard-up, like our father. I shouldn't wonder if he were to give us diamond arrow brooches."

Hetty had seen a diamond arrow in Lady Hartley's bonnet-strings, and had conceived a passion for that ornament.

"What do you bet that it will be diamond arrows?"

"There's no use in betting. If you lose, one never gets paid."

"I don't often have any money," Peggy replied naively; and then came a knocking at the lath and plaster partition, and Sophy's sharp voice remonstrating—

"Are you children never going to leave off chattering? You are worse than the swallows in the morning."

* * * *

204

There was one blissfullest of days for Peggy during the week before the wedding, a balmy June morning on which Vansittart came in a dog-cart to take Eve and her youngest sister to Haslemere station, whence the train carried them through a smiling land, perfumed with bean blossoms and those fragrant spices which pine woods exhale under the summer sun, to Liss, where another dog-cart was waiting for them, and whence they drove past copse and common to Merewood, Vansittart's very own house, to which he brought his future wife on a visit of inspection—"to see if she would like any alterations," he said.

"As if any one could want to alter such a lovely house," exclaimed Peggy, who was allowed to run about and pry into every hole and corner, and open all the wardrobes and drawers, except in Mrs. Vansittart's rooms, where everything was looked at with almost religious reverence.

There were boxes packed already in this lady's dressing-room, the note of departure already sounded.

"My mother talks of a house at Brighton," said Vansittart. "She has a good many friends settled there, and the winter climate suits her."

"I am sorry she should feel constrained to go away," said Eve, looking ruefully round the spacious morning-room, with its three French windows opening on to a wide balcony, a room which could have swallowed up half the Homestead. "It seems as if I were turning her out. And I am sure there would have been ample room for both of us in this big house."

"So I told her, love; but English mothers don't take kindly to the idea of a joint ménage. She will come to us often as our guest, I have no doubt, but she insists upon giving up possession to you and me."

They loitered in all the lower rooms, drawing-room and anteroom, library, billiard-room—an unpretentious country house, spread over a good deal of ground, roomy, airy, beautifully lighted, but boasting no art collections, no treasures of old books, unpretentiously furnished after the fashion of a century ago, and with only such modern additions as comfort required. The drawing-room would have appeared shabby to eyes fresh from London drawing-rooms; but the colouring was harmonious, and the room was made beautiful by the flowers on tables, chimney-piece, and cabinets.

"I dare say you would like to refurnish this room by-and-by," said Vansittart.

"Not for worlds. I would not change one detail that can remind you of your childhood. I remember the drawing-room in Yorkshire, and how dearly I loved the sofas and easy-chairs—the glass cabinets of old blue china. It would grieve me to go back and see strange furniture in that dear old room; and I love to think that your eyes looked at these things when they were only on a level with that table"—pointing to a low table with a great bowl of roses upon it.

"Not my eyes alone, but my father's and grandfather's eyes have looked from yonder low level. I am glad you don't mind the shabby furniture. I confess to a weakness for the old sticks."

"Shabby furniture!" repeated Eve. "One would think you were going to marry a princess. Why, this house is a palace compared with the Homestead; and yet I have contrived to be happy at the Homestead."

"Because Heaven has given you one of its choicest gifts—a happy disposition," said Vansittart. "It is that sunny temperament which irradiates your beauty. It is not that tip-tilted little nose, so slender in the bridge, so ethereal in its upward curve, nor yet those violet eyes, which make you so lovely. It is the happy soul for ever singing to itself, like the lark up yonder in the fathomless blue."

"I shouldn't think you cared for me, if you didn't talk nonsense sometimes," answered Eve, gaily; "but it *is* a privilege to be happy, isn't it? Sophy and I have had the same troubles to bear, but they have hurt her ever so much more than they hurt me. Jenny and I sometimes call her Mrs. Gummidge. I think it is because she has never left off struggling to be smart, never left off thinking that we ought to be on the same level as the county families; while Jenny and I gave up the battle at once, and confessed to each other frankly that we were poor and shabby, and the daughters of a scampish father. And so we have managed to be happy. I love to think that I am like Beatrice, and that I was born under a star that danced."

"You were born under a star that brought me good luck."

They were in the flower-garden, a delightful old garden of velvet turf and herbaceous borders, a garden brimful of roses, standard roses and climbing roses and dwarf roses, arches of roses that made the blue sky beyond look bluer, alleys shaded with roses, like the vine-clad berceaux of Italy. It was a garden shut in by walls of ilex and yew, and so secluded as to make an *al fresco* saloon for summer habitation; a saloon in which one could breakfast or dine, without fear of being espied by any one approaching the hall door.

Eve was enchanted with her new home. She poured out her confidence to him who was so soon to be her husband, with the right to know her inmost thoughts, her every impulse or fancy. It was not often that she talked of herself; but to-day she was full of personal reminiscences, and Vansittart encouraged her innocent egotism.

"I don't think you realize that you are playing the part of King Cophetua, and marrying a beggar-maiden," she said. "I don't think you can have any idea what a struggle my life has been since I was twelve years old—how that dear Nancy and I have had to scheme and manage, in order to feed four hungry girls. You remember how Hetty and Peggy giggled when you talked about dinner. We scarcely ever had a meal which you and Lady Hartley would call dinner. We were vegetarians half our time—we abstained when it wasn't Lent. We had our Ember days all the year round. Oh, pray don't look so horrified. We had the kind of food we liked. Vegetable soups, and savoury messes, salads and cheese, cakes and buns, bread and jam. We had meals that we all enjoyed tremendously—only we could not have asked a dropper-in to stay and lunch or dine—could we? So it was lucky people took so little notice of us."

"My darling, you were the pearls, and your neighbours were the swine."

"And then our dress. How could we be neat tailor-made girls when a ten-pound note once in a way was all we could extort from father for the whole flock? Ten pounds! Lady Hartley would pay as much for a bonnet as would buy gowns for all five of us. And then you bring me to this delicious old house—so spacious, so dignified, with such a settled air of wealth and comfort—and you ask if I can suggest improvement in things which to my mind are perfect."

"My dearest, I want you to be happy, and very happy; and to feel that this house is your house, to deal with as you please."

"I only want to live in it, with you," she answered shyly, "and not to disappoint you. What should I do if King Cophetua were to repent his romantic marriage, and were to think of all the brilliant matches he might have made?"

"When we are settled here I will show you the girls my mother would have liked me to marry, and you will see that they are not particularly brilliant. And I do not even know if any of them would have accepted me, had I been minded to offer myself."

"They could not have refused you. No one could. To know you is to adore you. Come, Jack, you have been talking rodomontade to me. It is my turn now. You are not extraordinarily handsome. I suppose, as a sober matter of fact, Mr. Sefton is handsomer. Don't wince at the sound of his name. You know I have always detested him. I doubt if you are even exceptionally clever—but you have a kind of charm—you creep into a girl's heart unawares. I pity the woman who loved you, and whom you did not love."

207

Vansittart thought of Fiordelisa. Perhaps in every man's life there comes one such ordeal as that—love cast at his feet, love worthless to him; but true love all the same, and priceless.

* * * *

Eve Marchant's wedding gifts were few but costly. She had no wide circle of acquaintances to shower feather fans and ivory paper-knives, standard lamps and silver boxes, teapots and cream-jugs, fruit spoons and carriage clocks upon her, till she sat among her treasures, bewildered and oppressed, like Tarpeia under the iron rain from warrior hands. Neighbours had stood aloof from the family at the Homestead, and could hardly come with gifts in their hands, now that the slighted girl was going to marry a man of some standing in an adjoining county, and to take her place among the respectabilities. The givers therefore were few, but the gifts were worthy. Mrs. Vansittart gave the pearl necklace which she had worn at her own bridal—a single string of perfect pearls, with a diamond clasp that had been in the family for a century and a half. Lady Hartley gave a set of diamond stars worthy to blaze in the fashionable firmament on a Drawing-Room day. Sir Hubert gave a three-quarter bred mare of splendid shape and remarkable power, perfect as hack or hunter, on whose back Eve had already taken her first lessons in equitation. And for the bridegroom! His gifts were of the choicest and the best considered; jewels, toilet nécessaire, travelling bag, books innumerable. He watched for every want, anticipated every fancy.

"Pray, pray don't spoil me," cried Eve. "You make me feel so horribly selfish. You load me with gifts, and you say you are not rich. You are ruining yourself for me."

"A man can afford to ruin himself once in his life for his nearest and dearest," he answered gaily. "Besides, if I give you all you want now, I shall cure you of any incipient tendency to extravagance."

"I have no such tendency. My nose has been kept too close to the grindstone of poverty."

"Poor, pretty little nose! Happily the grindstone has not hurt it."

"And as for wants, who said I wanted Tennyson and Browning bound in vellum, or a travelling bag as big as a house? I have no wants, or they are all centred upon one object, which isn't to be bought with money. I want you and your love."

"I and my love are yours—have been yours since that night in the snowy road, when you entered into my life at a flash, like the sunlight through Newton's shutter, like Undine, like Titania."

208

* * * *

One of the few wedding presents was embarrassing alike to bride and bridegroom, for it came from a man whom both disliked, but whom one of the two would rather not offend.

Eve's appearance in the family sitting-room just a little later than usual one morning was loudly hailed by Hetty and Peggy, who were squabbling over a small parcel which had arrived, registered and insured, by the morning post.

"It is a jeweller's box in the shape of a crescent," cried Peggy. "It must be a crescent brooch. How too utterly lovely! But it is not from Mr. Vansittart."

They called him Mr. Vansittart still, although he had begged them to call him Jack.

"It would be too awfully free and easy to call so superb a gentleman by such a vulgar name," Hetty said, when the subject came under discussion.

"I say it is from Mr. Vansittart," protested Hetty. "Who else would send her a diamond crescent?"

"How do you know it's diamonds?"

"Oh, of course. Bridegrooms always give diamonds. Did you ever see anything else in the weddings in the *Lady's Pictorial*?"

"Bother the *Lady's Pictorial*! it ain't his handwriting."

"Ain't it, stupid? Who said it was? It's the jeweller's writing, of course—with Mr. Vansittart's card inside."

"Perhaps you will allow me to open the parcel, and see what it all means," said Eve, with the eldest sister's dignity.

The two young barbarians had had the breakfast-table to themselves, Sophy and Jenny not having appeared. There were certain operations with spirit-lamp and tongs which made these young ladies later than the unsophisticated juniors.

"I shall scold him savagely for sending me this, after what I told him yesterday," said Eve, as she tore open the carefully sealed parcel.

She was of Hetty's opinion. The gift could be from none but her lover.

"Oh, oh, oh!" they cried, all three of them, in a chorus of rapture, as the box was opened.

The crescent was of sapphires, deeply, darkly, beautifully blue, without flaw or feather. Small brilliants filled in the corners between the stones, but these hardly showed in that blue depth and darkness.

209

The effect was of a solemn, almost mysterious splendour.

"Oh, how wicked, how wilful of him, to waste such a fortune upon me!" cried Eve, taking the crescent out of its velvet bed.

Under the jewel, like the asp under the fig-leaves, there lay a visiting-card.

"From Mr. Sefton, with all best wishes."

Eve dropped the brooch as if it had stung her.

"From him?" she cried. "How horrid!"

"I call it utterly charming of him," protested Hetty, who had adopted as many of Lady Hartley's phrases as her memory would hold. "We all know that he admired you, and I think it too sweet of him to show that he bears no malice now that you are marrying somebody else. Had he sent you anything paltry I should have loathed him. But such a present as this, so simple yet so *distingué*, in such perfect taste——"

"Cease your raptures, Hetty, for mercy's sake!" cried Eve, wrapping the jewel-box in the crumpled paper, and tying the string round it rather roughly. "Would you accept any gift from a man you hate?"

"It would depend upon the gift. I wouldn't advise my worst enemy to try me with a sapphire crescent—such sapphires as those!"

"You are a mighty judge of sapphires!" said Eve, contemptuously; after which unkind remark she ate her breakfast of bread and butter and home-made marmalade in moody silence. And it was a rare thing for Eve to be silent or moody.

Vansittart's step was heard upon the gravel before the curling-tongs were done with in the upper story, and Eve ran out to the porch to meet him, with the jeweller's parcel in her hand. They walked about the garden together, between rows of blossoming peas and feathery asparagus, by borders of roses and pinks, talking of Sefton and his gift. Eve wanted to send it back to the giver.

"I can decline it upon the ground that I don't approve of wedding presents except from one's own and one's bridegroom's kindred," she said. "I won't be uncivil."

"I fear he would think the return of his gift uncivil, however sweetly you might word your refusal. Wedding gifts are such a customary business; it is an unheard-of act to send one back. No, Eve, I fear you must keep the thing," with a tone of disgust; "but you need not wear it."

"Wear it! I should think not! Of course I shall obey you; but I hate the idea of being under an obligation to Mr. Sefton, who—well, who always made me feel more than any one else that I wasn't one of the elect. His friendliness was more humiliating than other people's stand-offishness. I wonder you mind offending him, Jack. I know you don't like him."

"No; but he is my sister's neighbour; and he and the Hartleys are by way of being friendly."

"Ah, I see! That is a reason. I wouldn't for the world do anything to make Lady Hartley uncomfortable. He might go to her and tax her with having an unmannerly young woman for a sister-in-law. So I suppose I must write a pretty little formal letter to thank him for his most exquisite gift, the perfect taste of which is only equalled by his condescension in remembering such an outsider as Colonel Marchant's daughter. Something to that effect, but not quite in those words."

She broke into gay laughter, the business being settled, and stood on tiptoe to offer her rosy lips to Vansittart's kiss; and all the invisible fairies in the peaseblossom, and all the microscopic Cupids lurking among the rose leaves, beheld that innocent kiss and laughed their noiseless laugh in sympathy with these true lovers.

"I have a good mind," said Eve, as she ran back to the house, "to give Peggy the blue crescent to fasten her pinafore."

* * * *

The wedding at Fernhurst Church was as pretty a wedding as any one need care to see, although it was a ceremony curtailed of all those surroundings which make weddings worthy to be recorded in the Society papers. There was no crowd of smart people, no assemblage of smart gowns stamped with the mantua-maker's cachet, and marking the latest development of fashion. No long train of carriages choked the rural road, or filled the little valley with clouds of summer dust. Only the kindred of bride and bridegroom were present; but even these made a gracious group in the chancel, while the music of the rustic choir and the school children with their baskets of roses were enough to give a bridal aspect to the scene.

Eve, in her severely simple gown, with no ornaments save the string of pearls round her full firm throat, and the natural orange blossoms in her bright hair, was a vision of youthful grace and beauty that satisfied every eye, and made the handsome bridegroom in all his height, and breadth, and manly strength, a mere accessory, hardly worth notice. The four sisters, in their gauzy white frocks and Gainsborough hats, when clustered in a group at the church door, might

211

have suggested four cherubic heads looking out of a fleecy cloud, so fresh and bright were the young faces, in the unalloyed happiness of the occasion—happiness almost supernal, for, regardless of precedent, and mysteriously divining Peggy's desire, the bridegroom had given them watches, dainty little watches, with an "E" in brilliants upon each golden back—E, for Eve; E, for Ecstasy; E, for Everlasting bliss! Peggy felt she had nothing more to ask of life. And for spectators, who need have wished a friendlier audience than honest Yorkshire Nancy, and the cottagers who had seen Eve Marchant grow up in their midst, and had experienced many kindnesses from her—the cottagers whose children she had taught in the Sunday-school, whose old people she had comforted on their death-beds, and for whose sake she had often stinted herself in order to take a jug of good soup, or a milk pudding, to a sick child?

Colonel Marchant made a dignified figure at the altar, in a frock-coat extorted from the reviving confidence of a tailor, who saw hope in Miss Marchant's marriage. He did all that was required of him with the grace of a man who had not forgotten the habits of good society. The modest collation at the Homestead was a success; for everybody was in good spirits and good appetite. Even Mrs. Vansittart was reconciled to a marriage which gave her son so fair a bride, content to believe that, whatever evil Harold Marchant might have done upon the earth, no shadow from his dark past need ever fall across his sister's pathway.

And so in a clash of joy-bells, and in a shower of rice from girlish hands, Eve and Vansittart ran down the steep garden path to the carriage which was to take them to Haslemere, whence they were going to Salisbury, on the first stage of their journey to that rock-bound coast

> *"Where that great vision of the guarded mount*
> *Looks o'er Namancos and Bayona's hold."*

CHAPTER XVIII.

"THE SHADOW PASSETH WHEN
THE TREE SHALL FALL"

What a happy honeymoon it was, along the porphyry walls of Western England; what joyous days that were so long and seemed so short! There never was a less costly honeymoon, for the bride's tastes were simple to childishness, and the bridegroom was too deeply in love to care for anything she did not desire. To ramble in that romantic land, staying here a few days, and there a week, all along the wild north coast, from Tintagel to St. Ives, southward then to Penzance, and Falmouth, and Fowey, was more than enough for bliss. And yet in all Eve's childish talk with her sisters of what she would do if ever she married a rich man, the honeymoon tour in Italy had been a leading feature in her programme; but in those girlish visions beside the schoolroom fire the husband had been a nonentity, a mere purse-bearer, and all her talk had been of the places she was to see. Now, with this very real husband, all earth was paradisaic, and Sorrento could not have seemed more like a dream of beauty than Penzance. She was exquisitely happy; and what can the human mind require beyond perfect bliss?

These wedded lovers lingered long over that summer holiday. It was an ideal summer—a summer of sunshine and cloudless skies, varied only by an occasional thunderstorm—tempest enjoyed by Vansittart and Eve, who loved Nature in her grand and awful as well as in her milder aspects—and a tempest from the heights above Boscastle, or from the grassy cliffs of the Lizard, is a spectacle to remember. They spun out the pleasures of that simple Cornish tour. There was nothing to call them home—no tie, no duty, only their own inclination; for the dowager Mrs. Vansittart was staying at Redwold, absorbed in worship of the third generation, and was to go from Redwold to Ireland for a round of visits to the friends of her early married life. The lovers were therefore free to prolong their wanderings, and it was only when the shortening days suggested fireside pleasures that Vansittart proposed going home.

"Going home," cried Eve; "how sweet that sounds! To think that your home is to be my home for evermore; and the servants, your old, well-trained servants, will be bobbing to me as their mistress—I who never had any servant but dear old motherly Nancy, who treats me as if I were her own flesh and blood, and an untaught chit for a parlour-maid, a girl who was always dropping knives off her tray, or smashing the crockery, in a most distracting manner. We had only the cheapest things we could buy at Whiteley's sales, with a few relics of former splendour; and it was generally the relics that suffered. I cannot imagine myself the mistress of a fine house, with a staff of capable servants. What an insignificant creature I shall seem among them!"

"You will seem a queen—a queen out of the great kingdom of poetry—a queen like Tennyson's Maud, in a white frock, with roses in your hair, and an ostrich fan for a sceptre. Don't worry about the house, Eve. It will govern itself. The servants are all old servants, and have been trained by my mother, whose laws are the laws of Draco. Everything will work by machinery, and you and I can live in the same happy idleness we have tasted here."

"Can we? May we, do you think? Is it not a wicked life? We care only for ourselves; we think only of ourselves."

"Oh, we can mend that in some wise. I'll introduce you to all my cottage tenants; and you will find plenty of scope for your benevolence in helping them through their troubles and sicknesses. You can start a village reading-room; you can start—or revive—a working man's club. You shall be Lady Bountiful—a young and blooming Bountiful—not dealing in herbs and medicines, but in tea, and wine, and sago puddings, and chicken broth; finding frocks for the children, and Sunday bonnets for the mothers—flashing across poverty's threshold like a ray of sunshine."

* * * *

Life that seems like a happy dream seldom lasts very long. There is generally a rough awakening. Fate comes, like the servant bidden to call us of a morning, and shakes the sleeper by the shoulder. The dream vanishes through the ivory gate, and the waking world in all its harsh reality is there.

Eve's awakening came in a most unexpected shape. It came one October morning in the first week of her residence at Merewood. It

214

came in a letter from her old servant, a letter in a shabby envelope, lying hidden among that heap of letters, monogrammed, coroneted, fashionable, which lay beside Mrs. Vansittart's plate when she took her seat at the breakfast table.

She left that letter for the last, not recognizing Nancy's penmanship, an article of which the faithful servant had always been sparing. Eve read all those other trivial letters—invitations, acceptances, friendly little communications of no meaning—and commented upon them to her husband as he took his breakfast—and finally opened Nancy's letter. It was October, and Vansittart was dressed for shooting. October, yet there was no house-party. Eve had pleaded for a little more of that dual solitude which husband and wife had found so delightful; and Vansittart had been nothing loth to indulge her whim. November would be time enough to invite his friends; and in the mean time they had their pine woods and copses and common all to themselves; and Eve could tramp about the covers with him when he went after his pheasants, without feeling herself in anybody's way. October had begun charmingly, with weather that was balmy and bright enough for August. They were breakfasting with windows open to the lawn and flower-beds, and the bees were buzzing among the dahlias, and the air was scented with the Dijon roses that covered the wall.

"Why, it is from Nancy," exclaimed Eve, looking at the signature. "Dear old Nancy. What can she have to write about?"

"Read, Eve, read," cried Vansittart. "I believe Nancy's letter will be more interesting than all those inanities you have been reading to me. There is sure to be some touch of originality, even if it is only in the spelling."

Eve's eyes had been hurrying over the letter while he spoke.

"Oh, Jack," she exclaimed, in a piteous voice, "can there be any truth in this?"

The letter was as follows, in an orthography which need not be reproduced:—

"HONOURED MADAM,

"I should not take the liberty to write to you about dear Miss Peggy, only at Miss Sophy's and Miss Jenny's age they can't be expected to know anything about illness, and I'm afraid they may pass things over till it's too late to mend matters, and then I know you would blame your old servant for not having spoken out."

"What an alarming preamble!" said Jack. "What does it all mean?"

"It means that Peggy is very ill. Peggy, who seemed the strongest of all of us."

She went on reading the letter.

"You know what beautiful weather we had after your marriage, honoured Madam. The young ladies enjoyed being out of doors all day long, and all the evening, sometimes till bedtime. They seldom had dinner indoors. It was 'Picnic basket, Nancy,' every morning, and I had to make them Cornish pasties—any scraps of meat was good enough so long as there was plenty of pie-crust—and fruit turnovers; and off they used to go to the copses and the hills directly after breakfast. They were all sunburnt, and they all looked so well, no one could have thought any harm would come of it. But Miss Peggy she used to run about more than her sisters, and she used to get into dreadful perspirations, as Miss Hetty told me afterwards, and then, standing or sitting about upon those windy hills, no doubt she got a chill. Even when she came home, with the perspiration teeming down her dear little face, she didn't like the tew of changing all her clothes, and I was too busy in the kitchen—cooking, or cleaning, or washing—to look much after the poor dear child, and so it came upon me as a surprise in the middle of August when I found what a bad cold she had got. I did all I could to cure her. You know, dear Miss Eve, that I'm a pretty good nurse—indeed, I helped to nurse your poor dear ma every winter till she went abroad—but, in spite of all my mustard poultices and hot footbaths, this cough has been hanging about Miss Peggy for more than six weeks, and she doesn't get the better of it. Miss Sophy sent for the doctor about a month ago, and he told her to keep the child warmly clad, and not to let her go out in an east wind, and he sent her a mixture, and he called two or three times, and then he didn't call any more. But Miss Peggy's cough is worse than it was when the doctor saw her, and the winter will be coming on soon, and I can't forget that her poor ma died of consumption: so I thought the best thing I could do was to write freely to you.—Your

216

faithful friend and servant,

"Nancy."

* * * *

"Died of consumption!" The words came upon Vansittart like the icy hand of Death himself, taking hold of his heart.

"Is that true, Eve?" he asked. "Did your mother die of consumption?"

"I never heard exactly what her complaint was. She was far away from us when she died. I remember she always had a cough in the winter, and she had to be very careful of herself—or, at least, people told her she ought to be careful. She seemed to fade away, and I have always fancied that her grief about Harold had a good deal to do with her death."

"Ah, that was it, no doubt. It was grief killed her. Her son's exile, her change of fortune, were enough to kill a sensitive woman. She died of a broken heart."

Anything! He would believe anything rather than accept the idea of that silent impalpable enemy threatening his beloved—the horror of hereditary consumption—the shadow that walketh in noonday.

"My sweet Peggy!" cried Eve, with brimming eyes. "I have been home a week, and I have not been to see my sisters—only an hour's journey by road and rail! It is nearly three months since I saw them, and we were never parted before in all our lives. May I go to-day—at once, Jack? I shall be miserable——"

"Till you have discovered a mare's nest, which I hope and believe Nancy's letter will prove," her husband interjected soothingly. "Yes, dear, we'll go to Haslemere by the first train that will carry us, and we'll telegraph for a fly to take us on to Fernhurst. There shall not be a minute lost. You shall have Peggy in your arms before lunch-time. Dear young Peggy! Do you suppose she is not precious to me, as well as to you? I promised I would be to her as a brother. Your sisters are my sisters, Eve."

He rang the bell at the beginning of his speech, and ordered the dog-cart at the end.

"We must catch the London train, at 10.15," he told the footman. "Let them bring round the cart as soon as it can be got ready. And now, dearest, your hat and jacket, and I am with you."

There was comfort in this prompt action. Eve rushed upstairs, threw on the first hat she could find, too eager to ring for her maid, with whose attendance she was always willing to dispense, as a novel and not always pleasant sensation. She came flying down to the hall ten minutes before the cart drove round, and she and Vansittart walked up and down in front of the porch, talking of the sisters, she breathless and with fast-beating heart, protesting more than once at the slowness of the grooms.

"My dearest, for pity's sake be calm. Why should you think the very worst, only because Nancy is an alarmist? These people are always full of ghoulish imaginings. Peasants gloat over the idea of sickness and death. They will stab one to the heart unwittingly; they will look at one's nearest and dearest, and say, 'Poor Miss So-and-so does not look as if she was long for this world.' Long for this world, forsooth! Thank Heaven the threatened life often outlasts the prophet's. Come, here is the cart. Jump in, Eve. The drive through the fresh air will revive your spirits."

She was certainly in better spirits by the time the cart drew up at the railway station, and in better spirits all the way to Haslemere; but it was her husband's hopefulness rather than the crisp autumn air which revived her. Yes, she would take comfort. Jack was right. Nancy was the best of creatures, but very apt to dwell upon the darker aspects of life, and to prophesy evil.

Yes, Jack was right; for scarcely had the fly stopped at the little gate when Peggy came dancing down the steep garden path, with outstretched arms, and wild hair flying in the wind, and legs much too long for her short petticoats—that very Peggy whom Eve's fearful imaginings had depicted stretched on a sick-bed, faint almost to speechlessness. No speechlessness about this Peggy, the real flesh and blood Peggy, whose arms were round Eve's neck before she had begun the ascent of the pathway, whose voice was greeting her vociferously, and who talked unintermittingly, without so much as a comma, till they were in the schoolroom. The arms that clung so lovingly were very skinny, and the voice was somewhat hoarse; but the hoarseness was no doubt only the consequence of running fast, and the skinnyness was the normal condition of a growing girl. Yes, Peggy had grown during her sister's long honeymoon. There was decidedly an inch or so more leg under the short skirt.

Eve wept aloud for very joy, as she sat on the sofa with Peggy on her lap—the dear old Yorkshire sofa—the sofa that had been a ship, an express train, a smart barouche, an opera-box, and ever so many other things, years ago, in their childish play. She could not restrain her tears as she thought of that terrible vision of a dying Peggy, and then clasped this warm, joyous, living Peggy closer and closer to her heart. The other sisters had gone to a morning service. She had this youngest all to herself for a little while.

"I don't go to church on weekdays now," said Peggy, "only on Sundays. It makes my chest ache to sit so long."

Ah, that was like the dull sudden sound of the death-bell.

"That's because you're growing so fast, Peg," said Vansittart's cheery voice. "Growing girls are apt to be weak. I shall send you some port which will soon make you sit up straight."

"You needn't trouble," said Peggy. "I could swim in port if I liked. Sir Hubert sent a lot for me—the finest old wine in his cellar—just because Lady Hartley happened to say I was growing too fast. And they have sent grapes, and game, and all sorts of delicious things from Redwold, only because I grow too fast. It's a fine thing for all of us that I grow so fast—ain't it, Eve?—for, of course, I can't eat all the grapes or the game."

Peggy looked from wife to husband, with a joyous laugh. She had red spots on her hollow cheeks, and her eyes were very bright. Vansittart heard the death-bell as he looked at her.

The sisters came trooping in, having seen the fly at the door and guessed its meaning. They were rapturous in their greetings, had worlds to say about themselves and their neighbours, and were more eager to talk of their own experiences than to hear about Eve's Cornish wanderings.

"You should just see how the people suck up to us, now you are Lady Hartley's sister-in-law," said Hetty, and was immediately silenced for vulgarity, and to make way for her elder sisters.

Vansittart left them all clustered about Eve, and all talking together. He went out into the garden—the homely garden of shrubs and fruit and flowers and vegetables, garden which now wore its autumnal aspect of over-ripeness verging on decay, rosy-red tomatoes hanging low upon the fence, with flabby yellowing leaves, vegetable marrows grown out of knowledge, and cucumbers that prophesied bitterness, cabbage stumps, withering bean-stalks—a wilderness of fennel: everywhere the growth that presages the end of all growing, and the long winter death-sleep.

It was not to muse upon decaying Nature that Vansittart had come out among the rose and carnation borders, the patches of parsley and mint. He had a purpose in his sauntering, and made his way to the back of the straggling cottage, where the long-tiled roof of the kitchen and offices jutted out from under the thatch. Here through the open casement he saw Yorkshire Nancy bustling about in the bright little kitchen, her pupil and slave busy cleaning vegetables at the sink, and a shoulder of lamb slowly revolving before the ruddy coal fire—an honest, open fireplace. "None of your kitcheners for me," Nancy was wont to say, with a scornful emphasis which recalled the fox in his condemnation of unattainable grapes.

Vansittart looked in at the window.

"May I have a few words with you, Nancy?" he asked politely.

"Lor, sir, how you did startle me to be sure. Sarah, look to lamb and put pastry to rise," cried Nancy, whisking off her apron, and darting out to the garden. "You see, sir, you and Miss Eve have took us by surprise, and it's as much as we shall have a bit of lunch ready for you at half-past one."

"Never mind lunch, my good soul. A crust of bread and cheese would be enough."

"Oh, it won't be quite so bad as that. Miss Eve likes my chisscakes, and she shall have a matrimony cake to her afternoon tea."

"Nancy, I want a little serious talk with you," Vansittart began gravely, when they had walked a little way from the house, and were standing side by side in front of the untidy patch where the vegetable marrows had swollen to huge orange-coloured gourds. "I am full of fear about Miss Peggy."

"Oh, sir, so am I, so am I," cried Nancy, bursting into tears. "I didn't want to frighten dear Miss Eve—I beg pardon, sir, I never can think of her as Mrs. Vansittart."

"Never mind, Nancy. You were saying——"

"I didn't want to frighten your sweet young lady in the midst of her happiness; but when I saw that dear child beginning to go off just like her poor mother——"

"Oh, Nancy!" cried Vansittart, despairingly, with his hand on the Yorkshirewoman's rough red arm. "Is that a sure thing? Did Mrs. Marchant die of consumption?"

"As sure as you and I are standing here, sir. It was a slow decline, but it was consumption, and nothing else. I've heard the doctors say so."

CHAPTER XIX.

"HE SAID, 'SHE HAS A LOVELY FACE'"

December's fogs covered London as with a funeral pall, and hansom and four-wheeler crept along the curb more slowly than a funeral procession. It was the winter season, the season of cattle-shows, and theatres, and middle-class suburban gaieties, and snug little dinners and luncheons in the smart world, casual meetings of birds of passage, halting for a few days between one country visit and another, or preparing for migration to sunnier skies. There were just people enough in Mayfair to make London pleasant; and there were people enough in South Kensington and Tyburnia to fill the favourite theatres to overflowing.

A new comic opera had been produced at the Apollo at the beginning of the month, and a new singer had taken the town by storm.

The opera was called *Fanchonette*. It was a story of the Regency; the Regency of Philip of Orleans and his *roués*; the age of red heels and lansquenet, of little suppers and deadly duels; a period altogether picturesque, profligate, and adapted to comic opera.

Fanchonette was a girl who sang in the streets; a girl born in the gutter, vulgar, audacious, irresistible, and the good genius of the piece.

Fanchonette was Fiordelisa—and Fiordelisa in her own skin; good-natured, impetuous, a creature of smiles and tears; buoyant as a sea-gull on the crest of a summer wave; rejoicing in her strength and her beauty as the Sun rejoiceth to run his race.

What people most admired in this new songstress was her perfect *abandon*, and that abundant power of voice which seemed strong enough to have sustained the most exacting *rôle* in the classic repertoire, with as little effort as the light music of opera bouffe—the power of a Malibran or a Tietjens. The music of *Fanchonette* was florid, and the part had been written up for the new singer. Manager, artists, and author had thought Mervyn Hawberk, the composer, reckless almost to lunacy when he elected to entrust the leading part in his new opera to an untried singer; but Hawberk had made Signora Vivanti rehearse the music in his own music-room, not once, but many times, before he resolved upon this experiment; and having so resolved, he turned her over to Mr. Watling, the author of the libretto, to be coached in the acting of her part; and Mr. Watling was fain to confess that the young Venetian's vivacity and quickness of apprehension, the force and fire, the magnetism of her southern nature, made the work of dramatic education a very different thing to the weary labour of grinding his ideas into the bread-and-butter misses who were sometimes sent to him as aspirants for dramatic fame. This girl was so quick to learn and to perceive, and struggled so valiantly with the difficulties of a foreign language. And her Venetian accent, with its soft slurring of consonants, was so quaint and pretty. Mr. Watling took heart, and began to think that his friend and partner, Mervyn Hawberk, had some justification for his faith in this untried star.

The result fully justified Hawberk's confidence. There were two principal ladies in the opera—the patrician heroine, written for a light soprano, and the gutter heroine, a mezzo soprano, whose music made a greater call upon the singer than the former character, which had been written especially for the Apollo's established prima donna, a lady with a charming birdlike voice, flexible and brilliant, but a little worn with six years' constant service, and a handsome face which was somewhat the worse for those six years in a London theatre. There could have been no greater contrast to Miss Emmeline Danby, with her sharp nose, blonde hair, sylph-like figure and canary-bird voice, than this daughter of St. Mark, whose splendour of colouring and fulness of form seemed in perfect harmony with the power and compass of her voice. The town, without being tired of Miss Danby, was at once caught and charmed by this new singer. Her blue-black hair and flashing eyes, her easy movements, her broken English, her girlish laughter, were all new to the audience of the Apollo, who hitherto had been called upon to applaud only the highest training of voice and person. Here was a girl who, like the character she represented, had evidently sprung from the proletariat, and who came dancing on to the London stage, fresh, fearless, unsophisticated, secure of the friendly feeling of her audience, and giving full scope to her natural gaiety of heart.

Signora Vivanti's personality was a new sensation; and to a *blasé* London public there is nothing so precious as a new sensation. Signor Zinco proved a true prophet. That touch of vulgarity which he had spoken of deprecatingly to Vansittart had made Lisa's fortune. Had she come straight from the Milan Conservatorio, cultivated to the highest pitch, approved by Verdi himself, she would hardly have succeeded as she had done, with all the rough edges of her grand voice unpolished, and all the little caprices and impertinences of a daughter of the people unchastened and unrestrained.

Lisa took the town by storm, and "Fanchonette," in her little mob cap and striped petticoat, appeared on half the match-boxes that were sold by the London tobacconists; and "Fanchonette," with every imaginable turn of head and shoulder, smiled in the windows of the Stereoscopic Company, and of all the fashionable stationers.

Among the many who admired the new singer one of the most enthusiastic was Wilfred Sefton, who generally spent a week or two of the early winter in his bachelor quarters at Chelsea, for the express purpose of seeing the new productions at the fashionable theatres, and of dining with his chosen friends.

Sefton was passionately fond of music, and knew more about it than is known to most country gentlemen. The loftiest classical school was not too high or too serious for him; and the lightest opera bouffe was not too low. He had a taste sufficiently catholic to range from Wagner to Offenbach. He was a profound believer in Sullivan, and he had a warm affection for Massenet.

Fanchonette was by far the cleverest opera which Mervyn Hawberk had written; and Sefton was at the Apollo on the opening night, charmed with the music, and amused by the new singer. He went a second, a third, a fourth time during his fortnight in town; and the oftener he heard the music the better he liked it; and the oftener he saw Signora Vivanti the more vividly was he impressed by her undisciplined graces of person and manner. She had just that spontaneity which had ever exercised the strongest influence over his mind and fancy. He had passed unmoved through the furnace of the best society, had danced and flirted, and had been on the best possible terms with some of the handsomest women in London, and had yet remained heart-whole. He had never been so near falling in love in all seriousness as with Eve Marchant; and Eve's chief charm had been her frank girlishness, her unsophisticated delight in life.

Well, he was cured of his passion for Eve, cured by that cold douche of indifference which the young lady had poured upon him; cured by the feeling of angry scorn which had been evoked by her preference for Vansittart; for a man who, in worldly position, in good looks, and in culture, Wilfred Sefton regarded as his inferior. He could not go on caring for a young woman who had shown herself so deficient in taste as not to prefer the dubious advances of a Sefton to the honest love of a Vansittart. He dismissed Eve from his thoughts for the time being; but not without prophetic musings upon a day when she might be wearied of her commonplace husband,

and more appreciative of Mr. Sefton's finer qualities of intellect and person. He was thus in a measure fancy free as he lolled in his stall at the Apollo, and listened approvingly to Lisa's full and bell-like tones in the quartette, which was already being played on all the barrel-organs in London, a quartette in which the composer had borrowed the dramatic form of the famous quartette in *Rigoletto*, and adapted it to a serio-comic situation. He was free to admire this exuberant Italian beauty, free to pursue a divinity whom he judged an easy conquest. He and the composer were old friends—Hawberk being a familiar figure at all artistic gatherings in the artistic suburb of Chelsea—and from the composer Sefton had heard something of the new prima donna's history. He had been told that she was a daughter of the Venetian people, a lace-maker from one of the islands; that she had come to London with her aunt, to seek her fortune; and that her musical training had been accomplished within the space of a year, under the direction of Signor Zinco, the fat little Italian who played the 'cello at the Apollo.

Such a history did not suggest inaccessible beauty, and there was a touch of originality in it which awakened Sefton's interest. The very name of Venice is a sound of enchantment for some minds; and Sefton, although a man of the world, was not without romantic yearnings. He was always glad to escape from beaten tracks.

He had been troubled and perplexed from the night of Signora Vivanti's *début* by the conviction that he had seen that brilliant face before, and by the inability to fix the when or the where. Yes, that vivid countenance was decidedly familiar. It was the individual and not the type which he knew—but where and when—where and when? The brain did its work in the usual unconscious way, and one night, sitting lazily in his stall, dreamily watching the scene, and the actress whose image seemed to fill the stage to the exclusion of all other figures, the memory of a past rencontre flashed suddenly upon the dreamer. The face was the face of the foreign girl he had seen on the Chelsea Embankment, hanging upon Vansittart's arm.

"By Heaven, there is something fatal in it," thought Sefton. "Are the threads always to cross in the web of our lives? He has worsted me with Eve; and now—now am I to fall in love with his cast-off mistress?"

He had been quick to make inferences from that little scene on the Embankment; the girl hanging on Vansittart's arm, looking up at him pleadingly, passionately. What could such a situation mean but a love affair of the most serious kind?

Had there been any doubt in Sefton's mind as to the nature of the intrigue, Vansittart's evident embarrassment would have settled the question. Mr. Sefton was the kind of man who always thinks worst about everybody, and prejudice had predisposed him to think badly of Eve's admirer.

This idea of the singer's probable relations with Vansittart produced a strong revulsion of feeling. An element of scorn was now mixed with his admiration of the lovely Venetian. Until now he had approached her with deference, sending her a bouquet every evening, with his card, but making no other advance. But the day after his discovery he sent her a diamond bracelet, and asked with easy assurance to be allowed to call upon her.

The bracelet was returned to him, with a stately letter signed Zinco; a letter wherein the 'cello player begged that his pupil might be spared the annoyance of gifts, which she could but consider as insults in disguise.

This refusal stimulated Sefton to renewed ardour. He forgot everything except the rebuff, which had taken him by surprise. He put the bracelet in a drawer of his writing-table, and turned the key upon it with a smile.

"She will be wiser by-and-by," he said to himself.

He went back to the country next day, and tried to forget Signora Vivanti's eyes, and the thrilling sweetness of her voice, tried to banish that seductive image altogether from his mind, while he devoted himself to the conquest of an untried hunter, a fine bay mare, whose pace was better than her manners, and who showed the vulgar strain in her pedigree very much as Signora Vivanti showed her peasant ancestry.

The season was not a good one, and after a couple of days with the hounds a hard frost set in, and the bay mare's evolutions were confined to the straw-yard, where she might walk on her hind legs to her heart's content; while her owner had nothing to do but brood upon the image that had taken possession of his fancy. It was only when he found himself amidst the tranquil surroundings of his country seat that he knew the strength of his infatuation for the Venetian singer.

He looked back upon his life as he strolled round the billiard table, cue in hand, trying a shot now and then yawningly, as the snow came softly down outside the Tudor windows, and gradually clouded and muffled garden and park. He looked back upon his life, wondering whether he had done the best for himself, starting from such an advantageous standpoint; whether, in his own careless phraseology, he had got change for his shilling.

He had always had plenty of money; he had always been his own master; he had always studied his own pleasure; and yet there had been burdens. His first love affair had turned out badly; so badly that there were people in Sussex who still gave him the cold shoulder on account of that old story. He had admired a good many women since he left Eton; but he had never seen the woman for whom he cared to sacrifice his liberty, for whose sake he could bind himself for all his life to come. He knew himself well enough to know that all his passions were short-lived, and that, however deeply he might be in love to-day, satiety might come to-morrow.

He was ambitious, and he meant to marry a woman who could bring him increase of fortune and social status. He was not to be drifted into matrimony by the caprice of the hour. Much as he had admired Eve Marchant, he had never thought of marrying her. A penniless girl with a disreputable father and a bevy of half-educated sisters was no mate for him. He had allowed himself full license in admiring her, and in letting her see that he admired her; and he had wondered that she should receive that open admiration as anything less than an honour.

And then a fool had stepped in to spoil sport—a besotted fool who took this girl for his wife, careless of her surroundings, defiant of Fate, which might overtake him in the shape of a blackguard brother. He felt only contempt for Vansittart when he thought over the story.

"He might have been content with his Venetian sweetheart," he thought. She is ever so much handsomer than Eve, and she obviously adored him; while that kind of ménage has the convenience of being easily got rid of when a man tires of it.

The snow lay deep on all the country round before nightfall, and Sefton went back to his nest in Chelsea on the following afternoon, and was in a stall at the Apollo in the evening. He tried to persuade himself that the music was the chief attraction.

"Your music is like a vice, Hawberk," he told the composer, at a tea-party next day. "It takes possession of a man. I go night after night to hear *Fanchonette*, though I know I am wasting my time."

"Thanks. *Fanchonette* is a very pretty opera, quite the best thing I have done," replied Hawberk, easily; "and it is very well sung and acted. The singing is good all round, but Lisa Vivanti is a pearl."

"You are enthusiastic," said Sefton; and then smiling at the composer's young wife, who went everywhere with her husband, and whose province was to wear smart frocks and look pretty, "You must keep your eye upon him, Mrs. Hawberk, lest this Venetian siren should prove as fatal as the Lurlei."

"No fear," cried Hawberk. "Little Lisa is as straight as an arrow and as good as gold. She lives as sedately as a nun, with a comfortable dragon in the shape of an aunt. She would hardly look at a ripping diamond bracelet which some cad sent her the other day. She just tossed bracelet and letter over to her old singing master, and told him to send it back to the giver. She has no desire for carriages and horses and fine raiment. She comes to the theatre in a shabby little black frock, and she lives like a peasant on a third floor in this neighbourhood."

"That will not last," said Sefton. "Your *rara avis* will soon realize her own value. The management will be called upon to provide her with a stable and a chef, and diamonds will be accepted freely as fitting tribute to her talents."

"I don't believe it. I think she is a genuine, honest, right-minded young woman, and that she will gang her ain gait in spite of all counter influences. There may have been some love affair in the past that has sobered her. I think there has been; for there is a little boy who calls her mother, and for whom she takes no trouble to account. I will vouch for my little Lisa, and I have allowed Mrs. Hawberk to go and see her."

"She is quite too sweet," assented the lady; "such a perfectly naïve little person."

"Upon my honour," said Hawberk, as his wife fluttered away and was absorbed in a group of acquaintances, "I believe Vivanti is a good woman, in spite of the little peccadillo in a sailor suit."

"I am very glad to hear it, for I want you to introduce me to the lady."

"Oh, but really now that is just what I don't care about doing. She is keeping herself to herself, and is working conscientiously at her musical education. She is a very busy woman, and she has no idea of society, or its ways and manners. What can she want with such an acquaintance as you?"

"Nothing; but I very much want to know her; and I pledge myself to approach her with all the respect due to the best woman in England."

"To approach her, yes; I can believe that. No doubt Lucifer approached Eve with all possible courtesy; yet the acquaintance ended badly. I don't see that any good could arise from your acquaintance with my charming Venetian."

"I understand," said Sefton, with an aggrieved air; "she is so charming that you would like to keep her all to yourself."

"Oh, come now, that's a very weak thing in the way of sneers," exclaimed the composer. "I hope I am secure from any insinuations of that sort. Look here, Sefton, I'm just a bit afraid of you; but if you promise to act on the square I'll get my wife to send you a card for a Sunday evening, at which I believe she is going to get Vivanti to sing for her. That is always the first thing Lavinia thinks of if I venture to introduce her to a singer."

"That would be very friendly of you, and I promise to act on the square. I am not a married man, and I am my own master. If I were desperately in love——"

"You wouldn't marry a Venetian lace-maker, with a damaged reputation. I know you too well to believe you capable of that sort of thing."

"Nobody knows of what a man is capable; least of all the man himself," said Sefton, sententiously.

* * * *

Mr. and Mrs. Hawberk lived in a smart little house in that dainty and artistic region of Cheyne Walk, which even yet retains a faint flavour of Don Saltero, of Bolingbroke and Walpole, of Chelsea buns and Chelsea china, Ranelagh routs, and Thames watermen. Mr. Hawberk's house was in a terrace at right angles with the Embankment, but further west than Tite Street. It was a new house, with all the latest improvements, and all the latest fads—tiny panes to Queen Anne windows, admitting the minimum of light and not overmuch air; a spacious ingle nook in a miniature dining-room, whereby facetious friends had frequently been heard to ask Mrs. Hawberk which was the ingle nook and which was the dining-room.

The house was quaint and pretty, and being entirely furnished with Japaneseries was a very fascinating toy, if not altogether the most commodious thing in the way of houses. For party-giving it was delightful, for less than a hundred people choked every inch of space in rooms and staircase, and suggested a tremendous reception: so that the smallest of Mrs. Hawberk's parties seemed a crush.

Sefton arriving at half-past ten, only half an hour after the time on Mrs. Hawberk's card, found the drawing-rooms blocked with people, mostly standing, and could see no more of Signora Vivanti than if she had been on the other side of the river; but the people in the doorway were talking about her, and their talk informed him that she was somewhere in the innermost angle of the back drawing-room, behind the grand piano, and that she was going to sing.

Then there came an authoritative "Silence, please," from Haw-berk, followed by a sudden hush as of sentences broken off in the middle, and anon a firm hand played the symphony to Sullivan's *Orpheus*, and the grand mezzo soprano voice rolled out the grand Shakesperean words set to noble music. The choice of the song was a delicate compliment to Hawberk's master in art, who was among Mrs. Hawberk's guests.

The Venetian accent was still present in Lisa's pronunciation, but her English had improved as much as her vocalization, under Haw-berk's training. He had taken extraordinary pains with this particular song, and every note rang out clear as crystal, pure as thrice-refined gold. The composer's "Brava, bravissima!" was heard amidst the ap-plause that followed the song.

Sefton elbowed his way through the crowd—as politely as was consistent with a determination to reach a given point—and con-trived to mingle with the group about the singer. She was standing by the piano in a careless attitude, dressed in a black velvet gown, which set off the yellowish whiteness of her shoulders and full round throat. Clasped round that statuesque throat, she wore a collet neck-lace of diamonds, splendid in size and colour, a necklace which could not have been bought for less than six or seven hundred pounds.

"So," thought Sefton. "Those diamonds don't quite come into Hawberk's notion of the lady's character."

Mr. Sefton did not know that, after the manner of Venetian women, Lisa looked upon jewellery as an investment, and that near-ly all her professional earnings since her *début* were represented by the diamonds she wore round her neck. She and la Zia were able to live on so little, and it was such a pleasure to them to save, first to gloat over the golden sovereigns, and then to change them into pre-cious stones. There was such a delightful feeling in being able to wear one's fortune round one's neck.

Mr. Hawberk had accompanied the singer, and he was still sitting at the piano, when Sefton's eager face reminded him of his promise.

"Signora, allow me to introduce another of your English admir-ers. Mr. Sefton, a connoisseur in the way of music, and a cosmopoli-tan in the way of speech."

Lisa turned smilingly to the stranger. "You speak Italian," she said in her own language, and Sefton replying in very good Tuscan, they were soon on easy terms; and presently he had the delight of taking her down to the supper-room, where there was a long narrow table loaded with delicacies, and a perpetual flow of champagne.

Lisa enjoyed herself here as frankly as she had enjoyed herself at the sign of the Black Hat, in the Piazza di San Marco. She was the same unsophisticated Lisa still, in the matter of quails and lobster mayonnaise, creams and jellies. She stood at the table and eat all the good things that Sefton brought her, and drank three or four glasses of champagne with jovial unconcern, and talked of the people and the gowns they were wearing in her soft southern tongue, secure of not being understood, though Sefton warned her occasionally that there might be other people in the room besides themselves who knew the language of Dante and Boccaccio.

Never had he talked to any beautiful woman who was so thoroughly unsophisticated; and that somewhat plebeian nature had a curious charm for him. He could understand Vansittart's infatuation for such a woman, but could not understand his giving her up for the sake of Eve Marchant, whose charms as compared with Lisa's were

"As moonlight unto sunlight, or as water unto wine."

He hoped to discover all the history of that intrigue by-and-by, seeing how freely Lisa talked of herself to an acquaintance of an hour. He meant to follow up that acquaintance with all the earnestness of which he was capable.

"There are no finer diamonds in the room than your necklace," he said, when she had been praising an ancient dowager's jewels, gems whose beauty was not enhanced by a neck that looked as if its bony structure had been covered with one of the family parchments.

"Do you really like them?" asked Lisa, with a flashing smile.

"She doesn't even blush for her spoil," thought Sefton.

"I'm so glad you think them good," continued Lisa. "They are all my fortune. The jeweller told me I should never repent buying them."

"What, Signora, did you buy them? I thought they were the offering of some devoted admirer."

"Do you suppose I would accept such a gift from any one except—except somebody I cared for?" she exclaimed indignantly. "A man sent me a diamond bracelet one night at the theatre—I found it in my dressing-room when I arrived—with his card. I sent it back next morning—or at least Zinco sent it back for me."

"And I dare say you have even forgotten the man's name?" said Sefton.

"Yes. Your English names are very ugly, and very difficult to remember. They are so short; so insignificant."

And then she told him the history of her diamonds; how the manager of the Apollo had first doubled, and then trebled, and quadrupled her salary; how she had kept the money in her trunk, all in gold, sovereigns upon sovereigns, and how she and her aunt had counted the gold every week, and how only last Saturday she and la Zia had gone off in a cab to Piccadilly, with a bag full of gold, and had bought the diamonds, which were now shining on Fiordelisa's throat.

"We had less than half the price of the necklace," concluded Lisa, "but when the jeweller heard who I was, he insisted that I should take it away with me, and pay him by degrees, just as I find convenient, so I shall pay him my salary every Saturday until I am out of debt."

"It sounds like a fairy tale," said Sefton. "Do you and your aunt live upon rose leaves and dew, Signora; or how is it that you can afford to invest all your earnings in diamonds?"

"Oh, we have other money," answered Lisa, with a defiant glance at the questioner. "I need not sing unless I like."

"Indeed!" exclaimed Sefton, strengthened in his conviction that Signora Vivanti was not altogether so "straight" as Hawberk believed, or affected to believe.

Mr. Sefton was not so confiding as the composer. He was a man prone to think badly of women, and he was inclined to think the worst of this brilliant Venetian, much as he admired her. He followed her like a shadow for the rest of the evening, escorted her up the narrow staircase, and stood near the piano while she sang, and then took her from the stifling atmosphere of the lamp-lit house to the semi-darkness of the garden, which Mrs. Hawberk had converted into a tent, shutting out the wintry sky, and enclosing the miniature lawn and surrounding shrubbery; a tent dimly lighted with fairy lamps, nestling among the foliage. Here he sat talking with Lisa in a shadowy corner, while three or four other couples murmured and whispered in other nooks and corners, and while Hawberk, feeling he had done his duty as host, smoked and drank whisky and soda with a little group of chosen friends—an actor, a journalist, a playwright, and a brace of musical critics, who had an inexhaustible flow of speech, and a delicious unconsciousness of time.

Sefton too was unconscious of time, talking with Lisa in that soft Italian tongue, having to bend his head very near the full red lips in order to catch the Venetian elisions, the gentle, sliding syllables.

The hum of voices, the occasional ripples of laughter, the music and song, dwindled and died into silence—even the lights in the lower windows grew dim, and gradually Sefton awakened to the fact that the party was at an end, and that he and Signora Vivanti, and Hawberk's Bohemian group yonder, were all that remained of Mrs. Hawberk's musical evening. He bent down to look at his watch by one of the fairy lamps.

Three o'clock.

"By Jove, we are sitting out everybody else," he said, with a pleased laugh, triumphant at the thought that he had been able to amuse and interest his companion. "Three o'clock. Very late for a musical evening. You did not know it was so late, did you, Signora?"

"No," answered Lisa, carelessly; "but I don't mind. I've been enjoying myself."

"So have I; but it's rather rough on Mrs. Hawberk, who may want to rest from her labours."

"I am quite ready to go home as soon as I get my shawl," said Lisa, rising from the low wicker chair, straight as a dart, her neck and shoulders and long bare arms looking like marble in the glimmer of the toy lamps. Sefton stood and looked at her, drinking her loveliness as if it had been a draught of wine from an enchanted cup. Oh, the charm of those Italian eyes; so brilliant, yet so soft; so darkly deep! Could there be any magic in fairyland more potent than the spell this Calypso was weaving round him?

"May I call your carriage?" he asked.

"I have no carriage. I live close by."

"Let me see you home, then."

She shrugged her shoulders with a gesture which meant that the question wasn't worth disputing, and Sefton followed her across the little bit of grass to the house door. Hawberk stopped her on her way.

"What, my Vivanti not gone yet!" he cried. "I would have had another song out of you if I had known you were there. What have you and Mr. Sefton found to say to each other all this time?"

"We have found plenty to say. He has been talking Italian, which none of you stupid others can talk. It is a treat to hear my own language from some one besides la Zia. Good night, Signor. Shall I find la Signora to wish her good night?"

"No, child. La Signora Hawberkini retired to rest an hour ago, when all the respectable people had gone. She did not wait to see the last of such night-birds as you and Sefton, and these disreputable journalists here."

"I love the night," said Lisa, in no wise abashed. "It is ever so much nicer than day."

The servants had vanished, but she found her wrap lying on a sofa—an old red silk shawl, a Bellagio shawl, whose dinginess went ill with her velvet gown and diamond necklace; but she wrapped it about her head and shoulders, nothing caring, and she looked a real Italian peasant as she turned to Sefton in the light of the hall lamps. He admired her even more at this moment than he had admired her before—he liked to think of her as a peasant; with no womanly sensitiveness to suffer, no pride to be wounded; divided from him socially by a great gulf of difference; and so much the more surely, and so much the more lightly to be won.

They went out into the street together. It was moonlight, a February moon, cold, and sharp, and clear, with a hoar frost whitening the wintry shrubs and iron railings. Lisa caught up her velvet train, and tripped lightly along the pavement in bronze beaded slippers and bright red stockings, Sefton at her side. She would not take his arm, both hands being occupied, one clutching the silk shawl, the other holding up her skirt. The walk was of the shortest, for Saltero's Mansion was only just round the corner; nor could Sefton detain her on the doorstep for any sentimentality about the moonlit river. She had her key in the door in a moment, and as he pushed the big, heavy door open for her, she vanished behind it with briefest "Grazie, e buona notte, caro Signor."

There had not been time for the gentlest pressure of her strong, broad hand, or for his tender "Addio, bellissima mia," to be heard.

But to know where she lived was something gained, and as he walked homeward humming "la donna è mobile," he meant to follow up that advantage. He had told her that he was her near neighbour. He had gone even further, and had asked her if she would sing for him at a little tea-party, were he to give one in her honour; on which she had only laughed, and said that she had never heard of a man giving a tea-party.

The acquaintance begun so auspiciously gave Wilfred Sefton a new zest for London life. He hailed the hardening frosts of February with absolute pleasure, he for whom that month had hitherto been the cream of the hunting season. He cared nothing that his latest acquisitions, the hunters in whose perfections he still believed, whose vices he had not had time to discover, were eating their heads off in his Sussex stables. He was in his stall at the Apollo every night; and Lisa's singing and Lisa's beauty, and the "quips and cranks and wanton wiles" which constituted Lisa's idea of acting, were enough for his contentment.

He waited till Wednesday before he ventured to call upon his divinity. He would gladly have presented himself at her door on Mon-

233

day afternoon; but he did not want to appear too eager. Tuesday seemed a long blank day to his impatience, although there was plenty to do in London for a man of intellect and taste; pictures, people, politics, all manner of interests and amusements.

Lisa had told him about the aunt who lived with her and kept house for her. There could be no impropriety in his visit. He made up his mind indeed to ask for the elder lady in the first instance; but all uncertainty was saved him, as it was la Zia who opened the door. Those diamonds of Lisa's could not have been earned so speedily had the Venetians taken upon themselves the maintenance of a servant. What was she there for, argued la Zia—when Hawberk suggested the necessity of a parlour-maid—except to sweep and dust, and market and cook? An English servant, who would want butcher's meat every day, and would object to the cuisine *à l'huile*, would be a ruinous institution.

La Zia was not too tidy in her indoor apparel, since her love for finery was stronger than her sense of the fitness of things. She had one gown at a time, a gown of silk or plush or velveteen, which she wore as a best gown till it began to be shabby or dilapidated, when Lisa bought her another fine gown, and the old one was taken for daily use.

Lisa's taste had become somewhat chastened since she had lived at Chelsea. A casual word or two from Vansittart, whose lightest speech she remembered, had made her scrupulously plain in her attire—save on such an occasion as Mrs. Hawberk's party, when her innate love of finery showed itself in scarlet stockings and beaded shoes. This afternoon Sefton found her sitting on the hearthrug in front of the bright little tiled grate, in the black stuff gown she had worn when he first saw her, and with just the same touch of colour at her throat, and in her blue-black hair.

She and the little boy were sitting on the rug together, dividing the caprices of a white kitten, the plaything of mother and son, mother and son laughing gaily, with laughter which harmonized and sounded like music. The boy made no change in his sprawling attitude as Sefton entered; but he looked up at the stranger with large dark eyes, wondering, and slightly resentful.

"*His* boy," thought Sefton, and felt a malignant disposition to kick the sprawling imp, hanging on to the mother's skirts, and preventing her from rising to greet her visitor.

"Let go, Paolo," said Lisa, laughing. "What with you and the kitten, I can't stir."

She shook herself free, transferred the kitten to the boy's eager

234

arms, rose, and gave Sefton her hand, with a careless grace which was charming from an artistic point of view, but which showed him how faint an impression all his attentions of Sunday night had made upon her. A woman who had thought of him in the interval would have been startled at his coming. Lisa took his visit much too easily. There was neither surprise nor gladness in her greeting.

"I saw you in the stalls," she said, "last night, and the night before. Aren't you tired of *Fanchonette?*"

"Not in the least."

"You must be monstrously fond of music," she said, always in Italian.

"I am—monstrously; but I have other reasons for liking *Fanchonette*. I like to see you act, as well as to hear you sing."

"So do other people," she answered, with frank vanity, tossing up her head. "They all applaud me when I first come on, before I have sung a note. I have to stand there in front of the lights for ever so long, while they go on applauding like mad. And yet people say you English have no enthusiasm, that you care very little for anything."

"We care a great deal for that which is really beautiful; most of all when it is fresh and new."

"Ah! that's what Mr. Hawberk says—I am all the better because I am not highly trained like other singers. My ignorance is my strength."

"But she has worked," interposed la Zia; "ah! how hard she has worked! At her piano; at the English language. She has such a strong will. She has but to make up her mind, and the thing is done."

"One can read as much, Signora, in those flashing eyes; in that square brow and firmly moulded chin," said Sefton, putting down his hat and cane, and establishing himself in one of the prettily draped basket-chairs. "And pray how did it happen that you two ladies made up your minds to seek your fortunes in London?"

"It was the impresario who brought us. We were at Milan, and we came to London to sing in the chorus at Covent Garden. It was good fortune which brought us so far from home."

"And you hate London, no doubt, after Italy?"

"No, indeed, Signor. London is a city to love—the wide, wide streets; the big, big houses; the great squares—ah! the Piazza is nothing to your square of Trafalgar—and the shops, the beautiful shops! Your sky is often gloomy, but there are summer days—heavenly days—when the wind blows down to the sea, and sweeps all the darkness out of the heavens, and your sky grows blue, like Italy.

235

Those are days to remember."

"True! They are rare enough to be counted on the fingers of one hand," answered Sefton, stooping to take hold of the boy, who had been pursuing his kitten on all-fours, and had this moment plunged between Sefton's legs to extract the animated ball of white fluff from under his chair. He felt nothing but aversion for the handsome, dark-eyed brat; but he felt that he must take some notice of the creature, if he wanted to stand well with the mother.

"Che sta facendo, padroncino?"

The boy was friendly, and explained himself in a torrent of broken speech. The cat was a bad cat, and wouldn't stay with him. Would the Signor make him stay? Sefton had to stoop and risk a scratching from the tiny claws, in a vain endeavour to get hold of the rebellious beast, which rolled away from him, hissing and spitting, and finally scampered across the room and took refuge behind the piano. Sefton lifted the boy on to his knee, and produced his watch, that unfailing object of interest to infancy, usually denominated, on the principle of all slang nomenclature, "tick-tick." Once interested in the opening and shutting of the "tick-tick," Paolo sat on the visitor's knee, *comme un image*, and allowed Sefton to talk to Lisa and her aunt.

He was careful to make himself agreeable to the elder lady, who was charmed to find an Englishman who understood her native tongue. She had contrived to learn a little English, but had made no such progress as her niece, and it was a labour to her to talk. What a pleasure, therefore, to find this suave, handsome Englishman, with his courtly manners, quick comprehension, and ready replies.

From la Zia he heard a good deal about Lisa's early life; yet there was a certain wise reticence even on that loquacious lady's part. She breathed no word of Lisa's Englishman, the first Mr. Smith, or of the second. In all her talk of their old life, in Venice, at Milan, there was no hint of any one but themselves. They appeared to have been alone, unprotected, dependent on their own small earnings.

After waiting in vain for any allusion to Vansittart, Sefton came straight to the point, with a direct question.

"I think you know a friend of mine, Signora," he said to Lisa. "Mr. Vansittart?"

"Vansittart?"

Lisa repeated the name slowly, with a look of blank wonder.

"Have you never heard that name before?"

"Never."

"So," thought Sefton, "she knew him under an alias. That means

236

a good deal, and confirms my original idea."

He put the boy off his knee almost roughly, and rose to depart.

"Good-bye, Signora. You will let me call in again some day, I hope?"

"If you like. Why did you think I knew your friend, Mr. Van—sit—tart?"

"Because last May I saw you in Cheyne Walk talking to a man whom I took for Vansittart. A tall man, with fair hair. You seemed very friendly with him; your hands were clasped upon his arm: you were smiling up at him."

This time Lisa blushed a deep carnation, and her face saddened.

"Oh, that," she stammered—"that was some one I knew in Italy."

"Not Vansittart?"

"No."

"But the gentleman has a name of some kind," persisted Sefton.

"Never mind his name," she answered abruptly. "I don't want to talk about him. I may never see him again, perhaps." And then, brushing away a tear, and becoming suddenly frivolous, she asked, "How did you come to remember me—after so long?"

"Because that moment by the river yonder has lived in my memory ever since—because no man can forget the loveliest face he ever saw in his life."

With that compliment, and with a lingering clasp of the strong hand, he concluded his first visit to Saltero's Mansion, la Zia accompanying him to the door and curtsying him out.

CHAPTER XX.

PEGGY'S CHANCE

If there were blue skies now and then in a London February, what was February along the Riviera but the most exquisite spring-time? And perhaps on all that favoured shore, Cannes has the richest firstfruits of the fertile year, for it is then that the mimosas are in their glory, and the hill of Californie is a yellow fairyland, an enchanted region, where all the trees drop golden rain.

Eve and her lover husband were at Cannes. Delicious as the place was at this season, and new as the shores of the Mediterranean were to Eve, she and her husband had not come there for their own pleasure. They had come at the advice of the doctors—to give Peggy a chance. That was what it had come to. Peggy's only chance of living through the winter was to be found in the south. One doctor had suggested Capri, another Sorrento; but for some unexplained reason Vansittart objected to Italy, and then Mentone or Cannes had been talked about; and finally Cannes was decided upon, for medical reasons, in order that Peggy might have the watchful care of Dr. Bright, which might give her an additional chance in the hand-to-hand struggle with her grim adversary.

Vansittart had offered, in the first instance, to send Peggy to the south in the care of one of her elder sisters and an experienced travelling-maid, who should be also a skilled nurse; but Eve had been so distressed at the idea of parting with the ailing child, that of his own accord he had offered to accompany his youngest sister-in-law on the journey that was to give her a chance—alas! only a chance. None of the doctors talked of cure as a certainty. Peggy's family history was bad; and Peggy's lungs were seriously affected.

It was almost inevitable that the youngest child—born after the mother's health had begun to fail—should inherit the mother's fatal tendency to lung disease; but things were altogether different in the case of Eve, the eldest daughter, born before her mother had begun to develop lung trouble. For Eve there was every chance. This was what a distinguished specialist told Vansittart, when he asked piteously if the hereditary disease shown too clearly by Peggy, were likely to appear by-and-by in Eve's constitution. He was obliged to take what comfort he could from this assurance. He would not alarm Eve by suggesting that her chest should be sounded by the physician who had just passed sentence upon her sister. Perhaps he did not want to know too much. He was content to see his young wife fair and blooming, with all the indications of perfect health, and to believe that she must needs be exempt from inherited evil.

She was enraptured when he offered to take her to the south with Peggy.

"You are more than good, you are adorable," she cried. "Now I feel justified in having worshipped you. What, you will leave Hampshire just when the hunting is at its best? You will forego all your plans for the spring? And you will put up with a sick child's company?"

"I shall have my wife's company, and that is enough. I shall see you happy and at ease, and not wearing yourself to death with anxieties and apprehensions about Peggy."

"Yes, I shall be ever so much happier with her, should things come to the worst"—her eyes brimmed over with sudden tears at the thought—"it will be so much to be with her—to know that we have made her quite happy."

They went to Haslemere next morning, and there was a grand scene with Peggy, who screamed with rapture on hearing that Eve and Jack were going to take her to Cannes their very own selves. She, who fancied she had lost Eve for ever, was to live with her, to sleep in the next room to her, to see her every day and all day long.

Then came the journey—the long, long journey, which made Eve and Peggy open wondering eyes at the width of France from sea to sea. They travelled with all those luxuries which modern civilization provides for the traveller who is able and willing to pay. And every detail of the journey was a surprise and a joy for Peggy, who brought upon herself more than one bad fit of coughing by her irrepressible raptures. The luncheon and dinner on board the rushing *Rapide*; the comfortable *wagon-lit* to retire to at Lyons, when darkness had fallen over the monotony of the landscape—and anon the surprise of awaking at midnight in a large bright room where two small beds were veiled like brides in white net curtains, and where piled up pine-logs blazed on a wide open hearth, such as Peggy only knew of in fairy tales.

How comforting was the basin of hot soup which Peggy sipped, squatting beside this cavernous chimney, while Benson, the courier-maid, skilled in nursing invalids, who had been engaged chiefly to wait upon Peggy, unpacked the Gladstone bag, and made everything comfortable for the night. Peggy had slept fitfully all the way from Lyons, hearing as in a dream the porters shouting "Avignon," at a place where they stopped in the winter darkness, and faintly remembering having heard of a city where Popes lived and tortured people once upon a time. She woke now and again in her white-curtained bed at Marseilles; for however happy her days might be her nights were generally restless and troubled. The new maid was very attentive to her, and gave her lemonade when her throat was parched, but the maid was able to sleep soundly between whiles, when Peggy was lying awake gazing through the white net curtains, and half expecting Robin Goodfellow to come creeping out of the wide black chimney, where the spark had faded from the heap of pale grey ashes on the hearth.

Towards morning Peggy fell into a refreshing slumber, and when she opened her eyes again the room was full of sunshine, and there was a band playing the "Faust Waltz" in the public gardens below.

"Why, it's summer!" cried Peggy, clapping her hands, and leaping out of the parted white curtains, and rushing to the open window.

The maid was dressed, and Peggy's breakfast was ready for her. "Oh, such delicious coffee!" she told Eve afterwards, "in a sweet little copper pot, and rolls such as were never made in humdrum England."

Yes, it was summer, the February summer of that lovely shore. The Vansittarts stayed nearly a week at Marseilles, to rest Peggy after her forty-eight hours' journey; and to see the Votive Church on the hill, and that famous dungeon on the rock which owes more of its renown to fiction than to fact; and the parting of the ways where the ships sail east and west, to Orient or Afric, the two wonderworlds for the untravelled European. Eve and Peggy looked longingly at the great steamers vanishing on the horizon, hardly knowing whether, if the choice were put to them, they would go right or left—to the country were the Great Moguls, the jewelled temples, the tiger hunts, the palanquins, the tame elephants with castles on their backs are to be found; or to the country where the Moors live, and where modern civilization camps gipsy-fashion among the vestiges of earth's most ancient people.

"Where would you like to go best, India or Africa?" asked Eve, as she and Peggy sat side by side in a fairy-like yawl, that went dipping and dancing over those summer waves, and seemed like a toy boat as it sailed under the lee of an Orient steamer bound for Alexandria.

"Oh, I think I would rather go up a pyramid than anything,"

gasped Peggy, breathless at the mere thought. "Don't you remember 'Belzoni's Travels,' that tattered little old book which once was mother's, and how they used to grope about, Belzoni and his people, and lose themselves in dark passages, and make discoveries inside the Pyramids? And then the Nile, and the crocodiles, which one could always run away from, because they can't turn, don't you know? Oh, I think Egypt must be best of all."

Peggy and her companions were out driving along the Corniche road or sailing over the blue waters every day, and all day long; and the invalid made a most wonderful recovery during that week.

Her nights were ever so much quieter, her appetite had improved. Peggy's chance began to look like a certainty, and hope revived in Eve's breast. Hope had never died there. She could not believe that this bright, happy young creature was to be taken away from her. There was such vitality in Peggy, such vigour in those thin arms when they clasped themselves round Eve's neck, such light and life in the full blue eyes when they looked out upon the movement and variety of the Rue Cannebière, or the bustle of the quays.

They went on to Cannes, and alighted first at one of the most comfortable hotels in Europe, the Mont Fleuri, so as to take their time in the selection of a home; for they meant to stay in Provence till there was an end of cold weather in England, to go back only when an English spring should have done its worst, and the footsteps of summer should be at hand. If Cannes should grow too warm, there was Grasse; and there were cool retreats perched still higher on the mountain slopes, where they might spend the last month or so of their sojourn. There were reasons why Eve would be glad to escape from the little world in which she was known, reasons why she should prefer the absolute retirement of a villa in a strange land, where she need receive no more visitors than she chose, where she might let it be known among the little community of British residents that she did not desire to be called upon.

They found just the retreat that suited them, high on the eastern hill, which at this season was cloaked with the mimosa's golden bloom as with a royal garment. The villa stood on higher ground than the Hotel Californie, and all the gulf of San Juan lay at its feet, and the ships at anchor looked like toy ships in the distance of that steep descent, where palm and pine, cypress and olive, lent their varying form and colour to the rough grey rocks, and where garden below garden spread a carpet of vivid flowers, hedges of roses, beds of pink and purple anemones, the scarlet and orange of the ranunculus, amidst the gloom of rocky gorge and pine forest.

Beyond the gulf rose the islands, shadowy at eventide, clear and sunlit in those early mornings when Peggy watched the red fires of dawn lighting up far away yonder towards Italy. She shared Eve's imaginings about that neighbouring country, and thought with wonder of being so near the border of that mystical land. All her ideas of Italy were derived from "Childe Harold," the more famous passages of which she had read and learnt diligently under Eve's instruction, the eldest daughter carrying on the education of the youngest in a casual way, after the homely governess had vanished from the scene.

The villa was small and unpretentious, flung down carelessly, as it seemed, in a spacious garden, a garden which had been neglected of late years, since much smarter villas had risen up, white and ornamental, upon the heights of Californie. But the garden had once been cared for. It was full of roses and ivy-leaved geranium, anemones and narcissi, and, what pleased Peggy most of all, there was a grove of orange trees, where she could lie upon the grass and let the mandarin oranges drop into her lap. Eve and her young sister sat among the oranges for hours at a stretch, Eve working at one of those tiny garments which it was her delight to make—"dressing dolls," Vansittart called it; Peggy pretending to read, but for the most part gazing at sky or sea, watching the white clouds or the white ships sailing by in the blue.

"Don't you think heaven must be very like this?" Peggy asked, one quiet noontide, when the sky was of its deepest sapphire, and the air had the warmth and perfume of an English midsummer.

"What, Peg, do you suppose there are orange trees in the 'Land of the Leal'—orange trees, and smart villas, and afternoon parties?"

"No, no—only the blue sky, and the sea, and the hills jutting out, one beyond another, till they melt into the sky. It looks as if one could never come to the end of it all. It looks just like heaven."

"Endless, and without limits, like Eternity," said Vansittart, smiling at her, unconscious that Eve's head was bending lower and lower over her work to hide the streaming tears. "A pretty fancy. But that boundless-seeming sea is only a big round pool after all; and think how clever it was of Columbus to find his way across the great ocean, and what rapture for Cortez to discover a second ocean, bigger than the first. And yet this earth of ours is only like a grain of sand in the multitude of worlds."

"Don't," cried Peggy, with her fingers in her ears. "You make my head ache. I can't bear to think of the universe. It's much too big. Mütterchen used to tell me about it when I was a small child. She made me dream bad dreams. Why isn't there one nice, comfortable world for us to live in, and one lovely heaven for us to go to after we are dead, and one horrid hell for the *very* bad people, just to prevent their mixing with the good ones? That's what the Bible means, doesn't it? I can't bear to think of anything more than that."

"Don't think, darling," said Eve, sitting down on the grass beside her, and drawing the fragile form close against her own—"don't think. Only be happy. Breathe this delicious air, bask in this delightful sun, be happy, and get well."

"Oh, I am getting well as fast as ever I can. Except for my tiresome cough, I am as well as anybody can be. I wonder what they are doing at Fernhurst. Skating on Farmer Green's pond, perhaps, or crouching over the fire. You know how Hetty would always sit with her head hanging over the coals, in spite of all you could say about spoiling her complexion. And here we spoil our complexions in the sun. Isn't it wonderful?"

"Everything in our lives is wonderful, Peggy. Most of all, that I should have such a husband as Jack."

Eve held out her hand to that model husband, smiling at him, with eyes that were veiled in tears, more grateful for his goodness to this ailing child than for all the love that he had lavished upon herself.

What a happy season this would have been on the lovely hill beside the tideless sea, if hope had never been dashed with fear! But, alas! there were moments, even at Peggy's best, when the shadow of doom fell dark across the summer glory of a land that knows not winter. Sometimes, in the midst of her joyous delight in the things around her, a sudden paroxysm of coughing would surprise the poor child, shaking her as if some invisible demon had seized the wasted form by the narrow shoulders, and were trying to tear it piecemeal.

"My enemy has been very cruel to me to-day," Peggy would say afterwards, with a serio-comic smile. "I thought Dr. Bright would get the better of him."

At first she used to call that wearing cough her enemy, as she had heard old people talk of their gout or their rheumatism. Later, she talked of her cough as the dragon, and of Dr. Bright as St. George; but although the medical champion might get the better of the dragon now and again, he was a sturdy monster, and harder to kill than the toughest crocodile along the sandy shores of old Nile. Peggy was wonderfully patient, wonderfully hopeful about herself, even when hope began to wax faint in the hearts of her companions, when the trained attendant could tell of sorely troubled nights, and when Eve, creeping in from her adjoining bed-chamber half a dozen times between night and morning, was saddened at finding the fevered head tossing unquietly upon the heaped-up pillows, the blue eyes wide open, and the parched lips uttering speech that told of semi-delirium.

However bad Peggy's nights were, her days were generally cheerful. She was never tired of the hillside paths, the luxury of ferns, and palms, and aloes, the glory of the golden-tufted mimosas, the peach blossom, the anemones, the silvery threads of water creeping down the rocky gorges, such narrow streamlets, cleaving Titanic rocks. To Peggy these things brought no satiety; while the more earthly enjoyment of afternoon tea at Rumpelmeyer's, sitting out of doors, and eating as many cakes and bon-bons as ever she liked, was only a lesser revelation of a world where all was beauty. Eve and her husband saw the crowds at Rumpelmeyer's with an amused interest. They looked on at this curiously blended smart world, this odd mixture of Royal Duchesses and Liverpool merchants, millionaires and impecunious *cavalière servente*, Parisian celebrities, the old nobility of France and England—old as the Angevin kings, when England and France were one monarchy—and the newly-gotten wealth of New York and Chicago. Eve and Vansittart looked on and were amused, and then drove back to the villa on the hill, and rejoiced in the seclusion of their own garden, which it had been their delight to improve and beautify. Everything grew so quickly—the rose-trees they planted throve so well that it was like gardening in fairyland.

They were not intruded upon by that smart world which they saw at the tea-shop on the Croisette. At Cannes two things only count as worthy of regard or reverence—the first, fashion; the second, money. Eve and her husband had neither one nor the other. A Hampshire squire, with three thousand a year and a young wife, was a person who could interest nobody. Had he been a bachelor and a dancing man, he would have been eligible and even courted; for dancing men are in a minority, and a ball at the Cercle Nautique is apt to recall Edwin Long's famous picture of the Babylonian Marriage Market, women of all nationalities waiting to be asked to dance. A Hampshire squire, living quietly with his wife and her sister in one of the cheapest villas in Californie was a person to seek, and not to be sought. If the Vansittarts wanted to be in society they should have brought letters of introduction, observed a Jewish Plutocrat whose garden joined the Vansittarts' modest enclosure. "We can't be expected to take any interest in people of whom we know absolutely nothing."

It would have been difficult, if not impossible, for the leaders of Cannes society, the owners of palatial villas, and givers of luncheons and dances, to understand that these pariahs did not desire to enter the charmed circle where wealth was the chief qualification, and where the triple millionaire, however humble his origin, and however dubious the source of his gold, was sure of welcome. Granted that such millionaires were talked of lightly as "good fun." The smart people who laughed were pleased to eat their luncheons, and dance at their balls, or drive on their coaches, or sail in their yachts. For the smart world of Californie and La Route de Frejus February meant a round of luncheons and teas, dinners and dances. Everybody complained of the "strain," of being "dragged" from party to party, of having "so much to do;" these butterflies treating the futilities of life as if they were penal servitude without option. To these the tranquil happiness of such a couple as Eve and Vansittart was unthinkable. Of course the poor things would be in society if society would have them. Cannes must be very dreary for such as they. It was really a pity that this kind of people did not stop at St. Raphael or go on to Alassio.

While society—looking at the "pretty young woman with the rather handsome husband" from afar, through a tortoiseshell merveilleuse—compassionated their forlorn condition, Eve and Vansittart found the resources of the neighbourhood inexhaustible, had schemes and delights for every day, and Peggy was never tired of comparing the Maritime Alps to heaven. What less in loveliness than heaven could be a land where one could picnic in February? For Peggy's sake there were many picnics—now in a rocky gorge on the road to Vallauris, where one could sit about the dry bed of a cataract, and set out one's luncheon on great rocky boulders, screened by feathery palm trees that suggested the South Sea Islands; now on the hilltop at Mougins, with the pinnacled walls of Grasse looking at them, across the deep valley of flower fields and mulberry orchards, blossoming lilies and budding vines; and now, with even more delight, in some sheltered inlet on the level coast of St. Honorat, some tiny cove where the water was brilliant as the jasper sea of the Apocalypse. Sometimes they landed and took their picnic luncheon under the pine trees, or on the edge of the sea—Peggy keenly interested in everything she saw, the time-worn fortress-monastery that rose tall above the level shore, and the modern building with its low-roofed cells and modest chapel, a building whose monastic rule forbade the entrance of Peggy and all her sex, and which therefore inspired the liveliest curiosity on her part. Not less delightful was the sister island of St. Marguerite, with its thrilling mystery of the nameless prisoner, whom Peggy would allow to be none other than a twin brother of the great Louis, and whose faded red velvet chair she looked at with affection and awe.

"To think of his meekly worshipping in this chapel, with an iron mask upon his face, when he might have been reigning over France and making war all over Europe, like the great King."

"But in that case Louis must have been here. You wouldn't have a brace of monarchs, Peggy. One brother must have gone to the wall," argued Vansittart.

"They needn't have shut him up in a dungeon, and made him wear a mask," said Peggy.

"True, Peggy; the whole story involves a want of common sense which makes it incredible. I no more believe in a twin brother of Louis Quatorze than in a twin brother of our Prince of Wales, languishing in the Tower of London at this present moment."

"But you believe there was a masked prisoner," exclaimed Peggy, with keen anxiety.

"Oh yes, I am willing to believe in the Italian exile. The record of that gentleman's existence seems tolerably reliable, and a very bad time he had of it. They managed things wonderfully well in those days. A political agitator, or the writer of an unpleasant epigram, could be promptly suppressed. They had prison walls for inconvenient people of all kinds."

Peggy sighed. She did not care about the Italian politician. She had read her Dumas, and had a settled belief in the royal twin. She liked to think that he had lived and suffered in that cold grey fortress. She cared nothing for Marshal Bazaine, and his legendary leap from the parapet, which the soldier guide recited with his tongue in his cheek. She despised Vansittart for being so curious about such a humdrum incident—an elderly general creeping out of captivity under the nose of guardians who were wilfully blind, and slipping quietly off in a steamer.

Those tranquil days on the islands or on the sea would have been as exquisite for Eve as for Peggy if the heart of the elder sister had not been heavy with anxiety about the younger. During the first few weeks in that soft climate Peggy's chance had seemed almost a certainty of cure. Even Dr. Bright had been hopeful for those first weeks, surprised by the marked improvement in his patient; but of late he had been grave to despondency, and every consultation strengthened Eve's fears.

Indeed, there was little need of medical science to reveal the cruel truth. Every week that went by left something of Peggy's youth and strength behind it. The walks which were easy for her in February were difficult in March, and impossible in April. The ground that was lost was never regained. Eve looked back, and remembered how Peggy had walked to the Signal with her a fortnight after their arrival. They had walked very slowly, and they had sat down to rest several times in the course of the journey; but the ascent had been accomplished without pain, and Peggy had been wild with delight at the prospect which rewarded them at the top.

"We'll come up here often, won't we, Eve?"

"As often as you like, darling."

The second ascent was made in March, when the peach trees and anemones were all in bloom, and the gold of the mimosas was a glory of the past. This time Peggy found the winding walks long and wearisome, and although, in spite of Eve's entreaties, she persisted in reaching the summit, the journey had evidently been too much for her. She sank exhausted on a bench, and it was nearly an hour before she was rested enough to mount the little platform on which the telescope stood, and explore the distance, looking for the French squadron which was rounding the point of the Esterelles, on its way to Toulon. Poor little Peggy! She was the only person who did not believe in the seriousness of her case.

"You and Dr. Bright make too much fuss about me," she said to Eve, seeing tears in the fond sister's eyes. "I am only growing. See how short my frock is! I have grown inches since Christmas."

She stretched out her thin legs—so thin as to make the feet look abnormally big, and contemplated the spectacle with a satisfied air.

"I am going to be very tall," she said. "I have only outgrown my strength. That is all that is the matter with me. Sophy and Jenny always said as much. And as for the cough which seems to frighten you so, it's only a stomach cough. Sophy said so."

Vansittart had procured every contrivance which could make Peggy's life easier. He bought her a donkey, on whose back she could be carried up to the Signal, and when her own back grew too weak to endure the fatigue of sitting on the donkey he bought her a wheel chair, which a patient Provençal two-legged beast of burden was willing to drag about all day, if Peggy pleased. And at each stage of her weakness—at each step on the downward road—he found some contrivance to make locomotion easier, so that Peggy might live out of doors, in the sunshine and on the sea.

Alas! there came a day when Peggy no longer cared to be carried about, when even the ripening loveliness of the land, the warmth and splendour of the southern spring, the white-sailed skiff with its quaint old sailors talking their unintelligible Cannois, and chivalrously attentive to Peggy's lightest wish—the time came when even these things could not tempt her from the couch in the garden, where she lay and watched the opening orange blossoms, and wondered who would be there to mark the first change from green to gold in the turn of the year, or thought of Eve's wedding and the orange wreath in her hair, and marvelled to remember how strong her young limbs felt in that gladdest of midsummers, and how slight a thing it had been to walk to the Roman village upon Bexley Hill, or to the pine-crowned crest of Blackdown. And now Vansittart had to carry her to the sofa in the orange grove, and she lay there supine all through the golden afternoon, while Eve, who was said to be herself in delicate health, sat in a low chair near her, and read aloud from Dumas' historical novels, or some fairy tale.

But this increasing weakness was of no consequence, Peggy protested, when she saw Eve looking anxious about her. She had only outgrown her strength. When she had done growing she would be as strong as ever, and able to climb those Sussex hills just as well as ever. But she would not be here to see the flower change to the fruit. That miracle of Nature's handicraft would be for other eyes—for the eyes of some other weakling, perhaps, passing, like Peggy, through the ordeal of overgrowth. But there was something far more wonderful than tree or flower, which had been whispered about by Peggy's nurse. There was the hope of a baby nephew or a baby niece in the first month of summer, a baby that was to open its eyes on some cool Alpine valley, to which Mr. and Mrs. Vansittart and their charge would migrate, when the plane trees by the harbour had unfolded their broad leaves, and the sun that looked upon Cannes was too fierce for any but the hardy natives of the old fishing village. In that sweet summer time a baby was to appear among them, and take its place in all their hearts and on all their knees, and was to reign over them by the divine right of the firstborn. Peggy's nurse told her that, were it only for the sake of this new-comer, she ought to take care of herself, and get well quickly.

"You wouldn't like not to see the baby, would you, Miss Margaret?"

Peggy always felt inclined to laugh when her prim attendant called her Miss Margaret. She had never been addressed by her baptismal name by any one else; but Benson was a superior person, who had lived only in the best families, and who did everything in a superior way.

"Like not to see Eve's baby? Why, of course I shall see it—see it and nurse it, every day of my life," answered Peggy.

"Of course, miss, if you are well enough when June comes."

"If—I—am—well—enough," Peggy repeated slowly, turning towards the nurse with an earnest gaze. "Perhaps you mean that I may not live till June. I heard you say something about me to the housemaid yesterday morning when she was making your bed. I was only half asleep; though I was too drowsy to speak and let you know I could hear all you were saying. You are quite wrong—both of you. I have only outgrown my strength. I shall grow up into a strong young woman, and I shall be very fond of Eve's baby. I shall be the first aunt he will know."

She stopped to laugh—a hoarse little laugh, which it pained Benson to hear.

"Isn't that absurd?" she asked. "I am calling the baby 'he.' But I do hope it will be a boy—I adore little boys—and I'm afraid I rather hate little girls."

"A son and heir," said the nurse, placidly. "That will look nice in the newspapers."

"Yes, baby will have to be in the newspapers," agreed Peggy. "His first appearance upon any stage. I should so love to make something for him to wear. Eve is always working for him; though she contrives to keep her work a secret, even from me. 'Mothers'-meeting work,' she said, when I asked her what she was so busy about. As if I didn't know better than that! One doesn't use the finest lawn and real Valenciennes for mothers'-meeting work. Let me make something for Eve's baby, Benson, there's a dear. I would take such pains with my stitches."

"It would tire you too much, Miss Margaret."

"No, no, it won't. My legs are weak—not my fingers. Let me make something, and surprise Eve with it when it is finished."

"I don't think Mrs. Vansittart would like you to know, miss. It is a secret."

"Yes, but Eve knows that I know. I told her that I had been dreaming about her, and that I dreamt there was a baby. It was after I heard you and Paulette whispering—I really did dream—and Eve kissed me, and cried a little, and said perhaps my dream might come true."

Peggy being very urgent, her nurse brought her some fine flannel, as soft as silk, and cut out a flannel shawl for the unknown, and instructed Peggy as to the manner in which it was to be made, and Peggy was propped up with pillows, and began a floss-silk scallop with neat little stitches, and with an earnest laboriousness which was a touching spectacle; but, alas! after ten minutes of strenuous labour, great beads of perspiration began to roll down Peggy's flushed face, and the thin arm and hand trembled with the effort.

"Oh, Miss Margaret, you mustn't work any more," cried Benson, shocked at her appearance.

"I'm afraid I can't, Nurse; not any more to-day," sighed Peggy, sinking back into the pillows, breathless and exhausted. "But I'll go on with baby's shawl to-morrow. Please fold it up for me and keep it in your basket. Eve mustn't see it till it's finished. The stitches are not too long, are they?"

No, the stitches were very small, but crowded one upon another in a manner that indicated resolute effort and failing sight.

"I feel as if I had been making shawls all day, like the poor woman in the poem," said Peggy. "'Stitch, stitch, stitch, with eyelids heavy and dim!' How odd it is that everything seems difficult when one is ill! I thought it was only my legs that were weak, but I'm afraid it's the whole of me. My finger aches with the weight of my thimble—the dear little gold thimble my brother-in-law gave me on Christmas Day."

She put the little thimble to her lips, and kissed it as if it were a sentient thing. Vansittart came into the room while she was so engaged.

"Oh, there you are," she said. "Do you know what I was thinking about?"

"Not I, quotha," said he, sitting down by Peggy's couch and taking her thin little hand in his. "Who can presume to thread the labyrinth of a young lady's mind, without the least little bit of a clue? You must give me a clue, Peg, if you want me to guess."

"Well, then, I was thinking of you. Is that a clue?"

"Not much of a one, my pet. You might be thinking any-thing—that my last coat is a bad fit about the shoulders—a true bill, Peggy; that I am growing stupid and indolent in this inconsistent climate, where one sleeps half the day and lies awake more than half the night."

"I was thinking of your goodness to Eve, and to all of us. My gold thimble; your bringing us here when you would rather have stayed in Hampshire to hunt. And I was thinking how different our lives would have been if you had never come to Fernhurst. Eve would just have gone on slaving to make both ends meet, cutting out all our frocks, and working her Wilcox and Gibbs, and bearing with father's temper, and going without things. I should have out-grown my strength all the same; but there would have been no one to bring us to Cannes. I should never have seen the Mediterranean, or the Snow Alps, or mother's grave. I should never have seen Eve in pretty tea-gowns, with nothing in the world to do except sit about and look lovely. You have changed our lives."

"For better, Peggy?" he asked earnestly.

"Yes, yes; for worlds and worlds better," she answered, with her arms round his neck.

Benson had crept off to her dinner; Peggy and her brother-in-law were alone.

"God bless you for that assurance, Peggy dear. And—if—if I were not by any means a perfect Christian—if I had done wicked things in my life—given way to a wicked temper, and done some great wrong, not in treachery but in passion, to a fellow-man—could you love me all the same, Peggy?"

"Of course I could. Do you suppose I ever thought you quite per-fect? You wouldn't be half so nice if you were outrageously good. I know you could never be false or treacherous. And as for getting in a passion, and even hitting people, I shouldn't love you one morsel the less for that. I have often wanted to hit people myself. My own sister Sophy, for instance, when she has been too provoking, with her superior airs and high-flown notions. Kiss me, Jack, again and again. If you were ever so wicked I think I should love you all the same."

* * * *

That was Vansittart's last serious talk with Peggy. It was indeed Peggy's last serious talk upon this planet, save for the murmured conversation in the dawn of an April day, when the London vicar, who was doing duty at St. George's, came in before an early cele-bration to sit beside Peggy's pillow and speak words of comfort and promise, words that told of a fairer world, whither Peggy's footsteps were being guided by an impalpable Hand—a world where it might be she would see the faces of the loved and lost—those angel faces, missed here, but living for ever there.

"Do you really believe it, sir?" Peggy asked eagerly, with her thin hand on the grave Churchman's sleeve, her imploring looks perusing the worn, elderly face. "Shall I really see my mother again—see her and know her in heaven?"

"We know only what He has told us, my dear. 'In My Father's house there are many mansions'—and it may be that the homes we have lost—the firesides we remember dimly—the faces that looked upon our cradles—will be found—again—somewhere."

251

"Ah, you are crying," said Peggy. "You would like to be-lieve—just as I would. That is the only heaven I care for—to be with mother—and for Eve and Jack to come to us by-and-by."

* * * *

This day, when the vicar came in the early morning, was thought to be Peggy's last on earth, but she lingered, rallied, and slowly sank again, a gradual fading—painless towards the end; for the stages of suffering which she had borne so patiently were past, and the last hours were peaceful. She could keep her arms round Eve's neck and listen to the soothing voice of sorrowing love, till even this effort was too much, and the weak arms relaxed their hold, and were gen-tly laid upon the bed in that meek attitude which looked like the fi-nal repose. She could hear Eve still—speaking or reading to her in the soft, low voice that was like falling waters—but her mind was wandering in a pleasant dreamland, and she thought she was drift-ing on a streamlet that winds through the valley between Bexley Hill and Blackdown; through summer pastures where the meadow-sweet grew tall and white beside the water, and where the voices of hay-makers were calling to each other across the newly cut grass.

"I should like to have lived to see your child," were Peggy's last words, faltered brokenly into Eve's ear as she knelt beside the bed.

There were long hours of silence; the mute faint struggles of the departing spirit; but that wish was the last of Peggy's earthly speech.

* * * *

Eve was broken-hearted. She never knew till the end came how she had clung to some frail thread of hope; in spite of the Destroyer's palpable advance; in spite of the physician's sad certainty; in spite of her husband's gentle warnings, striving to prepare her for the end. The blow was terrible. Vansittart trembled for life and reason when he saw the intensity of her grief. Always highly strung, she was in a condition of health which made hysteria more to be dreaded. The brief delay between death and burial horrified her; yet to Vansittart that swift departure of the lifeless clay seemed an unutterable relief. For just a few hours the wasted form lay on the rose-strewn bed; and then in the early dimness, before the mists had floated up from the valley, before harbour and parish church stood out clear and bright in the face of the morning sun, came the bearers of the coffin, and at nine o'clock Vansittart went alone to see the loved youngest sister laid in the cemetery on the hill, in the secluded corner he himself had chosen—near the mother's grave—as a spot where Eve might like to sit by-and-by, when sorrow should be less poignant, a nook from which she could see the shallow bay, and the cloud-capped islands jutting out into the sea, and the tall white lighthouse of Antibes, standing up above the crest of the hill, glorified in the afternoon sun, as if it were nearer heaven than earth.

In everything that Vansittart did at this time his thought was of Eve and her feelings. His grief for her sorrow was no less keen than the sorrow itself. He had been very fond of poor little Peggy, and had grown fonder of her as her weakness increased, and strengthened her claim upon his compassion. But now he saw with Eve's eyes, thought with Eve's mind, and every sigh and every tear of hers wrung his heart afresh.

Those earnest words of Peggy's, spoken with the wasted arms about his neck, were very precious to him. It seemed as if they were in some wise his absolution for the wrong which he had done in keeping the secret of Harold Marchant's death. Peggy had told him that she and her sister owed comfort and happiness to him—that he had changed the tenor of their lives from struggling penury to luxury and ease. He knew that over and above all these material advantages he had given Harold Marchant's sister a profound and steadfast love—a love which would last as long as his life, and which was and would be the governing principle of his life—and he told himself that in keeping that dark secret he had done well.

Tranquillized by this assurance he put aside the old fear as something to be forgotten. But there was a nearer fear, a fear which had grown out of Peggy's illness and death, which no casuistry could lessen or thrust aside. The fear of hereditary phthisis came upon him in the dead of night, and flung its dark shadow across his path by day. He had talked long with Dr. Bright after Peggy's death, and the kind physician had calmly discussed the probabilities of evil; had held nothing back. Fear there must needs be, in such a case; but there was also ground for hope. Vansittart told the doctor of Eve's buoyant spirits and energy, her long walks and untiring pleasure in natural scenery. "That does not look like hereditary disease, does it?" he asked, pleading for a hopeful answer.

"Those are good signs, no doubt. Your wife is of an active temperament, highly nervous, but with a very happy disposition. Her sister's fatal illness has tried her severely; but we must look to the arising of a new interest as the best cure for sorrow."

"Poor Peggy! Yes, we shall brood less upon her loss when we

have our little one to think about."

The thought of Eve's coming happiness as a mother was his chief comfort. She could not fail to be consoled by the infant whose tender life would absorb her every thought, whose sleeping and waking would be a source of interest and anxiety. But before the consoler's coming there was a dreary interval to be bridged over, and this was a cause of fear.

There was a journey to be taken, for the climate of Cannes would be too hot for health, or even for endurance, before mother and child could be moved. Thus it was imperative that they should move without delay. Indeed, Vansittart thought they could not too soon leave the scene so closely associated with the image of the dead—where everything recalled Peggy, and the alternating hopes and fears of those gradual stages on her journey to the grave. On this path her feet had tripped so lightly last February, when her illness was talked of as "only a cough." Under this giant eucalyptus her couch had been established in April, when walking had become a painful effort, and she could only lie and absorb the beauty of her surroundings, and talk of the coming days in which she would be strong again, and able to go up to the Signal with Jack.

Vansittart fancied that Eve would catch eagerly at the idea of leaving that haunted house; but her grief increased at the thought of going away.

"I like to be here in the place she loved. I can at least console myself with remembering how happy she was with us; and what a joy Californie and the wild walks above Golfe Juan were to her. Sometimes I think she is in the garden still. I lie upon the sofa here and watch the window, expecting to see her come creeping in, leaning upon the stick you gave her—so white and weak and thin—but so bright, so patient, so lovable."

Then came the inevitable burst of tears, with the threatening of hysteria, and it was all her husband could do to tranquillize her.

"The comfort you get here is a cruel comfort, dearest," he said. "We shall both be ever so much better away from Cannes—at St. Martin de Lantosque, in the cool mountain air. Our rooms are ready for us, we shall have our own servants, and if the accommodation be somewhat rough——"

"Do you think I mind roughness with you? I could be happy in a hut. Oh, Jack, you are so patient with my grief! There are people who would say I am foolish to grieve so much for a young sister; but it is the first time Death has touched us since mother went. We were such a happy little band. I never thought that one of us could die, and that one the youngest, the most loving of us all."

"Dearest, I shall never think your grief unreasonable; but I want you to grieve less, for my sake, for the sake of the future. Think, Eve, only think what it will be to have that new tie between us, a child, belonging equally to each, looking equally to each for all it has of safety and of gladness upon this earth."

CHAPTER XXI.

"FROM THE EVIL TO COME"

Vansittart and his wife never went to the village in the mountains, where all things had been made ready for their coming. Eve spent that afternoon which should have been her last at Cannes in the burial-ground on the hill, now in its glory of May flowers, a paradise of roses and white marble, a place full of tenderest memorials to the early dead, a spot which seemed especially dedicated to those whom the gods love best, the holy ones and pure of spirit, removed from the evil to come for hard middle-life and selfish old age. Eve gave herself up to the luxury of grief on that last day, taking her fond farewell of that quiet bed where, under a coverlet of pale roses, the happy child slept the everlasting sleep. She lingered, and lingered, as the sun sloped towards the dark ridge of hills; lingered when the great flaming disc touched the rugged line, until there was only the afterglow to light her back to Californie. Vansittart had trusted her alone with the steady Benson, now promoted from Peggy's nurse to be Eve's own maid. He had cheques to write and final arrangements to make; and he thought that there would be greater tranquillity for Eve in solitude, with only an attendant. It was better there should be no one to whom she could expatiate on her grief, for her talk with him had always tended to hysteria. Thus convenience and prudence had both counselled his leaving her to herself; and it was only when the clock on the mantelpiece chimed the quarter before eight and the shadows deepened in the corners of the room that he felt he had been imprudent. He went hurriedly out to the terrace in front of the villa, and felt that creeping chillness in the air which follows quickly upon sundown on this southern shore. The carriage stopped at the gate as he went out, and Eve was in his arms, to be welcomed first and scolded afterwards.

"It is with you I am most angry, Benson," he said to his wife's attendant; "you ought to have been wiser."

"I won't have you scold Benson," remonstrated Eve; "it is my fault. She teased me to come home ever so long ago, and I wouldn't. I wanted to stay with Peggy till the last moment. It was like bidding her good-bye again. And now I have left her lying in her quiet grave, near the poor mother whom she hardly knew. I didn't know how late it was till we were in the carriage coming home, and I began to feel rather chilly."

"You are shivering now, Eve. You should have remembered what Dr. Bright said about sunset."

"Ah, that was on Peggy's account. It is different for me."

"Well, I won't try to frighten you into a cold. Run to your mistress's-room, Benson, and make a good fire. I ordered tea to be ready."

He almost carried Eve upstairs, and with his own hands manipulated the olive logs, and set the merry pine cones blazing and crackling, while she lay on the sofa in front of the fireplace and watched the flames; but the shivering continued in spite of the cheery wood fire, and eiderdown coverlet, and hot tea; so Dr. Bright was sent for hurriedly, and came to find his patient with a temperature that indicated grave disturbance. He came, and left only to come back again, with another English doctor, who did not leave his patient all night; and between midnight and morning the young wife's existence trembled in the balance, and the husband, pacing to and fro and in and out on the lower floor, ground his teeth and beat his head in a passion of self-reproach, hating himself for having allowed that perilous visit to the cemetery, cursing himself for his folly in not having gone with her if she must needs go.

"There is a blight upon us and upon our love," he told himself in his despair. "Nemesis will have her due."

* * * *

His fondest hope was blighted—the hope of a living link which should bind him closer to his wife and make severance impossible—a child, whose innocent eyes should turn from father to mother, and plead to the mother for the father's sin—the child who, in direct contingency, was to be his champion and his saviour. He passed through an ordeal of such agony and apprehension on his wife's account as to make him for the time being comparatively indifferent to the loss of his son, who came upon this mortal scene only to vanish from it for ever; but when at last, in mid-June, while Californie and her fir woods were baking under a tropical sun, his wife was restored to him, strong enough to travel to cooler regions in the shadow of the great Alps, there fell upon him the sense of an irreparable loss.

They went by easy stages to Courmayeur, and established themselves there for the rest of the summer, in a reposeful solitude, keep-

257

ing aloof from the climbers and explorers and the race of tourists generally. They had their own rooms, in a Dépendance of the hotel, rooms whose windows commanded valley and mountain. Here Eve first felt the tranquillizing influence of Alpine scenery, and her quiet rambles with Vansittart soon brought back the bloom of her girlish beauty, and restored something of the frank gladness of those younger years when she and her sisters used to ramble over the undulating ridge of Bexley Hill, and think it a mountain.

"Dear old Bexley," sighed Eve, with her eyes dreamily contemplating Mont Chetif; "I hope I shall never begin to despise you, even though you are a hill to put in one's pocket as compared with these white giants."

The peaceful days, the perfect union between husband and wife, revived Eve's spirits and did much to restore her health, sorely shaken by the ordeal through which she had passed. Fever had raged fiercely in the battle between life and death, and the long bright hair, which had made so fair a diadem in the days of her poverty, had been shorn from the burning head. She looked quaintly pretty now, with her boyish crop, framing the broad white forehead with crisp short curls. She laughed when Vansittart talked of next season, when his mother was to lend them the house in Charles Street.

"You can never appear in society with a cropped head for your companion," she said. "People will say you have married a lady doctor, or some other learned monstrosity from Girton. I shall be tabooed in the smart world where ignorance is *de rigueur*, and to know anything about books is a sign of inferiority."

"What care I if they think my sweet love a senior wrangler disguised as a fine lady? You are pretty enough to set the fashion of cropped heads."

* * * *

They moved slowly homeward in the late autumn, loitering beside the great Swiss lakes till the October mists began to make Pilatus invisible and to hang low over the steep gables of Lucerne. They lingered under Mr. Hauser's hospitable roof so long that the great black St. Bernard lifted his head and howled an agonizing farewell when the carriage drove off to the station with Eve and her husband. That leonine beast was sagacious enough to know that the trunks and travelling-bags and bustle of departure meant something more than the daily drive, and that he was to see these kind friends no more, and eat no more sweet biscuits out of Eve's soft white hands.

It was late in October when they found themselves among the pine woods and hillocks of Hampshire, and insignificant as the hills were there was pleasure in feeling one's self at home. Eve's mother-in-law was at Merewood to receive them, and to make much of her son's wife, whom she found thinner and more fragile-looking than when she left for the Riviera, but with all the beauty and brightness which had captivated her lover. Mrs. Vansittart's welcome had in it more of affection than she had ever given her son's wife in the past.

"I think you are beginning to love me," Eve said, too sensitive not to feel the change.

"My dear child, I always loved you."

"Only a very little," argued Eve. "You liked me pretty well in the abstract, I dare say, but you did not care for me as Mrs. John Vansittart. It was very natural. You had your own favourites, any one of whom you would have liked Jack to marry; dear, nice girls who always wear tidy frocks, play the 'Lieder ohne Worte,' and visit the poor. I was altogether a detrimental."

"It was not you, Eve—only your people."

"My people—meaning my father. Yes, he was a stumbling-block, no doubt—a man who had gone down in the world, and about whom malevolent people said cruel things. Well, he has not been obtrusive, has he? He has kept himself in the background."

"My dear, he has been admirable, and your sisters, when I came to know them and understand them, proved altogether unobjectionable. We saw a good deal of each other while you were away."

"Sophy told me how kind you had been. Yes, they are good girls. Their faults are all on the surface. But the flower of the flock is gone—the brightest and the most loving. She was all love."

"Take comfort, dear; there is deep sorrow, but there can be no bitterness in the thought of a child's death."

"Ah, that is what you religious people say," cried Eve, rebelliously, "but I have not faith enough to feel that. Why should she be taken? Life was all before her, full of happiness, of beautiful sights and sounds, and joys untasted. She was taken from the evil to come, you will say—but there might be no evil. There has been no evil in your life! See how peacefully it has glided by."

"You forget, Eve, that I have had to sorrow for a beloved husband."

"Oh, forgive me. Yes, you have felt the burden—the shadow has fallen upon you too—the shadow, and the burden of death. Why did the Creator make a beautiful world, and then spoil it?"

"Eve, this is blasphemy."

"The heart must rebel sometimes; one must ask these questions. 'The fool hath said in his heart, There is no God.' Is it only the fool who says that? Is it not the bitter cry of all humanity at some time or other?"

"Eve, you are writhing under your first sorrow. Let it turn your heart to God, not away from Him. Do you think the unbeliever's creed will give you any comfort?"

"Comfort? No. There is no comfort in religion, or in unbelief. Religion only means obedience, and public worship, and kindness to the poor, and a good orderly life. It doesn't mean the certainty of getting back our dead—somewhere, somehow, and being happy again as we have been."

"We can rest in the hope of that, Eve, knowing that we are immortal."

"Knowing? But we don't know. Nobody has ever come back to tell us. Oh, if but once, only once, for one moment in a year, our dead could come back and look at us, and speak to us, death would not be death."

Mrs. Vansittart spoke no more of comfort. It was better perhaps to let the troubled heart tire itself out with grieving. Tranquillity would come afterwards.

"And our son, our son who breathed only to die. He did not live even long enough for baptism. He was dead when the Bishop came hurriedly from his house on the hill. You think perhaps—you who are a strict Anglican—that his soul is in limbo—that he will never see the throne of God. We were going to be so fond of him, Jack and I—and Peggy wanted to live long enough to see him—but she was gone before he came, and he didn't care about living. If she had been well and happy all things would have been different. They would have been running about together in a year or two from now. And now she would have been carrying him about in her arms. He would have been beginning to notice people, and to laugh and coo like that cottager's child we saw yesterday, just about as old as my baby would have been now."

"My dearest, do you suppose I am not sorry for your loss and for your husband's? But God never meant us to rebel, even in our grief. That must not be."

"I know I am wicked," said Eve, with a long-drawn sigh. "I have my fits of wickedness. In church yesterday, on my knees at the altar, I thought that I was resigned, I almost believed in the heaven where we shall see and know our friends again."

The dark hour passed, and at sunset, when Vansittart came home from a long day in the plantations, his wife received him with her brightest smile. His coming back after a few hours' absence meant the fulness of joy.

She had spent a day at Fernhurst, and the sight of her three sisters in their somewhat ostentatious mourning had renewed her grief. She had sent them money for mourning, which largesse they had spent conscientiously, and so were swathed in crape and distinctly funereal of aspect.

There were Peggy's sisters, whose very existence recalled her image too vividly; and there was Peggy's room, the room which she had shared with Hetty; and the little bed where she had slept so peacefully, with her nose almost touching the sloping roof, before the cruel cough took hold of her, and disturbed those happy, childish slumbers, with their visions of fairyland, or of castles in the air which seemed solid and real to the dreamer. Everything in that cottage chamber suggested her who slept in a far lovelier spot.

The room remained just as the child had left it. Peggy's things were sacred. There was her workbox, the substantial, old-fashioned rosewood box, inlaid with mother-o'-pearl, and lined with blue silk, the old, old blue, a colour such as modern taste holds up to scorn—for the box was nearly half a century old, and had belonged to Peggy's grandmother first and to her mother afterwards. It had been given to Peggy because she was the youngest, and the little stock of trinkets was exhausted by the time her four sisters had each received a souvenir. The amethyst earrings, utterly unwearable, for Eve; the watch which had not gone for years, to Sophy; and a couple of poor little brooches for Jenny and Hetty. After these jewels had been dealt out there remained only the workbox for Peggy. It had been to her a source of infinite delight. What treasures of doll's clothing, what varieties of fancy-work; kettle-holders, never to be polluted by a kettle; mats, never finished; Berlin-wool cuffs, and point-lace handkerchiefs. Peggy had seldom finished anything; but the rapture of beginning things had been intense, a fever of enjoyment.

There were her books upon a little carved Swiss shelf, by her bed. Her lesson-books, thumbed and dog's-eared, everybody else's lesson-books before they descended to her; that "Grammaire des Grammaires" over which the whole family had toiled, and the Primers which make learning easy and people the world with smatterers. There were gift-books, birthday presents from governess or sisters; the immortal Family Robinson, Grimm, Hans Andersen, Bluebeard, Cinderella. How many a summer dawn Peggy had lain upon that pillow, reading the old fairy-tales before a foot was stirring in the house. Her bed was there, with the prettiest of Bellagio rugs laid over it, sacred as a shrine. The little room would have been far more convenient for Hetty if that bed had been taken down and put away; but no one dreamed of removing it. There would have been unlovingness in the mere suggestion.

Well, they had all to do without Peggy henceforward. There was one link gone from the chain of love. Vansittart looked round at his sisters-in-law's faces with an agonized dread. Who would be the next? Which among that tainted flock would be the first to show the inherited poison, the first to feel the cold hand of the destroyer?

They all looked bright and healthy. They had all the fair complexion and fine roseate bloom which mark the typical English beauty, a loveliness of colour which can almost afford to dispense with perfection of form. They were slenderly made. In a doctor's parlance, there was not much of them to fall back upon—not much in hand at the beginning of a long illness. They were tall and willowy, rather narrow-chested, Vansittart noted with a pang. Yes, assuredly Eve was the flower of the flock. Her chest was broader, her throat fuller and more firmly moulded than the chests and throats of her sisters. The poise of her head was more decided, her whole bearing argued a stronger constitution. She was the offspring of her mother's youth, before any indication of disease had darkened the young life. She was the offspring of her father's early manhood. The doctors had augured well for her on this account.

* * * *

The winter was spent very quietly at Merewood. Vansittart hunted and shot, and he often went home earlier in the winter dusk than became him as a sportsman, in order to take tea with Eve beside the fire. His mother lingered at Merewood, so that Eve should not be alone, the link between the two women strengthening day by day. The sisters came over from Haslemere, and enjoyed all the luxuries of a well-appointed house. Eve and her husband went for two or three short visits to Redwold Towers, and Sir Hubert and Lady Hartley came to Merewood; he for the last of the pheasants—having pretty nearly cleared his own woods, extensive as they were—she for the pleasure of being with Eve, to whom she was sincerely attached.

And so the winter went by, a not unhappy winter. How could a young wife be unhappy, adoring and adored by her husband? Hymen's torch glowed with gentlest light beside that hearth where the pine logs were heaped so liberally, pine logs from Vansittart's paternal woods.

Eve was in high health at Easter, radiant, full of life and spirits, albeit in no wise forgetful of that grave on the hill where the Maréchal Niel roses were growing so luxuriantly, and which was being carefully tended by stranger hands. There are those at Cannes who take a loving pride in that Garden of Death, whose care it is that this place of rest should be for ever beautiful, a paradise of peace, the very memory whereof should be sweet in the thoughts of the bereaved. Eve could think now with resignation of that tranquil spot, and of the young life which had come to a sudden pause on earth. Was it a full stop, or only a hyphen? Was it the end of the book, or only the bottom of the page, with the last word repeated over-leaf, to carry on the story without a break?

Mrs. Vansittart insisted that her children should have the free use of the house in Charles Street for the London season. She wanted Eve to enjoy the privileges of her position as the wife of a man of good family and good means. She had also a lingering hope that in the high pressure of London society her son might awaken to some worthy ambition—political or social, and might try to make his mark in the world. She had always been ambitious for him—had always wanted him to do something more than shoot his own pheasants, improve the cottages on his estate, and live within his means. For a young man of his social status, the political arena offered fair scope for ambition, and Mrs. Vansittart had the common idea that any man of good abilities can succeed in politics.

CHAPTER XXII.

"SO VERY WILFUL"

Another Easter over, another season beginning, and with all the usual auguries of a season of exceptional splendour—auguries to be exchanged later for dismal elegies upon a season of surpassing dulness and stagnation, which had disappointed everybody, and all but ruined the West End tradesmen. As this jubilant vaticination and these melancholy wailings are repeated year after year, they have come to be of little more significance than the chirping of the newly arriving swifts under the eaves, or the twittering of the swallows assembled for their autumnal flight. Seasons come and seasons go. People are hopeful before the fact, and disappointed after the fact; the great chorus of humanity goes on. Such is life. A season of hope and disillusion. Contemplate existence from the severest standpoint of the agnostic metaphysician, or from the most exalted platform of the Christian saint, and the ultimate fact is the same. We begin in hope to end in sorrow.

For Signora Vivanti the after-Easter season began under cheeriest conditions. Her success at the Apollo had been unbroken. The longer she acted a part, the more spirited her acting became. Ignorant and uncultured as she was, she possessed the gift of "gag," knew when and where to introduce a word or a look which delighted her audience; and the management and her brother and sister artists—more especially the brothers—gave her full scope. These little inspirations of hers became licensed liberties, and her *rôle* grew and strengthened under her hands. She was the most popular actress who had appeared at the Apollo since the building of the theatre.

So at Easter the impresario increased the lady's salary for the fourth time since her *début*. He knew what tempting offers had been made to her by managers and by agents—how eager one was to send her to America, what dazzling lures another held out for Australasia. Happily, la Vivanti liked London—big, dirty, bustling London—and was content to make her fortune within the sound of Big Ben, whose mighty voice came booming along the tide to Chelsea when the wind blew from the Essex marshes and the German Ocean.

Lisa was making her fortune as fast as a young woman of moderate desires could wish to make it. To herself she appeared inordinately rich. The collet necklace had now a fine half-hoop bracelet to keep it company in the strong box under Lisa's bed, and she had a number of brooches which studded her corsage like a constellation. What the outside world said of Lisa's diamonds was very different from the truth; but the Venetian neither knew nor cared what the outside world was saying. The people in the theatre were all very kind to her. They knew that she was what Mr. Hawberk called "straight," and that the gems she flashed upon the public eye were honestly come by, the result of an economical existence. She and la Zia were able to live upon so little. A few shreds of meat, messed up in some occult manner with their perpetual pasta, sufficed for dinner. A breakfast of coffee and rolls; a supper of highly odorous cheese, with sometimes for a festa a dish of cheap pastry from the Swiss confectioner's in the King's Road. Such a cuisine did not make much impression upon Signora Vivanti's salary. She had no servant, except a slovenly female, with depressing manners, who came two mornings a week to scrub floors, clean windows, and black-lead grates. La Zia did all the rest, and delighted in her work. To sweep and dust those palatial apartments was a perpetual joy to her, second only to the delight of tramping up and down the King's Road, exploring every greengrocer's shop till she secured the cheapest vegetables, and lamenting the Rialto, where three lemons could be had for two soldi, and where the pale, bloodless asparagus was less than a quarter the London price of that luxury. Pleasant also was it to la Zia to take the 'bus for Coventry Street, and to prowl about the foreign settlement between the churches of St. Anne and St. Giles; but oh, what a dull and dismal aspect had the restaurants and *table d'hôtes* in this quarter, as compared with the Cappello Nero and the movement and brightness of the Piazza.

La Zia was happy, but in spite of an altogether phenomenal success, and of wealth that far surpassed her dreams of fortune, the same could not be said of Fiordelisa. There was that lacking in her young life which changed her gold to dross, her laurels to worthless weeds. She had loved, and loved passionately, with all the force of her undisciplined heart, and her love had been rejected. She had steeped her soul in the promise of bliss, had told herself again and again that the kindnesses she received from the man she loved could only be given by a lover. Her notion of ethics was not exalted enough to comprehend Vansittart's desire to atone for a great wrong, or to understand that so much gentleness and generosity could be lavished upon her by any one less than a lover. She had built her soul

265

a palace—not of art, but of love—and when the unreal fabric fell her disappointment had been as crushing as it was unforeseen.

After that passionate scene with Vansittart Lisa gave herself up to the luxury of grief. For days she would hardly eat enough to sustain life; for many nights she tossed sleepless on her bed, sobbing over her vanished hopes, as an undisciplined child weeps for the loss of a promised pleasure. It was only good little Tomaso Zinco's strenuous arguments which ultimately brought her to reason. La Zia could do nothing with her. She turned her face to the wall, like David, and her long blue-black hair was tangled with tossing on her pillow, and wet with her passionate tears. She would not get up, or put on her clothes, or even wash her face. It was her way of scattering ashes on her head, and rending her garments. Her grief had all the fervid unreasonableness of Oriental mourning.

La Zia was obliged to take the 'cello player into the bedroom, and show him this spectacle of angry despair.

"He has deserted her—the father of her child," muttered Zinco, in the vestibule, as la Zia tried to explain the situation. "That is bad, bad, bad. Very bad."

"No, no," said la Zia, shaking her head vehemently; "it is not that. He has done no wrong. He has paid for her lessons, paid her rent, he has done much for us. Only she loved him, and he did not love her. She is like a child. She will not be consoled."

Zinco nodded a vague assent, but did not believe the good aunt's assurance. Of course this man was the father of her child. Of course she had been his mistress. He had brought her from Venice, and established her in these comfortable lodgings, and now he was tired of her. These things always end so. "Chi va all'acqua si bagna, e chi va a cavallo cade."

The good little Zinco crept into the room as softly as a cat, and seated his stout and oily person by the bed, where Lisa was lying face downwards, her tearful countenance buried in the pillow, and nothing but a mass of tangled black hair visible above the gaudy Mexican blanket. He gently patted her shoulder, which acknowledged the attention with an angry shrug.

"Come, come, cara mia," pleaded the singing-master. "Is not this a mere childishness, to cry for the moon, when we have good fortune almost at our feet? To cry because just one foolish young man among all the men in the world is not wise enough to know that there is no more beautiful woman than us in London! And not to eat, and not to sleep, and to cry and sob all day and night. Ahimé, che bestia! This is just the very way to lose our voice, to become mute as one of those nightingales whose tongues were cut out to flavour the pasta for Vitellius. Was there ever such foolishness? Were I a beautiful girl with a fine voice, I would be queen of the world. If he has been cold and cruel show him what a pearl he has lost. It is not by lying here and crying that you will bring him to reason. Get up and dress yourself, and come to the piano. I'll wager you will not be able to take the upper C in 'Roberto.'"

Lisa listened in sullen silence, but she did listen, and it seemed to her that the words of Zinco were the words of wisdom. To lose her voice—her voice which was her fortune—and to lose her good looks, which alone had lifted her from the herd of peasants, living in penury, toiling from sunrise to sunset, unknown and ill-clad, and dying uncared for, save by creatures as poor and as hopeless as themselves! Yes, Zinco was right; that would indeed be foolishness, and not the way to win him whose love her sick soul longed for. Perhaps if she were a public singer, and all the world admired her, he would admire her too. He would see in the eyes of other men that she was handsome, and worthy to be admired. He would hear on the lips of other men that she was worthy of praise.

"I'll get up," she said, without lifting her tear-stained face from the pillow. "Go into the sala and wait for me. I won't be long. You shall see I haven't lost my voice."

"Bene, benissimo, Si'ora," cried the master, rubbing his fat little hands, "now she speaks like a woman of spirit. She is not going to give up the world for love, like Marc Antony at Actium."

He shuffled off to the sitting-room, seated himself at the piano, and began to play the symphony of "Una Voce" with that grandly decisive style of a man who has played all his life in an orchestra. It was a refreshment to Lisa's weary spirit to hear that sparkling music, light, gay, capricious as summer wavelets.

She joined her teacher at the piano in a much shorter time than a young Englishwoman would have needed to complete her toilet, yet she looked fresh enough in her southern beauty, and there were glittering water-drops in her hair which gave a suggestion of a young river goddess.

"Now, then, sir, play 'Roberto' and you will see if my voice is broken."

She attacked the scena with wonderful dash and spirit, and was, in sporting phraseology, winning easily till she came to that C in alt—but here her voice snapped. She tried a second time, and a third time—but the note was gone. She gave a cry of rage, and then burst into tears.

"Ecco," exclaimed Zinco, with a triumphant air, "that is what your love-sick nonsense has done for you. You have been singing as false as a prima donna at a *café chantant* in the Boulevard St. Michel, and your upper C is gone. It would have been worth £40 a week to you, but you have thrown it away."

At this; Lisa continued her lamentation, deeply sorry for herself.

"There's no use in crying," said Zinco; "that only makes things worse. Bisogna sempre aver pazienza in questo mondo. You had better dry your tears and eat a beefsteak—bleeding—and drink a pint of port-beer. Malibran used to drink port-beer. In one of her great scenes she had her quart pot on the stage, hidden behind a set piece—a rock, or what not—and after her cavatina she would fall on the stage as if fainting, and drag herself to the back of the rock and drink; ah, how she would drink!"

"I don't want to lose my voice," sobbed Lisa, to whom Malibran was but an empty name.

"No. Yet you go just the right way to lose it. Come, cheer up, Si'ora. Eat much steaks, drink much stout, for the next three days. Andiamo adagio. Don't sing a note till I come next Saturday afternoon to give you your lesson."

Zinco's policy prevailed. Lisa fretted sorely at the thought of losing that voice which was to be her fortune. She had told herself in her despair that fame and fortune would be useless without the man she loved—that she had only wished to succeed as a singer in order to please him. And now she began to see the situation in a new light. She wanted to be admired and famous like the singers whom she had seen at Covent Garden, curtsying behind a pile of bouquets, while the house resounded with applause. She wanted to be applauded like those famous singers, so that the cruel Smith might see her, and be sorry that he had refused her his heart. Who could tell? Perhaps seeing her so admired, hearing her voice ring clear and sweet through the theatre, he might abandon his tuneless English sweetheart, and come back to Lisa, come back as lover, as husband. Zinco had told her that a fashionable prima donna could not look too high. She would have all London at her feet. It would be for her to choose.

Lisa had a strong will, and a wonderful power of self-command when she really wanted to command herself; so she dried her tears, ate British beef, almost raw, and drank British stout; and under this régime her nerves speedily recovered from the rude shaking which passion had given them, and when the good little 'cello player came to give her the Saturday lesson, her voice rang out sound as a bell, and B natural was produced with perfect ease—a round and perfect note.

"We'll wait till next Tuesday for the C," said Zinco, "and we won't try 'Roberto' for a week or so. Stick to the Solfeggi."

"And I have not lost my voice, caro?"

"No more than I have lost a thousand pounds, poveretta."

After this things went smoothly. Life seemed very dreary to Fiordelisa without the friend whose rare visits had been her delight; but her mind was braced and fortified by a steady purpose. She meant to win the great British public; and behind that indefinite monster there shone the image of the man she loved. He would go to the theatre where she sang. He would see her, and understand at last that she was beautiful and gifted, and worthy to be loved.

"And then he knows that I love him with all the strength of my heart," she said to herself. "That ought to count for something. Yet when I told him of my love he shrank from me, as if he hated me for loving him. That is his cold English nature, perhaps. An Englishman does not like unasked love."

* * * *

Lisa was two years older than in that day of despair, and Zinco's promises had been realized. She had the town at her feet; and if the coronet matrimonial had not yet been laid there she had received plenty of that adulation and of those advances which cannot be accepted without peril. All such advances Lisa had repulsed with a splendid scorn. Carriages, servants, West End apartments, and St. John's Wood villas had been offered her; but she still rode in penny omnibuses or twopenny steamers, or trudged valiantly in cheap shoes. She might have had an open account with any silk mercer in London. She might have had her frocks made by the dressmaker on the crest of fashion's changeful wave—but she was content to wear a black stuff gown, with a bit of bright ribbon tied round her neck, and another bit twisted in her hair. When she wanted to look her best she put on her bead necklace—one of those necklaces which the man she loved bought for her in the Procuratie Vecchie on that fatal night. The idea that he had bought the murderous dagger at the same shop in no wise lessened her pleasure in these gifts of his.

Among her numerous admirers one only had been received by the lady and her aunt, and that was Wilfred Sefton, who had contrived to establish a footing in the Signora's drawing-room before Zinco could protest against his admission. He had so managed as to be regarded as a friend by both aunt and niece, and the boy, whom he detested, had grown odiously fond of him. He had known Lisa for a year and a half, had seen her often, had spent long summer days in her company, and in all that time he had never addressed her as a lover. He knew, too well, from many a subtle sign and token, that his going or coming affected her not at all; that she liked him and welcomed him only because his presence and his attentions made a pleasant variety in the dulness of her domestic life. He knew this. He knew that whatever she might have been in the past, she was a virtuous woman in the present, that she courted no man's admiration, and was tempted by no man's gold. Convinced of this, finding her as remote in her quiet indifference as if she had been some young patrician pacing her ancestral park in maiden meditation, fancy free, his desire to win her intensified until she seemed to him the only woman in the world worth winning. Had she been easily won he might have been tired of her before now. His grandes passions in the past had been of short duration. Unspeakable weariness had descended upon him as a blight; the loathing of life and all it could yield him. Lisa's indifference gave a piquancy to their relations. He told himself that he could afford to bide his time. He had done a good deal of mischief in the world; but he was not a vulgar profligate. His love was an unscrupulous but not a vulgar love.

* * * *

The white kitten, a thoroughbred Persian, and a gift from Mrs. Hawberk, had grown into a great white cat, stolid, beautiful, resentful of strange caresses, but devotedly attached to Lisa and her boy. He was called Marco, after the patron saint of Venice; and he looked like the white cat of fairy tale, who might be transformed at any moment into Prince Charming.

By the time Marco had grown up Mr. Sefton had made himself accepted as a trusted and familiar friend, and in this season of ripening spring, when the lilacs and laburnums filled the suburban gardens with perfume and colour, and when the hawthorn bushes were beginning to break into clusters of scented blossom here and there, it was his business and his pleasure to afford some glimpses of a fairer world to the little family at Chelsea.

The holiday which Fiordelisa and her belongings most enjoyed was a day on the river. They would have taken boat at Chelsea, if Sefton had allowed them, and would have been content to be rowed to Hammersmith Bridge; but he insisted on introducing them to Father Thames under a fairer aspect; so they usually took the train to Richmond, and from Richmond Bridge Sefton rowed them to Kingston or Hampton, where they lunched at some quiet inn, and sat in some rustic inn garden, or sauntered in those lovely old Palace gardens by the river, till it was time to go back to the boat and the train. Sefton was too punctual and business-like to permit any risk of the singer's non-appearance. He took care that Lisa should always be at the Apollo in time for her work.

These days were very delightful to him, even in spite of Paolo, whose attentions were sometimes boring. Happily, Paolo loved the water with an instinctive hereditary passion, the instinct of amphibious ancestors, born and bred on a level with the lagunes—reared half on sea and half on land. It was amusement enough for him to sit in the stern of the skiff and dabble a bare arm in the stream, or to watch the little paper boats which la Zia made for him, or the great white swans which hissed menaces at him with horizontal necks as they paddled slowly by, sacrificing grace and stateliness to unreasoning anger. Sefton put up with Paolo, and was happy in the society of two ignorant women, delighting in Lisa's *naïveté*, finding a delicious originality in all her remarks upon life and the world she lived in, her stories of green-room quarrels and side-scene flirtations. Talk which might have sounded silly and vulgar in English was fascinating in Italian—all the more fascinating in that Venetian dialect which so languidly slurred the syllables, lazily dropping the consonants, and which had in its soft elisions something childlike that touched Sefton's fancy. He took pleasure in Lisa's talk almost as if she had been a child, while those sudden flashes of shrewdness, natural to the peasant of all countries, assured him that she was no fool.

He thought of Emma Hamilton, and wondered whether the charm which held Nelson till the hour of death, and made his Emma the last thought when life grew dim, were some such childlike spontaneous charm as this of Lisa's, the charm of unsophisticated womanhood, adapted to no universal pattern, cut and polished in no social diamond-mill.

Yes, she had charmed him in their first interview, sitting out in the chilly tent, amidst the glimmer of fairy lamps. She charmed him still, after a year and a half of familiar friendship. She, the ignorant and low-born; he, the modern worldling, who had touched the highest culture at every point, strained his intellect to reach every goal, measured himself against every theory of life here and hereafter, and found happiness nowhere. She pleased him all the more because she was not a lady, and made none of the demands which the modern lady makes over-strenuously—the demand to be treated as a boon companion and yet worshipped as a goddess; the demand of your money, your mind, your time, your wit, your trouble. Lisa had no idea of women's rights, and she was grateful for the simplest festa which her admirer offered her. Never had a grande passion cost him so little. This girl, who had worked in the lace factory at Burano for a few pence per day, and had lived mostly on polenta, sternly refused anything in the shape of a gift, even to a bunch of flowers, if she thought they were costly.

"I like the cheap flowers best," she said, "the blue and yellow ones that they sell in the streets, or the great red poppies la Zia buys, which flame in the fireplace, ever so much brighter than a real fire."

Often, in a casual way, he had tried to make her talk of Vansittart, but in vain. She would say nothing about him, yet she was curious to know all that Sefton could tell her about the man with whom he had seen her talking. Sefton took his revenge by a studious reticence.

"Yes, I know the man," he said, when the subject was mooted in the early days of their acquaintance.

"Do you know him intimately? Is he your friend?"

"No."

"You look and speak as if you did not like him."

"I look and speak as I feel."

"Why don't you like him?" urged Lisa.

"Who knows? We all have our likings and our antipathies."

"But if he has never injured you——"

"That is a negative merit. I dislike a good many people who have never done me any harm."

"He is going to be married, I hear."

"He is married. He was married last summer."

"Do you know his wife?"

"Yes."

"Is she beautiful?"

"Not so beautiful as you; but she has a complexion like the inside of a sea-shell. You know those pale shells, almost transparent, with a rosy flush that is less a colour than a light. She has pale gold hair, which shines round her low, broad forehead like a nimbus in one of Fra Angelica's pictures of Virgins and angels. She is rather like an old Italian picture, of that early school which chose a golden-haired ideal and left your glowing Southern beauty out in the cold. She is not so handsome as you, bellissima."

"Yet he liked her better than he liked me. What is the good of my being handsome? He did not care," said Lisa, passionately.

It was the first time she had betrayed herself to Sefton. He smiled, and glanced from the mother's angry face to the boy, who was hanging about her knee, unconsciously reproducing the attitude of many an infant St. John.

"Yes, there can be no doubt," he told himself, "Vansittart is the man she loved, and this brat must be Vansittart's offspring."

Lady Hartley had told him that her brother had been a rambler in Italy and the Tyrol for years before her marriage.

CHAPTER XXIII.

THE LITTLE RIFT

It was summer-time in London; the butterfly season, in which the metropolis of the world puts on such a splendour of gaiety and luxury that it is hard to remember the fog and damp and dreariness of a long winter; hard to believe that this stately West End London can ever be otherwise than beautiful. Are not her hotels palaces, and her parks paradises of foliage and flowers, fashion and beauty—with only an occasional incursion from the Processional Proletariat? Country cousins seeing the great city in this joyous season may be excused for thinking that life in London is always delectable; and, bored to death in their country quarters in the dull depth of an agricultural winter, or suffering under the discomforts of a ten-mile journey behind a pair of "boilers," on a snow-bound road, to a third-rate ball, may not unnaturally envy the children of the city their January and February dances, and dinners, and theatres, all, as these rustics imagine, within a quarter of an hour's drive.

Eve Vansittart thoroughly enjoyed the pleasures of a London season; the jaunts and excitements by day; Hurlingham, Sandown, Ascot, Henley, Lord's, Barn Elms; the ever-delightful morning ride, the evening drive in the Park, with its smiling flower-beds, ablaze with gaudy colour that rivalled the scarlet plumes and shining breast-plates flashing past now and again between the close ranks of carriages. Yes, London was brilliant, vivid, noisy, full of startling sights and sounds by day; and by night a city of enchantment, where one might wander from house to house to mingle in a mob of more or less beautiful women, and beautiful gowns, and diamonds that took one's breath away by their magnificence. A city of fairyland, with awnings over stately doorways, and gardens and balconies aglitter with coloured lamps; and gorgeous reception-rooms where one heard all that there is of the most exquisite in modern music—violin and 'cello, tenor and soprano—the stars of opera and concert-hall, breathing their finer strains for the delight of these choicer assemblies.

There are circles and circles in London, as many as in the progressive After-life of Esoteric Buddhism, and it is not to be supposed that a small Hampshire squire, with a paltry three thousand a year, was in the uppermost and most sacred heaven; but the circles touch and mingle very often in the larger gatherings of the season, and though Eve Vansittart was not on intimate terms with duchesses, she often rubbed shoulders with them, and for an evening lived the life they lived, and thrilled to the same melodious strains, and melted almost to tears to the same music of Wolff or Hollmann, till pleasure verged upon pain, and borne upon the long-drawn notes of violin or 'cello, came sad, sweet memories of the years that were gone. Vansittart knew plenty of people who were decidedly "nice," and these included a sprinkling of the nobility, and a good many givers of fine parties. His wife's beauty and charm of manner ensured her a prompt acceptance among people outside that circle of old friends who would have accepted her as a duty, even had she been neither lovely nor amiable.

The most enjoyable parties must at last produce satiety, if they come every night, and sometimes two or three in a night; and there came a time when Eve's strength began to flag, and her spirits to droop a little in the midst of these pleasures, this paradise of music and Parisian comedy, of dances after midnight, and coaching meets at noon.

Vansittart noticed the pallid morning face and purple shadows under the dark grey eyes.

"We are doing too much, Eve," he said anxiously. "I am letting you kill yourself."

"It is a very pleasant kind of death," answered Eve, smiling at him across the small breakfast-table, where a grilled chicken for him, a dish of strawberries for her, comprised the simple repast, a repast over which they always lingered as long as their engagements allowed, since it was the only confidential hour in the day. At luncheon people were always running in; or there was a snug little party invited for that friendly meal. Dinner was rarely eaten at home, except when they had a dinner-party. "It is a very delicious death, and I shall take a long time killing. Perhaps when I am as old as Honoria, Duchess of Boscastle, I shall begin to feel I have had enough."

"My dearest, I love to see you happy and amused, but I mustn't let you wear yourself out. We must have a quiet day now and then."

"As many quiet days as you like, as long as they are spent

with you. Shall we go to Haslemere and take the girls for a picnic—this very day? No, there is Maud's dinner-party to-night. Fernhurst would be too far. We could not get home to dress, without a
rush, if we took a really long day on Bexley Hill."

"Fernhurst and the sisters will keep till the autumn, especially as
you will be having Sophy here to-morrow."

"Yes, I shall be having Sophy"—with a faint sigh. "We shall
have no more cosy little breakfasts like this for a whole week."

"Nonsense. We can send Sophy's breakfast up to her room, with
strict injunctions not to get up till eleven. People who ain't used to
parties always want a lot of sleep in the morning. Sophy shall be
made to sleep. But, for to-day, now? What should you say to a long,
lazy day on the river? We can take the train to Moulsey, and row
down to Richmond."

"Too delicious for words. But there is a tea-party in Berkeley
Square, and another at Hyde Park Gardens. I promised to go to
both."

"Then you will go to neither. You can send telegrams from
Moulsey to say you are seedy, and your doctor ordered a quiet day
in the country—I being your doctor for the nonce. We'll steep ourselves in the mild beauty of Old Father Thames, a poor little river
when one remembers Danube and Rhine; but he will serve for our
holiday."

He rang for a time-table, found a train that was to leave Waterloo
at eleven, and ordered the victoria to take them to the station.

"Now, Eve, your coolest frock, and your favourite poet to read
in your luxurious seat in the stern, while I toil at the oar. Be sure you
will not read a page during the whole afternoon! The willows and
rushes, the villa gardens dipping to the water's edge, the people in
the passing boats, the patient horses on the tow-path—those will be
your books, living, moving, changing things, compared with which
Keats and Musset are trash, Endymion colourless, La Carmago a
phantom."

"I'll take Musset," said Eve, pouncing upon a vellum-bound
duodecimo—a *chef d'œuvre* of Zaehnsdorf's, which was one of Vansittart's latest gifts. "He has opened a new world to me."

"A very wicked world for your young innocence to explore; a
world of midnight rendezvous and early morning assassinations; a
world of unholy loves and savage revenges—the dagger, the bowl,
the suicide's despair, the satiated worldling's vacuity. Yet he is a poet—ain't he, Eve?—the greatest France ever produced. Compared
with that fiery genius Hugo is but a rhetorician."

They were at Hampton before noon, and on the river in the fierce golden sunlight, when Hampton Church clock struck the hour, Eve leaning back in her cushioned seat, gazing dreamily at the lazy rower midships. They had the current to help them, so there was no need for strenuous toil. The oars dipped gently; the church and village, Garrick's Temple, the gaily decked house-boats with gardens on their roofs and bright striped awnings, barracks, bridge, old Tudor Palace, drifted by like shadows in a dream. Eve did not open De Musset, though the ribbon marked a page where passion hung suspended in tragic possibilities; a crisis which might well have stimulated curiosity. She was too happy to be curious about anything. It was her first holiday on the river, they two alone.

"If this is your idea of resting let us rest very often," said Eve.

She would not hear of landing at Kingston for luncheon. She wanted nothing but the river, and the sunshine, and his company, all to herself. She would have some tea, if he liked, later; and seeing an open-air tea-house a little lower down the river, and a garden where at this early hour there were no visitors, Vansittart pushed the nozzle of his skiff in among the reeds, and they landed, and ordered tea and eggs and bread and butter to be served in a rustic arbour close by the glancing tide.

"I dare say there are water-rats about," said Eve, gathering her pale pink frock daintily round her ankles, "but I feel as if I should hardly mind one to-day."

They both enjoyed this humble substitute for their customary luncheon. It was a relief to escape the conventional menu—the everlasting mayonnaise, the cutlets hot or cold, the too familiar chicken and lamb. The tea and eggs in this vine-curtained bower had the most exquisite of all flavours—novelty.

"I am so happy," cried Eve, "that I think, like Miss de Bourgh in 'Pride and Prejudice,' I could sing—if I had learnt."

"Your face is my music," said her husband, his face reflecting her happy smile; "your laughter is better than singing."

"Oh, you mustn't, you really mustn't talk like that; at least, not till our silver wedding," protested Eve. "You will have to make a speech, perhaps, on that anniversary, and you might incorporate that idea in it. 'What, ladies and gentlemen, in returning thanks for your kind compliments and this truly magnificent epergne, can I say of my wife of five and twenty blissful years, except that I love her, I love her, I love her? Her face is my music; her laughter is better than singing.' How would that do, Jack?"

Her clear laugh rang out in the still summer air. No female of the

277

great Bounder tribe could have enjoyed herself more frankly. Vansittart would hardly have been surprised if she had offered to exchange hats with him.

"Five and twenty years! A quarter of a century," she said musingly. "I wonder what we shall be like, three and twenty years hence—what the world will be like—what kind of frocks will be worn?"

"Will the cylinder hat be abolished?"

"Shall we still travel by steam, or only by electricity?"

"What gun-maker will be in vogue?"

"What kind of lap-dog will be the rage?"

In this wise they dawdled an hour away, having garden and arbour all to themselves, till after three o'clock, when a couple of Bounder-laden boats came noisily to the reedy bank, and their human cargo landed, scrambling upon shore, hilarious, exploding into joyous cockney jests, with the true South London twang.

"Come," said Vansittart, "it is time we were off."

"Are you sure you have rested?"

"From my Herculean labours? Yes."

They drifted down the river, praising or dispraising the villas on the Middlesex shore, inhaling the sweetness of flowering clover from the Surrey fields; he leaning lazily on his sculls, she prattling to him, as much lovers as in the outset of their wooing; and so to Teddington Lock, where they had to wait for a boat to come out, before their boat went in.

It was the laziest hour of the day, and scarcely a leaf stirred among the willows on the eyot hard by. There was only the sound of the water, and the voices of the rowers, muffled by the heavy wooden gates and high walls of the smaller lock. Suddenly the doors opened. A skiff with four passengers slowly emerged from the yawning darkness, and a voice, strong, yet silvery sweet, broke upon the quiet of the scene, a voice at whose first word Vansittart started as if he had been shot.

The speaker started too, and gave a cry of surprise that was almost rapture. A girl, hatless, with dark hair heaped carelessly on the top of her small head, a girl with the loveliest Italian eyes Eve had ever seen, leaned forward over the gunwale, stretching out both her gloveless hands to Vansittart.

"It is you," she cried in Italian; "I thought I should never see you again;" and then, with a quick glance at Eve, and in almost a whisper, "Is that your wife?"

"Si, Si'ora."

The girl looked at Eve with bold unfriendly eyes, and from her looked back again to Vansittart, as his boat passed into the lock. Her manner had been so absorbing, her beauty was so startling, that it was only in this last moment that Eve recognized the man rowing as Sefton, and saw that the other two passengers were a stout middle-aged woman and a little boy, both of them dark eyed and foreign looking, like the girl.

When Eve and Vansittart looked at each other in the gloom of the lock both were deadly pale.

"Who is that girl?" she asked huskily.

"An Italian singer—Signora Vivanti. You must have heard of her; she is the rage at the Apollo."

"But she knows you—intimately. She was enraptured at seeing you. Her whole face lighted up."

"That is the southern manner; an organ-grinder will do as much for you if you fling him a penny."

"How did you come to know her?"

"In Italy, years ago, before she began to be famous."

They were out of the lock by this time, and in the broad sunshine. Eve could see that her husband's pallor was not an illusive effect of the green gloom in that deep well they had just left.

He was white to the lips.

Sefton! Sefton and Fiordelisa hand in glove with each other! That was a perilous alliance. And Lisa's manner, claiming him so impulsively, darting that evil look at his wife! He saw himself hemmed round with dangers, saw the menace of his domestic peace from two most formidable influences: on the one hand Lisa's slighted love; on the other Sefton's hatred of a successful rival. The fear of untoward complications, coming suddenly upon the happy security of his wedded life, was so absorbing that he was unconscious of Eve's pallor and of her suppressed agitation while questioning him.

"You knew her in Italy," said Eve, her head bent a little, one listless hand dabbling in the sunlit water that reflected the vivid colouring of the boat in gleams of lapis and malachite. "In what part of Italy? Tell me all about her. I am dying of curiosity. There was such odious familiarity in her manner."

"Again I must refer you to any organ-grinder as an example of southern exuberance."

"Yes, yes, that is all very fine, but Signora Vivanti must belong to a higher grade than the organ-grinder. She is not to be judged by his standard."

"There you are wrong. She is of peasant birth."

"Indeed. She certainly looks common; beautiful, but essentially common. Well, Jack, where and when did you meet her?"

"Years ago, as I told you. Where?" hesitatingly, as if trying to fix a vague memory, while lurid before his mental vision there rose the scene at Florian's, the lights, the crowd, the Babel of music from brass and strings, mandoline and flute, every stone of the city resonant with varied melodies. "Where?" he repeated, seeing her looking at him impatiently. "Why, I think it was in Verona."

"You think. She had a very distinct memory of meeting you, at any rate"—with a little scornful laugh. "If you were her bosom friend her greeting could not have been warmer."

"Mere Celtic impulsiveness. One meets with as much warmth in the south of Ireland. Hotel waiters have the air of clansmen, who would shed their blood for us. Hotel acquaintances seem as old friends."

"How did you come to know this girl—peasant born, as you say?"

"She was in a factory, and I was going over the factory, and I talked to her, and she told me her troubles, and I was interested and——The same sort of thing happens a dozen times on a Continental tour. You don't want chapter and verse, I hope. That memory is immeshed in a tangle of other memories. I should only deceive you if I went into particulars."

He had recovered himself by this time, and the colour had come slowly back to his face. Eve sat dumbly watching him as he bent over the sculls, rowing faster than he need have done, much faster than on the other side of the lock. He was ready to lie with an appalling recklessness if he could by so doing set up a barrier of falsehood between his wife and the true story of that night in Venice. He looked at her presently, and saw that she was troubled. He smiled, but there was no answering smile.

"My darling, you are not by way of being jealous, I hope," he said gaily. "You are not unhappy because a peasant girl held out her hands to me."

"Signora Vivanti has been long enough in England to know that a woman does not behave in that way to an almost stranger," said Eve. "Why did you look frightened at the sound of her voice when the boat came out of the lock? Why did you turn pale when she spoke to you?"

"Did I really turn pale? I suppose I was a little scared at her demonstrative address, fearing lest it should offend you. One has time to think of so many contingencies in a few moments. But I did not imagine you would take the matter so very seriously. Come, dearest, I think you know I have but one divinity below the stars, and worship at only one shrine."

"Now, perhaps—but what do I know of the past?"

"If in the past I have admired and even fancied I loved women less admirable than yourself, be sure this woman was not one of them. No ghost of a dead love looks out of her eyes, beautiful as they are."

"I must believe you," sighed Eve. "I want to believe you, and to be happy again."

"Foolish Eve. Can it be that an irrepressible young woman's greeting could interfere with your happiness?"

"It was foolish, no doubt. Women are very foolish when they love their husbands as I love you. There are scores of women I meet who think of their husbands as lightly as of their dressmakers. Would you like me to be that kind of wife—to be lunching and gadding, and driving and dancing in one direction, while you are betting and dining and card-playing somewhere else? I should be nearer being a woman of fashion than I am now."

"Be ever what you are now. Be jealous, even, if jealousy be a proof of love."

"There was a child in the boat—a handsome black-eyed boy. Is he her child, do you think?"

Having affected ignorance at the outset, Vansittart was forced to maintain his attitude.

"Chi lo sa?" he said, with a careless shrug.

"Was it not odd that Mr. Sefton should be escorting her?"

"Not especially odd. She is a public character, and has troops of admirers, no doubt. Why should not Sefton be among them?"

"I never heard him mention her when he was talking of the theatres."

"Men seldom speak of the woman they admire—especially if the lady is not in society—and Sefton is reticent about a good many things."

After this they talked of trifles, lightly, but with a somewhat studied lightness. Eve seemed again content; but her gaiety was gone, as if her spirits had drooped with the vanishing of the sun, which now at five o'clock was hidden by threatening clouds.

At Richmond Bridge they left their boat, to be taken back by a waterman, and walked through the busy town to the station. An express took them to London in good time for dressing and dining at Lady Hartley's state dinner. She had a large house in Hill Street this year, and was entertaining a good deal.

"My dear Eve, you are looking utterly washed out," she said to her sister-in-law in the drawing-room after dinner. "You must come to us at Redwold directly after Goodwood—you could come straight from Goodwood, don't you know—and let me nurse you."

"You are too kind. I think, though, it would be a greater rest if I were to go to Fernhurst for a few days, and let the sisters and Nancy take care of me. A taste of the old poverty, the whitewashed attics, and the tea-dinners would act as a tonic. I am debilitated by pleasures and luxuries."

"You were looking bright enough last night at Mrs. Cameron's French play."

"Was I? Perhaps I laughed too much at Coquelin cadet, or eat too many strawberries."

* * * *

Lady Hartley had an evening party after the dinner, and it was a shock for Vansittart on coming into the drawing-room at half-past ten, after a long-drawn-out political discussion with a big-wig of Sir Hubert's party, to find Sefton and Eve sitting side by side in a flowery nook near the piano, where at this moment Oscar de Lampion, the Belgian tenor, was casting his fine eyes up towards the ceiling, preparatory to the melting strains of his favourite serenade—

"And them canst sleep, while from the rain-washed lawn
  Thy lover watches for thy passing shade
Across the blind, and sobs and sighs till dawn
  Glows o'er the vale and creeps along the glade.
And thou canst sleep—thou heedest not his sighing;
And thou canst sleep—thou wouldst if he were dying;
Yes, thou canst sleep—canst sleep—sleep. "

There was a second verse to the same effect, exquisitely sung, but worn threadbare by familiarity, which Vansittart heard impatiently, watching Eve and her companion, and longing to break in upon their seclusion. They were silent now, since they could not with decency talk while De Lampion was singing.

There were only two verses. De Lampion was too much an artist to sing lengthy songs, although too lazy to extend his repertoire. He liked people to be sorry when he left off.

Vansittart dropped into a chair near his wife. The rooms had not filled yet, so there was a possibility of sitting down, and this quiet

282

corner, screened by an arrangement of palms and tall golden lilies, was a pleasant haven for conversation in the brief intervals between the music, which was of that superior order which is heard in respectful silence by everybody within earshot, though the people outside the room talk to their hearts' content, a buzz of multitudinous voices breaking in upon the silence whenever a door is opened.

Sefton and Vansittart shook hands directly the song was over.

"I was told you were to dine here," said Vansittart, as an obvious opening.

"Lady Hartley was kind enough to ask me, but I had an earlier engagement in Chelsea. I have been dining with the Hawberks—the composer, don't you know. Sweet little woman, Mrs. Hawberk—so sympathetic. You know them, of course."

"Only from meeting them at other people's houses."

"Ah, you should know Hawberk. He's a glorious fellow. You must spare me an hour or two to meet him at breakfast some Sunday morning, when Mrs. Vansittart doesn't want you to go to church with her."

"I always want him," said Eve, with a decisive air.

"And does he always go?"

"Always."

"A model husband. I put down the husbands who attend the morning service among the great army of hen-pecked, together with the husbands who belong to only one rather fogeyish club. But that comes of my demoralized attitude towards the respectabilities. Well, it shall not be a Sunday, but you must meet Hawberk *en petit comité* before the season is over. He is a very remarkable man. It was he who invented Signora Vivanti, the lady who claimed your acquaintance so effusively to-day."

"Indeed!" said Vansittart, with a scowl which did not invite further comment; but Sefton was not to be silenced by black looks.

"Did Mr. Hawberk bring Signora Vivanti from Italy?" asked Eve; and Sefton could see that she paled at the mere mention of the singer's name.

"I think not. She was established in very comfortable quarters at Chelsea when Hawberk first heard of her. Some good friend brought her to London and paid for her training. The rest of her career is history. Hawberk finished her artistic education, and had the courage to trust the fate of a new opera to an untried singer. The result justified his audacity, and the Vivanti is the rage. She is original, you see; and a grain of originality is worth a bushel of imitative excellence!"

"I should like to hear her sing," said Eve.

"Then you are in a fair way of being gratified. She is to sing to-night. Lady Hartley has engaged her."

"Really! How odd that Lady Hartley never mentioned her when she was telling me about her programme."

"The engagement was made only two or three days ago, after I met Lady Hartley at Lady Belle Teddington's evening party. It was my suggestion. Musical evenings are apt to be so dismal—Mendelssohn, de Beriot, Spohr, relieved by a portentous Scotch ballad of nine and twenty verses by a fashionable baritone. Vivanti has sentiment and humour, chic and fire. She will be the bouquet, and send people away in good spirits."

A duet for violin and 'cello began at this stage of conversation, and when it was over Vansittart moved away to another part of the room, and talked to other people. It was past eleven. He knew not how soon the Venetian might appear upon the scene; but he was determined to keep out of her way. He would not risk another effusive greeting; and with a woman of her type there was no reliance upon the restraints of society. She might be as demonstrative in a crowded drawing-room as on the river Thames. Of all irritating chances what could be more exasperating than this young woman's appearance at his sister's house, even as a paid entertainer? And it was Sefton's doing; Sefton, who had seen him with Fiordelisa two years ago on the Embankment, and who doubtless remembered that meeting; Sefton, who had admired Eve and had been scorned by her, and who doubtless hated Eve's husband.

Nothing could be more disquieting for Vansittart than that Sefton should have made himself the friend and patron of Fiordelisa—even if he were no more than friend or patron. If he were pursuing the Venetian girl with evil meaning it would be Vansittart's duty to warn her. He had urged her to lead a good life—to redeem the error of her girlhood by a virtuous and reputable womanhood. It would be the act of a coward to stand aside and keep silence, while her reputation was being blighted by Sefton's patronage. True that her aunt and son had been the companions of to-day's river excursion; true that their presence had given respectability to the jaunt; yet with his knowledge of Sefton's character Vansittart could hardly believe that his intentions towards this daughter of the people could be altogether free from guile. He hated the idea of an interview with Lisa; but he told himself that it was his duty to give her fair warning of Sefton's character. She might have been Harold Marchant's wife, perhaps, with a legitimate protector, but for his—Vansittart's—evil passions. This gave her an indisputable claim upon his care and kindness—a claim not to be ignored because it involved unpleasantness or risk for himself.

He went back to Eve presently, and asked her to come into the inner drawing-room, where there were people who wanted to see her; an excuse for getting her away from Sefton, who still held his ground by her chair.

"I shall lose my place if I stir," she said; "and I want to hear Signora Vivanti."

"I'll bring you back."

"There'll be no getting back through the crowd. Please let me stay till she has sung."

"As you please."

He turned and left her, offended that she should refuse him; vexed at her desire to hear the woman who had already been a bone of contention between them. He went back to the inner drawing-room, as far as possible from the piano and the clever German pianist who had arranged the programme for Lady Hartley, and who was to accompany—somewhat reluctantly—the lady from the Apollo, whose performance might pass the boundary line of the *comme il faut*, he thought.

Vansittart stood where he could just see Lisa, by looking over the heads of the crowd. She took her stand a little way from the piano, with admirable aplomb, though this was her first society performance. She was in yellow—a yellow crape gown, very simply made, with a baby bodice and short puffed sleeves; and on the clear olive of her finely moulded neck there flashed the collet necklace which represented the firstfruits of her success. Vansittart shuddered as he noted the jewels, for he had the accepted idea of actress's diamonds, and he began to fear that Lisa had already taken the wrong road.

She sang a ballad from the new serio-comic opera, *Haroun Alraschid*, a ballad which all the street organs and all the smart bands were playing, and which was as familiar in the remotest slums of the east as in the gardens of the west.

> *"I am not fair, I am not wise,*
> *But I would die for thee;*
> *My only merit in thine eyes*
> *Is my fidelity.*
> *Oh, couldst thou kill me with thy frown,*
> *That death I'd meekly meet,*
> *For it were joy to lay me down*
> *And perish at thy feet."*

It was the song of a slave to her Sultan, and glanced from the supreme of sentiment to the absurdity of burlesque. The song was the rage, but it was the power and passion of the singer that made it so. The sudden silvery laugh with which she finished the second verse, changing instantaneously from pathos to mocking gaiety—with a sudden change of metre—was a touch of originality that delighted her audience, and the song was applauded to the echo. Vansittart had moved into the music-room while she sang, as if drawn irresistibly by the power of song, and he was near enough to see his wife and Sefton talking to the singer; praising her, no doubt; uttering only the idle nothings which are spoken upon such occasions; but the idea that Eve should get to know this woman's name, that they should talk together familiarly, and above all, that Lisa should know his name, and be able to approach wife or husband whenever some wild impulse urged her attack, was dreadful to him. How could he be sure henceforward that his secret would remain a secret? Was the Venetian a person to be trusted with the power of life or death?

He went back to the inner room, and was speedily absorbed in the duty of attending two colossal dowagers with monumental necks and shoulders, and diamonds as large as chandelier drops, to steer whom down a London staircase, past a stream of people who were ascending, was no trifling work. In the dining-room the débris of dessert and the ashes of cigarettes had given place to old Derby china, peaches, grapes, and strawberries, chicken salad, and *foie gras* sandwiches, and to this light refreshment people were crowding as eagerly as if dinner were an obsolete custom among the upper classes. Blocked in between two great ladies, pouring out champagne for one, and peeling a peach for another, Vansittart was secure from being pounced upon by Fiordelisa. He saw Sefton sitting with her at a little table in a corner, as he piloted his aristocratic three-deckers to the door. Sefton was plying her with champagne and lobster salad, and her joyous laugh rang out above society's languid jabber.

He hated Sefton with all his heart that night; and he was too angry with Eve to speak to her, either as they waited in the hall for their carriage, or during the short drive home.

Never before had he treated her with this sullen rudeness. She followed him into his den, where he went for a final smoke before going upstairs. She stood by his chair for a few minutes in silence, watching him as he lighted his cigar, and then she said gently—

"What is the matter with you to-night, Jack? Have I vexed you?"

"I don't know that you have vexed me—but I know that I am

vexed."

"About what?"

"I didn't like to see you so civil to Signora Vivanti. It is all very well for dowagers and fussy matrons to take notice of a public singer, but it is a new departure for you."

"I could hardly help myself. She sang so delightfully, and I was pleased with her, and then Mr. Sefton introduced her to me. What could I do but praise her, when I really admired her?"

"No, you were blameless. It was Sefton's fault. He had no right to introduce her to you."

"But is she not respectable?"

"I cannot answer for her respectability. I know nothing of what kind of life she has led since she made her *début*. She wears diamonds, and that is not a good sign."

"She does not look like a disreputable person," said Eve, very thoughtfully. "There is something frank and simple about her. That boy must be hers, he is so like her. Do you know if she was ever married—if the boy's father was her husband?"

"I know very little about her, as I told you to-day; but I should say not."

"Poor thing! I am very sorry for her."

"Don't waste your pity upon her. She seems perfectly happy. A peasant girl, reared upon polenta, does not consider these things so tragically as they are considered in Mayfair."

"How scornfully you speak of her. I am sure she is a good girl at heart. She remembered seeing me in the boat to-day, and she asked me if I was your wife. She repeated my name curiously, as if she had never heard it before. Did not she know your name when you met her in Verona, or wherever it was?"

"Very likely not. I was an Englishman. That might have been a sufficient distinction in her mind."

"I hope she is not leading a wicked life," said Eve, with a sigh. "She has a good face."

"Do not let us trouble about her any more," said Vansittart, looking earnestly up at the thoughtful face that was looking down at him. "She has almost brought dissension between us—for the first time."

"Only almost. We could not be angry with each other long, could we, Jack? But you must own it was enough to take any wife by surprise. A beautiful Italian girl stretching out both her hands in eager greeting, almost throwing herself out of her boat into ours. Any wife caring very much for her husband would have felt as I did—a sudden pang of jealousy."

"Any wife must be a foolish wife if she felt that pang, knowing herself beloved as you do."

"Yes, I think that now you are honestly fond of me. Ah, how can I think otherwise when you have been so indulgent, so dear? Yet in the past you might have loved that dark-eyed girl. You never pretended I was your first love. And if you did care for her, do please be candid and tell me. I should be happier if I knew the worst. It could not matter much to me, you see, Jack, that you should have been fond of her—once. Dearest, dearest," she repeated coaxingly, with her head bent down till her soft cheek leaned against his own, "tell me the worst."

"Eve, how often must I protest that I never cared for this girl—that she was never anything to me but a friendless woman—friendless except for an aunt as poor and as ignorant as herself. She was never anything to me—never. Are you satisfied now? As far as Fiordelisa is concerned you know the worst."

"I am satisfied. But if you did not care for her she cared for you. She could not have looked as she looked to-day—her whole face lighting up with rapture—if she had not loved you. Only love can smile like that. But I won't tease you. The thought of her shall never again come between us."

"So be it, Eve. We have had our much ado about nothing. We will give Signora Vivanti a holiday. Sophy will be with you to-morrow, and will want no end of amusement—exhibitions all day and a theatre every night, with an evening party afterwards. I know what country cousins—or country sisters are. Besides, it will be Sophy's *début*, and she will expect to make an impression."

"I hope she will not be too fine," said Eve, remembering Sophy's strivings to be smart under difficulties.

"She will be as fine as the finest, be sure of that. She will expect matrimonial offers—to be a success in her first season. Why don't you marry her to Sefton?"

"I don't like Mr. Sefton."

"But Sophy might like him, and he is rich and well born. If he is not a gentleman that is his own fault—not any flaw in his pedigree."

CHAPTER XXIV.

"POOR KIND WILD EYES SO DASHED
WITH LIGHT QUICK TEARS"

Sophy arrived next day with portentous punctuality, in time for luncheon, intent on pleasure, and dressed in a style which she believed in as the very latest Parisian fashion; for this damsel credited herself with an occult power of knowing what was "in" and what was "out," and, with no larger horizon than a country church and an occasional rustic garden-party, set up as an authority upon dress, and gave her instructions to the village dressmaker, who made up ladies' own materials, and worked at ladies' houses, with the air of a Kate Reilly directing an apprentice.

Eve had been very generous, and Sophy's costume was a great advance upon those days when Lady Hartley had talked of the sisters as Colonel Marchant's burlesque troupe. Eve had sent down a big parcel of materials from a West End draper's, the newest and the best, and Sophy had exercised her fingers and her taste in the confection of stylish garments; yet it must be owned there was an unmistakable air of home dress-making—of fabrications suggested by answers to correspondents in a ladies' newspaper—about those smart gowns, jackets, capes, and fichus which Sophy wore with such satisfaction. This showed itself most in an unconscious exaggeration of every fashion; just as a woman who rouges exceeds the bloom of natural carnations. Sophy's Medici collars were higher than anybody else's. The military collar of Sophy's home-made tailor gown was an instrument of torture. Sophy's waistcoats and sleeves were more mannish and sporting than anything the West End tailors had produced for Eve. In a word, there was a touch of Sophy's personality about every garment; just as in every picture there is the individuality of the painter.

But Sophy, flushed with the delights of a London season, was quite pretty enough to be forgiven a little provincialism in her dress and manners, and she was well received by Eve's friends.

It was good for Eve that she should be obliged to exert herself in order to amuse Sophy, and that the sweet solitude of two was no longer possible for her and Vansittart.

He said nothing further about his wife's need of repose. He was glad to see her occupied from morning till long past midnight, showing Sophy what our ancestors used to call "the town;" but which now includes a wide range of the suburbs, and occasional garden-parties as far off as Marlow or Hatfield. He was glad of anything which could distract his wife's thoughts from too deep a consideration of his relations with Signora Vivanti, and he encouraged Sophy in every form of dissipation, until he found, to his annoyance, that an evening had been allotted to the Apollo.

The fame of *Haroun Alraschid* and of Signora Vivanti's beauty and talent had penetrated beyond Haslemere, and Sophy had written to her sister imploring her to secure places for an evening during her visit. A box had been taken six weeks in advance, and Eve, who was always indulged in every theatrical fancy, had not thought it necessary to inform her husband of the fact.

To forbid the occupation of that box would have been too marked an exercise of authority; to absent himself from the party would have made Eve uneasy; so he went with his wife and sister-in-law, and saw Lisa on the stage for the first time since he had watched her in the chorus at Covent Garden.

The box was one of the best in the house, and very near the stage. Vansittart felt assured that Lisa would recognize his wife and would see him standing behind her chair; and with a young woman of Lisa's temperament he knew not what form that recognition might assume.

Fortunately Lisa had now become too much of an artist to do anything which would take her "out of the picture." She gave Vansittart one little look which told him he was seen in the shadow where he stood; and for the rest she was no longer Lisa, the Venetian, but Haroun's devoted slave-girl, bought from a cruel master, during one of Haroun's nocturnal explorations of the city, and following him ever after with a devoted love, watchful, ubiquitous, his guardian angel in every danger, his resource and protection in every serio-comic dilemma. Her singing, her acting, were alike instinct with passion and genius, a genius unspoiled by that higher culture which is too apt to bring self-consciousness and over-elaboration in its train, and so to miss all broad and spontaneous effects. Fiordelisa flung herself into her *rôle* with a daring energy which always hit the mark.

Sefton was in the stalls, attentive, but not applauding. He left all noisy demonstration to the British public. It was enough for him to know that Lisa liked to see him there, tranquil and interested. The highest reward she had ever given him for his devotion was the confession that she missed him when he was absent, and found something wanting in her audience when his stall was empty. For the most part he went as regularly to hear Lisa sing as he took his coffee after dinner. The dinner-party must be something very much out of the common run of dinners which could draw him from his place at the Apollo; and people remarked that for the last two seasons Mr. Sefton was seldom to be met in society until late in the evening.

He went to Mrs. Vansittart's box between the acts, and made himself particularly agreeable to Sophy, whom he had not seen since her sister's marriage.

"This is your first season, ain't it, Miss Marchant?" he said. "What a large reserve fund of enjoyment you must have to spend!"

Sophy was not going to accept compliments upon her ignorance.

"Fernhurst is so near town," she said. "One sees everybody, and one breathes the town atmosphere."

"Ah, but you only see people on their rustic side. They wear tailor gowns and talk about fox-hunting and sick cottagers. They leave their London intellect in Mayfair, like the table-knives rolled up in mutton fat, to come out sharp and bright next season. You don't know what we are like in town if you see us only in the country."

"I don't find a remarkable difference in *you*," said Sophy, pertly. "You always try to be epigrammatic."

"Oh, I am no one—a poor follower of the fashion of the hour, whatever it may be. How do you like the music?"

"For music to hear and forget I think it is absolutely delightful."

"There are some numbers which the piano-organs and the fashionable bands won't allow you to forget—Zuleika's song, for instance, and the quartette."

"I rather hate all but classical music," replied Sophy, with her fine air, "and I find your famous Signora Vivanti odiously vulgar."

"Deliciously vulgar, you should have said. Her vulgarity is one of her attractions. To be so pretty, and so graceful, and so clever, and at the same time a peasant to the tips of her fingers—there is the charm."

"I hate peasants, even when they are as clever as Thomas Carlyle."

Sefton looked at the pert little face meditatively. She was like Eve, but without Eve's exceptional loveliness—the loveliness that consists chiefly in delicacy and refinement, an ethereal beauty which makes a woman like a flower. She had Eve's transparent complexion and changeful colouring. There was the same type, but less beautifully developed. She was quite pretty enough for Sefton to find amusement in teasing her, although all his stronger feelings were given to Signora Vivanti. He called in Charles Street on the following afternoon. It was Mrs. Vansittart's afternoon at home; and she could not shut her door even against her worst enemy.

Sefton found the usual feminine gossips—mothers and daughters, maiden aunts, and cousins from the country, with fresh-coloured cheeks, and unremarkable faces—the usual sprinkling of well-dressed young men. Among so many people he could secure a few confidential words with Eve, while she poured out the tea, a duty she always performed with her own hands. It was the one thing that reminded her of the old life at Fernhurst, and those jovial teas which had stood in the place of dinner.

She spoke frankly enough of the performance at the Apollo, praised the music and the libretto, declared she had enjoyed it more than any serio-comic opera she had heard during the season; yet Sefton detected a certain constraint when she spoke of Signora Vivanti, which told him that the meeting of the two boats was not forgotten, and that the little scene had left almost as angry a spot upon her memory as that which burnt in his.

"And had you really never seen her on the stage before last night?" he asked.

"Never!"

"How very odd. I think you and Vansittart must have been about the only people at the West End who have not seen *Haroun Alraschid*—and yet you are playgoers."

"I was saving the Apollo for my sister," she answered, perfectly understanding his drift.

She knew that he was trying to give her pain, that he wanted to make her distrust her husband. Lisa's conduct had impressed him as it had impressed her, and now he was gloating over her jealous agony.

She turned from him to talk to an aristocratic matron, a large and grand-looking woman, who would have looked better in peplum and chiton than in a flimsy pongee confection which she called her "frock." The matron had heard the word Apollo, and had a good deal to say about Signora Vivanti, whose performance she deprecated as too realistic.

"Dramatic passion is all very well in a classic opera like Gluck's *Orphée*," she said authoritatively, "but that mixture of passion with broad comedy is too bizarre for my taste."

"My dear Lady Oriphane, that is just what we want nowadays. We all languish for the bizarre. If we travel we want Africa and pigmy blackamoors. If we go to the play we want to be startled by the outrageous, rather that awed by the sublime. The stories we read must have some strange background, or be dotted about with unknown tongues. An author can interest us in a footman if he will only call him a Kitmutghar. With us the worship of the bizarre marks the highest point of culture."

Mr. Tivett was there, and chimed in at this stage of the conversation with his pretty little lady-like voice.

"It all means the same thing," he said; "Neo-paganism. We are the children of a decadent age. We have come to the top of the ladder of life—life meaning civilization and culture—and there is nothing left for us but to climb down again. All the strongest spirits are harking back to the uncivilized. That is at the bottom of the strong man's passion for Africa. The strong men will all go to Africa, and in a few generations Europe will be peopled by weaklings and hereditary imbeciles. Then the strong men will come back and pour themselves over the civilized world, as the Vandals poured themselves over Italy, and London and Paris will be the spoil of the Anglo-African."

"Why not the Dutch-African, or the Portuguese-African?" asked Sefton, when everybody had laughed at little Mr. Tivett's gloomy outlook.

"Oh, the Anglo-Saxon race will prevail on the Dark Continent, just as they have prevailed in the East. Our future kings will style themselves Emperor of India and Africa. No other race can stand against us in the game of colonization. We have the courage which conquers, and the dogged patience which can keep what boldness has won."

Mr. Tivett was not allowed to indulge in any further prophecies, for Sophy absorbed him in a discussion about the plays she ought to see, and the music she ought to hear while she was in town.

"You are too late for Sarasate," he said tragically. "Last Saturday was his final performance. He leaves us in the flood-tide of the season, leaves us lamenting. But there are plenty of good things left. Clifford Harrison gives some of his delicious recitations next Saturday. Be sure you hear him. Hollmann and Wolff are to be heard almost daily. And then there is the opera three nights a week. I hope you have no horrid dinner-parties to prevent your enjoying yourself."

"Only one this week, I am thankful to say," said Sophy, who was dying to see what London dinners were like, and was deeply grateful to that one generous hostess who, hearing of her expected visit, had sent her a card for the stately feast to which the Vansittarts were bidden.

Eve had refused other dinner invitations during her sister's visit. She made all engagements subservient to Sophy's pleasure. Vansittart was not rich enough to give his wife an opera-box for the season, but he had taken a box for four evenings in the fortnight that Sophy was to spend in Charles Street, and four operas, with different sets of artists, for a young woman who had never heard an opera in her life, was an almost overpowering prospect. It needed all Sophy's aplomb to talk of operas of which she only knew the overtures, and an occasional hackneyed scena, as if every page of the score were familiar to her; but Sophy was equal to the occasion, and discussed the merits of sopranos, tenors, and baritones with as critical an air as if her opinions were the growth of years of experience, rather than the result of a careful study of *Truth* and *The World*, sent her regularly by Eve, so soon as they had been read in Charles Street.

Sefton joined in the conversation between Sophy and Mr. Tivett, and had a good deal of advice to offer as to the things that were worthy of the young lady's attention; the result of which advice appeared to be that there was really very little to be heard worth hearing, or to be seen worth seeing.

* * * *

While tea and gossip occupied Eve and her friends in Charles Street, Vansittart had taken advantage of his wife's "afternoon," an occasion which he rarely honoured with his presence, and had driven to Chelsea to see Lisa and her aunt, and to impart that warning which he had resolved upon giving, at any hazard to himself. It was dangerous perhaps, in his position, to renew any relations with the Venetian; yet on the other hand it might be needful to assure himself of her loyalty, now that she had been brought suddenly into the foreground of his life, and might, at any hour, reveal his fatal secret to her from whom he would have it for ever hidden.

All things considered, after two days and nights of anxious thought, it seemed to him best, for his own sake, as well as for Lisa's, that he should have some serious talk with her.

He heard the prattle of the child as la Zia opened the door to him, and the mother's voice telling him to be quiet. La Zia received him with open arms, and praised his kindness in coming to see them after such a long absence.

"If it had not been for the discovery that the rent was paid when we took our money to the agent on Our Lady's Day, we should have thought you had forgotten us," said la Zia.

She had her bonnet on, ready to take Paolo to Battersea Park, where she took him nearly every afternoon, while Lisa practised, or slept, or yawned over an English story-book. She would read nothing but English, in her determination to master that language; but history was too dull, novels were too long, and she cared only for short stories in which there was much sentimental love-making, generally by lords and ladies with high-sounding titles. These she read with rapture, picturing herself as the heroine, Vansittart as the highborn lover. She could not understand how so grand a gentleman could have missed a title. In Italy he would have been a Marquis or a Prince, she told herself.

She started up at the sound of his voice, and welcomed him joyously, pale but radiant.

"Why would you not come near me the other night?" she asked. "I was in your sister's house—Mr. Sefton told me that the gracious lady is your sister—and you were there, and you hid yourself from me."

"I was afraid, Si'ora," he answered, coming to the point at once. "You know what lies between you and me—a secret the telling of which would blight my life—and you are so reckless, so impetuous. How could I tell what you might say?"

She looked at him with mournful reproachfulness.

"Do you know me so little as that?" she said. "Don't you know that I would cut my tongue out—that I would die on the rack, as tortured prisoners died in Venice hundreds of years ago—rather than I would speak one word that could hurt you?"

"Forgive me, Si'ora. Yes, yes, I know that you would not willingly injure me—but you might ruin my life by a careless speech. You have aroused my wife's suspicions already—suspicious of she knows not what—vague jealousies that have made her unhappy. She could not understand your impulsive greeting; and I could not tell her how much you were my friend, without telling her the why and the wherefore. I am hemmed round with difficulty when I am questioned about you. If you were old and ugly it would be different—but I dare not avow my interest in a young and beautiful woman without revealing the claim she has upon my friendship—and in that claim lies the secret of my crime. Do you understand, Lisa?"

"Yes, I understand," she answered moodily.

Her aunt lingered on the threshold of the door, the boy tugging at her skirts, and urging her to go out. Battersea Park was his favourite playground. He carried a wooden horse with a fine development of head, but with only a stick and a wheel to represent his body, which equine compromise he bestrode and galloped upon in the course of his airing. La Zia carried his pail and the shovel with which he was wont to scrape up the loose gravel in the roadway as blissfully as if he had been disporting himself beside the waves that roll gaily in to splash the children at play on the sands.

La Zia looked at her niece interrogatively, and the niece nodded "go," whereupon aunt and boy vanished. She was always bidden to stop when Sefton was the visitor.

"You need not be frightened," said Lisa. "We are not likely to meet again, as we met on the river. It was so long since I had seen you! I was taken by surprise, and forgot everything except that it was you, whom I thought I should never see again. I shall be wiser in future, now that I know more about you, and now that I have seen your wife."

"That is my own good Lisa! She is a sweet wife, is she not? Worthy that a man should love her?"

"Yes, she is worthy; and she is fair and beautiful, like the Mary-lilies. I don't wonder that you love her. And she has never done any evil thing in her life, has she? If a young man had said to her, 'Come with me to Venice, and be my little wife,' she would not have believed him, as I did. She would have said, 'You must marry me first in the church.' She would have believed in nothing but the church and the priest. She was not ignorant and poor, like me."

"Lisa, do you suppose that I was making any unkind comparisons? I said only that she is worthy to be loved—that all men and women must love and honour her, and that her husband must needs adore her. And now, Si'ora, promise me that you will respect her jealousy, which is only the shadow cast by her love, and that you will do or say nothing that can make her unhappy."

"I will do or say nothing to hurt you," Lisa answered, somewhat sullenly. "She has little need to be unhappy, having all your love. But she is very sweet, as you say. She spoke to me graciously the other night, although she had a curious look, as if she were half afraid of me. Yes, she is beautiful. Did you know her and love her long before that day on the Lido, when you were so friendly with my aunt and me?"

"No, Si'ora."

"What! your heart was free then?"

"Free as air."

"And afterwards—when I saw you at the opera? When you came to our lodgings?"

"Ah, then I had seen her, I was captive. I loved her at first sight, but went about foolishly hiding my chains, trying not to love her. And now that we understand each other fully upon one point—now that I can trust my happiness in your hands, I want to talk to you about yourself, Lisa. I am not over-fond of that Mr. Sefton with whom you are so friendly."

"No more am I over-fond of him. He is kind to us. He brings toys for Paolo; and he takes us on the river. He is the only friend little Zinco has allowed me to have."

"He gives Paolo toys? And he gave you that diamond necklace, did he not?"

"Gave me my necklace! I should think not! Do you suppose I would be beholden to him, or to any one? Do you know how many bracelets and brooches I have sent back to the fools who bought them for me? Diamonds, emeralds, rubies, sapphires—all the colours of the rainbow. I just look at them and laugh, and carry them off to little Zinco, and he packs them up and sends them back to the giver, with his compliments, and his assurance that Signora Vivanti is not in the habit of accepting gifts. Mr. Sefton give me my neck-lace! Why, my necklace is my fortune!"

And then she told him how she and la Zia had scraped and saved, and lived upon pasta and Swiss cheese, in order to buy that necklace from Mr. Attenborough, who had allowed her to pay a considerable part of the price by weekly instalments. It was a bankrupt Contessa's necklace—a Contessa who had run away from her husband.

"I am very glad to hear that," said Vansittart. "I was afraid all was not well when I saw my little Si'ora blazing in diamonds."

"Did they blaze?" she cried, delighted. "You thought that I was like some of the singers who spend all their salary on a carriage, and grand dinners, and fine silk gowns—a hundred pounds for a single gown! I wanted to buy something that would last, something that I could turn into money whenever I liked."

"But your diamonds yield no interest, Si'ora, so they are hardly a wise investment."

"I don't want interest; I want something that is pretty to look at. Did my diamonds blaze? Your sister's is the only grand house I have sung at. I sing for Mrs. Hawberk, but her house is not grand, and I take no money for singing at her parties. But I had ten guineas for singing at Lady Hartley's—ten guineas for two little songs."

"Bravissima, Si'ora! There are plenty of drawing-rooms in London where you may pick up gold and silver. There is a freshness about you and your singing that people will like, as a pleasant relief, after a grand opera. But now, Cara, I would earnestly warn you to have very little to do with Mr. Sefton, to keep him at the furthest possible distance. Believe me, he is a dangerous acquaintance."

"Not to me," said Lisa, snapping her fingers. "He is nothing to me, niente, niente, niente! My heart has never beat any faster for his coming. I am never sorry when he goes. He is kind to Paolo, and my aunt thinks him a delightful gentleman. He tells us stories about the lords and ladies he knows, and he helps me with my English. He makes me read to him. He tells me the meaning of words, and teaches me how to pronounce them. I should not have got on nearly so fast without his help."

"Dangerous help, Si'ora. You are encouraging a traitor. His kindness springs from no good motive. He doesn't want to marry you."

"Do you think I want him for a husband?" exclaimed Lisa, with supreme contempt. "I shall never marry. No one will ever have the right to question me about Paolo's father."

There was a dignity in this assertion which showed that the unsophisticated daughter of the Isles had made some progress in social science. She knew at least that a husband was a person who might call her to account for her past life.

"I tell you that I don't care for Mr. Sefton; but he amuses la Zia and me, and our lives would be very dull without him."

"Better dulness than danger. The man is bad, Lisa, bad to the core. Some men are made so. In the county where he was born, among the neighbours who respected his father and mother, and who tolerate him for his name's sake, he is neither trusted nor liked. Before he left the University, when he had only just come of age, there was a village tragedy in which he was known to be implicated, a tenant-farmer's pretty daughter drowned in the mill-dam with her nameless child. The girl's father was a tenant on the Sefton estate, as his father and grandfather had been before him. A connection of that kind with most young men would be sacred—but Wilfrid Sefton had no compunction. He was saved from exposure, for the love that the sufferers bore to his people; but the scandal became pretty well known in the neighbourhood, and the friends of his family who might have pitied him for the awful consequences of his sin, were disgusted by the indifference with which he treated the tragedy—living it down with a brazen front, and later, when he was owner of the estate, turning the girl's father out of his holding, on the flimsiest excuse. Do you think such a man as that is worthy to be admitted to the home of an unprotected woman on a footing of friendship?"

"No, no, he is not worthy. If you tell me to shut my door against him, the door shall be shut. But is it true? Did this poor girl really drown herself because she could not bear to live disgraced? Are there women in England like that?"

"Yes, Lisa. There have been many such women. This girl belonged to the yeoman class—her forefathers had been settled in the land for two hundred years, sons of the soil, respected by their neighbours, and as proud of their good name as if it had been a patent of nobility; and this girl was young and sensitive. I have heard her story from those who saw her grow up from infancy to womanhood—gentle, yielding, guileless—an easy prey for an unscrupulous young man with a handsome face and a winning manner. He won her, blighted her, murdered her. Yes, Lisa, his crime came nearer murder than that dagger-thrust at Florian's."

"Don't speak of that," she cried, putting her fingers on his lips. "We must forget it. There never was such a thing—or at least you had nothing to do with it. It was Fate, not your will, that he should die like that. It was to be. Non si muove foglia che Iddio non voglia. I am glad you have told me about that girl. I never liked Mr. Sefton—never really liked him. However pleasant he was I had always a feeling that he was hiding something. There is a light in his eyes as if he were laughing at one. He is like Mephistopheles in the opera. It is not in his nature to be sorry for any one."

"And you will give him his *congé*?"

"Yes; he shall come here no more. I shall not let him know that you have told me that poor girl's story. He might want to fight a duel with you, if he knew what you have said of him."

"I don't think he would, Lisa; but it is wiser to tell him nothing. You can say you have been told you are compromising yourself by receiving his visits."

"Little Zinco does not love him," said Lisa; "he will be pleased to see him dismissed. He says I should have no friend but him and my piano."

"Zinco is a worthy soul."

"Is he not? He pretends to be very proud of my success. For the first year of my engagement at the Apollo I used to give him a quarter of my salary; but now I only pay him for my lessons. He goes on teaching me grand opera. It broadens and refines my style, he tells me—but Mr. Hawberk implores me never to leave off being vulgar. It would be my ruin, he says."

"Be yourself. Lisa—bright, candid, and original. Your transparent nature will always pass for genius, from its rarity. And now good-bye. I must not come here any more. I came to-day because I felt I had a duty to do as your friend, but my wife would not like to hear of me as your visitor. She and I love each other too well not to be easily jealous."

"It has been sweet to see you," answered Lisa, gravely, "but I will not ask you to come again. Yes, yes," she added musingly. "I understand! Love is always jealous."

She gave him her hand, and bade him good-bye, with a gentle resignation which touched him more deeply than her passionate moods had ever done. The beautiful dark eyes looked into his, and said, "I love you still—shall love you always," in language which a man need not be a coxcomb to understand. And so they parted, each believing that this might be a final parting.

Vansittart looked at his watch as he ran downstairs. It was nearly six o'clock. At the bottom of the last flight he met Sefton, who was entering with an easy air and self-satisfied smile, which changed to a frown as he recognized Lisa's departing visitor.

"I have just come from Charles Street," he said, recovering himself instantly, "where I expected to find you. But I dare say you have been more amused here than you would have been there. The narrow footpaths and shady woodland walks are generally pleasanter than the broad high-road."

"Is that a truism, or an allegory? If the latter, it bears no application to my visit here."

"Doesn't it really? You don't mean that you, Mrs. Vansittart's husband, call upon Signora Vivanti in the beaten way of friendship?"

"In friendship, at least, if not in the beaten way; but whatever my motive in visiting that lady, I don't admit your right to question me about it; or"—with a laugh—"to resort to allegory. Good day to you."

He ran down the steps to his hansom, and Sefton went slowly up the three flights of stone stairs which led to Signora Vivanti's bower, brooding angrily upon his encounter with Vansittart. He had never been able to extort any admissions from Lisa about this man. She had been secret as the grave; yet he was convinced that her past history was the history of an intrigue with Vansittart; and after that effusive greeting from the boat, and remembering the expression of her face more than two years ago, as she hung upon his arm on the Embankment, he was convinced that she loved him still, and that this passion was the cause of her coldness to him, Wilfred Sefton.

300

CHAPTER XXV.

"AND EVERY GENTLE PASSION SICK TO DEATH"

Although in his leisurely ascent to the third story Mr. Sefton had time to recover the appearance of serenity, he was by no means master of himself as he waited for Lisa's door to be opened. Still less was he master of himself when the door was opened by Lisa herself, looking flushed and excited, her eyes brilliant with newly shed tears.

He went through the little vestibule and into the sunlit drawing-room with the air of a man who had the right to enter unbidden, and flung himself sullenly into one of Lisa's basket chairs, which creaked under his weight.

"It is very late," said Lisa, evidently fluttered and uneasy. "I ought to be starting for the theatre."

"You needn't hurry," Sefton answered coolly. "It isn't six o'clock; and you don't come on the stage till half-past eight. You'd better sit down and take things easily. You don't look much like going into the street, with that crying face. You'd better get over your scene with your lover before you go out of doors."

"I have no lover," Lisa answered indignantly, tossing up her head.

In Sefton's eyes she had never looked lovelier than at that moment; every feature instinct with passion; red lips and delicate nostrils faintly quivering; a rich carmine flushing the pale olive of her cheeks; the great dark eyes brightened by tears; the haughty pose of the head giving something of aristocracy to that uncultured beauty. He loved her with a passion which every fresh indication of her cold indifference had stimulated to increasing warmth. He loved her first because she was lovely and fascinating in her childish simplicity. He loved her next and best because she, who by every common rule of life should have been so easily won, had proved invincible. The greatest princess in the land—the woman most hedged round by conventionalities—could not have held herself more aloof than Lisa had done, even while condescending to accept his friendship. She had held herself aloof; and she had shown him that she was not afraid of him.

He saw her now under a new aspect, saw her deeply moved, with all the potentialities of tragedy in those tremulous lips and shining eyes. He saw now in all its reality the passion which informed her acting, and gave pathetic reality to all that there was of sentiment in her *rôle*. He saw the moving spring which had made it so easy for her to represent in all its touching details the passion of hopeless love.

"You have no lover? You are an audacious woman to make that assertion to me when I have seen you in his company, after an interval of years, and when each time I saw you, your face has been a declaration of love. I met the man on your staircase just now; and I can read the history of his visit in your eyes. Do you mean to tell me that he is anything less than your lover?"

"I mean to tell you nothing. Che diavolo! What are you to me that you should call me to account? Signor Zinco said I was very foolish to let you come here. It was only because my aunt and the boy liked you that I let you come. And you took us on the river, which was pleasant. One must have some one."

"You will have me no more until we understand each other," cried Sefton, furiously. "Voglio finirla. I will not be fooled. I will not be duped. I will not be your abject slave as I have been, going night after night to feast upon your beauty, to drink the music of your voice, giving you my whole mind and heart, and getting nothing for my pains, not even the assurance that you are growing fonder of me, that love will come in good time. Do you think I am the man to endure that sort of torture for ever?"

"I do not think at all about you. Voglio finirla, io! I have made up my mind that it will be better for you not to come here any more. We shall miss you and your clever talk, and the days on the river—but we can live without you—and as for love, that is over and done with. I shall never love anybody but Paolo and la Zia. I have cared for two people in this world—and my love ended badly with both. The one who loved me died. The one I loved the most never loved me. There, you have my confession without questioning. Are you satisfied now?"

"Not quite. The man you love is the man who left you just now—Paolo's father?"

He came nearer to her as he asked this daring question; the question he had been longing to ask from the beginning of things. He took hold of her arm almost roughly, and drew her towards him, scrutinizing her face, and trying to read her secret in her eyes.

She answered him with a mocking laugh.

"You are very clever at guessing riddles," she said. "I have made my confession. You will get no more out of me. And now, with your permission, I will put on my hat. It takes me a long time to get to the theatre—I always go by the steamboat on fine evenings—and it takes me a still longer time to dress for the stage."

She went to the door and opened it for him, waiting with a courteous air for him to go out; but he took hold of her again, even more roughly than before, shut the door violently, and drew her back into the room.

"There is time enough for you to talk to me," he said. "I will answer for your being at the theatre—but you must hear me out. We must have an explanation. I never knew how fond I was of you till just now, when I met that man leaving your house. I was satisfied to go dangling on—playing with fire—so long as I was the only one. But now that he is hanging about you, there must be no more uncertainty. I must know my fate. Lisa, you know how I love you. There is no use in talking of that. If I were to talk for an hour I could say no more than every word I have spoken for the last year and a half—ever since we sat together in the tent that Sunday night at Hawberk's—has been telling you. I love you. I love you, Lisa: with a love that fuses my life into yours, which makes life useless, purposeless, hopeless without you."

He had not loosened his hold. That strong, sinewy hand of his was grasping her firm, round arm, his other hand and arm drawing her against his heart. She could feel how furiously that heart was beating; she could see his finely cut face whitening as it looked into hers; his eyes with a wild light in them. He stood silent, holding her thus, like a bird caught in a springe, while she struggled to release herself from him. He stood thinking out his fate, with the woman he loved in his arms.

In those few moments he was asking himself the crucial question, Could he live without this woman? Passion—a passion of slow and silent growth—answered no. Then came another question, Would she be his mistress? Was it any use to sing the old song, to offer her the market price for her charms—a house at the West End, a carriage, a settlement; all except his name and the world's esteem? Common sense answered him sternly no. This woman, struggling to escape from an unwelcome caress, was not the woman to accept dishonourable proposals. She had been showing him for the last year and a half, in the plainest manner, that he was positively indifferent to her. She was no fonder of him now than at the beginning of their acquaintance. Love could not tempt her. Wealth could hardly tempt her, since she could earn an income which was more than sufficient for her needs. To such a woman as this, peasant born as she was, uncultivated, friendless, he must offer the highest price—that price which he had told himself he would offer to no woman living. He must offer his name, and he must enter upon that solemn contract between man and woman which had always seemed to him an anomaly in the legislature of a civilized people—a contract which only death or dishonour could break.

"Lisa," he said, "I am not the enemy you think me. There is no sacrifice I would not make for you. You know so little of the world that perhaps you hardly know how much a man of good birth sacrifices when he takes a wife who can bring him nothing but his heart's desire. Try and understand that, Lisa. I love you too well to count the cost—too well to care that marriage with you cuts me off from all chance of marrying a woman whose money would quadruple my fortune and buy me a peerage. I could make such a marriage as that to-morrow if I choose, Lisa. It has been made very plain to me that I should be accepted by a lady who will carry a million sterling to the husband of her choice. Don't think me a snob for telling you this. I want you to understand that I am worth something in the world's market. Be my wife, Lisa. I am a rich man. I can take you to a fine old country house, as large as one of the palaces on the Canal Grande. I can give you all things women value—horses and carriages, fine rooms, pictures, silver, jewels—and I give you with them the devotion of a man who has loved many women with a light and passing love, but who never knew what the reality of love meant till he knew you, who never until now has asked a woman to be his wife."

He released her with those last words, and they stood looking at each other, she breathless with surprise.

"Do you really mean that?" she asked.

"Really, really, really. Say yes, Lisa. Kiss me, my beloved, kiss me the kiss of betrothal"—holding out his arms to her pleadingly. "We can be married two or three days hence, before the registrar, and afterwards in any church you like. You will throw up your engagement at once. We will go to the Tyrol, bury ourselves in the hills and the woods, and in November I will take you home, and let all the county envy me my lovely wife."

"You would marry me—me, the lace-girl of Burano; common, oh, so common! And so poor; brought up among ragged children, earning seven soldi a day, living on polenta. You would marry Paolo's mother?"

"Yes, I would marry Paolo's mother, without even knowing the secret of Paolo's parentage. I would marry you because I love you, Lisa—madly, foolishly, obstinately, with a love that does not count the cost."

"And I should be a great lady? I should drive about in a grand carriage, and have footmen—powdered footmen like Lady Hartley's—to wait upon me?"

"Yes, child, yes—frivolous, foolish child. Come! Come to my heart, Lisa! Non posso stare senza te!"

He would have taken her to his heart triumphantly, believing himself accepted; but she stretched out her two hands with a repelling gesture as he approached her, and held him at arm's length.

"Not if you could make me a queen," she said. "You do not know Fiordelisa, when you try to tempt her with house and land. Your English ladies marry like that, I have heard, for houses and jewels and horses, to be called Principessa or Contessa—but I will never belong to a man I don't love. I have belonged to one man, and he was a hard master, and I felt like a slave with a chain. My life was not my own. I know what it is to belong to a man. It doesn't mean paradise. But I loved him dearly at the first, when he was kind to me, and took me away from work and poverty. I loved him a little to the last even, though he was a hard master."

"I would never be hard with you, Lisa. I could never be your master. Love has made me your slave. Carissima mia, be not so foolish as to deny me. Think how gay, how luxurious, how happy your life may be."

He was pleading to her in her own dulcet language, the soft Italian, softened to even more liquid utterance by those elisions he had caught from her Venetian tongue.

She stood a few paces from him, her arms folded tightly across her breast, defying him. Marco, the cat, had awakened from his long afternoon sleep in a luxurious basket—Sefton's offering—and was arching his back and rubbing his soft white fur against his mistress's black gown. She looked like a witch, Sefton thought, standing there in her defiant beauty, shabbily clad in rusty black, and with the white cat protecting her, glaring and spitting at him in unreasoning anger.

"My life could never be happy with a man I did not love," she said resolutely. "Even if I believed in your promises I would not marry you. I would not accept your generous sacrifice. But I don't believe in your grand offers. I have been warned. I know your character better than you think. You are trying to deceive me with promises that you don't mean to keep, as you deceived the farmer's daughter, who drowned herself because of your lies."

305

"Ah!" he cried furiously. "You have heard that village slander. It could only reach you from one source—the lips of the man who left you just now. Don't you know that when a poor man's daughter goes wrong it is always the richest man in the neighbourhood who is accused of seducing her? I dare say that rule holds good in Italy as well as in England. I am in earnest, Lisa. I mean no less than I say. Meet me next Monday at the registrar's office, with your aunt, and with Signor Zinco if you like, to see that the marriage is a good marriage, and we will leave that office as man and wife."

"No," she answered doggedly. "Even if you are in earnest it can make no difference to me. I don't want to be a great lady. People would laugh at me, and I should be miserable. You wouldn't like la Zia to live in your fine house, would you now?"

"We could make her happy in a house of her own, or send her back to Venice with a comfortable income."

"Just so. You would want to get rid of la Zia. That would not do for me. She and I have never been parted. And Paolo; you would marry Paolo's mother; but you would want to send him back to Venice with la Zia, I dare say."

"It would be the simplest way of solving a difficulty; but if he were necessary to your happiness he should stay with us, Lisa. I would do anything to make you happy."

She looked at him with a touch of sadness, and shook her head.

"You are a generous lover," she said, "if you mean what you say; but it is all useless. You could not make me happy; and I could not make you happy. You would very soon be sorry for your sacrifice. You would regret the English lady and her million. I am content as I am—content if not happy. I have as much money as I want, and this room is fine enough for me. If you saw the hovel in which I was reared you would think me a lucky woman to have such a beautiful home. In ten years I shall have saved a fortune, and la Zia and I can go back to Venice and live like ladies on the Canal Grande; or I can go on singing if I'm not tired, and then I shall grow richer every day."

"Lisa, Lisa, how cold and how cruel you are—cruel to a poor wretch who adores you. To me you are ice, but to Vansittart you are fire. Your face lighted, your whole being awoke to new life, at sight of him."

Lisa shrugged her shoulders, irritated by his persistency, and provoked into candour.

"Suppose I like him and don't like you, can I help it? God has made me so," she said carelessly. "Ah, here is la Zia—la Zia whom you would banish," she cried, clapping her hands as a key turned in the vestibule door.

"It looked like rain," said la Zia, as she came in, "so Paolo and I made haste home."

Lisa caught the boy up in her arms, and kissed him passionately. Never had she felt so glad to see him. Her active imagination had pictured herself separated for ever from her son, living in an atmosphere of pomp and powdered footmen, learning to forget her fatherless boy.

He had thriven on English fare, and the mild breezes of Battersea Park, and frequent airings upon the Citizen steamers. He was a great lump of a boy, with large black eyes, and long brown hair, and his mother's Murillo colouring. The only traces of the other parentage were in the square Saxon brow and the firm aquiline of the nose. He was a magnificent outcome of a mixed race, and a fine example of what a boy of four years old ought to be. Lisa dropped into a chair with her burden, still hugging him, but borne down by his weight.

"Santo e santissimo!" exclaimed la Zia. "You will be late at the theatre. You must take a cab, quanto che costa."

The Venetians had a horror of cabs, which were not alone costly, but fraught with the hazard of vituperation from fiery-faced cabmen. They delighted in the penny distances of road cars and other public conveyances. To exceed the limit of a penny ride was to la Zia's mind culpable extravagance. A cab was only to be thought of in emergencies.

"Pardon, Signor," she said, "the pleasure of your most desired company has made my niece forget her duties."

She bustled into the adjoining room, and returned with Lisa's black lace hat and little merino cape. There was no chorus girl at the Apollo who dressed as shabbily as the Venetian prima donna. La Zia bundled on the hat and tied on the cape, and dismissed her niece with a kiss.

"Zinco will bring you home, as always," she said.

The 'cello lived in a shabby old street hard by, and was Lisa's nightly escort from the Apollo to Chelsea. On fine nights they walked all the way, hugging the river, and praising the Embankment, which Zinco declared to be as much finer than the Lung 'Arno, as London was in his opinion superior to Florence.

Lisa and Sefton went downstairs together, both silent. He hailed a crawling hansom a few paces from the house-door, and put her into it, without a word. When she was seated he lifted his hat, and bade her good night; and it seemed to her that there was deadly hatred in the face which had looked at her a little while ago transfigured by passionate love.

Hatred of some one; herself, perhaps; or it might be of a fancied rival. Her heart grew cold as she thought of Vansittart. Unreasoning jealousy on her account had cost one man his life, and had burdened the life of another man with inextinguishable remorse. Would Sefton, whose love expressed itself with appalling vehemence, try to injure the one man she cared for, the man for whose sake she would give her life? It would be well to warn him, perhaps. To warn him? But how? She did not even know where he lived; but she knew his sister's house, and his sister's servants would be able to tell her his address. She knew his real name now—Vansittart, a grandly sounding name. She repeated it to herself with a kind of rapture as the cab rattled along the King's Road, taking her to the Apollo.

She wrote to Vansittart next day, telling him that Sefton had offered to marry her, and that she had refused him.

"He is jealous and angry about you," she told him, in conclusion. "He fancies because I was so pleased to see you that day on the river that it is my love for you that made me refuse him, and I think he would like to kill you. His face looked like murder as he bade me good-bye—and I'm afraid it is you he wants to murder, not me. Pray be on your guard about him. He may hire some one to stab you in the street, after dark. Please don't go out at night except in your carriage. Forgive me for writing to you; but when I think that your life may be in danger, I cannot refrain from sending you this warning. You warned me of my danger, which was no danger, because I never cared for the man. I warn you of yours."

With this letter in her pocket, Lisa put herself into one of her favourite omnibuses, which took her to Albert Gate, and from Albert Gate she found her way across the Park to Hill Street. She remembered the number, though she would hardly have known the house in its morning brightness of yellow marguerites and pale blue silk blinds.

The haughtiest of footmen opened the door, and looked at her from head to foot with the deliberate eye of scorn. Her beauty made not the faintest impression upon his rhinoceros hide. She was on foot, and shabbily clad, and he took her for a work-girl.

"I have a letter for Mr. Vansittart," she began timidly.

The footman interrupted her with stern decisiveness. "This is not Mr. Vansittart's 'ouse. This is Lady 'Artley's."

"I want to know where Mr. Vansittart lives."

"Charles Street. Number 99a."

"Please tell me the way."

The magnificent creature stalked slowly to the doorstep, moving with the languid hauteur which befitted one whose noble height and well-grown legs gave him first rank in the army of London footmen. He was not ill-natured, but he took what he called a proper pride in himself, conscious that his livery was made by one of the most expensive tailors in the West End, and that his shoes came from Bond Street.

Lifting his arm with a haughty grace, he indicated the turning which would be Lisa's nearest way to Charles Street.

She thanked him and tripped lightly away, he watching her with a languid gaze, too obtuse to recognize the brilliant Venetian prima donna—whose eyes, and shoulders, and diamonds he had approved the other night, when he hung over her with peaches and champagne—in the young person in rusty black.

Lisa found 99a, again a house with flowers in all the windows, and dainty silken blinds—a house of brighter and fresher aspect than the houses of Venice, where the effects of form and colour are broader, bolder, and more paintable, but lack that finish and neatness which distinguish a well-kept house at the West End of London: a house where no expenditure is spared in the struggle between the love of beauty and colour, and the curse of coal fires and gloomy skies. Another footman looked at Lisa with the cold eye of indifference, less haughty than Lady Hartley's superb menial only because Vansittart's smaller means did not afford prize specimens of the footman genus.

"Any answer?" asked the youth, as Lisa delivered her letter.

No, there was no answer required—but would he be sure to give the letter to Mr. Vansittart?

There was a rustle of silken skirts on the stairs as she spoke, and two ladies came tripping down, talking as they came.

"The carriage is not there yet," cried Sophy, glancing at the open doorway. "I'm afraid we shall be late for luncheon."

Eve followed her, and was in the hall in time to see Lisa as she turned from the door—to see her and to recognize her as the woman who had brought perplexity and apprehension into the clear heaven of her life.

The victoria came to the door. The footman stood ready to hand his mistress to her carriage and to take his place beside the coachman.

"What did that person want?" asked Eve, sharply.

"She brought a letter for my master, ma'am."

"Where is it? Give it to me."

She took the letter, and looked at it frowningly.

"Mr. Vansetart!" The woman could not even spell his name, and yet was able to darken his wife's existence.

"What a shabby letter!" cried Sophy, struggling with the top button of a tight glove. "It must be a begging letter, I should think. But what a pretty dark-eyed woman that was. I seem to remember her face. Really, really, Eve, we shall be late! Mrs. Montford told us her luncheons are always punctual. She wouldn't wait for a Bishop."

Eve was staring at the letter. Vansittart was out, or she would have gone to him with it. She wanted to put it into his hands, and to see how he took its contents; but she did not even venture to keep the letter in her possession till they met. She ran into her husband's study, and put the odious letter on the mantelpiece, in a spot where he might overlook it. If it were overlooked until the afternoon she might be with him when he opened it.

She went into society with her heart aching. Whatever her husband's feelings might be, this shameless Italian was running after him. What insolence! What consummate audacity! To come to his house, to pursue him with letters, even in his wife's presence! And Sefton had introduced this brazen creature to her; and she—Vansittart's wife—had been weak enough to be civil.

Sophy's perpetual prattle agonized her all the way to Grosvenor Gardens; nor was the smart luncheon which awaited them there less agonizing. She had to brace herself for the ordeal, to smile and talk, and laugh at good stories, pretending to see the point of them; laughing when other people laughed; pretending to enjoy that happy mixture of society to be met at some hospitable tables—a dash of literature and art, a fashionable priest and a fashionable actor, an archæological Dean from a grave old Midland city, a young married beauty, a Primrose League enthusiast, a foreign diplomatist, and a sporting peer owning a handsome slice of the shires.

Mr. Sefton came in after they were seated, and dropped into the one vacant chair beside Sophy.

"You are always late," Mrs. Montford said reproachfully. "I suppose that is because you are the idlest man I know."

He was a favourite of Mrs. Montford's—*l'ami de la maison*—and allowed to come and go as he pleased. When he gave a tea-party it was generally Mrs. Montford who invited half the company, helped him to choose the flowers and to receive the guests.

"You have hit the mark," he said. "A man who has no specific occupation never has time to be punctual. Nobody respects him. He

310

can't look at his watch in the middle of a friend's prosing and pretend important business. I think I shall article myself to a civil engineer; and then when people are boring I can say I am waited for about the caissons for the new bridge. What bridge? My dear fellow, no time to explain! One springs into a hansom, and is gone. Your idler can't extricate himself from the Arachne web of boredom. His time is everybody's property."

"Elaborate, but not convincing," said Mrs. Montford, smiling at him, as he helped himself with a leisurely air to a cutlet en papillote. "I would wager all the gloves that I shall wear at Etretat that you were lying in your easiest chair, with your feet on that high fender of yours, reading Maupassant's new story."

"For once in your life you have succeeded as a reader of character—or no character. I was reading 'Le Pas Perdu.' Don't you see how red my eyelids are?"

"Exactly. You are the kind of man who can weep over a book and refuse a sovereign to a poor relation."

"That," said Sefton, "was almost unkind."

Sophy now claimed her right of being talked to.

"Why were you not at Lady Dalborough's last night?" she asked.

"My dear Miss Marchant, you can't expect to see me at all the stupidest parties in London."

"The party was rather dull," assented Sophy, who until this moment had thought it brilliant, "but there was some good music."

"One can have that for filthy lucre at the St. James's Hall. I adore Oscar de Lampion's love ditties, but not at the price of perspiring in a mob of second-best people."

"It was my fault that we went to Lady Dalborough's," said Sophy, remorsefully.

"Oh, I forgive anybody for going there—once. You will be wiser next year."

His eyes were watching Eve across the table, while he talked with Sophy. She was very pale, and instead of the delicate blush rose of her complexion there were hectic spots under the eyes, which accentuated her pallor. He who once cared for her almost to the point of passion, felt a thrill of pain at seeing in a face a hint of the consumptive tendency which he had heard of about Peggy. "Those girls are all consumptive," some village gossip had said to him, with the morbid relish of gloomy possibilities which is an outcome of village monotony. He was shocked to think that she, too, perhaps, was doomed; but the thought suggested no pity for her husband—not even that pity which would have prevented him striking at his enemy through her. The rage that consumed him knew no restraining power. If he had lived in the Middle Ages that rage would have meant murder—but bloodshed in the nineteenth century involves too many inconvenient possibilities to be thought of lightly by a man of landed estate. It means throwing up everything for the rapture of gratified revenge—melting all the pearls of life into one fiery draught.

"Why is not Vansittart with you?" he asked Sophy, still looking at Eve.

"He had business in the City this morning."

"Business—in the City? What could take Vansittart to the City? That seems quite out of his line."

"Yes, it does, don't it," said Sophy, impressed by the significance of his tone, which seemed to veil a deeper meaning. "What should a Hampshire squire have to do in the City?"

Sefton did not dwell upon the question. He saw that he had awakened vague suspicions in Sophy's mind, the first faint hint of a domestic mystery. He talked of other things—of people—lightly, delightfully, Sophy thought. He told her of two marriages which had just occurred, on the summit of the fashionable mountain—took her behind the scenes, as it were, and introduced her to the inner life of the chief actors in those elegant ceremonials—the impecunious father of one bride selling his daughter to a man she hated, the angry mother of the bridegroom in the other marriage raging against the girl her son had chosen.

"You don't know the bad blood which was hidden among the champagne bottles on the buffet," he said.

Sophy was charmed to hear about these smart people—charmed most of all at the idea that they were miserable—that the women whose toilettes her soul sickened for often wore the hair-shirt of the penitent under a gown which Society papers extolled.

Sefton was very attentive to Sophy, albeit his furtive glances were always returning to the lovely face on the other side of the table. Poor Sophy thrilled at startling possibilities. He had admired Eve in the past, had seemed devoted almost to the point of proposing. And she, Sophy, had been told she was growing daily more like Eve. More wonderful things had happened than that he should fall in love with her—the old fancy for Eve reviving for Eve's younger sister. Now that the detrimental father had taken up his abode permanently on the Continent, his domestic responsibilities much lightened by Eve's liberality to her sisters, there could be less objection to an alliance with the house of Marchant. Mr. Sefton was his own master. He had lost Eve by his hesitancy and hanging back. Might he not act more nobly in his dealings with Eve's sister? That low, thrilling note which he knew how to put into his voice, which was a mere mechanism of the man, touched Sophy's senses like exquisite music. Her eyelids sank, her cheek kindled, though he talked only of common things.

He had seen enough of Eve, while thus entertaining Sophy, to be assured that she had lately suffered some painful experience—a quarrel with Vansittart, perhaps. Or it might be that silent jealousy had been gnawing at her heart since that day on the river. No woman could see Lisa's behaviour and not be jealous. The husband would explain, no doubt, but explanations go for very little in such a case. They are accepted for the moment; wife and husband "kiss again with tears;" and the next morning at the breakfast-table the husband sees brooding brows, and knows that there is a scorpion coiled in his wife's heart. Her faith in him has been shaken. He may scotch the snake, but he cannot kill it.

* * * *

Eve was glad when Mrs. Montford gave the signal for a move to the drawing-room. The men stayed behind to smoke, all but Sefton, who followed the ladies, a proceeding which Sophy ascribed to his interest in her conversation. At the luncheon-table Eve had been all talk and gaiety, deceiving every one except the man who watched her face in its occasional moments of repose. In the drawing-room she abandoned all effort, sank into a chair near the window, evidently sick at heart, glancing first at the clock on the chimney-piece and then at the street to see if her carriage were approaching. She had ordered it for a quarter past three. She started up the instant it was announced, and went over to Mrs. Montford to make her adieux, that lady being deep in a murmured discussion of the latest Mayfair scandal with a brace of matrons, while Sophy was being taken round the rooms by Sefton, to look at the pictures and curios.

"You needn't have been in such an absurd hurry to come away," remonstrated this young lady in a lugubrious tone, as they drove homeward. "Nobody else was moving."

"They will be gone in a quarter of an hour. Only the bores ever linger after a London luncheon. Everybody has something to do."

"We have nothing to do till five o'clock; unless you go to Lady Thornton's at home before five. The card says four till seven."

"Then we can go at six. That will be quite early enough."

"And what are we to do in the interval? It isn't half-past three

313

yet."

"Rest, Sophy; sleep if you can. We are going to a theatre to-night, and a dance afterwards."

"It is so near the end of the season," sighed Sophy. "People are all rushing off to Germany for their cures. One feels quite out of it when one has no complaint to talk about."

* * * *

Vansittart was at home. Eve went straight to his den, sure to find him there, smoking over a book or a newspaper.

He looked up at her smilingly, but she thought he looked weary and worn out, and when the smile was gone there was a troubled expression.

"Was it a lively luncheon, Eve?" he asked, giving her his hand as she took up her favourite position behind his high-backed chair.

It was a colossal chair, with cushioned arms, upon one of which she sometimes seated herself, liking to nestle against him, yet not so loquacious as to interrupt his reading; sometimes reading with him; dipping into some French novel which he read from sheer idleness, not because he had any taste for the thinly beaten gold-leaf of Maupassant or Bourget.

To-day she stood behind his chair, silent, meditative, while he read and smoked.

"Was it pleasant—your party?" he asked presently, repeating the question she had left unanswered.

"Oh, it was pleasant enough. Sophy will tell you that it was delightful. I leave her to expatiate upon the people and the dishes and the talk. I was not in a very pleasant mood. There is a letter for you on the mantelpiece. You have not seen it, perhaps?"

"No," he said, startled by the angry agitation in her tone. "Is there anything particular about the letter?"

He put down his pipe and stood up, looking at her inquiringly. She was very pale, always with the exception of that hectic spot which Sefton had noticed, and which burned more fiercely now.

He stretched out his hand to take the letter, half hidden by a little bronze Buddha with malevolent onyx eyes.

He recognized Lisa's unformed scrawl at the first glance.

"What is the matter with the letter?" he asked coldly.

"She brought it here herself, Jack,—that Italian woman—Signora Vivanti. I was coming downstairs while she was at the door. I saw her give the letter to James. What can she have to write to you about?

314

Why should she bring the letter with her own hand? How could she dare come to the house where your wife lives?" She flamed up at the last question, and her voice trembled at the word wife.

"I don't see why my wife's presence should alarm her, if she had need of immediate help from me."

"What should she want? Why should she come to you for help? Because you helped her once, in Italy, when she was poor and friendless? Is that a reason why she should pester you now?"

"If you will let me read her letter I may be able to tell you," he answered gravely.

It was a long letter, for in writing to the man she adored, Lisa let her pen run away with her. Nothing would ever induce her to marry Sefton, she told him; her heart was given to another; he knew who that other was, and that she could never change. Then came the warning of his danger. Sefton's savage hatred. It was a letter he could under no circumstances show to his wife. And there she stood waiting for the letter to be shown her, raging with jealousy, the love which had made her so angelic in her self-abnegation now transformed into a fire that made her almost diabolical.

"Well! May I see her letter?"

"No, Eve. The letter is confidential. She asks nothing from me—except perhaps approval of the course she has taken. She has had an offer of marriage—an offer that most young women in her position would accept without a second thought."

"And she has refused?" cried Eve, breathlessly.

"She has refused."

"Because she loves some one else—some one who can't marry her—but who can carry on an intrigue with her—an old intrigue—begun years ago. Some one whom she is trying to get into her net again. The net is spread—before my very eyes. That letter is to make an appointment."

He tore the letter across and across, and dropped the pieces into his waste-paper basket.

"Your thought is as far from the truth as it is unworthy of you, Eve," he said, with grave displeasure. "This young woman has never been more to me than I have told you. A woman in whom I was interested, chiefly because she was friendless."

"Chiefly," she cried, catching at the qualifying word; "and the other reason?"

"If there was another reason, it had nothing to do with love. Does that satisfy you?"

"No," she answered gloomily. "Nothing you can say will prevent my being miserable. That woman has come into my life and spoilt it."

"Only because you are unreasonably and absurdly jealous. You are miserable of your own choice. You have me here, your faithful husband, unchanged in thought, act, or feeling since the day we rowed down the river; and yet you choose to torture yourself with vile suspicions, unworthy of a lady, unworthy of a wife."

"I cannot help it," she said. "We all have some latent sin, I suppose. Perhaps jealousy is mine. I never knew what it was to feel wicked before. Forgive me, Jack, if you can."

She took up his hand, kissed it, and then sank sighing into her chair, the chair she had christened Joan, while his, the colossal arm-chair, was Darby.

"I forgive you with all my heart, Eve, on condition that this little storm is the last outbreak. I should be sorry to think our married life was to be a succession of tempests in teacups."

"I promise to behave better in future. I hate myself for my folly."

Vansittart resumed his newspaper, too much disturbed to court conversation. He felt himself living upon the crust of a volcano. This ceaseless jealousy was a matter of trivial moment in itself. He could have laughed it off, as too absurd for serious argument; but this jealousy brought Eve to the brink of that revelation which might wreck two lives. The horror in front of him was a horror that meant doom.

Eve bore with the silence for a few minutes, took off her bonnet, and carefully adjusted the petals of an artificial rose, studied the little fantasy of lace and flowers as if it were the gravest thing in the world, then flung it impatiently on a chair, and began to smooth out her long suède gloves on her soft, silken knee. Her nerves were strung to torture. She had pretended to be satisfied, while the tempest in her heart was still raging. She looked at her husband as if she hated him. Yes; it was hateful to see him sitting there, silent, imperturbable, reading his newspaper, while she was in the depths of despair. The fact that he had refused to show her that letter seemed almost an admission of guilt. If the thing which he had told her was true, the letter would have borne witness to his truth. He would have been eager to show it to her. "Here," he would have said, "under the woman's own hand, you will see that she is nothing to me."

She brooded thus for about ten minutes, and then her irritation could submit to silence no longer.

"What was the City doing?" she asked. "The City which deprived me of your company at Mrs. Montford's luncheon."

"It was not the City's fault. I surrendered my place to Sophy."

"Oh, that's nonsense. There is always room enough and a welcome at Mrs. Montford's luncheons; but no doubt on a warm July morning the City is more attractive than Mayfair."

"Certainly, for those who are making or losing money," he answered, throwing down his paper and preparing to be sociable, though there was that in his wife's tone which told him her heart was not at ease. "What was the City doing?" he repeated. "Buying and selling, getting and losing. It is not half a bad place on a summer morning, though you speak of it with the voice of the scorner. I walked across St. Paul's Churchyard. They have turned an old burial-ground into a flower-garden; and there were nurses and children, and homeless ragamuffins lying asleep in the sun, and pigeons—tame pigeons—that fed out of the children's hands. It might have been Venice."

He started and turned deadly pale. It was the first time he had ever pronounced the name of the fatal city, voluntarily, in his wife's hearing. His nerves were overstrained—as much as hers, perhaps—and the mere name took his breath away.

Eve saw the startled look, the sudden pallor.

"I understand!" she cried passionately. "It was at Venice you met that woman. Venice, not Verona. The very name of the place agitates you! The very name of the place where you knew her and loved her moves you more than all I have said to you—than all my pain!"

"You are a fool," he said roughly, "like Fatima, the type of all woman-fools."

"It was Venice."

"It may have been Venice. Who cares; or what does it matter?"

"It may have been! What hypocrisy! Do you think I am a child, to be hoodwinked by your feeble prevarications? Every look, every word, tells me that you have loved that woman better than you ever loved me—that you are still in her net."

"It was at Venice, then, if you will have it," he answered, beside himself. "At Venice, on a Shrove Tuesday, in Carnival time, five years ago. Are you satisfied now? That is the first half of the riddle."

His pale cheek grew whiter, his head fell back upon the velvet cushion, his whole frame collapsed. He was as near fainting as a strong man could be.

Eve rushed to a little table, where she was privileged to write her letters now and then—business letters, she called them, chiefly relating to spending money. Here, among silver ornaments and fanciful cutlery, there was a big bottle of eau de Cologne, which she half emptied over her husband's temples.

"Thanks," he murmured. "You meant it kindly; but you've almost blinded me. I'm all right now. It was only a touch of vertigo. I've had no luncheon; and a man can't live upon tobacco and emotional arguments."

CHAPTER XXVI.

"CLOSER AND CLOSER SWAM
THE THUNDER-CLOUD"

Eve was very sorry for her husband after that tragical scene in the study; but what profiteth a jealous wife's sorrow if she is unconvinced; if heart and brain are still racked with doubts and angry questionings, while her calmness, her submission are only on the surface, the subterranean fires still burning?

Vansittart took a high hand with the woman he loved. There must be no more quarrels, he told himself. He could not control his tongue even in his own interests, if she were to goad him any further. In their next encounter the secret would explode. He could not live this slave's life for ever. It was not in him to go on prevaricating and fencing with the truth.

He told her, gently but firmly, that she must torment him no more with false imaginings. If she could not believe in his fidelity it would be wiser for them to part. Better to be miserable asunder, than to live together in an atmosphere of distrust.

At this hint of parting she flamed up, her doubt changed for a moment to conviction.

"Part!" she cried. "Perhaps that is what you would like?"

"I would like anything better than this madness, Eve," he answered wearily. "We cannot be worse than utterly wretched, and we are that now, and shall be as long as you harbour unworthy suspicions."

His face looked like truth, his voice rang true. She flung herself on her knees beside his chair, and clasped and cried over his hand.

"I will not torment you. I will not plague and torture myself any more," she sobbed. "It is only because I love you too much, and a breath makes me fear I may lose you. I will trust you, Jack, in spite of your mysteriousness, in spite of your refusing to show me that letter, which I had a right to see, a right as your wife. No husband should receive a letter from any woman which he dare not show his wife."

"I did not choose to show you that letter."

"Well, you did not choose, perhaps. It was temper, I dare say. I

319

was like the children who are refused a thing because they don't ask properly. I did not ask properly, and you snubbed me, and treated me as a child. But I won't be Fatima again, Jack. If there is a blue chamber in your life, I won't tease you for the key."

"That's my own good wife. Remember how happy we were at Bexley Hill, Eve, in our courting days, when you knew me so little and trusted me so much. Surely after two years of wedlock you should trust me more and not less—two years in which you and I have been all the world to each other."

"Yes, yes, I was foolish. I hate myself for my mad jealousy. You have found the ugly spot in my character, Jack. I did not know it was there."

"Shall I be angry with my love for loving me too well?" he said, as he folded the slender form to his heart.

How slender, how ethereal she was, the tall slip of a girl whose graceful shape had never developed matronly solidity. A thrill of fear ran through him at the thought of her fragility, too frail a sapling to stand firm against the storms of life.

"God keep her from knowing the truth," he prayed dumbly, as she hung upon his breast. "It would break her heart."

After this there came a halcyon interval. Eve was convinced that she was beloved, and what more could a woman want in this world? There was only one thing that stood in the way of perfect peace. Vansittart had business in the City on two other mornings, and those disappearances Citywards worried her. The City, as Sefton had said, was not in her husband's line.

When she questioned him about the business that drew him eastward he answered lightly that he went to his stockbroker's to make some small changes in his investments. That very lightness of his, which was meant to spare her a serious anxiety, awakened her suspicions. The actual cause of Vansittart's unusual interest in the money market was sufficiently serious. A panic had occurred in some South American Railway Stock from which some part of his income was derived, and he was watching the market and the tide of affairs in Brazil, waiting the hour when it might be needful to sell out and snatch the remnant of his capital, or the turn of the tide which should justify his holding on and hoping for a renewal of the good days gone.

To this end he went to his stockbroker's every day, and heard the latest news, the last opinions, dawdling in the office, hearing the wise men of the East and their counsel. The hazards, the suspense, excited him. He grew interested in the money market, and felt all the gambler's keenness. The City drew him like the loadstone rock that took the nails out of Sinbad's ship. It was better than Monte Carlo. A third of his fortune trembled in the balance.

He would not tell Eve the whole truth, believing that it would worry her into a fever. She would exaggerate this fear as she had exaggerated her jealous doubts. She would foresee beggary, and dream of houselessness and starvation. He did not know that to a woman money-troubles are the lightest of all woes. A husband suspected of infidelity, a child down with measles, will afflict the average woman more than the loss of a fortune.

* * * *

Sophy was enjoying herself to her uttermost capacity of enjoyment. This was life indeed. It was the last week of the season, the week before Goodwood, and there was a sense of the end of all things in the air. A good many of the people who were not going to Goodwood were going away, starting for Homburg, Marienbad, Wildbad, Auvergne, or the Pyrenees, in advance of the universal rush which would make sleeping-cars impossible, and travelling odious. It annoyed Sophy to hear people talk of getting away; as if London were worn out and done with, London which she was enjoying so intensely. This was the fly in the ointment for Sophy. She felt aggrieved that her sister should have invited her at the end of the season. Yet there was one compensating delight. The sales were on: those delicious drapery sales, which had always been Sophy's highest ideal of earthly happiness, even when her strained resources had compelled her to turn with unsatisfied longing from a counter where odd lengths of silk and velvet were being all but given away. She had lain broad awake in her attic chamber at Fernhurst regretting those bargains, which would have made her a richly dressed woman at the most moderate cost. The counters of Marshall, and Debenham, and Robinson, and Lewis, at the end of the season, were to Sophy as the board of green cloth to the gambler. She felt that fortunes were to be won for those who had money to stake, fifteen guinea frocks for three pounds, two guinea parasols at nine and eleven-pence.

Eve took her sister to the sales, and financed the situation. With a judicious expenditure of twenty pounds Sophy secured treasures that would last her through the coming autumn and winter, and, with Eve at her elbow, resisted the allurements of unsuitable finery. These shopping mornings were rapture to Sophy, and not without pleasure to Eve. It was pleasant to see Sophy's joyous excitement, as she hung tremulously between two fabrics which the shopman exhibited for her choice—a bengaline at three and ninepence, which had been seven shillings—a watered silk at two and eleven-pence, which had been eight and sixpence. After intense consideration Sophy settled on the watered silk, not because she liked it best, but because of the "had been." The original price decided her—not taking into account that the price was reduced in the exact ratio of the material's un-fashionableness, and that she might find herself next winter the only young woman in watered silk. There was for Eve also the pleasure of buying presents for Jenny and Hetty, the two sisters who were pining in their rustic bower, while Sophy was draining the wine-cup of London gaieties. It was delightful to Eve to feel that a few pounds could buy them happiness: and she brought all her knowledge of good and evil to bear upon her selections for those absent ones.

"You have such a very quiet taste," said Sophy, rather regretfully. "I call those cottons and foulards you have chosen almost dowdy."

"You won't think so when you see them made up. I'm afraid your scarlet pongee will look rather too showy for country lanes."

"My dear Eve, I shall keep it for garden-parties till it begins to get shabby. Scarlet gives just the right touch of colour in a land-scape."

"Yes, but I think one would always rather that somebody else should give the touch."

"Mr. Sefton said yesterday that fair-haired women should wear scarlet."

Sefton was Sophy's great authority. He had been very polite to her, very pleasant, very confidential, talking to her about London society as if she were to the manner born, and had been brought up in the very midst of these people whom she saw to-day for the first time. This flattered her; indeed, his whole speech was made up of flattery, that subtle adulation which did not express itself in mere words, but which was indicated rather by a deference to her opinion, a quickness in laughing at her little jokes, an acceptance of her as on his own intellectual level. "You and I know better than the common herd," was expressed in all his conversation with her.

When they met in the evening it was only natural she should tell him her sister's plans for the next day, whether they were going to spend the morning in the Park or at the picture-galleries. Sophy was eager for picture-seeing when there was nothing better to be done. Those galleries would give her so much to talk about at autumn tea-parties, such a superior air among women who thought they did a great deal for art when they fatigued themselves at the Royal Academy.

If they sat in the Park for an hour or so before luncheon Sefton contrived to find them there—if they were picture-seeing he dropped into the gallery, and criticized the pictures in technical phraseology which provided Sophy with a treasury of art talk especially adapted for country use. If they were at a theatre in the evening he was there too. Eve warned Sophy that he was only a philanderer.

"You remember how disagreeably attentive he was to me," she said, reddening at the recollection, "and yet, you see, he never meant anything."

"We were worse detrimentals then than we are now," argued Sophy. "Your marriage has altered our position, and now that the father lives abroad a man need not be afraid of marrying one of us. I don't mean to say that Mr. Sefton is going to make me an offer; but he is certainly very attentive."

"Yes, he is very attentive, I admit. He likes being attentive to girls. Nothing pleases him better than to try the effect of that musical voice of his, and his nicely chosen phrases, upon any girl who will listen to him—like Orpheus leading the brute beasts with his lyre. I doubt if he cares any more for the girls than Orpheus cared for the beasts. He is false for falsehood's sake."

"You are very bitter against him, Eve," retorted Sophy. "Yet I dare say you would have married him if he had asked you."

"I think not."

"Oh, nonsense. You would not have refused to be mistress of the Manor. Merewood is a hovel in comparison."

"Merewood has the man I love for master. If Jack had been the lodge-keeper I would have married him, and washed and cooked and mended for him, and opened the gate and curtsied to the gentry, and been happy."

"Bosh!" said Sophy, very angry. "That's the way girls talk when they are first engaged. It sounds ridiculously sentimental from an old married woman like you. You are absurdly prejudiced against Mr. Sefton."

"Call it prejudice, if you like. I call it instinct. Birds are prejudiced against cats. I look upon Mr. Sefton as my natural enemy."

"And I suppose, if he should call, you will be uncivil, and spoil my chances?"

"No, I will not spoil your chances—such as they are."

"How disagreeably you say that. One would think you were jealous of an old admirer."

"No, I am not jealous; only I don't like to see you duped by meaningless attentions. I have no doubt Mr. Sefton does admire you—I only fear his admiration is worthless—but I will do everything that a sister can do to encourage him."

After this conversation Eve was particularly polite to Mr. Sefton. Poor Sophy was so terribly in earnest in her desire to make a good marriage. The elder sister's success had been so startling, so easy a conquest, so delightful a settlement in life, that it was natural the younger sister should cherish hopes on her own account. People told Sophy that she was growing more and more like Eve. Hope's flattering tale told her that she was quite as pretty, while vanity suggested that she had more *savoir faire*. Poor Sophy had always prided herself upon her *savoir faire*, though how a quality which is, as it were, the final polish produced by society friction, could have been acquired by a young lady in a cottage at Fernhurst, must needs remain a mystery. Eve looked at her sister, and saw that she was prettier than the ruck of girls to be met in a London season. Her beauty had the dewy freshness that comes of a rustic rearing; her eyes were brighter than the eyes of the hardened fashionable belle. Her complexion had the delicacy of colouring which was characteristic of Colonel Marchant's daughters—which had been, alas! Peggy's chief beauty.

Sophy, dressed as Eve had dressed her, and with her somewhat rebellious hair treated artistically by the skilful Benson, was certainly a very attractive young woman; and it seemed to Eve not impossible that Sefton, beginning the flirtation without any serious aim, might end by asking Sophy to be his wife. He was entirely his own master, could marry to please himself, without consideration of worldly advantage; only, unhappily, those are just the men who marry for self-aggrandizement rather than for simple inclination. It is not as if all heiresses were hideous or disagreeable, ignorant or underbred. Even England can furnish richly dowered young women who are both handsome and amiable; so why, asks the youthful peer or landowner, should I marry some portionless beauty, when I may as easily add to my revenue or treble my acreage? The original possessor considers his estate as the nucleus of a great property, which he and each successive holder should increase by judicious alliances; until the rolling mass swells into a territory like the duchy of Cleveland, and its acres are reckoned by thousands. Eve had heard the mothers and fathers talk of their sons' views and duties, even if the sons themselves did not openly avow their intention of marrying to better themselves.

The only hope in Sophy's case lay in a certain eccentricity of temper in Wilfred Sefton which might show itself in a disadvanta-geous marriage. The very fact that he had remained so long a bach-elor indicated that he was not eager for a prize in the matrimonial market. He had been content to stand by and see many prizes carried off by men who were personally and socially his inferiors.

He had been a frequent visitor in Charles Street since Sophy's arrival. Her liveliness evidently pleased him; they were always talk-ing and laughing in corners wherever they met, and seemed to have worlds to say to each other.

"It is delightful to meet any one so fresh as your sister at the end of the season," he explained to Eve, "just when most of us are feel-ing dull and jaded, and almost ready to yawn in each other's faces, like my lord and my lady in the 'Marriage *à la Mode.*'"

He invited Mrs. Vansittart and her sister to a tea-party, given in honour of Sophy, who had expressed an ardent desire to see the house in Tite Street—the bachelor den which little Mr. Tivett had de-scribed to her in glowing colours. Eve hesitated about accepting the invitation, knowing that her husband disliked Sefton as much as she did herself; but the hesitation was overcome by Sophy's arguments.

"He is giving the party on purpose for me," she pleaded. "The invitation arose out of my wish to see his library, which Mr. Tivett had been praising. He could not pay me a more marked attention, could he now?"

"It is certainly an attention," assented Eve, distressed by Sophy's sanguine hopes, so likely to end in disappointment.

"Don't spoil all my chances by refusing," urged Sophy. "He would be offended—and men are so easily choked off."

"Not a man who is really in earnest."

"Perhaps not—but he may not be quite in earnest yet. He may not have made up his mind. Of course I should be a very bad match. He cannot forget that all at once. There is a stage in which a man who is inclined to fall in love lets himself drift, don't you know, Eve? He may be drifting—and it would be a pity to discourage him."

Every woman is at heart a matchmaker. Eve yielded, and accept-ed Sefton's invitation for five o'clock tea and a little music.

"Shall you have any singing?" she asked, with a sudden fear of meeting Signora Vivanti.

No—there would be no singing.

"I only asked the American banjo man to amuse you," said Mr. Sefton. "He is a capital fellow, and he does the most wonderful things with his banjo. He is a Paganini among banjoists. That, with the inevitable piano, will be more than enough music."

The afternoon, at the end of a brilliant July, was delightful, and the Embankment, with its red-brick palaces and its little bit of old Chelsea, looked just the one perfect place in which to live; to live an idle, artistic life, *bien intendu*, and bask in sunshine reflected from blue water. The tide was at the flood, the gardens were full of gaudy July flowers.

"How horrid Fernhurst will be after this!" sighed Sophy. "What a lucky man Mr. Sefton is to have a house in Tite Street, as well as the Manor!"

"Ah, but it is only a bachelor den, remember," said Eve. "He will do away with it when he marries."

"Not if his wife has any sense—unless she makes him change it for a larger house facing the river."

Mr. Sefton's house was near the corner, and commanded a side-long view of the Thames from all the front windows, and a still better view from an oriel in the library, which projected so as to rake the street. Sophy thought this small house in Tite Street, with its rich and sombre furniture and subdued colouring, one of the most enchanting houses she had ever entered, second only to the Manor House, which she had seen some years before on the never-to-be-forgotten occasion of a Primrose League garden-party given by Mr. Sefton in the interests of the cause. The Manor House and its splendours of art, its old gardens, and antique furniture, were the growth of centuries, and owed their existence to Seftons who were dust. This twelve-roomed house in Tite Street was an emanation of the man himself. His temperament, his education, his tastes were all embodied here. This was the pleasure dome which he had built for himself—this was his palace of art.

She went about peeping and peering at everything, escorted by Mr. Tivett, who expatiated and explained to his heart's content, pointing out the workmanship which made a mahogany table as precious as jasper or ivory; the artistic form of those high-backed chairs, copied from an old French model; the Gobelin tapestry, which had neither the glow nor sheen of silken fabrics, and yet was six times as costly.

"This house of Sefton's just serves to remind one of what a parvenu's house is not," said little Tivett, sententiously.

Sophy looked at the titles of the books. How ignorant they made her feel! There was hardly one that she had ever seen before; and yet no doubt they were the very cream of classic and modern literature, not to have read which stamped one as illiterate.

"I have been looking at your books," she said, when Sefton came in with Eve. "They are too lovely."

"Rather nicely bound, aren't they?" he said, smiling gently at her enthusiasm. "They are a somewhat scratch collection, not quite family literature; but those vellum bindings with the blue labels give a nice tone of colour against the prevailing brown."

"That is so like Sefton," said Mr. Tivett. "He values his books from an æsthetic standpoint. Thinks of the effect of their bindings, not of the literature inside."

"As one gets older reading becomes more and more impossible. There is a satisfaction in possessing books, but one's chief pleasure is in their outsides. I sit here sometimes after midnight, smoking the pipe of the lotus-eater and looking at my bindings, and I feel as if that were enough for culture."

"I dare say that is quite the pleasantest way of enjoying a library," said Mr. Tivett, as if he saw the matter in a new light.

"Of course it is. There's no use in thinking of the lifetime it would need to read all the great books. That way madness lies. De Quincey went into the question once arithmetically, and to read his bare statement is distraction. I think it was that calculation of his which first put me off reading."

"Then your books are only ornaments?" said Sophy, disappointed.

"My books are a dado by Riviere and Zaehnsdorf. There are a great many of them with the leaves unopened. I take out a volume now and then, and peep between the pages. One gets the best of a book that way—the flavour without the substance of the author. But I came to take you down to tea, Miss Marchant. My banjoist has arrived, and Lady Hartley and Mrs. Montford are doing all they can to spoil him."

"Is Lady Hartley here? How nice!" exclaimed Sophy, to whom Lady Hartley's dress, manners, and way of thinking were a continual study.

Eve's sister-in-law was Sophy's ideal fine lady.

"Lady Hartley is always nice to me," replied Sefton. "She never misses one of my afternoons if she is in town. She would sacrifice the Marlborough House garden-party for my tea and muffins."

"Ah, but I dare say you contrive to make your tea-parties exceptional. This banjoist, now. Everybody is dying to hear him."

They went down to tea, which was served in a little bit of a room at the back of the dining-room, from which it was divided only by a curtain of old Italian tapestry; a mere alcove in which eight or ten people made a mob. Flowers, ices, tea, chocolate, cakes, china, silver, damask embroidered by industrious Bavarians, everything was the choicest of its kind; and Mr. Sefton's valet, with a footman and a smart parlour-maid, waited admirably. The squeeziness of the room made the entertainment all the more enjoyable. The banjoist stood in the centre of the crowd, talking in the true American style, with an incisive cleverness, and a clear metallic enunciation which made everybody else's speech sound slipshod and slovenly.

People were amused and delighted. He told anecdotes, firing them off as fast as the crackers which demon boys explode on the pavement. The admiring circle forgot that his distinction was the banjo, and began to accept him as a wit. Mrs. Montford asked him to lunch; Lady Hartley booked him for her next cosy little dinner.

After tea they all trooped up the narrow staircase to the library which had to serve Mr. Sefton for a drawing-room. More people dropped in—neighbours, most of them, including Mervyn Hawberk and his wife—and the room filled before the banjoist began to play.

He played wonderfully, surprising the metallic instrument into melodious utterances. He sang and accompanied himself; he played in a concertante duet for banjo and piano—a delightful arrangement of the serenade from *Don Giovanni*, in which the banjo was now the melody, and now the accompaniment; he played on his banjo with a bow, as if it had been a violin, and produced an effect which was remarkable, although somewhat distressing. His banjo laughed; his banjo cried; and with those wailing notes there stole over the senses of his audience a dream of weary Ethiopians resting from their labours amidst the sunlit verdure beside some broad Virginian river.

Mr. Sefton's visitors, who were chiefly feminine, flocked round the American, praising and descanting upon his talent. Little Tivett went about explaining, after his wont. He talked as if he had invented the banjoist.

"Did you really know him in America?" inquired Mrs. Montford, deluded by this little way of Mr. Tivett's.

"No, no; I was never in America in my life; but I knew him when first he came to London, before people began to talk about him. I told him what a hit he was going to make."

While Society was prostrating itself before a novel entertainer, Mr. Sefton and Sophy had drifted through the curtained archway to the little back room, which seemed, from its smallness, a kind of inner temple, where the treasures of the house might be found; as in the smallest rooms in old Italian palaces one looks for the choicest gems in the princely collection.

Sophy was talking and laughing with her host, radiant and happy. This tea-party seemed to her full of meaning. It was assuredly given for her pleasure. Mr. Sefton had said so. She had expressed a curiosity about his small house in Chelsea, and he had said instantly, "You must come and see it. I will ask some people to tea." What more could a man do for the woman he meant to marry? Sophy was intoxicated with this delicate token of subjugation. She imagined herself looked at and talked about as the future Mrs. Sefton. Unconsciously she gave herself some small airs of an affianced wife; chiding him; making little jokes at his expense; pretending to underrate his surroundings—the pretty childish graces and little pettish tricks which come naturally to the weaker sex before marriage, as if they were recompensing themselves in advance for the iron heel under which they are to exist afterwards.

They sauntered into the inner room, brushing against the tapestry curtains, and one glance at the sanctuary sent the blood to Sophy's cheeks in a hot, angry blush.

The most prominent position in the room was filled by an easel draped with orange and gold brocade, and on the easel appeared a full-length portrait of Signora Vivanti in her character of "Fanchonette."

It was a bold sketch in water-colours, suggested by a photograph, but with all the grace and power of a picture painted from the living model. The painter had caught the fire and sparkle of the Italian face, the richness of colouring, the wealth of a somewhat vulgar beauty. The photographer had seized a happy moment of graceful abandon—not a photographer's pose.

She was half reclining in her chair, with averted shoulder, and looking backward out of the picture with a most provoking smile—Fanchonette's audacious smile, which had taken the town by storm.

The velvet bodice set off the bust and shoulders in all their beauty, the blue and white striped petticoat was short enough to show the well-shaped leg and large useful foot in scarlet stocking and neat buckled shoe. A grisette's little white muslin cap sat airily upon the splendid coils of blue-black hair. Beauty of the plebeian type could go no further. Eyes, hair, complexion, figure, all were perfect; and over and above all there was the charm of mutinous lip and flashing smile, a look that was bold without immodesty, the frank outlook of a nature unacquainted with guile.

Sefton watched Sophy's face as she stared at the portrait, and her pinched lips, her sickly pallor, smote him with a sudden remorse. He had been fooling this rustic for his own purposes, making her an instrument in his scheme of evil. He felt that he had gone too far. Poor simpleton! What had she done that he should give her pain? Eve had slighted him; Eve's husband had come between him and the woman who was his passion; but this simpering, chattering, giggling girl had done him no wrong; and it was a base treachery to have deluded her with flattering speeches and meaningless attentions. However, the harm was done, done with deliberate purpose; and he had only to carry out his plan to the end. He meant Sophy to be his means of communication with Eve. He meant to reach the wife's ear through the sister.

"I'll make his life as miserable as he has made mine, if I can," he said to himself.

Sophy stood before the portrait, dumb with misery. What did he mean—what could he mean by placing the singer's portrait there, the crowning gem of his luxurious rooms, a portrait which even her ignorant eye told her must be by the brush of a master, so bold and brilliant was the handling? Even the easel, with its costly draping of orange and gold, was a work of art. What right had he to exhibit such a portrait; the portrait of an improper young woman, in all probability?

She felt sorry that she had accepted his invitation. She felt as if she had been brought to a house which was hardly fit for her to enter. And yet there were the Montfords and Lady Hartley chattering at their ease in the next room; so it could hardly be "bad form" to come here.

"What do you think of the likeness?" asked Sefton, lolling against a tall Versailles chair, and contemplating the brilliant face in the picture with a smile.

"I suppose it is a very good likeness," said Sophy, "but of a vulgar face—very handsome, no doubt; nobody can deny that—but quite *peuple*."

"Yes, it is *peuple*. That is one of its charms. It has all the fire and freshness of an unsophisticated race, generations of fishermen, sailors, gondoliers, all that there is of a frank free life between sea and sky. You can't get such beauty as that from a race reared indoors. It is an open-air loveliness, as rich in grace and colouring as one of those sea-flowers that unfold their living petals under the clear bright water."

"You admire her very much?" faltered Sophy.

"Yes, I admire her very much. You and I have got on so well together, Miss Marchant, that I feel I may talk to you with all the freedom of friendship—and confide in you as I have confided in no one else. I do admire that woman, have admired her ever since she made her first appearance at the Apollo. I began by liking to hear her sing, liking to watch her bright spontaneous acting, like the acting of a clever child in its naturalness. Even her beauty charmed me less than that delicious spontaneity which struck a new chord in the genius of the stage. I went night after night to see her and hear her, without fear of danger; and one day I awoke and found myself her slave. I love her as I never loved before—not even when I used to fancy myself in love with your charming sister. Against every other love, a selfish desire to retain my liberty, a vacillating temper, which made the desire of to-morrow unlike the desire of yesterday, have prevailed; but against the love I bear that woman," pointing to the laughing face in that picture, "reason has been powerless. Another man in my position might have tried to do what other men have been doing, ever since the first girl-Desdemona disgusted John Evelyn and began the long line of actresses who have charmed the civilized world. Another man might have tried to win her by dishonourable means. I was not base enough for that."

Sophy crimsoned, remembering that dark story of the farmer's daughter, which Nancy had related to her, that well-meaning woman not being over scrupulous in her communications to the ear of girlhood.

She waited silently, and Sefton went on, looking at the portrait, not at the woman to whom he was talking. An angry glow was on his cheek. An angry light was in his eyes. The thought of the social sacrifice he had been prepared to make and the futility of his offer lashed him to fury.

"I would not degrade her by a dishonourable proposal. No—though I knew she was not spotless—though I knew her as the mother of a nameless child. She was all the world to me, and what social consideration should a man set against that which is his all of happiness or hope? I asked her to be my wife, offered her my place in society, my passionate love, a life's devotion; and she refused me—refused me after more than a year of friendship, a friendship which had seemingly brought us very near to each other."

"She refused you?" exclaimed Sophy, beholding in one comprehensive glance this charming house in Tite Street, the Manor, and all its belongings dead and alive, together with this remarkably handsome and agreeable man to whom these things belonged! "She refused you! Why, what a preposterous minx she must be!"

"Yes, that's the word, Miss Marchant. It seems preposterous, doesn't it, that a Venetian peasant, with only her voice and good looks—and the hazardous fortunes of an opera singer—should refuse an English gentleman with a handsome rent-roll. But the thing is true all the same. She refused me. Can you guess why?"

"I can only imagine that she is a brainless idiot," said Sophy, feeling that she might be tempted to take out her bonnet pin and run it into that vivid face, if it were not for the glass which protected the picture.

She was too angry with Signora Vivanti for having won Mr. Sefton's affections to be grateful to her for having refused his hand.

"There is always a reason for everything," said Sefton, after a backward glance at the other room, which showed him that there was no one near enough or unoccupied enough to overhear or observe him; the banjoist being still the centre of attraction, and everybody grouped about him in the neighbourhood of the piano. "There is always a reason if one will only look for it. Signora Vivanti refused me because she was in love with another man, the man she knew and loved in Venice, the man who brought her to London and established her in the house she occupies, and had her trained for the stage. Forgive me, Miss Marchant, if I go a step further and say the man who is the father of her son!"

Sophy drew herself up with an offended air, and flashed an angry look at him.

"You have no right to talk to me in this way, Mr. Sefton. I don't understand why you should select me for your confidante," she said icily, moving towards the next room.

"Pray forgive me. You are clever and sympathetic. I have no sister, and in certain crises of life a man feels the need of a woman's sympathy. And then there were other reasons; or at least there was another reason."

He stopped, embarrassed, looking at her with a curious hesitation; looking from her to the group by the piano, where Eve's face shone out among the rest, smiling at the American's last ebullition.

"You are hinting at something dreadful," Sophy said, with a scared look. "Do you mean that the man is—is some one I know?"

"Don't tell her, Miss Marchant. I would not for worlds have her know. It would do no good. It might make her miserable. Women are so sensitive, even about the past, and I fear this affair is going on in the present."

"Don't tell her!" echoed Sophy. "You mean my sister! And the man is—Jack! Oh, what a wretch he must be!"

"Weak rather than wicked, perhaps. Don't be too hard upon him in your innocence of life. When a man has forged fetters of that kind it ain't easy to break them."

"A man so fettered has no right to marry. It would break her heart if she knew."

"She need not know. You won't tell her; and you may be sure I shan't. But you are a girl with strong sense; and you love your sister. I thought it only right that you should know."

"You may be mistaken."

"Hardly likely. It is an open secret that he established her in lodgings and paid for her education. And over and above that evidence there is the fact that he still visits her. I met him leaving her rooms only a few days ago."

"The wretch! The hypocrite! He seems to idolize Eve!"

"And your sister is happy in that idolatry. For pity's sake, Miss Marchant, don't let her see the seamy side of a husband's character."

Eve came towards the archway at this moment.

"You have lost ever so many amusing stories," she said to Sophy. "Your banjoist is the most entertaining person I have met this season, Mr. Sefton, and he has made us all oblivious of time. I have just discovered that it is ever so much past six."

"'Ever so much' meaning a quarter of an hour," retorted Sefton, laughing.

He dropped a fold of the brocade drapery as Eve drew near, and the portrait was hidden before her face appeared in the curtained arch.

He looked at her, trying to recall his feelings of a time gone by, when he had been—or had fancied himself—in love with her. Oh, what a weak, hesitating love that had been, as measured against his devotion to this scum of the lagunes—this gutter-bred minx who had scorned him!

"A preposterous minx!" he repeated to himself by-and-by, when he was alone. "I thank thee, child, for teaching me that word. Well, I have sown the wind; I wonder whether I shall have a prosperous harvest, and reap the whirlwind?"

333

CHAPTER XXVII.

"THOU MAYST BE FALSE
AND YET I KNOW IT NOT"

Before addressing his confidences to Sophy Marchant, Mr. Sefton had assured himself that she did not belong to that exceptional order of womankind who, in honour and discretion, are on a level with wise and honourable men. He had known the young lady quite long enough to know that, although sharp and clever, she was shallow-brained, impulsive, and emotional. He was very sure that with every desire to spare her sister pain she would end by telling Eve of her husband's infidelity. The secret would be kept for some days, perhaps, or even for some weeks; but it would be as a consuming fire, and would ultimately burst into flame—a flame that would devastate his rival's home.

The more scathing that whirlwind which was to come from the wind of his sowing, the happier the result for Sefton. It was in vain that Lisa had denied her son's paternity. In Sefton's mind there was no shadow of doubt that Vansittart had been, and even now was her lover—and it was for love of Vansittart that his, Sefton's, honourable attachment had been scorned by her. King Cophetua had offered himself to the beggar-maid, and the beggar-maid had refused him. Was that a humiliation for a man to forgive? Was that a disappointment to go unavenged? All the latent malignity of Sefton's nature was aroused into active life by that fierce passion of jealousy.

He had not misinterpreted Sophy's character. She was very silent during the homeward drive with her sister, lolling back in the victoria, looking vacantly at the carriages and the people as they passed.

"How tired you look, Sophy!" Eve said, as they crossed the path, where the carriages and riders and loungers had dwindled considerably within the past week. "I fancy even you begin to feel you have had enough of gadding about?"

"Yes, I have had enough, more than enough," Sophy answered, with a little choking sob.

She could no more suppress her own feelings, bear her own troubles, and be dumb, than a child can. It was quite as much as she could do to keep herself from crying, in the broad light of summer evening and Hyde Park.

"My poor Sophy, what has happened to distress you?" Eve asked affectionately. "You and Mr. Sefton had such a long confabulation in that inner room. I really thought the crisis had come."

"There was no crisis; there never will be. You were right. He was only fooling me. All his fine speeches, his sentimental talk—his way of holding one's hand as if he would like to squeeze it, and was only prevented by his deep respect for one—he *did* squeeze it at the carriage door that night when we stayed so late at Mrs. Macpherson's dance—it all meant nothing—less than nothing."

"But how do you know, Sophy?" Eve asked earnestly. "He can't have told you that he doesn't care for you?"

"No; but he can have told me that he is in love with another woman—a low-born, ignorant creature, who can do nothing but sing and strut about the stage in the boldest, horridest way, showing her lace petticoats and her legs," said Sophy, disgustedly, forgetting how she had admired Signora Vivanti.

"Do you mean the singer at the Apollo?" asked Eve.

"Yes, Signora Vivanti. He is in love with her, if you please, and she has refused him."

Eve remembered her husband's explanation of Lisa's letter.

"He told you this—chose you for his confidante. How odd!"

"Rather bad form, wasn't it? I fear I had been too—what young Theobald calls—coming on. I thought he liked me, and I encouraged him, and he rewards me by confiding his attachment to that creature."

"And she has refused to marry him. Why?" asked Eve, very pale.

"Who knows? Mere airs and graces, I dare say. She thinks she has all London at her feet, and that she can pick and choose. How I wish I were on the stage! I can sing pretty well, can't I, Eve? And I have often been told that I am like Ellen Terry."

In her angry excitement, Sophy saw a vision of herself as the queen of a theatre, all the town rushing to see her act, as they went to see this Venetian peasant. Surely a young lady with good blood in her veins must be better than a girl bred in a hovel. Sophy did not pause to consider that it was the rough freshness, the primitive vigour of the peasant which constituted Signora Vivanti's chief claim to notice.

Sophy had exercised no small amount of self-control in restraining her tears during the homeward drive; but once safe in the sanctuary of her bedroom she let loose the flood of her emotions, with its cross-currents of anger and sorrow, disappointed ambition, and

335

disappointed love. Yes, love. Considering Mr. Sefton, in the first instance, only from the social point of view, with the mercenary feelings engendered by a youth of poverty, she had allowed herself to be beguiled by his attentions, and had entered at the golden gate of that fool's paradise which first love creates for its victim—a world of fevered dreams, where nothing is but what is not. Walking in the enchanted groves of that paradise, she had seen Wilfred Sefton in the light that never was on land or sea—the light that beautifies all waking dreams—and she had interpreted every speech of his after her own fashion. Words lightly spoken took the deepest meaning—not his meaning, but hers. She told herself again and again that, if he had not actually asked her to be his wife, he had spoken words which a man only speaks to the woman whose life is to be interwoven with his own.

Eve came to her sister's door and insisted upon being admitted.

"Oh, what streaming eyes! Sophy, dearest, I am so sorry you have allowed yourself to care for him. I warned you, dear; I warned you."

"Yes," retorted Sophy, irritated beyond measure at a form of speech which is always irritating, "but you didn't warn me of anything like the truth. You didn't tell me that he was passionately, ridiculously, degradingly in love with that Venetian girl."

"My dearest, how could I warn you of what I did not know?"

"Don't dearest me. I am almost out of my mind—indeed, I should not be surprised if I were to have brain fever, or something. When I remember how I have lowered myself—letting him see that I cared for him; for I have no doubt he did see, and that was why he made me his confidante this afternoon, and told me about that creature—a woman with a nameless son. Do you think I can ever get over the degradation of being talked to about such a subject?"

Eve did not answer. She sank down upon the sofa, while her sister stood before the looking-glass, frowning at her tear-stained face as she unbuttoned the bodice of her gown, that gown which she made a point of calling her "frock."

Her nameless son. Eve remembered the boy in the boat, the Murillo-faced boy, looking up with big wondering eyes as his mother and Vansittart clasped hands. Her nameless son. She remembered that curious speech of Vansittart's a week ago—"Yes, it was at Venice we met. That is the first half of the riddle." What was the second half? The parentage of that boy, perhaps. His son—his son—another woman's and his. And she, his adoring wife, had no son to place in his arms, no child to gratify the well-born man's desire to see his race prolonged.

"If I live to be an old woman he may die without an heir," she thought. "There may be no more Vansittarts of Merewood. Hannah's husband did not hate her because she was childless—but then he had other wives."

She pictured her husband loving that alien's son, making him his heir perhaps by-and-by, desiring to bring him into his home, asking her to receive Hagar's child, to let him call her mother. She had heard of such things being done.

"No, no, no, not for worlds," she protested to herself. "I could not do it."

She got up and walked about the room, while Sophy bathed her eyes, and tried to undo the damages her emotions had inflicted on her delicate prettiness.

"I can't go to the party looking like this," exclaimed Sophy, ruefully contemplating her swollen eyelids in the glass.

"We need not go till half-past ten. Eleven o'clock would be early enough. There is time for you to get back your good looks. Benson shall bring you a light little dinner, and then you had better lie down and take a long nap."

"Do you think I can eat or sleep in my state of mind?" protested Sophy; but a quarter of an hour later, when Benson appeared with an appetizing meal, the victim of misplaced affection found that violent emotions are not incompatible with hunger.

She eat her dinner, cried a little now and then between whiles, and at half-past ten went down to the drawing-room in her most attractive frock, and with her light fluffy hair piled as high as she could pile it, and sparkling with those dainty paste stars which Eve had sported at the memorable hunt ball.

"Sophy," cried Vansittart, "I vow you look almost as pretty as Eve looked that night in the snow. And what do I see? Surely I know those quivering starlets! You are wearing the family diamonds."

Sophy rewarded him with a most ungracious scowl, and moved to the other side of the room. Vansittart was looking at an evening paper, and was serenely unconscious of the change in his sister-in-law's manner; but Eve saw that angry glance and movement of avoidance, and wondered what could have caused such rudeness. Temper, perhaps; only poor Sophy's petulant temper, which had never been discriminating in its outbursts.

This was Sophy's way of keeping a secret. Her visit to Charles Street ended two days later. She was studiously uncivil to her host up to the hour of her departure; and in her farewell talk with her sister, being closely questioned by Eve as to the reason of this change in her manner, she prevaricated, hesitated, said things and unsaid them; and finally, in a flood of compassionate tears, she protested that it was only on Eve's account she was angry with Eve's husband. Mr. Sefton had told her that Vansittart still visited that odious woman. Mr. Sefton had met him leaving her house only a few days previously; and Mr. Sefton had assured her that it was he, Eve's husband, who had brought Signora Vivanti to London, and paid for her musical education.

"Can you wonder that I am angry with him, Eve, loving you as I do? You have been so good to me, so generous. It would be wicked of me to go away without warning you. I hated the idea of telling you. I have thought over it again and again. I promised Mr. Sefton that I would tell you nothing; but I could not bear the idea of your being hoodwinked by an unfaithful husband. It was right to tell you, wasn't it, dear? It is better for you to know the truth, is it not?"

"Yes, yes, it is better for me to know," Eve answered, in a hard, cold voice.

"How quietly she takes it!" thought Sophy, as the footman announced the carriage.

Benson had gone on with Sophy's luggage in a four-wheel cab; twice as much luggage as Sophy had brought from Fernhurst.

"I shall never forget your kindness to me," said Sophy, with her parting kiss.

"And I shall never forget your visit," answered Eve.

* * * *

Eve was not at home at luncheon time, so Vansittart went off to his club, and only returned to Charles Street at Eve's usual hour for afternoon tea, when he was told that Mrs. Vansittart had gone out at three o'clock, and had left a note for him in the study.

The note was a letter.

"I am taking a step which will no doubt make you angry," Eve began, "but I cannot help myself. I cannot go on living as we are living now. Every hour of my life increases my misery. I have been told that you visit that woman—that woman who is the cause of all my unhappiness. I have been told that it is you who brought her to London, and had her educated for the stage; that her child is your child. I ought to have known all this without being told; but I shut my eyes to the truth. I wanted so to believe in you. I clung so desperately to that which makes the happiness of my life. You accuse me of unreasoning jealousy; but could any wife help being jealous, seeing what I have seen, hearing what I hear? That woman's face and manner spoke volumes. I tried to accept your explanation—tried to believe you. I had even begun to feel happy again, when I learnt this hateful fact of your visit to her house. I cannot believe that you would have gone there, knowing my feelings on the subject, if this love of the past had not been more to you than your love for me, your wife. There is but one thing for me to do, only one thing which can set my mind at rest, or make me wretched for ever; and that is to see this woman, and hear her story from her own lips. I have no fear that I shall fail in getting at the truth when she and I are face to face. Woman against woman, wife against mistress, I know who will be the stronger.

"If I have wronged you, my beloved, your wife in penitent love. If you have wronged me, your wife no longer—Eve."

A pleasant letter to greet a husband on his home-coming.

"Woman against woman, face to face, those two!" thought Vansittart. "She will discover—not that which she fears to discover, but a darker secret—and then it will be as she has said, my wife no longer."

He stood with his finger on the button of the bell till a servant came.

"A hansom instantly, but be sure you get a good horse," he said, and went into the hall to wait for the man's return.

CHAPTER XXVIII.

IN THE BLUE CHAMBER

Eve had learnt Madame Vivanti's address from Lady Hartley the day after the singer's appearance in Hill Street. So her letter to her husband written, and her mind made up, she had only to drive to Don Saltero's Mansion, and to make her way to that upper floor in which the singer had her bower. The door was opened by Fiordelisa herself, who gave a little look of surprise at seeing her visitor, and then stood in mute wonder, waiting for Eve to speak, smiling faintly, and evidently embarrassed.

She wore her accustomed black stuff gown, with a yellow silk handkerchief knotted carelessly on her breast. The boy was hanging on to her gown, and peeping shyly at the strange lady, so pure and fresh looking in her soft grey silk, and dainty grey hat with pale pink roses. Lisa noted her rival's toilette in all its details, the long loose grey gloves, the grey parasol.

For a minute or so the two women stood thus, looking at each other in silence. Then, with an effort, Eve spoke.

"Are you alone, Madame Vivanti?"

"Alone, all but Paolo, and I don't suppose you count him any-body, Eccellenza. La Zia has gone to London."

"I have come to talk to you—about my husband."

Lisa flushed crimson.

"Please take the trouble to sit down, Eccellenza," she said polite-ly, placing her prettiest armchair in front of the open window.

There were flowers in the balcony, a bed of marigolds, a flower which la Zia had discovered to be decorative and cheap. For perfume there were stocks and mignonette. The balcony was wide enough to hold plenty of flowers, and a couple of basket chairs in which Lisa and her aunt sat for many idle hours in fine weather, breathing the cool breezes from the river, and submitting to the blacks. They thought of their attic window in the Campo, and the life and move-ment in the paved square below, the passing and repassing of the light-hearted crowd to and fro on the Rialto, the twanging of a guitar now and then, the tinkling of wiry mandolines, the nasal tones of a street-singer. Here they had a wider horizon, but a murkier sky, and not that concentration of gaiety which makes every campo in Venice a busy little world, self-contained and self-sufficing. Eve looked round the room, noting the pretty furniture, obviously chosen by a person of taste; the open piano; the glimpse of a somewhat untidy bedroom through a door ajar. Her husband had chosen the furniture, Eve told herself. He had built this nest for his singing-bird.

"I am looking at your rooms," she said, with pale lips; "the rooms my husband furnished for you."

Lisa had not even the grace to attempt a denial.

"He was very good, very generous," she faltered, her eyes suffused with tears, those tears which came so readily to Lisa's eyes, on the stage or off. "There never was any one so good as he."

"He owed you at least as much as that," said Eve, sternly. "It was the least he could do."

"Ah, he has told you then," cried Lisa, eagerly; "he has told you his secret."

"No, he has not told me. He was too much ashamed to tell me of anything so infamous. He is not shameless like you," said Eve, trembling with indignant feeling.

It was all true then, all that Sefton had told her sister; all that her own jealous fears had suggested. This woman stood before her, unabashed, ready to expatiate upon her sin.

"He has told me nothing," she said, "or if he has spoken of you it has only been to deceive me. But there are some things that are easy to guess, when a woman has lived in the world as I have, and has heard other women talk. Two years ago perhaps I might have been fooled by his falsehoods; but I am wiser now. I knew from the first that you had been his mistress; that he was the father of that boy."

She pointed to the unconscious Paolo, sprawling on the floor, turning the leaves of a picture-book, and doing his utmost to destroy an indestructible "Jack the Giant Killer," printed on stout linen.

"You knew what was not true, then," said Lisa, drawing herself up, with crimson cheeks and flaming eyes. "You pretend to know that which is false, false, *una bugia indegna*. He was never anything to me but a friend, my generous and noble friend. He hired this apartment for us, for la Zia and me, and he furnished these rooms, and he bought me that piano, and he paid the good Zinco to teach me to sing. *E vero!* I owe him my fortune, and all I have in the world. I would walk barefoot all over this earth if I could make him happier by my toil. There is nothing in this world I would not do for him."

"And you ask me to believe that he did all this for friendship—mere friendship—he, an English gentleman, for an Italian peasant?"

"I don't ask you to believe anything, and I don't care what you believe. He is all the world to me. You are nothing—less than nothing!" cried Lisa, passionately. "I hate you. If it had not been for you he would have married me, perhaps. Who knows?"

"You think he would have married you! And yet he was only your friend, you say."

"He was only my friend."

"He brought you and your aunt from Italy and set you up in London; and yet he was only your friend."

"He did not bring us from Italy. We came to London of our own accord. He was only my friend. He was never any more than my friend. If he had been I would not disown him. I love him too well to be ashamed."

"You own that you love him?"

"Yes, I am not ashamed of my love. There are people somewhere who worship the sun. I am no more ashamed than they are. I told him of my love on my knees in this room, where you are sitting. I knelt at his feet and asked him to give me heart for heart. I thought then that he would hardly have been so kind unless he loved me. But he told me that he loved an English girl, and that she was to be his wife. There was no hope for me. I wanted to kill myself, but he stopped me with his strong arms. Yes, for just one moment I was in his arms! Only one moment, and then he flung me from him as if I were dirt."

"He must have been very chivalrous to do so much for friendship," said Eve, shaken, but not convinced.

The woman spoke with the accents of truth; but Eve remembered that she was an actress, trained in the art of simulated passion. No doubt it was easy for an actress to lie like truth.

"He wanted to help us," protested Lisa; "he blamed himself so much for——"

She stopped, coloured, and then grew pale. It was evident to her now that Vansittart's wife had been told nothing, and she, Lisa, had been on the point of betraying him.

"For what? Why did he blame himself?"

"Did I say 'blame'? I use wrong words sometimes," she said, quick to recover herself. "I hardly know your language. He pitied us: that is what I meant to say. He pitied us because we were alone and poor—two helpless women."

"And the father of your child, where was he?" Eve asked sternly, only half convinced. "Why did not he help you?"

Paolo had grown tired of his book, and had gone back to his

mother's knee. He stood half hidden in Lisa's gown, looking earnestly at the stranger, his infantile mind puzzled at the tone and manner of the two women, feeling dimly that there was a tempest in the atmosphere, feeling it as the birds feel when they twitter apprehensively before the coming of the thunder. Inquisitive as well as alarmed, and bold in his wonder, he went over to Eve, and took hold of her gown, and looked up in her face.

She looked down at him, and it was her turn to wonder.

Of whom did the face remind her? He was like his mother; but it was not her face he recalled to Eve. Nor was it Vansittart's face, though she tried, shrinkingly, to trace a resemblance there, looking for something she hoped not to see. No, the face recalled some other face, and the likeness, faint and indefinable as it was, thrilled her with a tremulous awe, as if she had seen a ghost.

"You had a claim upon this child's father," said Eve, her hand lightly touching the boy's head, and then shrinking away as from pollution; "the strongest possible claim, for he ought to have been your husband. Why did not he help you?"

"Because he was in his grave," said Lisa; and again the ready tears gushed out.

There was a pause, and then Eve spoke in a gentler tone.

"That was hard for you," she said, with a touch of pity.

"Yes, it was hard. He had promised to marry me. I think he would have married me, for Paolo's sake. My baby was not born till afterwards—after his father's death."

"Poor creature! All that was very sad. Was my husband—was Mr. Vansittart a friend of the man who died? Was it for his friend's sake he was so kind to you?"

"No, he was not a friend. It was for my sake, and la Zia's, that he was kind. I tell you again, he pitied us."

Eve sank into a chair, drooping, miserable. Even yet she could not believe in this story of Vansittart's chivalrous kindness to two foreign waifs who had no claim upon his friendship, not even the claim of country. She knew him to be benevolent, generous, full of compassion for all suffering of man or beast; but there was nothing Quixotic in his benevolence. That which he had done for Lisa was too much to be expected of any man who was not a millionaire or a musical fanatic. He could not have done so much without a strong motive. And then once again she reminded herself that Lisa was an actress, to whom all falsehoods and simulations must be easy. She started to her feet; indignant with this woman for deceiving her; angry with herself for being so easily duped.

"I don't believe a word you have told me," she cried. "I believe that Mr. Vansittart was your lover; my husband, John Vansittart, and no other; and when he came here the other day you had lured him back to your net."

"You don't believe—you don't believe in Paolo's dead father? Don't cry, Carissimo; she is a cruel woman, but she shan't hurt you." The boy had begun to whimper, scared by the angry voices. "I will make you believe. I will show you his likeness—the likeness I have never shown to any one else. It is a bad one; it does not make him half handsome enough. He was handsome; he had hair as light as yours, only redder, and he was very fair—a true Englishman. He was not as handsome as your husband—no, there is no one else like *him*. Shall I show you his picture? Will you believe me then?"

She did not wait for an answer, but ran into the adjoining room, pulled a heavy, iron-clamped box from under the bed—the box which contained her jewels—unlocked it, and came running back with a photograph in her hand.

"Ecco, Signora. It was taken at Burano, by a man who came from Venice one summer morning, and photographed the church, and the street, and the bridge, and as many of the people as would pay him a few soldi for a likeness. I have kept it hidden away since he died. It hurt me to look at it, remembering his end. But there!"—pushing the photograph in front of Eve's gloomy, distrustful countenance—"look at it to your heart's content, Signora. That man was the father of my child! Believe, or not believe, as you please."

Eve glanced with a careless contempt at the faded sun-picture—a bad photograph, which time had made worse—the blurred image of a face which, as her widening gaze fastened upon it, flashed back all the picture of her childhood upon the mirror of her memory.

"Oh, God!" she cried. "My brother Harold!"

The door opened as she spoke, and looking up she saw her husband standing on the threshold.

She appealed to him hopelessly in her bewilderment.

"Did you know?" she asked. "Was it for my sake you were kind to her? Was that the link between you?"

"No, Fatima," he answered sternly. "My Blue Chamber holds a ghastlier secret than that. I was kind to her because I killed her lover. Are you satisfied now? You wanted to know the worst. You would not be content. We were united, happy, adoring each other; the happiest husband and wife in all London, perhaps; but you would not be

satisfied. I entreated you to trust me. I assured you, with every as-
severation a man could make, that I was true to you. But you would
not believe. You were like your first namesake; you lent your ear to
the hiss of the snake. You were jealous by a woman's instinct, and
you let Sefton feed your jealousy. Well, you are content now, perhaps. You have his picture in your hand—the picture of the man I
killed."

"You killed him? You?"

"It sounds like madness, doesn't it, but it's true all the same. A
vulgar incident enough—nothing romantic about the story. The man
whose likeness you hold, and whom you recognize as your brother—that man and I met as strangers in a Venetian caffè, in Carnival time. This young woman here and her aunt were with me—the
chance acquaintance of the afternoon. We had known each other
only a few hours, had we, Fiordelisa? You did not even know my
name."

"Only a few hours," nodded Lisa.

"He had been on a journey, and had been drinking. He came on
us unawares; and he chose to take offence because Lisa and her aunt
and I were sitting at the same table. He was easily jealous—as you
are. It runs in the family, perhaps. He assaulted me brutally, and I
fought him almost as brutally. It would have all ended harmlessly
enough with a rough mauling of each other—perhaps a black eye, or
a broken nose—but as Fate would have it I had a dagger ready to my
hand—and exasperated at a little extra brutality on his part I stabbed
him. Luck was against us both. That casual thrust of a dagger might
have resulted in a slight flesh wound. It killed him."

"And you let me love you—you let me be your wife—knowing
that you had murdered my brother," said Eve, trembling in every
limb, white as death.

"No, Eve. It was not murder. It is the intention that makes the
crime. He was unarmed, drunk. I ought to have spared him, I suppose—but he fell upon me like a tiger. It was brute force against
brute force. The knife was an unlucky accident."

"He had just bought it in the Procuratie," explained Lisa; "he had
no thought of killing him. You do not know how violent the Englishman could be. He was cruel to me sometimes—he struck me many
times when he was angry."

"You take the part of the murderer against the murdered—though this man would have married you, would have made
you an honest woman."

"He had promised," said Lisa, doubtfully.

Eve put the photograph to her white lips and kissed it passionately, again, and again, and again.

"Oh, Harold," she said, "to have hoped so long for your return, to have prayed so many useless prayers! You were dead—dead before that child was born."

She looked at the boy, reckoning the years by the child's growth. Four years, at least, she told herself.

"And you dared to make me your wife, to let me love you with a love that was almost idolatry," she cried, turning upon Vansittart with dilated eyes, "knowing that you had killed my brother. You heard me talk of him—you pretended to sympathize with me—and you knew that you had killed him."

"I did not know. There was no such thing as certainty. When I asked you to be my wife I knew nothing of your brother's fate. Afterwards, when we were engaged, the idea was suggested to me by your officious friend Sefton—who wanted to put a stumbling-block in the way of our marriage. He succeeded in tracing your brother to Venice, and he read the story after his own lights. He thought Harold Marchant was the man who struck the fatal blow. He did not take him for the victim. But the links in his chain of evidence were not over strong—and I had ample justification for not accepting his assertions as certainties. And you loved me, did you not; and our marriage was likely to make your life fairer and brighter, was it not?"

"What of that? Do you think I should have weighed my own love or my own happiness against my brother's life? Do you think I would have married you if I had known the truth?"

"You would not, perhaps; and two lives would have been spoilt by your loyalty to the dead—who would sleep none the more peacefully because you and I were miserable. Did you owe him so much, this wandering brother of yours? What kindness had he ever shown you? What care had he ever taken of you?"

"He was my brother, and I loved him dearly."

"And did not I love you, and had not I some claim upon you?" asked Vansittart, indignantly. "Could you have let me go without a tear?"

"No, no, no. I adored you from the first—yes, that first night on the snowy road, and at the ball, when you were so kind. I began to love you almost at once, foolishly, ridiculously, without a hope of being loved again. But, let my love be what it would, the love of a lifetime, it would have made no difference. Nothing would have induced me to marry the man who killed my brother. Oh, God," she cried hysterically, "the hands that I have kissed so often—stained

346

with Harold's life-blood!"

"I thought as much," said Vansittart, doggedly. "I told myself that you would not marry me if you knew my secret. I told myself that two lives would be spoilt—it was a question, perhaps, of half a century of happiness for two people, to be sacrificed because of the angry passions of one night—of one minute. The deed was done in less time than the bronze giants of the clock-tower would have taken to strike the hour. Because once in my life, for one instant, under grossest provocation, I let my temper master me—because of that one savage impulse two hearts were to be broken. I spent a night of agony deliberating this question, Eve. Mark you, it was within a few weeks of our wedding-day that your kindred with the dead man was first suggested to me."

"You knew that you had killed a fellow-creature?"

"Yes, I knew, and I had suffered all the bitterness of a long remorse; and I had given myself absolution. And when I knew the worst, knew at least the probability that I had killed your brother, even then, after most earnest questioning, I told myself that it was best for both of us that we should marry. Our lives were our own. Neither of us was responsible to that dead man in his grave. But now, now that I see how dear he was to you, now that I know which way your heart turns, I wish to God that he had killed me, and that I were lying where he lies, among that quiet company by the lagune."

They were alone together, Lisa having slipped away, taking the boy with her, when she found the revelation inevitable. Let them fight it out, these two; and if this Englishwoman loved her dead brother better than her living husband, and chose to desert that noble husband, and thus show of what poor stuff she was made, there was Lisa who adored him, who would follow him through the world, if he would let her, with fidelity that neither time nor trouble could change.

Eve stood for a few moments mutely looking at the blurred photograph, the wretched production of an itinerant photographer's camera, in which one hand was out of focus, jointless, fingerless, monstrous. Poor as the image was, it brought back the days of her childhood as vividly as if it had been the finest work of art that Venice, in her golden age of Titian, Tintoret, and Veronese, could have produced. How well she remembered him! How dearly she had loved him! His holidays had been a season of boisterous gladness, his return to school or university a time of mourning. He had given interest and delight to all her childish amusements. He had taught her to ride. He had taught her to shoot with an air-gun, which was

one of his choicest possessions. He had taught her to serve at tennis, to play billiards on the worn-out table, where the balls rattled
against the cushions as on cast iron. He had done all these things in
a casual way, never sacrificing any inclination or engagement of his
own to her pleasure—but in after days, when he had vanished out of
her life, she knew not whither, it seemed to her that he had been the
kindest and most unselfish of brothers. And he was dead, had been
dead for years, cut off in the prime of his manhood by a remorseless
hand. He was dead, and the man who had slain him stood before her,
undaunted, impenitent—her husband.

And the boy whose treble voice sounded now and again from
the next room—the child from whose lightest contact she had shrank
with jealous abhorrence—that child was of her kindred, no matter
how basely born. He was all that was left to her of the brother she
had loved, and it was not for her to shrink from him.

CHAPTER XXIX.

"'TIS NOT THE SAME NOW, NEVER MORE CAN BE"

Vansittart was the first to break that agony of silence.

"Does this mean the end of love?" he asked. "Is all over and done with between you and me? Is love only a dream that we have dreamed?"

"Yes; it is a dream," she answered, looking at him with tearless eyes, which had more misery in them than all the tears he had ever seen in the eyes of women. "It is something perhaps to have believed one's self happy for two blessed years. You have been so good to me—so good to poor Peggy. She loved you almost as much as I did. You have been all goodness,—and you did not know that he was my brother. Yet, yet, when you killed him you must have known that some heart would be broken. No, I can never forget how good you have been—or how dear. Don't think that I can change in an hour from love to hate. No, no; that cannot be. To my dying day I must love you—but I cannot live with the man who killed my brother. I can never be your wife again. That is all over. We must be strangers on this side of the grave."

"A hard sentence, Eve; it could not be harder if I were a deliberate murderer. And yet perhaps it is no more than I deserve—perhaps even the gallows would be no more than my desert——"

"The gallows! Oh, God, could they kill you because——?"

The words died in her throat, choked by the agony of a great fear.

"But no one knows—no one will ever know," she cried. "She will never tell"—pointing to the door. "She loves you too dearly."

"No, she will not tell."

"Is there any one else who knows?"

"Only her aunt, who may be trusted. No, I don't think I am in any danger from the law," he said carelessly, as if that hardly mattered. "But you—you are my supreme judge; and you look upon me as a murderer. Well, perhaps you are right. Let me sophisticate with myself as I will, in that one moment I was in mind and instinct a homicide. When I struck that blow I did not care about consequences. All the savage impulses within me were raging. Yes, I was a murderer. And you say that we must part! That is your sentence?"

349

She nodded yes.

"Very well; then I must do all I can to make our parting easy and reputable. The world will wonder and talk, but we must bear that. I think I know a way of lessening the scandal. You will live at Mere-wood, and I will travel. That will make things easy."

"Live at Merewood without you! Not for all the world. I can go back to Fernhurst to my sisters. What does it matter where I live? The worst is that I *must* live. You will let me give them some of my pin-money, I know, so that I may not be a burden upon them."

"Let you? Why, your pin-money is your own, to throw in the gutter if you like."

"No, no; it was meant for your wife. I shall have no claim upon it when we are parted. But I don't want to be a burden at the Homestead. I should like to give them fifty pounds a year. I shall not cost them so much as that."

"I dare say not. Why do you torture me with this talk of money? All the money I have is turned to withered leaves. Eve, Eve," he cried passionately, "you could not do this cruel thing if our child had lived!"

"Could I not? Would that have altered the fact that you killed my brother? No, for God's sake don't come near me," as he approached her with extended hand, trying to clasp her hand in his, passionately longing for reunion. "There is a ghost between us. I should hate myself if I could forget the dead."

"Ah, that is the worst sting of death," he cried bitterly, "the influence of the dead which blights the living. Is there no hope, Eve—no hope? Is your mind made up?"

"Alas! alas! I have no choice."

"Take time to think, at least, before you act."

"Time to think? Why, I have been thinking for an eternity. It is ages since that woman put this picture in my hand. Oh, I have thought, Jack. I have thought. If I could shut my eyes and say I forget—if I could say the past is past, and the dead are no better for our tears and our sacrifices, our crape gowns, or the roses we plant on their graves if I could be like the heathens who said, 'Let us be happy to-day, for to-morrow we die,' how gladly would I blot thought and memory from my brain! But you see while I live I must think and remember; and every hour of my life with you would be darkened by one hideous memory. I should see my brother in his blood-stained winding-sheet standing between us. There are some things that cannot be, that heart, and mind, and conscience cry out against, and our marriage is one of those things. Oh, it was wicked,

wicked, to marry me, knowing what you knew."

"Was it wicked? If it was, I don't repent of that sin. I repent my first crime—the crime of bloodshed—not my second, the crime of making you my wife. I have had two years of bliss. How many men can say as much? Well, since you are resolute—have weighed what you are doing, and still decide against me, I will leave you in peace. If the memory of those years cannot plead for me, all words are idle."

She heard the strangled sob in his voice as he turned from her and went slowly to the door: but she did not call him back. She stood like a woman of stone till the door closed on him, and the outer door opened and shut again. Then she clasped her hands above her head with a distracted gesture, and rushed out upon the balcony to see the last of him. She leant over the high iron rail to watch him as he sprang into the waiting hansom. She saw him drive away, and did not shriek to him to come back, though her whole being, brain, heart, nerves, yearned after him with despairing love. She watched till the cab vanished from her sight, hidden by the foliage on the Embankment, and then she dragged herself slowly back to the room, as a wounded animal crawls to its lair, and flung herself upon Lisa's sofa, a broken-hearted woman.

"Could I act otherwise,—could I, could I?" she asked herself. "My brother, my own flesh and blood! Even if I had not loved him, could I live with the man who killed him?"

Lisa crept into the room, while Eve sat sobbing, with her face hidden in the sofa pillow. Lisa crept to her side, and sat on the ground by her, pitying her, and looking up at her with mute doglike tenderness. "What have you done?" she asked at last. "Have you sent him from you—your husband who loves you?"

"Yes, he is gone. It is our fate."

"Fate!" cried Lisa, contemptuously. "What is fate? It is you, not Fate, that make the parting. If you loved him you would not let him go."

"If I loved him? Why, my whole being is made up of love for him."

"What then? And you send him from you for an accident—for something which no one could help. I was there—these eyes saw it. A moment and it was done! There was not time for thought. For that one instant of wrong-doing are you to make his life miserable?"

"He killed my brother. Do you understand that, Lisa? The man who ought to have been your husband was my brother. Did you care nothing for him—you, the mother of his child?"

"Si, si, I cared for him. When first he came to Burano I worshipped him as if he had been St. Mark. And when he said, 'Come to Venice with me, Lisa, and be my little wife,' I went. It was wicked, I know. I ought not to have left Burano till I had been to confession, and the priest had married us; but when I said, 'You will marry me, Signor Inglese,' he said, 'Yes, Lisa, by-and-by,' and that was what he always said till the last—'by-and-by.' He was not always kind to me, Si'ora, though he was your brother. He beat me sometimes when the luck had been bad at cards. When he had been sitting up half the night playing cards with his friends, and I crept into the room and begged him to play no more—he was not kind then. He would start up out of his chair, and swear a big English oath, and strike at me with his clenched fist. But am I sorry? Yes, of course I am sorry. It was dreadful to see him fall dead in a moment; but is that to be remembered against your husband years afterwards? He was brutal that night, so brutal that he deserved his death, almost. He flew at the strange Englishman like a tiger. He would not listen, he would not believe that I was not false to him. He was mad with drink and foolish anger. He was like a wild beast. And for an accident like that you would make the noblest of men unhappy. Ah, Si'ora, that is not love. If your husband belonged to me, and he loved me as he loves you, he might kill twenty men, and I would cling to him and love him still. What would their life be to me, or their death, if I had him?"

"You are a semi-civilized savage, and you can't understand," said Eve, sternly. "Life and death, good name, and honour, have no meaning for you."

"Love means more than all," said Lisa, doggedly.

"There is only one man you have the right to love," said Eve; "the man who ought to have been your husband. You must be indeed a wretch if you can love the man who killed him."

"Ah, madonna mia, we do not make our hearts. They are made for us," Lisa pleaded naively. "The Signor Inglese was very good to me at Burano in my poverty; but afterwards, at Venice, I had a good deal to suffer. It was a hard life sometimes. One had need be young, and able to laugh, and forgive and forget. But he—Signor Vansittart—he was always kind. His face haunted me after that Shrove Tuesday on the Lido, and when we met again—when la Zia and I were strangers in London, without a friend in the world—oh, how kind and generous he was! All that I have of fame and fortune I owe to him, and though he does not care for me so much as that," with a contemptuous wave of her fingers, "yet he is always gentle, always good. Do not tell me that I am to care more for the dead man who deceived me and beat me than for the living man who has been my benefactor, my guardian angel, and for whom I say a paternoster and two aves every night of my life. It is sweet to say these for his sake: that his sin may be forgiven."

"Ah, you do not understand. You do not know what death is," said Eve, with gloomy anger, getting up from the sofa, and rearranging her loosened hair with trembling hands.

"It must come to all of us," answered Lisa, with a philosophical shrug. "Better that it should come in a moment as his came, without suffering, without fear, than that we should live to be old and fat and full of maladies. People die of dreadful diseases that one shudders only to hear of, and that is called a natural death. How much better to be stabbed to the heart unawares."

"I cannot reason with you," said Eve, haughtily. "I loved my brother. You, his mistress, evidently cared nothing for him."

And with this verbal stab, she departed. Who shall say whether she was more indignant with the Venetian for loving Harold Marchant too little or for loving John Vansittart too much?

Her carriage was waiting for her; the servants were asleep in the afternoon sun. She was only just able to utter the monosyllabic "Home," in answer to the footman's question.

How strange the streets and all their movement of everyday life seemed to her, as she drove along the interminable King's Road, and by Sloane Street and the Park—how careless the faces of the people. Was there no other trouble in the world but her own? Was everybody else busy, and bustling, and happy? She felt as if she had been driving home from a funeral, wondering to find a world where there were no signs of sorrow. Had she not verily parted from her dead? The dead brother whom she had always pictured to herself as alive and happy in some far-off African wilderness, leading the adventurer's reckless life, caring for no one he had left in the civilized world, but destined to come back to her hereafter with that wild spirit tamed, and his home affections reviving with mature years. He was dead, and she would see him no more on earth—killed in a tavern brawl, for the sake of a worthless woman. And the husband she adored, he, too, was dead—dead to her for ever. She had renounced him, and he was free to go his own way, and lead his own life, and find consolation and happiness where he could. Her friends of Mayfair had told her that no man laments long for the loss of any woman; that one beautiful face blots out another; that there is no image, however cherished, which does not grow faint, and fade and vanish, as a circle widens and melts away upon still water.

Even the house in Charles Street had a strange aspect when she re-entered it. Should she find him there? Would he plead with her again, in their own house, where she had been so happy with him, where all mute things reminded her of the glad life he had given her? Would he plead with her once more, and renew the struggle between love for the living and loyalty to the dead? No; she was spared that ordeal. The servant who opened the door told her that his master had been summoned hurriedly to Southampton, and had left a letter for her. She caught up the letter eagerly, hungry, in her desolation, for some sign from him, some last link between them.

"I start by the mail for Southampton," he wrote. "Till nine I shall be within reach of a telegram at the Travellers, if you change your mind. Before to-morrow night I shall be outward bound; but till to-morrow night a wire to the Post Office at Southampton would find me. I have made no plans as yet, but you may think of me as an exile and a wanderer."

He was gone! She had been obeyed. The wrench was over; and now she had to face life calmly and deliberately without him. She had sacrificed all that was nearest and dearest to her on this earth to the shadow of the dead. She had made her choice between the dead and the living. Could she have chosen otherwise?

That was the question she asked herself when she had locked the door of her room and was alone with her misery, walking to and fro among the familiar surroundings which had been the background of a happy union. How could she have chosen otherwise?

"He killed him!" she repeated to herself with dogged insistency. "He killed my brother. What should I be if I could stay with him—call him husband, love him and obey him for the rest of my life—the man who killed my brother? Was it murder or not murder, he killed him. It was death. Oh, to think of my poor Harold—to think that he entered that fatal place in all the strength of his manhood; a young man, with a long life before him, perhaps; with all the chances of fortune and happiness which length of years can bring; and there in a moment he was breathing his last breath, stabbed to the heart!"

Memory recalled that fondly loved brother in the flush of his active boyhood—a cricket field shining in the sunlight, the white tents, the village crowd, and that tall, muscular form, the sunburnt face, blue eyes, and auburn hair, the type of English boyhood at its best. One scene after another of her childhood passed before her as in a panorama, and Harold was the central figure in every picture. So strong, so brave, so intelligent, so kind to her always, even when at war with others; loving her to the last, even when an outcast from his home.

How cruelly Fate had used him—an unkind father—a forced exile—an early and a violent death!

For more than an hour—for an eternity of suffering—she paced her room—or knelt beside the bed, not praying, nor yet crying—only thinking, thinking of the life that had been and that was over for ever—her childish life in Yorkshire while her brother was still the cherished son, the honoured heir—the later season of disgrace and parting—her life with the husband of her love.

"And Peggy," she thought, with a new agony of unavailing love, "oh, how good he was to my poor Peggy; but if she had known that the hand which smoothed her pillow was the hand that killed her brother—if she had known! Does she know now, I wonder, and know what I suffer, and pity me, from the far distance, in the land where there are no tears?"

* * * *

She refused admittance to her maid at the usual hour of dressing. She told Benson that she had a headache, and would not go down to dinner. Later in the evening she wandered about the house, looking at the rooms in which she had been so happy—remembering the days of her courtship, when those rooms were still new to her, and when they realized all she had ever imagined of luxury and refinement. She went about bidding the rooms good-bye, looking at them for the last time, as she believed, for she meant to depart on her journey early next morning.

To depart whither?

On thinking out the question of her future she rejected the notion of that return to the old home of which she had spoken to Vansittart.

She could not go to her sisters at Fernhurst, the refuge which she would instinctively have chosen, content to hide herself in the humble home of her girlhood, to live the old unluxurious life, to sit by the cottage hearth, and read the tattered old books, and try to think herself a girl again, a girl who had never seen the face of Jack Vansittart.

Fernhurst would not do. It was too near Lady Hartley; it was not remote enough from Merewood. She had to find some abiding place which should be unknown to all the world except the servant who went with her. She did not feel herself equal to travelling without a servant. The ways of wealth had spoiled her for the ways of penury. She was no longer the same young woman who used to head an early expedition from Haslemere to Waterloo, travelling third class, among soldiers and workmen, to be first in the scramble for bargains at a sale of drapery. She felt herself powerless, in her bruised and broken state, to face the confusion of a crowded railway station, the bewilderment of foreign travel, with its stringent demands upon the traveller's calmness and intelligence.

She found her good Benson waiting for her in her boudoir dressing-room with a tea-tray, and a meal of cold chicken, fruit and jelly, set out temptingly to beguile her into eating.

"You have had nothing since lunch, ma'am."

"I can't eat anything—yes," as Benson looked distressed, "some bread and butter. You can leave that and the tea—but take away all the rest, please. And then give me Bradshaw—and I want you to pack before you go to bed. It is not very late, is it?"—looking hopelessly at the watch on her chatelaine, but unable to see the quaint old figures with those tired eyes.

"Past eleven, ma'am; but I can pack to-night, if you like. Are we to leave early to-morrow?"

Eve turned the leaves of Bradshaw before she answered, and pored over a page for a few minutes.

"The Continental train leaves Charing Cross at eight," she said.

"Then I must certainly pack to-night, ma'am. Shall I take many dresses—evening gowns—tea-gowns? Shall you be going out much in the evenings?"

"I shan't be going out at all. Take my plainest walking gowns, and, yes, a tea-gown or two; one black evening gown will do. Take plenty of things. I shall be abroad a long time."

"It is very sudden, ma'am," faltered Benson, who was honestly fond of her mistress.

"Yes, it is very sudden. You must not ask me any questions. You must take it on trust that there is nothing wrong in my life."

"Oh, ma'am, I should never think that, whatever happened. I know you too well. Are we going to join Mr. Vansittart on the Continent?"

"No, Benson. We are going away from him. Mr. Vansittart and I have parted for ever. Please don't speak of it to any one downstairs. I want to avoid all talk and scandal. I tell you because you are going with me. You will share in my new life—if you like to go."

"I would go to the end of the world with you, ma'am. But, dear, dear, dear, to think that you and Mr. Vansittart can be parted—you who have been so happy together, like children almost! It can only be a temporary misunderstanding. I am sure of that."

"Benson, if you talk about my trouble I shall go alone. Can't you understand that there are griefs that won't bear to be spoken of? Mine is one of them. I am going abroad; I hardly know where as yet. To some quiet place in Brittany or Normandy most likely, where I can just exist."

"Oh, my dear young lady, you will kill yourself with grief," sobbed Benson, as she poured out tea for her mistress.

While Benson was packing, with all the dexterity and method of an accomplished packer, Eve was employed in writing the most difficult letter she had ever written in her life.

She was writing to her husband's mother, the woman who had received her at first reluctantly, but afterwards with motherly affection; the woman who had surrendered the son she adored to the wife he had chosen for himself, and who looked to that wife for the happiness of her son's future years. Penniless, the daughter of a disreputable father, with no social surroundings or family influence to recommend her, she had been accepted by Jack Vansittart's relations; petted and praised by his sister; lovingly cherished by his mother; and for recompense of their trust in her what was she going to give them?

She was going to spoil her husband's life in the heyday of youth and love; to leave him bound in wedlock and yet companionless; with a wife and no wife. He could not divorce her; she could not divorce him. His sin was not of the kind which breaks marriage bonds.

What could she say to her mother-in-law which could in any manner explain or justify the parting of husband and wife who until yesterday had been living together in seemingly happiest union? There was no explanation, no justification possible. The mystery of those two broken lives must remain for ever dark to their kindred and the world.

"My husband and I have agreed to part, and our parting must needs be for a lifetime," she wrote. "We can tell no one our reasons, not even you, mother, who of all people have the strongest right to question us. Unfaithfulness or lessening love has nothing to do with our separation. I never loved my husband better than I love him now; or, at least, I never knew the strength of my love for him so well as I know it now. What must be must be. It is Fate, and not our own will, that divides us. Wherever he may go my heart will go with him. Think of me with indulgence if you can; pity me if you can, for I have direst need of your pity."

She said nothing about her destination. She had not made up her mind yet where she was to go. She sat for an hour or more turning the leaves of the Continental time-table; now thinking she would go by Ostend, and to the Ardennes; and then again deciding upon Brittany. It mattered nothing to her where she went; all places were alike, except for her desire to avoid the people she knew.

Finally she decided upon crossing to St. Malo by the boat that left Southampton at five o'clock next day; and from St. Malo to Dinan or Avranches. She would avoid the seaside, where English visitors would be likely to be met at this season. The Norman and Breton towns she knew by repute as places where people lived quietly and economically, forgotten by the world.

* * * *

The same post which brought Mrs. Vansittart Eve's letter from London brought her a letter from her son, written from Southampton.

"You will be surprised at the address from which I write, and still more surprised when I tell you that Southampton is only the first stage on my journey to South Africa. I sail from here to the Cape, and from thence shall make my way to whichever portion of the Dark Continent promises best for health and enjoyment at this time of year. Do not be uneasy about me, my dear mother. I shall take counsel with experienced travellers before I turn my back upon the civilized world; and I shall not go to meet fever, famine, or assassination. You shall hear from me at each stage of my wanderings. I do not go as a scientific explorer, or as a sportsman in quest of big game, though I hope to make good use of my gun. I go with the desire to escape from civilization, monotony, and my own thoughts, which just now are of the saddest.

"A cloud has spread itself between Eve and me, and we two, who were so happy in each other's affection a little while ago, have agreed to part, I fear never again to live together. I cannot tell you our reasons, for they involve a secret the revelation of which would be disastrous to me—the only secret I ever kept from you. Eve is blameless—chaste and faithful as in the beginning of our wedded lives. I implore you to think of her always with affection; to shelter and cherish her if ever she appeal to your love or claim your protection. She is entitled to your respect and to your pity. The only sinner—never a deliberate sinner—is your son, who in his shattered domestic life pays the forfeit of one unhappy act."

CHAPTER XXX.

A DOUBLE EXILE

Hail, dark mother of wanderers, parched nurse of lions! Amidst thy romantic wildernesses grief and dishonour may forget themselves; with thee man is only man! He leaves that other half of himself, reputation, yonder in the crowd, and in these solitudes becomes a creature of thews and sinews, valuable only for his strength and endurance, for the range of his eye and the truth of his hand. He has done with the outward shows of life, and with all nice differences between good and bad. Here, worth is to be measured by the hunter's fleetness of foot, and honour by the marksman's aim. What a man is counts for but little; what he can do for much. In that aching misery which possessed him when he left England, John Vansittart looked to the desert as his best refuge. The hunter's life in Mashonaland gives scanty leisure for brooding over the ruins of a home in England. The early trek with the waggons, or the start on foot from the skerm; the hard day's tramp under the blazing sun; the need of providing meat for the boys—the long following on the spoor of giraffe or antelope, with the wild ride or cautious stalk at the end—which that need involves; the charm of the life, its poetry, its absolute novelty, and the ever-recurring vicissitudes which each new day brings forth, leave the head of the expedition briefest time for introspective thought. His slumbers are for the most part dreamless; or his dreams are of lions prowling by the camp-fire, or of the dark forms and wild gestures of those he has last seen dancing by its flickering light; not of the lost faces of home. Best of all, his conscience is at ease, for face to face with man in his most primitive aspect he loses the habit of weighing his past acts and comparing, with futile regret, the things he has done with the things he ought to have done.

For Vansittart there could have been no better refuge than the desert.

Here, if his heart wounds were not healed, his consciousness of

359

sin was deadened. Here, where no exaggerated value was set on human life, he could remember Harold Marchant's death with less intensity of pain. Here, where the native freely turned his gun or his assegai against his fellow-man, a mischance such as that of Florian's Caffè seemed a small thing—the fortune of war, a spurt of anger, an unlucky blow, and there an end. Every man must die somehow; and it may not be the worst doom to drop down in the fulness of youth and vigour, knowing not the slow agonies of gradual extinction, the torture of dying by inches.

Vansittart's thoughts were tempered by his surroundings. His character took new colours in that vivid life, in that lapse backward from the civilized and the complicated to the primitive stage of man's history. It was as if Time had turned his glass and the earth were young. The wild race of Cain, the outcast, could have been no wilder than these woolly-haired followers of his, who were faithful to him because he was a good shot.

Nature, the great consoler, helped him to forget his grief by forgetting himself. Here, face to face with Nature's mightiest forces, man's sense of his own personality dwindles to the faintest shadow in the vastness of his surroundings. Instead of Trafalgar Square he has the Falls of the Zambesi; instead of the languid club lounger he has the elephant and the lion for his companions—the purring growl of the lion instead of the gossip of the smoking-room; the trumpet of the elephant instead of the chatter of the dinner-table. Surely it is good for a man to be alone in the wilderness—alone save for the company of followers to whom, though he be their leader, he is as another being, a white man, a stranger in their land, between whose thoughts and feelings and their own a great gulf is for ever fixed. It is good for him to feel his own insignificance among men who value him only for his powder and shot, and who will lose their reverence for his white superiority with the spending of his last cartridge. Here he must needs forget that pride of place which at home was a part of his being. Here there are no tradesmen to fawn upon him, no servants to touch their hats to him, no women to praise him. Small food for vanity here, where the darkies call his smooth, flat hair dog's hair, and who liken his hairy arm to a baboon's arm. Here if the women fawn upon him it is not for his smiles or his favour, but for beads or printed calico, such vivid orange or scarlet fabrics, figured with stars or half moons, as Manchester weaves for the Torrid Zone. Here if the men are true to him it is because he can feed them and pay them. He is in a world of stern facts, where sentiment and sophistication are unknown.

The atmosphere suits him. The primitive interests of this primitive life help to shut off that other life where all is gloom, the life of thought and of memory. Sufficient for the day, that is the motto here: food for the day; safety for the day; wood for the fires, water for man and beast. Beside them, behind them, ahead of them, stalk dangers that Europe knows not. Danger from beasts of prey; danger from men as cruel; fever, starvation, death in many shapes—all the vicissitudes of a life between the desert and the sky.

Fortune favours him in his desolation of spirit. A happier man might have been less lucky. A man more careful of his life, with more to live for, might have hardly escaped scot-free from all the dangers of the hunter's life in an unknown land. Travellers far more experienced wondered afterwards when they heard the story of this man's travels, and the impunity with which he had done desperate things.

His daring had been the audacity of ignorance, they said. If he had known the extent of the peril in such unconsidered wanderings, with so small a party, with such inadequate preparation, he would have been a madman to set his life upon such chances. Had he answered them truthfully he would have told them that he was a madman when he turned his face towards the desert; mad with the agony of a life that was blighted; mad with the bitter memories of lost happiness.

* * * *

Of these wedded lovers, parted in the noontide of their love, one carried his wounded heart to the wilderness, and sought for tranquillity of spirit in a life of movement and peril; the other, the weaker vessel, had no such large resources. The life of adventure, the ever-changing horizon, were not for her. She could only creep to some quiet haven and sit alone and brood upon her grief.

She went first to Avranches; then late in the autumn she took a fancy to the solitude of Mont St. Michel, the quaint monastic citadel, the fortress on the rock; and here, when the last of the tourists had gone, and the equinoctial gales were roaring round the Gothic towers, she took up her abode in an apartment specially prepared for her by the cheery patronne of the Inn at the Gate, an apartment upon the ramparts, with windows looking wide over the sea towards Coutances and Jersey.

Benson, who had a constitution of iron, complained bitterly of this wind-swept rock, yet had to own later that her health had nev-

er been better. Eve stopped here late into the winter, sketching a little, reading a great deal, wandering on the sands in all weathers, and
sometimes wishing that her footsteps would take her unawares to
that portion of the bay, where, as in the Kelpie's flow, sorrow might
find a grave.

An imprudent ramble in the marshy fields between Pontorson
and the Mount, which left her belated in the mists of a November
evening, resulted in congestion of the lungs. She had contrived to
lose herself among those salt meadows as completely as ever her
husband had lost himself in Mashonaland, and it was eleven o'clock
when she and her whimpering attendant tottered along the causeway
leading to the gates of the fortress, footsore and weary, their shoes
worn out in that long tramp over coarse grass and sandy hillocks.

Benson telegraphed to Miss Marchant at Fernhurst, and Sophy
appeared on the scene as quickly as boat and rail, and a wretched fly
from Avranches, with harness eked out by bits of rope, could bring
her. Sophy was broken-hearted at this cruel turn which her sister's
bright fortunes had taken, and agonized with remorseful retrospec-
tion. It was she, perhaps, whose imprudent tongue had parted husband and wife, had destroyed that happy home. Sophy hated herself for the folly of that revelation. Why could she not have let well
alone? Why could she not have left undisturbed that happy state of
things by which she herself had profited so richly? Looking back upon her conduct of that fatal week, she saw that it was her own disappointment which had soured her, and her own selfish vexation which
had made her so angry with Vansittart.

It was a long time before Eve was well enough for serious talk
of any kind. She rallied slowly, and during the monotonous days of
her convalescence she was treated as a child, who must only hear of
pleasant things; but when she was well again, quite well—save for
that little hacking cough which seemed to have become an element
of her being—Sophy ventured to approach the subject of her domestic sorrows.

"I have been utterly miserable since the day I left Charles
Street," said Sophy, seated beside Eve's easy-chair, and resting her
forehead on the cushioned arm as she talked, so that her face was
invisible. "I have hated myself for speaking of your husband as I
did—only upon hearsay. After all, Mr. Sefton might have misinterpreted Jack's conduct. It might all have been a mistake."

"It was a mistake, Sophy."

"Oh, I am so glad. You found out at once that Mr. Sefton was
wrong."

"Yes."

"Thank God! But then"—looking up at her sister in blank astonishment—"if that is so, why are you parted, Jack and you?"

"That is our secret, Sophy."

"But why, but why? I can't understand. There could be only one reason for your leaving him when you loved him so dearly. Nothing but the knowledge of his infidelity would justify——"

"Stop, Sophy," said Eve, peremptorily. "There is nothing gained by speculating about other people's business. My husband and I have our own reason for taking different roads. We have never quarrelled; we have never ceased to care for each other. I shall love him with all my heart, and mind, and strength, till my last breath."

"I guess your reason," answered Sophy, nodding sagaciously. "He is an Atheist, and you, who have always been a good Churchwoman, could not go on living with an unbeliever. You are like poor Catherine in 'Robert Elsmere.'"

"Oh, Sophy, do you think I should forsake him because he was without hope or comfort from God? Why do you tease me with foolish guesses? I tell you again the reason of our parting is our secret. A secret that will go down with me to the grave."

Sophy's eager imagination ran riot in the world of mystery. Politics, Freemasonry, Hypnotism, Theosophy, Nihilism, hereditary madness, epilepsy, hydrophobia, a family ghost, a family fatality! That lively mind of hers touched each possibility, rejected each, and flew off to the next; and lastly, with a sigh of relief, she exclaimed—

"I am more thankful than I can say that it was not my imprudent tongue which parted you."

An hour later, walking alone on the ramparts, she told herself that in all probability this desolate wife was only throwing dust in her eyes, and that Vansittart's inconstancy had been clearly demonstrated in accordance with Sefton's story. It would be only like a devoted wife to violate truth in order to vindicate her husband. Pride and love would alike urge Eve to deny her husband's infidelity.

CHAPTER XXXI.

"OH TELL HER, BRIEF IS LIFE,
BUT LOVE IS LONG"

As soon as Eve was well enough to be moved she left the rock and went to finish the winter at Dinard. The doctor who attended her through her illness suggested the south of France, Cannes for instance, as the better climate for her; but she told him she had lost a sister at Cannes, and that all that lovely coast was associated with her loss.

"It is very beautiful," she said; "but I shall never go there again. My sister was sent there because she was consumptive; but my case is altogether different. It would be absurd to go to the south just because I have had a touch of congestion, in consequence of an autumnal ramble."

"It was a somewhat severe touch, madam," said the doctor; "but perhaps Dinard may suit you very well. There are some people who say the climate is almost as good as Provence."

Sophy went with her sister to Dinard, which she pronounced a considerable improvement upon Mont St. Michel, the mediævalism of which picturesque settlement had in no wise reconciled her to existence in a place without people and without shops. At Dinard there were smart residents even in winter, and if Eve had not been obstinately bent upon isolation they might have known people, as Sophy murmured regretfully.

Not knowing people, she soon wearied of Dinard, which was only the sands and the sea over again, when one had exhausted the town and the quaintness of shops which were unlike English shops, and had explored St. Malo and St. Servan, and excursionized, chaperoned by Benson, as far as Dinan, where she was more impressed by the bad drainage than by the fine architecture.

Sophy began to talk of her home duties. Jenny's letters had been most exasperating of late, and it was too evident she was interfering with Nancy, and making a mess of the housekeeping. Finally Sophy declared that things at Fernhurst could go on no longer without her. Jenny had been entertaining in a most reckless manner—people to luncheon, people to tea. "She will be giving dinner-parties next," said Sophy. "Nancy is so weak about her, because she saved her life in the measles—as if it was any merit of Jenny to have had measles worse than any of us."

Eve did not oppose her departure, being somewhat weary of that light talk which centred chiefly in self, one's own experiences, sensations, hopes, disappointments.

"How I wish you would go back with me, Eve!" urged Sophy, with very real warmth. "Surely you would be happier at Fernhurst than here, and it would be like the old days for us to have you again. You would be one of us, the head of the family once more. You would forget that you had ever left home."

"Ah, Sophy, if that were possible! If any one could forget! They can't, dear. They only harden their hearts and call it forgetting. Dear old Fernhurst! Yes, I should love to be there; to ramble over Blackdown again, and hear the wind whistling in the dark fir trees; to look over the weald far off to the faint streak of distant sea, just a line of light on the horizon and no more. But it can't be, Sophy. Fernhurst is too near Redwold Towers, too near Mr. Sefton's place, too near all the people I have done with."

"Poor Eve, it is sad to hear you talk of yourself as if you had committed a crime. It was most trying when Mrs. Vansittart came over to see us, and questioned us so closely about you. Did we think this or that? Had we known of any unhappiness between you and Jack? Had we any idea why you parted? I felt it more than the others, for I thought I was at the bottom of it all with my foolish speech about your husband. But I held my tongue. The others declared they knew nothing, could not even surmise a reason for your conduct. They adored Jack, thought him simply perfect as a husband, and Eve the luckiest girl of their acquaintance. And then there was Lady Hartley. Of course we had to go through the same kind of thing with her, not once but several times, for she is always nice in asking us to her house, and in coming to tea with us every now and then, and I know that she is very fond of you, in her light-minded way. But, indeed, Eve, I don't see any reason why you should not go home with me. Nobody will venture to question you, and Jack is in Africa——"

"No, no; I could not bear to see the people I know, or the old places. I should be miserable. I see them often in my dreams—hill and common, and lane, and cottage garden—and wake disappointed to find myself so far away. But I could not bear to be there again—without him. No, dear. Jack is travelling, and I am travelling. That is much the best arrangement."

"But you don't travel," remonstrated Sophy. "You bury yourself alive in a place like this, and walk up and down the same stretch of sand every day, or tramp along the same chalky road, or cross the same ridiculous ferry, and march round the same windy ramparts. Surely you don't call that travelling."

"I mean to do better by-and-by. I mean to go to Italy. Perhaps you would spare me Hetty for a travelling companion?"

"Spare her, indeed! You have but to ask her, and she will spare herself. She won't ask my leave. She is pining for a change. She even wanted to go into a convent by way of variety. She would think nothing of going over to Rome; and if you take her to Italy you will have to be very careful that the priests don't get hold of her."

"I will take care of her, Sophy. Benson and I will keep the priests at bay. Benson is a dragon of Protestantism."

It was settled that Hester should meet Eve and her maid in Paris early in April, and that they should travel from that city, slowly and at their ease, by Basle and Lucerne to Milan, and thence to the Italian lakes, or possibly to Venice. Eve trembled as she spoke the name of that fatal city. She had a morbid longing to go there to look upon her brother's grave before she died. She could afford to indulge any fancy in the way of travelling, for the pin-money sent her quarterly by the trustee to her marriage settlement was sufficient for her wants, and over and above this private income of hers the trustee, who was also her husband's solicitor, sent her a hundred and fifty pounds quarterly, in accordance with Mr. Vansittart's parting instructions. She had protested against this extra allowance, assuring the solicitor that the income under her settlement was sufficient for her maintenance, and the solicitor had replied that he was instructed to furnish her with six hundred a year during his client's absence from Europe, and that as his client was in Africa, beyond the reach of letters, it was impossible to depart from his instructions. Eve was thus richer than her needs, and was able to be generous to the sisters, whose letters informed her of the result of her bounty, in the shape of a much smarter style of living at the Homestead. They had a page to open the door; they dined at eight o'clock, and they always had dessert on the table. They had their afternoon; and carriages—chiefly pony—came from far distances to take tea with them, Jenny assured her sister.

"Your marriage lifted us all out of the mire," wrote Jenny; "but it is too sad to think of Jack in Africa and you a broken-hearted wanderer. It is awfully sad, and we can none of us guess the why or the wherefore. We feel that there must be some terrible secret. No light reason could have parted you. Mr. Sefton is at the Manor, hunting every day, and going long distances by rail when there are no hounds in the neighbourhood. We hear he has been paying attentions to Lord Haverstock's only daughter, who will be enormously rich. No doubt he will end by marrying for money. Poor Sophy turned deadly pale the first Sunday she saw him in church. We were earlier than usual, and we were seated in our pew as he came up the nave, staring about him as if he had been in a theatre."

* * * *

With Hetty for her travelling companion, Eve felt more her own mistress, and, therefore, happier than she had felt with Sophy. Hetty was only fifteen, and might be treated as a child, and, indeed, she still possessed some of the best attributes of childhood; was incurious about the future save when it promised some novelty, change of place, new possession, amusement or excitement; was deeply interested in trifles, and had no margin of mind left for serious things.

Such a companion may do much for a heart weighed down by the burden of unavailing regret. Hetty, when allowed to give full scope to her own absorbing individuality, left very little room for any one else's feelings. Her delight in travelling was so intense as to be almost contagious. Everything interested her, and the newness of things was a perpetual surprise. She paused in her raptures only to pity the people who are doomed never to travel. She kept a list of the towns through which she passed, were it only sitting in a railway carriage. She had brought the shabby old family atlas from the Homestead, and had it open on her lap in the railway carriage, poring over it till her eyes ached, and rarely able to find the place she was looking for in that pale and faded type.

They stopped a couple of nights at Basle, where the Rhine was rapture. They stopped a week at the Schweitzerhoff, and exhausted the drives and excursions about Lucerne, and explored the lake of the Forest Cantons, and climbed the Righi, and did all that the veriest Cockney tourist can do, personally conducted by Hetty, who read her Baedeker every morning, and gave her sister no rest till the day's excursion had been settled upon.

"Sophy said I was not to let you brood," explained Hetty. "I was to take care you went about and enjoyed the scenery."

Eve went about uncomplainingly, first to please Hetty, and next because days and weeks must be got rid of somehow, and sorrow must keep moving by day if it would court a few hours' respite by night. Eve had her little cough still—only a little cough; but the experienced Benson heard that dull, hacking sound with some anxi-

367

ety, remembering poor Peggy's chance, and how little it had done for her. Would it ever come to that pass with her young mistress, Benson wondered? Was the fatal strain in the blood of all these fair sisters, with their transparent complexions and hectic bloom? Half a year ago Eve had seemed in exuberant health, as well as in exuberant spirits, the fairest type of youthful womanhood, dancing along the flowery path of life with foot so light as never to touch the thorns, or disturb the snake asleep in the sun. The parting with the man she adored had changed her whole being, and the sound of her laughter was heard no more, despite of the lively Hetty's provocations to mirth.

They went from Lucerne to Como, and lingered in that enchanting region until the midsummer heat drove them into the mountains. They roughed it in the Dolomites till October, and then went down to Lake Leman, and established themselves for the winter at Lausanne, where Eve took her sister's education seriously in hand, and placed her as day-boarder in a very superior establishment "to be finished." Here they lived very quietly, Hetty interested in her work, and improving herself with a rapidity which astounded her mistresses, who had been scandalized at her benighted condition from the educational point of view, and who had not yet grasped the idea that a girl who has led a free out-of-door life until she is fifteen years old has a stock of brain power that makes education a much easier business for her between that age and twenty than it is for the victim of premature culture, who has been straining and exhausting the growing brain ever since she was five.

Hetty revived her juvenile French, and took to German and Italian as readily as to tennis or golf. Eve was delighted with her progress, and for Hetty's sake she stayed at Lausanne, with only a summer holiday in the Jura, until the second winter of her exile, when by her English doctor's advice she went up to St. Moritz, Hetty, who was growing a very pretty girl, accompanying her, and turning the heads of all the young men at the Kulm Hotel, most especially when she played one of poor Samary's characters in a little French duologue with the all-accomplished Dr. Holland.

Home letters told Eve that Vansittart was still in Africa, and that his mother was living very quietly at Merewood. From that lady, directly, Eve had not heard of late. She had answered her daughter-in-law's letter coldly and cruelly, as it seemed to Eve.

"I cannot enter into your domestic mystery," she wrote. "I only know that you took my son's life into your keeping, and that you have wrecked it. He was the only son of his mother, and she was a widow. We were very happy together till you crossed his path; and now he is an exile, and I do not even know the reason of his banishment. Forgive me if I say I wish he had never seen your face."

* * * *

Lord Haverstock's daughter was now the Honourable Mrs. Sefton, and her husband was said to have secured the highest matrimonial prize in Sussex. The lady's aristocratic features had the stamp of a shrewish temper, as plainly as ever a knife was stamped "Sheffield." She was proud of her birth and of her money, and a lesser man than Wilfred Sefton would have had a bad time with her, but he was reported to be equal to the situation. They entertained enormously, and were considered an acquisition to the neighbourhood. The Miss Marchants had been bidden to all their parties, and Sophy's cheerful tone in describing the high jinks at the Manor showed that she had outlived her disappointment.

"Everybody knows that he married for money," concluded Sophy, after a graphic account of a New Year's dance given by Mrs. Sefton, "and everybody admires the way he manages his wife. He is obviously supreme in everything. If he had married a curate's daughter he could not be more completely the master, although her income is nearly treble his, and they are always buying land, either adding to the Sefton property, or creeping over the county in other directions. They have no heir as yet, or promise of an heir, which is a disappointment to Lord Haverstock, who wanted a grandson immediately. I don't believe it is possible to imagine a more unhappy marriage, looked at from our point of view; but as, in my opinion, he never had a heart, in spite of his folly about the Venetian singer, it is just the kind of marriage to suit him.

"Lady Hartley's last baby is perfection—a girl—and I am asked to be godmother, a great compliment, considering her extensive circle and what snobs people are.

"Nancy sends you her dear love, and wants me to tell you that she always uses the lovely carved workbox, with the sleeping lion on the lid, which you sent her from Lucerne.

"Shall I secure you a few remnants at Marshall's or Robinson's before the January sales are over? You must pay outrageous prices for everything in Switzerland."

So much for news from home. The London papers afforded ample information about Signora Vivanti, who pursued her successful career unchecked, and rose a step or so in public estimation with

369

each new part she created—"created" was the word the critics used of this uncultured islander's impersonations. She had fresh whims, and eccentricities, and gaieties for each new character. She was *peuple* to the marrow of her bones, and she had all the cleverness and unflagging pleasure in life which belongs to the populace. Her London public adored her, and to provincial audiences she came as a revelation of what gaiety of heart really means. She seemed a well-spring of joyousness, and sent her audience home convinced that life was not so very dreary after all.

Could Eve have known more than the newspapers told her she would have known that the Signora was keeping herself what Mr. Hawberk called "straight." Slander had not breathed upon her name. She had loved, and her love had been rejected; and from the hour of that disillusion she had concentrated her affections upon that which never betrays or disappoints. Lisa and her aunt found the chief delight of their lives in the scraping and self-denial which enabled them to add to their hoard.

Lisa no longer bought diamonds, and wore her whole fortune upon her neck and arms. The diamonds were a very delightful form of investment, but the elementary theory of principal and interest had been gradually borne in upon her mind, and she now knew enough of finance to know that she ought to get something for her money. Reluctantly, and with serious misgivings, she followed the advice of her manager and opened a deposit account at the Union Bank, whither her light feet tripped gaily once a week, and where she handed in the major part of her salary to a clerk who could scarcely write the receipt under the too near radiance of those dazzling eyes.

Life was so cheap for two abstemious women and one little boy. Vansittart had paid three years' rent of the flat in advance before he left Southampton. Lisa and la Zia were on velvet, and while the deposit account was growing there came offers from America, which were intoxicating in their liberality. American agents had seen and heard the lovely Venetian; Anglo-American newspapers had written about her talents and her beauty; and the always enterprising agent-in-advance was eager to introduce her to the Western world.

Lisa carried the tempting offers to her London manager, who shrugged his shoulders, and raised her salary, for the sixth or seventh time.

"You will ruin me if I try to keep you, Signora," he said; "but I can't afford to lose you."

The prima donna and her aunt used to sit over their handful of fire in the small hours after a cheap but savoury supper of liver, or some other abomination, chopped up in a seething mass of macaroni, reeking of garlic and oil. There was no dish the smartest restaurant in London could have provided that they would have enjoyed better than their native kitchen. They came of a people who can make a feast out of a morsel of meat which the sturdy British workman would toss to his dog. Their luxuries and their pleasures were alike of the cheapest. A jaunt to Greenwich or Kew by river, a long day roaming about the Crystal Palace, idle afternoons on the grassy levels of Battersea Park, basking in the sunshine while Paolo made pies in the sand. Pleasures as simple as these sufficed for Lisa, while her fortune was growing at the Union Bank. By the kind manager's advice she had invested the bulk of her wealth in railway shares, to which she had added from time to time as her deposit account grew. She had at first been very chary of trusting the railway with her savings, preferring to confide in the bank, which looked solid and respectable; but on being assured that she would get better interest from the railway with equal security, she consented to become a shareholder. It was pleasant when sitting with her aunt in a third-class carriage on the way to Windsor or Richmond to be able to remind that good lady that she, Lisa, was part owner of the carriage, and indeed of the whole line.

Economical as the two women were their parsimony never degenerated into meanness. If their fare was humble they were always ready to share it with a friend. Little Zinco, who was a bachelor, dined with his pupil every Sunday, la Zia devoting the whole morning, after an early Mass in the chapel near Sloane Street, to the preparation of a little bit of beef stuffed with raisins, and a mess of rice and cheese, while Lisa in her best gown, escorted by the faithful Zinco, attended Mass at the Oratory or the Pro-Cathedral.

In their after-midnight talk by the fire, when autumnal or wintry nights made a fire a necessity, Lisa and la Zia built their castle in the air, and that castle was a small house on the Guidecca, a house of which they could let a couple of floors, reserving the piano nobile, or upper story, with its fine views over the blue water, for themselves, and furnishing the same gorgeously with carved chestnut wood and inlaid ebony, from one of the big manufactories on the Grand Canal. Here they were to live happily ever after, when once Fiordelisa had earned an income that would maintain them for the rest of their days, and pay for Paolo's education.

Already he had shown a passionate love of music, and Zinco saw in him the makings of a fine opera singer.

"He will be handsome, he will be big," said the 'cello, "and already at five years old he shows me that he has an ear as true as a bird's, or as yours. You will send him to the Conservatorio at Milan as soon as he is old enough to enter, and he will find his fortune in his larynx as you have."

CHAPTER XXXII.

"A SCENE OF LIGHT AND GLORY"

It was April, the third springtime after the parting of the wedded lovers, and to Eve it seemed as if many years had come and gone since she looked upon her husband's face. She had endured her life somehow, a life of mornings and afternoons, of twilight and sunrise, of moons that waxed and waned, of seasons that changed from hot to cold and back again, an existence like a squirrel's wheel, and having nothing in common with that happy wedded life in which her eyes opened every morning upon joy and love—the joy of knowing the beloved companion near, the love which seemed ever near and ever growing.

Hetty had been a comfort to her in all that time, and had shown herself so sympathetic that Eve had resolved never to part with her, except to a husband; and, as yet, among Hetty's numerous admirers there had been no one whom she cared for as a future husband. So far Hetty was heart-whole and devoted to her sister, more than ever devoted, alas! now, when the red flag of phthisis flaunted upon Eve's hollow cheeks, and too surely marked the beginning of the end.

She had borne up bravely in those years of exile, making the best of life in some of earth's pleasantest places, courting cheerfulness for her young sister's sake, and never wearing her widowed heart upon her sleeve. She had borne up bravely, though the enemy had been at work all the time, and the fatal strain which had developed so early in Peggy, showed itself in Eve by occasional illnesses, through which she battled successfully, with the aid of much careful nursing by the skilled Benson and the devoted Hetty. They had patched her up time after time, as Benson told her compatriots in the courier's room at the hotel, but the day was coming when patching would no longer serve—when the frail frame and the brave spirit must yield to the inevitable.

"Well, it'll have to come to all of us, in our time," said Benson, brushing away a tear or two, "but it seems hard it should come to her before she's six and twenty. So pretty, too, and such a sweet disposition. It'll be a long time before I shall get a mistress I shall like as well, though when I first took the place I thought I should find it strange like, after being used only to titled people. But there, we're all human, and there ain't much difference between a plain country gentleman's wife and a duchess when you're putting a poultice on her chest."

* * * *

In the bright April weather Eve and her sister came to Venice, the city to which all Eve's thoughts had been trending ever since she left England, nearly three years before. She had always meant to go there, always wished to look upon the scene of her brother's untimely death, and to kneel beside his nameless grave; but she had shrunk with an indescribable dread from the accomplishment of her desire, her heart aching even at the thought of the pain it must cost her to look upon that place, which was associated with all her misery.

Hetty had talked about Venice very often, in her ignorance of all painful associations, and Eve had put her off with promises. "Yes, dear, I mean to go there, sooner or later;" and Hetty hung over the coloured plan in Baedeker—the blue canal, with its curious serpentine curve—and longed to be there with all the intensity which pertains to the juvenile side of twenty. Venice, a name to conjure with! She repeated those lines of Rogers', the plain unvarnished statement—"There is a glorious city by the sea; the sea is in the broad, the narrow streets"—which brings that wonder-city before the eye of the mind more vividly than all the fire and fervour of Byron, or the word-painting of Dickens and Howells.

And now, now, in the beginning of the end, Eve knowing there was no time to lose, the sisters were here in the spring sunset, their gondola moving with the smooth, delicious motion which serves as a balm for troubled spirits, a cure for all the agitations of life, moving in and out of the labyrinthine rios, as the hansom cabman of Venice takes his short cut to the Riva degli Schiavoni, and the comfortable hostelry of Danieli, where at Benson's advice rooms had been secured on the entresol facing the lagoon, Benson professing familiarity with almost every hotel in Europe. She had stayed at Danieli's with her Duchess, stayed there for a month, occupying the piano nobilissimo, in the most palatial wing of that patchwork of palaces, where the traveller may either find himself ushered into the

374

mediæval splendour of a kingly chamber, or may be conducted by a labyrinth of passages to a garret looking out upon a slum that recalls St. Giles's. The wise traveller, of course, is he who gives Danieli ample notice of his coming, and for him the noble floors are reserved.

The entresol was cosy rather than palatial; the rooms were spacious, although low; and the windows opened directly upon all the life and movement of this noisiest and gayest spot of Venice, curiously suggestive of Margate in the Cockney season, save that it is cosmopolitan instead of Cockney, and that instead of the Jew of Houndsditch one may meet the Jew from Damascus or Cairo, from Ispahan or Hungary, from Frankfort or Rome. Here all nations meet and mingle, and all tongues are heard in the voices that mix with the tramp of passing footsteps from morning till midnight. For people who want the silence of the city by the sea, this entresol would be hardly the choicest portion of Danieli's rambling caravanserai; but to Hetty's mind those windows opened on a scene of enchantment.

The fishing-boats were coming in, their painted sails gaudier than the sunset, and an Italian man-of-war was lying between the Riva and the Island church yonder. How familiar that church of St. George the Greater seemed to Hetty, and the Custom House, and the dome of Santa Maria della Salute. She had known them all her life in pictures and photographs—sham Canalettis, books of engravings—but the glory of light and colour were as new to her dazzled eyes as if she had died unawares and had come to life again in Paradise.

"Lovely, lovely; quite too lovely," was all she could say, not having a Ruskinesque vocabulary at her command.

When she looked round, appealing to her sister for sympathy in this new delight, it was a shock to find the room empty.

She ran into the adjoining bedroom, where Benson was unpacking, and then into her own little room further on; but there was no sign of Eve.

"She must have gone out for a stroll," Hetty said ruefully. "She might as well have told me she was going. She ought to know that I am dying to see St. Mark's."

Hetty knew her sister's dislike of all public rooms in hotels, so she had very little hope of finding her in any of those lounges—reading-room, hall, salon—which Signor Campi has provided for his guests. There was no doubt in Hetty's mind that Eve had gone to look at St. Mark's, before the twilight shadows began to veil the splendour of the façade. Hetty went back to the window, and amused herself with the perpetual movement on the quay, and on the water, man-of-war, P. and O., fishing-boats, barges, gondolas moving diagonally across the crimsoned water towards the crimson sky, light and colour reflected upon all things, save where the dark cool shadows accentuated that sunset splendour.

CHAPTER XXXIII.

"BOTH TOGETHER, HE HER GOD, SHE HIS IDOL"

Pale, quiet, resolute, with her mind made up as to what she had to do, Eve Vansittart crossed the Piazzetta towards Florian's Caffè, and slowly, very slowly, passed in front of the windows, looking at the loungers seated here and there at the marble tables, and wondering whether this was the scene of her brother's fate. She had not been told the name of the caffè. She only knew that it was at Venice, in Carnival time, and at a crowded caffè that the fatal encounter had happened.

She passed Florian's, and a door or two further on was assailed by a photographer, who wanted to sell her views of the city at five francs a dozen, and who would not believe that she could exist without them. She looked at him absently for a minute or two while he showed his views, expatiating upon their beauty and cheapness, and after that thoughtful pause went into his shop, seated herself, and turned over the leaves of an album of specimen photographs, choosing a dozen at random—"this—and this—and this"—without looking at them.

"Have you had this shop long?" she asked.

"Fifteen years."

"Then you must remember something that happened in a caffè in the Piazza—Florian's, most likely—seven years ago. It was on a Shrove Tuesday, late at night. A young man was killed, accidentally, in a scuffle. Do you remember?"

The photographer shrugged his shoulders.

"That is a thing that might happen any year at Carnival time," he said lightly. "There is much excitement. Our people are good-natured, very good-natured, but they are hot-tempered, and a blow is quickly given, even a blow that may prove fatal. I cannot say that I remember any particular case."

"The man who was killed was an Englishman, and the man who killed him was an Englishman."

"Strange," said the photographer. "The English are generally cool and collected—a serious nation. Had it been an American I should be less surprised. The Americans are more like us. There is more quicksilver in their blood."

"Cannot you remember now? An Englishman, a gentleman, stabbed by an English gentleman," urged Eve. "Surely such things do not happen every day?"

"Every day? No, Signora. But in Carnival time one is prepared for strange things happening. I begin to recall the circumstance, but not very clearly. A young Englishman stabbed with a dagger that had been bought over the way a short time before. He had been drinking, and was jealous of a young woman who was present. He attacked his compatriot with savage violence. Yes, I recall the affair more clearly now. There were those present who said he brought his fate upon himself by his brutality. The man who stabbed him made a bolt of it, on a hint from a bystander—ran across the Piazzetta, jumped into the water, and swam for his life. No one in Venice ever knew what became of him. He must have been picked up by a gondola, and must have got away by the railroad. Who knows? He may have got ashore on the mainland, and made his way to Mestre, so as to avoid the railway station here, where the police might be on the watch for him. Anyhow, he got away. He had courage, quickness, his wits well about him."

"It was at Florian's that this happened?" asked Eve.

"Yes, at Florian's—where else? There is no caffè in Venice equal to Florian's."

That was all. She paid for her photographs and went back to Florian's, and peered in at the bright, pretty salons, where the Italians were lounging over their coffee, with here and there a group playing dominoes, and where tourists—English, American, German—were enjoying themselves more noisily. She wondered in which of those salons the tragedy had been acted. Was the stain of her brother's blood on the floor ineffaceable, like Rizzio's in the fatal room at Holyrood? She loitered for a few minutes, looking in through the open doors and windows shudderingly; and seeing she was observed, she moved quickly away, and presently was being followed across the piazza by a Venetian seeker of *bonnes fortunes*, she herself happily unconscious of the fact.

She looked at the shops in the Procuratie Vecchie, and was pestered by the touting shopkeepers after their Venetian manner. She looked in at all those Eastern toys and Italian gewgaws, and jewellery which has here and there a suggestion of Birmingham.

"Do you sell daggers?" she asked a black-eyed youth, who had entreated her earnestly to ascend to the show-room above, assuring her that the "to look costs nothing."

Her question startled him. "Daggers, yes, assuredly. Was it a jewelled dagger for her hair that the Signora desired? He had of the most magnificent."

No. She wanted no dagger, only to know whether he sold them, real daggers, strong enough to wound fatally.

He showed her a whole armoury of Moorish knives, any one of which looked as if it might be deadly.

"Do you remember a young Englishman being killed with such a dagger as this?" she said, pointing to one of the deadliest, "by accident, in Carnival time?"

He remembered, or affected to remember, nothing.

Leaving his shop, after buying half a dozen bead necklaces for civility, Eve found herself face to face with her Venetian admirer, upon whom she turned so dark a frown as to repel even that practised Lothario. She hurried back to Danieli's, and arrived there flushed and breathless, and far too much exhausted to do justice to the simple little dinner of clear soup and roast chicken which Benson had ordered, a dinner served in her own sitting-room, which privilege of dining alone was Eve's only extravagance in her travels.

Hetty questioned her sister closely, and reproached her for unkindness in going out unaccompanied; but Eve gave her no explanation of that excursion.

"You are not strong enough to walk about alone, dear," the sister said tenderly. "You want a giraffe like me to give you an arm." This was Hetty's way of alluding to the tall slim figure which had been so much admired on the tennis courts of St. Moritz and Maloja.

Eve engaged a gondola next morning. It was to be her own gondola, and the gondolier was to give allegiance to no one else, so long as Mrs. Vansittart remained in Venice. She set out alone in her gondola directly after breakfast, in spite of Hetty's remonstrances.

"I have some business in Venice that I must keep to myself, Hetty. It will be the greatest kindness in you to ask no questions."

"You are full of mysteries," said Hetty, "but I won't tease you. Only take care of yourself, dearest, and don't be unhappy about anything, for the sake of the sisters who idolize you."

Eve kissed her, and went away without another word. Hetty marched about all the morning with Benson, who showed her St. Mark's and the pigeons, and the Doge's Palace, whisking her rapidly through all the picture-rooms, but not letting her off a single dark cell on either side the Bridge of Sighs.

* * * *

379

Eve's first visit was to the chief office of the Venetian police, where she found an obliging functionary, who, at her desire, produced the record of the unknown Englishman's death.

The story was bald and brief. A scuffle, ending in a fatal wound from a dagger. The man who used the dagger had escaped. The weapon was in the possession of the police.

"Was every means taken to find the man who killed him?" Eve asked.

"Every means, although there was no extra pressure put upon us. Nobody came forward to identify the victim or to claim the body. He must have been a waif and stray; his name, Smith, is one of the commonest English names, I am told, and it may have been an assumed name in his case. He was a fine young fellow, but showed marks of having lived recklessly and drunk hard. The lines in his face were the lines that dissipated habits leave on young faces. It was a sad business. Has the Signora any personal interest in this unfortunate gentleman?"

"Yes, he was my relation. I have come to Venice on purpose to find his grave."

"That will be difficult, I fear. He belonged to nobody. His bones will have been mingled with other bones in the public grave ere now."

"Oh, that is hard," said Eve, in a broken voice. "A pauper's grave. He was a gentleman by birth and education. There were those in his own country who would have starved rather than let him lie in a nameless grave."

The official shrugged his shoulders with the true philosophical shrug.

"Does the Signora really think that it matters whether we have as grand a tomb as Titian or lie nameless and forgotten in some quiet corner? For my part, the finest monument that was ever set up would not console me for a short life. When these bones of mine are only aches and pains, and can carry me about no longer, away with them to the crematorium. The Signora will pardon me for venturing to state my own views, and if she desires it I will try to discover the exact circumstances of the Englishman's burial. It is possible that there may have been some one interested in his last resting-place, and the grave may have been bought. There was a young Venetian, the girl who caused the quarrel, who seems to have been attached to him. She may have done something. If the Signora will be good enough to wait till to-morrow I may be able to furnish her with better information."

Eve thanked him for his polite interest, and promised to recompense him for any trouble he might take on her behalf.

She received a letter from him the next morning.

"The grave is the last in the avenue leading due west by the side of the south wall in the cemetery at San Michele. There is a wooden cross, and the name Smith. The grave was bought and the cross erected at the expense of the Venetian girl."

Eve's gondola took her to the sea-girt burial-place in the morning sunshine. She carried a basket of roses and narcissus, to lay upon her brother's grave, and her mind was full of the hour when she saw him for the last time. How near in its distinctness of detail, of sensation even! how far in that sense of remoteness which made her feel as if she were looking across a gulf of death and time to another life! Was that really herself—that impetuous girl, whose arms had clung round her brother's neck in the agony of parting, and who had never known any other love?

To-day there was a conflict of feeling. There was the thought of the man whose crime had been the crime of a moment, whose punishment was the punishment of a lifetime.

"I know that he loved me," she told herself. "I know that I was necessary to his happiness, and yet I sent him away from me. Could I do otherwise? No. The man who killed my brother could not be my husband, I knowing what he had done. Ah, as long as I did not know, what a happy woman I was! And I might have lived happy in my ignorance to the end but for my own fault."

And then with bitterest smile she said aloud—

"Ah, Fatima, Fatima, how dearly you have paid for the turning of the key!"

She found San Michele, the quiet island of the dead, sleeping in the soft haze of morning on the bosom of the lagune. A little way off, the chimneys of Murano were tarnishing the clear Italian sky with their smoke; the barges were loading and unloading; the glass-makers were passing to and fro—women and girls flip-flopping over the damp stones in their quarter-less shoes! the children and the beggars were sprawling in the sun. There the stir and variety of life: here the silence and the sameness of death.

She found her brother's grave, and the monument which Fiordelisa and her aunt had set up in his honour. The grave was a mound on which the grass grew tall and rank, as it grows at Torcello, above the ruins of the mother city. The monument—poor tribute of faithful poverty—was a wooden cross painted black, with an inscription in white lettering, rudely done:—

SIR SMIZZ
MORTO A VENEZIA,
MARTEDI-GRASSO, 1885.

Below this brief description were seven of those conventional figures—in shape like a chandelier-drop—which often ornament the funeral drapery that marks the house of death. These chandelier-drops, painted white on the black ground of the cross, represented tears. They were seven, the mystic number, sacred to every Catholic mind.

These seven tears—seven heart-wounds—were all the epitaph Lisa could give to her lover. A wreath of immortelles, black with the blackness of years, hung upon the cross. It dropped into atoms as Eve touched it, was blown away upon the salt sea wind, vanishing as if it had been the spectral form of a wreath rather than the thing itself.

Eve sank on her knees in the hollow between two graves, and abandoned herself to a long ecstasy of supplication, praying not for the dead, at peace beneath that green mound where the grasshoppers were chirping, and the swift lizards gliding in and out,—not for the dead, but for the man who killed him, for the conscience-burdened wanderer, under torrid suns, far from peace, and home, and all the pleasures and comforts of civilization, seeking forgetfulness in the arid desert, in the fever-haunted swamp, among savage beasts and savage men, going with his life in his hand, lying down to sleep at the end of a weary day, with the knowledge that if his camp-fires were not watched he might wake to find himself face to face with a lion. Oh, what a life for him to lead, for him whose days had been spent so pleasantly in the busy idleness of a man whose only occupation is the care of a small landed estate, and whose only notion of hard work is the early rising in the season of cub-hunting, or the strenuous pleasures of salmon-fishing beyond the Scottish border.

When her prayer was done—her prayer that her beloved might be sheltered and guarded by a Power which guides the forces of Nature, and bridles the neck of the lion, and can disperse the pestilence with a breath—prayer is a dead letter for those who believe less than this—Eve sat upon the grass, under her Italian umbrella, the red umbrella which all the peasants use as shelter from sun and rain, and abandoned herself to thoughts of the wanderer.

She knew more of his wanderings than she had hoped to know

when Sophy's letter from Fernhurst first told her that he was travelling with a friend in the Mashona country; thanks to an occasional letter from his own pen which appeared in the *Field*, and over which his wife hung with breathless interest, and read and re-read, returning to it again and again long after the date of publication, as she returned to *Hamlet* or "In Memoriam." Week after week she searched the paper eagerly for any new letter, or any stray paragraph giving news of the wanderer; but the letters appeared at long intervals, and the last was nearly three months old. He had turned his face homeward, he said, in that last letter. Her heart thrilled at the thought that he might have returned ere now, that he might be at Merewood perhaps, in the rooms where they had lived together, in the garden which was once their earthly Paradise, in which she had watched the growth of every flowering shrub, and counted every rose, in that mild Hampshire where roses flourish almost as abundantly as in balmy Devon. She thought of the tulip tree she had planted on their favourite lawn, he standing beside her as she bent to her work, laughingly prophetic of the day when they should sit on a rustic bench together under the spreading branches of that sapling of to-day, to accept the congratulations of garden-party guests upon their golden wedding.

"'We must really go and speak to the old people,' some pert young visitor would say to a perter granddaughter of the house, 'only one hardly knows what to say to people of that prodigious age.'"

Eve remembered her feeling of vague wonder what it was like to be old, whilst Vansittart jestingly forecast the future.

Well, all speculation of that kind was at an end now. She would never know what it was like.

"Those the Gods love die young," she repeated to herself, dreamily. "I would not mind dying—any more than Peggy minded, happy-souled Peggy—if I could but see him before I die. There could be no harm in my seeing him—just at the end—no treason to my flesh and blood lying here."

She laid her wasted cheek upon the mound, and let her tears mix with the last lingering dew on the long grass. She wanted to be loyal to her dead; but her heart yearned with a sick yearning for one touch from the hand of the living, for one look from the eyes that would look only love. Love, and pardon, and fond regret.

It was a fortnight after that morning in the cemetery at San Michele, that in poring over her *Field* Eve came upon a two-line paragraph at the bottom of a column, a most obscure little paragraph—side by side with one of those little anecdotes of intensest

383

human interest which chill one at the end by the fatal symbol, "Advt."—a tiny scrap of news which any but the most searching reader would have been likely to overlook.

"Among the passengers on board the *City of Zanzibar*, which left Cape Town on the 3rd inst., for Alexandria and Brindisi, were Mr. Murthwait and Mr. Vansittart, returning from a hunting expedition to Lobengula's country."

Eve sent for her doctor that evening, the English doctor who had attended her at St. Moritz in January and February, and who was now taking a semi-professional holiday in Venice—willing to see old patients who might have drifted to the city in the sea, but not desiring new ones.

She submitted patiently to the necessary auscultation, while her sister stood by, pale and breathless, waiting to hear the words of doom.

The doctor's face, when he laid down the stethoscope, was grave even to sorrowfulness. He had been warmly interested in this case in the winter, had hoped against hope.

"Am I worse than I was in February?" Eve asked quietly.

"I am very sorry to have to say it—yes, you are worse."

"And you think badly of my case? You think it quite hopeless?"

"There is no such thing as hopelessness," said the doctor, responding to an appealing look from Hetty. "You are so young—have such a fine constitution, and even after what you told me of your family history—who knows?—there is always a chance."

"Yes, there was a chance for my youngest sister," answered Eve, with a faint smile. "Peggy's chance lasted six months."

"If there is anything you want to settle—any business matter, such as the disposal of property, which makes your mind uneasy—it is always well to set such anxieties at rest," answered the doctor, soothingly.

"Yes, I must see to that. My settlement gives me the right to dispose of my property—the property my husband gave me. I had none of my own. But it is not of that I am thinking. Oh, doctor, be frank with me. I have a reason for wanting to know. Do you think that I am dying?"

"Alas, dear lady! I cannot promise you many years of life."

"Or many months? Or many weeks? Oh, doctor, don't think I am afraid of the truth. I am not one of those consumptives who deceive themselves. I have no spurious hopes—perhaps because I do not set a great value on life. Only there is some one I want to see before I die."

"Send for him, then," said the doctor, divining that the some one was her husband. "Send for him, and set your mind at rest."

"I will," she answered resolutely, and before the doctor had left her half an hour she had written and despatched her telegram—

"John Vansittart, Steamer *City of Zanzibar*, Poste Restante, Brindisi.—I am at Venice, and would give much to see you on your way home.—Eve.—Danieli's."

The windows of Mrs. Vansittart's salon on the entresol at Danieli's opened upon a balcony—a balcony shaded and sheltered by a striped awning, under which Eve loved to sit at her ease, nestling among the cushions which Hetty arranged for her, on days when, in her own words, she felt hardly equal to the gondola. There had been many days since the despatch of that message to Brindisi when Eve had felt unequal to the gondola, and Hetty had by this time exhausted all the sights of Venice under the chaperonage of Benson—who gave herself as many airs as if she had been Ruskin—and had yawned as heartily in the Accademia as ever she had yawned in the National Gallery. She had wearied of Titian and Tintoretto. She had tried her hardest to admire Carpaccio, and to pin her mind to her limp little piratical edition of the "Stones of Venice." She thought of Ruskin religiously every day as she tripped past Figtree Corner. More fondly, perhaps, did she affect the shops in the Merceria, and all those wonderful little streets which to the Cockney of mature years recall all that was most precious—that is to say, most characteristic of the little industries and little trades of a great city—in the vanishing alleys and paved courts between Leicester Square and Oxford Street. Here there was always something to interest the girl from Sussex; and the Rialto, market and bridge, afforded never-failing pleasure. Thus the gondolier had an easy time of it, and slept away the brightening hours, and basked in the sun, and fattened on golden messes of polenta.

It was quite true that Eve felt less capable of exertion—even that slight effort of going downstairs and stepping from Danieli's doorstep into a gondola—than when first she came to Venice; but she had another and stronger reason for preferring her cushioned nest on the balcony to the Lido or the lagunes, lovely as those smooth waters were in the lovely May weather. She was waiting for the result of her telegram, she was watching for the coming of her husband. He would come to her. On that question she had no fear. If he lived to land at Brindisi and to receive her message, he would come to Venice. She would see him, and forgive, and be forgiven, before she died. Forgive him; forgive the wrong done to another?

For her own part there had never been anything less than pardon in her mind. She had made every excuse that love can make—love, the special pleader—the infallible advocate for a criminal at the court of a woman's conscience. She had excused his crime until it was no crime; but she had been firm in her conviction that she could not live with the man who killed her brother. Looking back now at the years of a double exile there was no wavering in her mind, no regret for what she had done. She felt only gratitude to Providence who had shortened the lonely years, and brought the end so near.

Three weeks of watching and waiting passed like a slow pensive dream—a dream of blue water—and lounging gondoliers—and flower-girls with baskets of ragged pink peonies, and the shriek and whistle of the steamer for the Lido, and the passing of many foot-steps, and sound of many voices, grey-coated tourists, American and British, for ever coming and going, so light-hearted, so light-mind-ed, so noisy, that one might think care and sorrow had no part in their lives or in their memories. To Eve, dwelling for ever on the memory of the life which had been, on the thought of the parting which was to be, all that tumultuous movement and gaiety seemed a thing of wonder.

"How happy they all are!" she said. "What a happy world it seems—for other people."

"Ah, but you see people must wear their happy side outermost," answered Hetty, "and I dare say even Americans know what care means, though they always seem wallowing in money and new clothes. I wish you would come down to the hall to-night, and hear the little concert we have every evening, and see my favourite young lady from Boston. She has all her frocks from Paris, and her waist is under nineteen inches. Yet she eats! Ah, what a privilege to be able to eat as much as she does, and yet keep one's waist under nineteen inches!"

The day had been almost oppressively warm, and the fishing-boats were coming home through a sea of molten gold in the un-speakable splendour of a Venetian sunset, when May has breathed the first breath of summer heat over land and water. Eve had been sitting in the balcony all day reading those little books of Howells' and his contemporaries, which seem especially invented for the trav-eller in fair countries, light, portable, dainty to touch and gracious to look upon, and eminently proper. She had read, and dreamed her waking dreams, and dozed a good deal at intervals—for her nights now were sadly broken, and sadly wakeful—quite as bad as poor Miss Margaret's nights, as Benson told her sympathetically. Miss

Margaret? Who was Miss Margaret? And then Eve remembered how the respectful Benson had insisted on calling Peggy by a name which no other lips had ever addressed to her.

Benson was an admirable nurse, wakeful, watchful, really attached to her mistress; but she was just a shade too business-like, and too much inclined to look upon Eve as a case rather than an individual. She watched the progress of decay with a ghoulish gusto, and told her mistress more about former patients than it was cheering for an invalid to know.

To-day, after the weariness of the night, and the long, long hours between sunrise and the breakfast hour of civilization, Eve's fitful slumbers were sound and deep, deeper than dreamland, deep as the dark abyss of unconsciousness. She had been falling into this gulf now and again all day, falling suddenly from her book or her daydream into that black pit of sleep.

A cooler breeze sprang up with the sinking of the sun, and the water between the Riva and the island church was stirred into bolder ripples as the dark gondolas stood sharply out against the reddening light. The salt breath of the Adriatic was blowing across the sandy bar yonder with revivifying freshness. Eve rose from her nest of pillows in the low canvas chair, and stood leaning against the balcony, looking at the animated scene. There was a paper lantern twinkling here and there with a pale fantastic light, in sickly contrast to that blaze of sunset colour, and as the crimson faded in the low western sky the little earthly lights brightened and grew bold, and there came the sound of that light music which Venetians love, music that seems only a natural accompaniment to the ripple of the incoming tide.

"How bright and gay it all looks!" said Eve. "Is there anything on earth to equal Venice? Oh, how strange that I should love this city so well!" she murmured, in self-reproach, remembering the purpose that had brought her there.

The charm of the city had crept upon her unawares. She was glad to live there, glad that she was to die there.

She looked towards the bridge by the Doge's Palace, and saw a man walking quickly down the steps—a bearded man, with a brown skin and a weather-beaten look. He was coming quickly towards the hotel; he was looking up at the windows, scanning the wide frontage with a sweeping glance, now high, now low, till his eyes lighted on the balcony where she stood, lighted on herself, and never unfixed their gaze.

Changed as he was, she had known him from the first instant. She had known him when he appeared at the top of the steps for John

Vansittart and no other. There was something in his walk, something in the carriage of his head, something which to the eyes of love seemed to distinguish him from all the rest of the world—characteristics that might have been invisible to all other eyes.

He ran towards the low doorway, and scarcely had he vanished from the outer world below when she heard a door bang at the end of the corridor and the rush of hurrying feet. How quick, how impetuous, what a creature of fire and name he seemed as he dashed into the room and clasped her in his arms!

"Are these your African manners?" she gasped, laughing and crying in the same moment.

"Oh, my love, my love, how sweet to hold you on my heart again and be forgiven! I am forgiven, am I not, dear? My calamity, or my crime—call it what you will—is forgiven. Oh, love, I have suffered. I have drunk the cup of atonement."

She was sobbing upon his shoulder, her face hidden, as she clung to him, with wasted arms wreathing his neck. In the blindness of his joy—for joy, like fortune, is stone blind—he had not noticed how pitiably thin those caressing arms had grown. Suddenly, scared by her silence, he withdrew himself from that caress, and held her from him at arm's length, and, looking into her face, saw the sign manual of death, and knew why she had summoned him.

By a heroic effort he commanded his countenance, and smiled faintly back her own faint smile.

"There is no question of the past between you and me," she said, "only love, a world of love."

He drew her to his breast again, cradling the thin cheek against his brown and bearded countenance, holding her to him as if he would hold her there against the grim assailant Death, breathing his own strong life into her as their lips met and their breath mingled. Surely between them there was life and vigour enough to ward off Death.

"My darling, my darling, my darling!"

It was all that he could say just yet. The rapture of reunion, the agony of an unspeakable dread were storming heart and mind. He felt like a man lashed to the mast in a hurricane, all the forces of Nature warring round him, unable to measure his danger or his chance of rescue.

To have her, to hold her again, loving him as of old. And then to lose her! But must he lose her? Could neither love nor science work a miracle, and snatch her from the jaws of the Destroyer?

He grew calmer presently, and they sat side by side in the deepening shadows, and began to talk to each other quietly, in soft hushed voices, while the music and the voices of the Riva mixed with their half-whispered sentences, and the footsteps went by with a gay spring in them as if all Venice were hurrying from pleasure to pleasure.

"Oh, dearest, it was time you sent for me; it was time," he said. "You have given me a long penance. Nothing but Africa could have helped me to bear my life. In a world less full of strange hazards I must have lost patience with calamity, and made a swift and sudden end of myself. Thanks to the Dark Continent I have lived somehow, as you see, and come back a semi-savage, a creature of thews and sinews."

"No, you are only rougher looking and browner. I can see the soul shining through your eyes. Africa has not altered that."

"But you, dear love," he said, with a thrill in his voice that marked the strangled sob, "you are altered. You are looking tired and ill. I am afraid you have been neglecting yourself. I shall take you to the Engadine, where we ought to have taken poor Peggy. The Riviera was a mistake. A winter at St. Moritz would have cured her. We will start to-morrow."

She did not answer for a minute or so, but nestled nearer to him, with her wan cheek leaning against his shoulder, and her waxen fingers clasping his strong wrist, hardened and roughened by weather and toil.

"The Engadine can do nothing for me, Jack—no more than it could have done for Peggy. South or north, mountain or valley, the end would have been the same. It is our family history, Jack. We were doomed from our birth. I was sent to the Engadine last winter, and Hetty and I only left St. Moritz in March. We stayed at Varese for nearly a month, and then came here. Hetty is with me, so bright, so active, so happy; but some day perhaps she will look in the glass as I have looked, and will see the summons written on her face. Dear husband, don't be too sorry for me. This parting must have come, even if we had escaped the other; even if I had never known what happened at Florian's; never knelt beside my brother's grave in the island cemetery. Let me lie near him, Jack: and whatever your future life may be—and God grant it may be rich in blessings, you have suffered enough for your sin—think of me sometimes; and sometimes, in your wanderings, go to San Michele and look upon my grave."

He clasped her close against his heart, with a shuddering sigh.

* * * *

Two days after, he took her away from the life and movement of the Riva to a palace on the Grand Canal, where the quiet of the Silent City had a soothing influence on her overwrought spirit. If any life could have been happy in which the end was so near, theirs would have been happy in that delicious beginning of the Venetian summer, a season when mere existence is a privilege. Whatever love which passeth understanding can do to smooth the last days of a fading life was done for Eve; and it may be that the footsteps of the invincible Enemy were slackened somewhat by that unsleeping watchfulness.

The end came slowly, and not ungently, and till the end her husband was her devoted nurse and companion, thinking no thought that was not of her.